THE MAN WHO DEALT IN DEATH

THE COLTON FEN SERIES

BOOK ONE

MARLENA FRANK

*For Kelley,
for supporting me throughout the many years it took for this
book to come to fruition. It never would have seen the light of
day without you.*

Dressed for the Hunt

Fire is one choice
but they come back enraged

Time is no good either
for they can never age

A fool will turn to water
but they refuse to drown

Death only greets a werewolf
in her finest silver gown.

PROLOGUE

TOO LATE

Hattie

HATTIE COULD TELL PAPA HAD BEEN DRINKING. She could smell it on him when he stepped through the door of their shanty, his beard thick with alcohol and sweat, stumbling over his own two feet. The squat wooden building shuddered as he shoved the door open. Dwindling orange sunlight trickled in, bringing with it dust and sand from the road. On instinct, Hattie shoved the bag of crackers she was munching on into the pocket of her skirt. Papa didn't need to see that, especially when he was drunk as a skunk. He would accuse her of stealing it, which she had, but that was beside the point. What did he expect her to do when the house didn't have a scrap of food? Sometimes he forgot he had a daughter at all.

Sitting up straighter, she swallowed down the remains of a cracker. "You're home early."

"Yeah, well, you ain't my boss," he grumbled. Hattie had to bite back a retort. She sometimes fancied telling Papa's boss that he liked to duck out of the mines and stay at the bar too late, but if she did that, there would be no shanty to return to. Papa tried to pull off one of his shoes, but ended up falling instead. He slammed onto the dusty floorboards, which creaked under his weight. He blinked for a moment as if slow to realize he was on the floor, then he threw his head back and laughed. His breath smelled rancid.

Hattie frowned. "You didn't get paid, did you?"

Papa stopped laughing and stared at her in confusion.

"Papa, please don't tell me you drank all our money again."

He scrunched up his face as he thought for a moment, then looked around the room. "We all out of food again? I thought we just got some. Did you eat it all already?"

Hattie sighed and sat back in the rickety wooden chair. "That was two weeks ago, Papa."

He looked at her again. A look of true embarrassment blanched his ruddy cheeks. "Hang on, I think I have some left." He pushed his fingers into his pocket and pulled out a sweaty dollar bill. A few bits fell and clattered on the floor. Hattie got to her feet and braved the smell, crouching to pick up the few coins.

Papa stared at her as she picked up each bit off the floor. "You put up with so much from your old Papa."

There was a warmth in his voice that she didn't get to hear very often these days. It reminded her of how it used to be, back before Mama died, back before he took to the drink like water. Hattie tried to smile. "I love you, Papa, even if you drink too much."

She had reached forward to pick up the last bit when Papa reached over and pulled the bag of crackers out of her pocket. "What's this?"

She closed her eyes for a moment. "It was a gift," she lied.

Papa put his head up and she could see the exhaustion on his face. "Hattie, you can't go stealing things. One of these days, someone is going to catch you, and I won't be able to do anything about it."

"What was I supposed to do?" She grabbed the bag back and stuffed it in her pocket.

"Do you know what they do to thieves in these parts?"

She knew, and she didn't care. No sheriff would hang a child, especially a hungry girl just looking for a box of crackers to get by. She picked up the last bit and headed for the door. Her father watched her with red-rimmed eyes.

"If your mother was alive, you'd have a better life here," he said.

"And you'd still be drunk all the time," Hattie spat before she hurried out of the house and down the steps, dodging any further words from him.

HATTIE HADN'T MEANT TO BE OUT SO LATE. SHE got caught up picking out groceries. It wasn't every day she got to wander the store and ogle all the food after living off crackers for days. Then the old grocer accused her of window shopping instead of buying. The look on his face when she pulled out Papa's dollar was priceless!

She had a whole crate of food, almost half her size. She wasn't used to carrying so much. When her arms got tired, she stopped by the Crimson Theater and peeked inside to watch the funny lady on stage. When everyone cheered and clapped, Hattie couldn't help but join in. She had never seen a lady on stage before and she wondered what it was like making so many people laugh and cheer. Maybe one day she would get to be on stage, too. Then her Papa would never drink all their grocery money again.

The red velvet curtains closed. She had been watching the show for a while. So she huffed a sigh and reached down again for the crate, resting it against her hip as she carried it back to the shanty. She watched her step to keep from stepping in any horse manure. As she left downtown Peridot, the dark night swept over her, chilled and windy. Stars flooded the night sky but they were distant lights, not enough to illuminate the shadows in this part of town. She walked down the dusty street, passing dozens of shanties like the one she lived in. Their wooden homes were barely built strong enough to keep out the wind. A few people eyed her from the shadows, but she wasn't afraid. Hattie had lived here all her life. She knew these people.

Finally, she reached her home. She put down the groceries on the bottom step and arched her back, feeling her muscles ache.

"Papa, I'm back!" She waited for him to come outside. Maybe he would be hungry after sleeping off his drink. But Papa didn't appear. She sighed and climbed the steps, pushing open the door in a huff. "Papa?"

The door leaned at an odd angle and the rickety wooden chair she had sat in earlier lay on its side. What concerned her most was that one chair leg was broken and hung on by a few splinters of wood. She crouched down beside it, trying to figure out what had happened. Then she saw the blood on the corner of the seat. Her heart pounded in her ears.

"Papa?" she called again, her voice filled with panic. Only silence replied. She grabbed the dangling chair leg and yanked it off the seat, then she went back outside.

She wanted to call to him again, but the darkness of the night seemed overwhelming now. Down the steps, she tripped over the crate of food in her panic. Most of the shanties out here were dark. The wind made a hollow sound and blew sand into her eyes. She wiped at them in annoyance, before she spotted movement farther down the street. A tall man, maybe Papa's height, stumbled between the houses and away from the main road.

It could be Papa, but it could have been whoever must have attacked him. She gripped the chair leg in her hand and ran after him.

Hattie was an excellent runner. Years of having to outrun angry shop owners and kids meant she was one of the fastest sprinters in Peridot. Sand kicked up as she dodged a pile of debris and leaped over a set of angled stairs. She could still make out the man's shape loping ahead, but not much farther.

Pushing black hair out of her face, she darted up toward him. That's when she realized he was dragging something behind him. No, not something, someone.

"Papa!" she cried, hoping he would wake up, fight back,

help her. Instead, the loping man turned around and his face was pale and gaunt. "Let go of my Papa!" she cried, crouching down beside her father and pulling on him.

"Hattie...?" Something dark and wet was on the side of Papa's face and he couldn't seem to open his eyes, but her heart soared at hearing his voice. Then she felt a painful tug on her arm and was lifted off the ground. She screamed as the man brought her up to his face, but she still held the chair leg in her other hand. She swung it with all her strength at his arm, his face, his head, but even when she slammed it into his mouth and split his lip, he didn't even wince. Then he flung her, and she slammed into the side of a shanty house. Splintering wood surrounded her as darkness consumed her.

The loping man picked her up under one arm, then he reached down and grabbed her Papa and dragged him. He took them far away from the shanties, away from prying eyes or ears, and away from the safety of Peridot.

PART ONE

PURSUED IN PERIDOT

CHAPTER 1

THE AGENCY FOR THE BETTERMENT OF SUPERNATURAL CREATURES

COLTON HATED WAITING ROOMS. HE DIDN'T enjoy sitting in a cage while someone more important carved out time to see him. It always rubbed him the wrong way and made him feel unimportant. It didn't help that waiting rooms were for things he didn't enjoy, such as seeing a doctor, being suspected of a robbery, or, in this case, meeting his new boss.

He drummed his fingers on the edge of the table beside him, ignoring the sweat marks left behind on the thick varnish. The room was full of chestnut furniture that smelled freshly polished. The oily scent clung to the back of his throat. It wasn't that strong to humans, but to werewolves, it was a mild form of torture. He tried to keep his leg from bouncing.

The heavy door at the end of the room opened and a tall man with dark, umber skin emerged. He wore an immaculate tan suit, quite rich, which was strange for someone who worked at the Agency.

"Mr. Fen," he said with a wide smile, "sorry to keep you

waiting. Come on in. I just have a few more things to finish before we can talk."

Colton rolled to his feet, removed his Stetson hat, and wiped his sweaty hand on his duster coat before shaking the man's hand. His new boss's wealth had taken him off guard, but it was Colton's inability to figure out what he was that made him uncomfortable. Almost every member of the Agency was some kind of supernatural being. He wasn't a werewolf, and he didn't smell like a vampire. Colton didn't have an inexplicable sense of dread come over him, so he couldn't be a wendigo, either. Nothing about him seemed unusual, and that normality made Colton uneasy. He was just a rich human who was far more put together than Colton.

"Not a problem, sir. I've got nowhere to be," he said.

His new boss chuckled. "It's good to meet you in person. Grady speaks highly of you."

"I'm surprised. Grady doesn't speak highly of anyone. It's a pleasure to meet you too, Mr. Tep."

"Please, call me Mekhu." He gestured into his office. "Why don't you come in and take a seat?"

Colton had the strange sensation of walking into a sacred space when he stepped through the threshold. While the waiting room smelled of buffed oils, this place was the exact opposite. The window was open, letting in the sounds of the bustling city below along with all the scents that came with it. Beneath the city smells of horses and the occasional automobile, some unusual ones lay just below the surface. It was difficult to resist openly sniffing the air. He wandered away from the open window and toward the bookshelves. There were some books, but what caught his eye were the trinkets sitting on a low shelf, intended to be missed by casual guests.

Little jars stood with various animal heads on top used as lids. One was a cat, another might have been a bird with a long beak. Colton was no historian, but he could tell they were ancient. He squatted down to look more closely at an ornamental human skull in the back, but he suspected there was more to it.

"Are you an anthropologist, Mr. Tep?" Colton asked.

Mr. Tep sat at his desk rifling through paperwork, and looked up to give a wide smile. "I see you've found my collection."

Colton stood up straight and put his hands into the pockets of his coat. "I guess that's where you got the money from, selling off whatever you stole from those tombs in Egypt?"

He laughed. "You're mistaken, Mr. Fen. I've never stolen once in my life, merely claimed what was mine."

Colton smirked. "I guess one man's otherworldly riches are another man's property."

Mekhu pursed his lips. "The Agency for the Betterment of Supernatural Creatures: we employ the skills and knowledge of many shades of the supernatural, as you know, Mr. Fen. That also means that it doesn't take much to offend."

It took Colton a minute to realize he had said something wrong, and he hadn't even sat down yet. "Sorry, sir."

Mekhu smiled again. "Why don't we just do what's best for both of us and start over? How does that sound?"

He swallowed down the lump in his throat and settled down in the seat opposite his new boss. "My apologies. I have a bad habit of poking around too much."

Mehku laced his fingers together. "Always the detective, I see. I understand your compulsion, Mr. Fen, but it's that attitude that will end up getting you killed on assignment in the Agency. You need more tact."

He resisted the urge to dig his nails into the wooden arms of his chair.

"Now I understand that on your first solo assignment down in Clarkville, Texas, you mistook starved vampires as gruesome monsters. Is that correct?"

Colton felt his heart skip a beat. This wasn't supposed to be a scolding, he wasn't supposed to be in any trouble. He was only supposed to come, meet his new boss, and get his next assignment. Somehow he had messed it up quick. His right leg bounced up and down.

"It wasn't quite like that, sir. I didn't know what they were until I was locked in with them."

Mehku shook his head. "Yes, and you almost got killed."

Colton sucked in a breath, trying to find the right words. "I don't know about that..."

Mehku sat back in his chair, steepling his fingers. "Grady speaks well of your detective skills, and your physical prowess. While I can attest somewhat to your sleuthing skills, I think your social skills are severely lacking."

Colton frowned.

"You haven't been assigned a partner yet either."

That wasn't a question, but a statement. Still, Colton felt compelled to answer. "No, sir."

Mehku got to his feet and walked over to one of the open windows. Looking out, he clasped his hands behind his back. The room fell silent, and Colton felt that strange sacred feeling settle over him again like a cloak.

"Do you know what I find sad, Mr. Fen? Every single one of our kind is damaged in some way. I encounter it every day amid our organization, and it frustrates me to no end. When the Agency began forty years back, I had hoped that it would help our kind to thrive even if it was under the nose of humans. I wanted us to succeed."

The silence stretched between them, and Colton searched for what to say.

"It might be sad, sir, but at least more of our kind are alive. I don't know where I would be if I wasn't here."

Mehku spun around with a smile. "That's it! I know who to pair you with." He rushed over to his desk with long strides and flipped through papers. "You need a partner who will balance out your social difficulties, someone who has a way with smoothing over your awkwardness. Your strength and detective skills should work well with his finesse and persuasiveness."

Colton forced himself to let go of the arms of his chair as he shifted to get a closer look. "I know this is probably a bad question, but do I have to have a partner?"

Mehku only glanced up from his papers. "Grady Walker, he's the werewolf who trained you, right?" He didn't wait for an answer. "He explained you have trouble working with others. Based on my brief interactions with you, he was spot on. Now I understand that even in the Clarkville incident, you struggled to control your wolfish side."

Colton sighed, hating how much he had underestimated this whole meeting. "But I did control it, sir, yes."

Mekhu nodded. "I'll take it. With your new partner, Mr. Dalton, at your side, it should help." He scribbled some notes out on a few pages, then leveled Colton with a powerful gaze. "I was not cursed to be part wolf, Mr. Fen. My curse was... different." He glanced away for a moment, and Colton saw only a brief reflection of fear in his face before it clouded over again. "I know how it feels to be overwhelmed by a curse. Just know that you aren't alone. We all struggle with our unique needs and desires. It's difficult sometimes, but remember: you have friends here willing to help. We must be strong and work together if we are to help our kindred."

Colton nodded, unable to find the right words. "Thank you, sir. I appreciate it."

Mekhu smiled. "I mean it. Now your new partner is a theater owner who lives in a little spit of a town known as Peridot back in Texas. Before I give you this assignment, I need your assurance, Mr. Fen."

Colton blinked. "What for?"

"I need to know that you and Mr. Dalton will work together. I need to know that you're willing to put in the effort. Otherwise, you're wasting your time here. This Agency is about helping others, and if you can't collaborate and work with others, you can't help here."

Colton clenched his jaw. One moment he'd felt like Mekhu was sympathetic to his cause, and the next, he was threatening him with getting canned. He pushed down the frustration and focused on choosing the right words. "I'll do my best, sir. I always do my best."

Mekhu nodded. "Good. I believe you're good for it. Please don't make me regret it."

Colton nodded and took a shaky breath.

"Now, we've had a string of disappearances out there, and although we know that some rogue werewolf packs live in the vicinity, I don't think that's the true cause. That's why we want a team to go out there and find out what's happening to the humans."

"Excuse me for asking, sir, but if only humans are targeted, then why are we being sent in? I thought we existed for the betterment of supernatural creatures, not humans."

"You know how humans are, Mr. Fen. You and I both used to be them. They're easily frightened, and once they learn about these disappearances, they'll aim their fear on anyone. They'll destroy any threat they come across. Unfortunately, our kind always become casualties when humans are afraid."

CHAPTER 2

———

THE NEW PARTNER

THE TRAIN WHISTLE SHRIEKED STEAM INTO THE purple evening sky. When Colton stepped off the train, his boots crunched on the gravel. He was one of only three people who disembarked at Peridot. Clearly, it wasn't a favored destination for travelers.

Judging by the gaps he could see between the boards that made up the walls of the train station, it was built quickly by people who probably didn't know what they were doing. That was a common story out west. The goal was to expand as quickly and efficiently as possible, not necessarily build a structure to last.

Colton walked past the building through the gravel and came to the dirt road that signified Peridot's main street. A little sign with handwritten letters confirmed it. Every little town out west had a Main Street, all looking like they had popped up overnight. A town always began with a road. Colton started down it, eyeing the surrounding shops.

Mr. Tep hadn't been joking when he called Peridot a

little spit of a town, either. But Peridot looked older than most of the towns he had visited out west. Despite the newness of the train station, shanties lay in the distance, looking at least twenty or thirty years old. It was a strange place, the mixture of new and old slammed together, all in the middle of nowhere.

As night advanced, the general stores were closed and most of Main Street was empty, save for the inn with its candles burning for weary, late-night travelers. The theater, though, glowed so brightly from all the lanterns that it lit up the street. It was clearly the biggest attraction in town.

Colton stepped up to the front of the place, eyeballing the stained bat-wing doors and the large sign above painted in shiny black and red paint with fancy lettering: The Crimson Theater. Colton shook his head. When Mr. Tep gave him the name of the theater that his new partner, Rennick Dalton, owned, he had thought it would be hard to find. He hadn't expected this.

The fancy sign up top didn't fit the faded wood of the neighboring shops. In fact, it didn't fit most of Peridot. It was too garish and rich for a place so embedded in the sand and grit of its surroundings. A trio of men stepped out of the theater, laughing loudly into the cool night air. One of them nearly tripped down the steps in a drunken haze. They dragged themselves down the street toward the shanties.

Music and more laughter came from inside the theater. There were probably a ton of people inside. His skin crawled at the thought. He tried to stay away from crowds on most days. It was too risky for a werewolf like him. But

Mr. Tep had told him he needed to be more social. He needed to get used to collaborating. Apparently it started here at The Crimson Theater.

He took a deep breath and steeled himself before stepping inside.

AS SOON AS COLTON STEPPED THROUGH THE doors, the thick tobacco smoke made his throat itch. His eyes burned for a moment as he adjusted to the cloud that permeated the upper half of the room. His gaze fell on the luxurious red curtain drawn closed on the stage. Another prop that appeared too good for the ramshackle town. Opposite the stage and along the wall to his left, the bar was thick with people. Colton had to step aside when someone pushed through the doors behind him and nearly ran him over on their way to the bar.

Realizing he wasn't ready to brave the crowd of people, he looked through the tables laid out in front of the stage. He tracked down a haggard waiter with a platter of glasses held overhead. He cocked an eyebrow. The waiter was a woman. Women weren't permitted to serve alcohol back East, but things were obviously different out here. She squeezed through pockets of people with the deftness of a house cat toward the back of the bar. Colton blocked her path, earning a scowl.

"My apologies, ma'am, but I'm looking for Rennick Dalton," Colton projected to be heard over all the people.

She jutted her chin to the far wall beyond the bar and snapped, "With the sharks."

With practiced ease, she slipped around him and into the crowd near the bar. Colton grumbled and followed her. Regardless of how many people were there, he needed to brave it to get to the gamblers on the other side. The crowd was so thick, Colton had to bring his arms in to squeeze past. He clenched his teeth at the crush of them. He squeezed around a group of four or five men who looked like they could barely walk straight. It was hard to tell if they really were though. Pickpockets would pretend to be drunk when they really weren't. Bars were the perfect hunting ground for thieves, something Colton had learned the hard way when he was younger. He had made sure to clean out his exterior coat pockets earlier, but he still thought he felt at least one attempt as he maneuvered through the crowd.

Through the thick mass of people, he could make out the card tables in the distance. He stepped down the few steps that separated the bar from the gambling tables and took a deep breath. Even though the air here reeked of equal parts smoke and sweat, it was still better than being crushed in the crowd.

Two large, round card tables sat near the wall, both packed with poker players. At the farthest one sat Rennick Dalton. It wasn't his expensive, light blue suit that made him so identifiable, or the three buxom women who were huddled around his chair. Werewolves could always pick out a vampire in a crowd, and vice versa. Outside of the Agency, werewolves and vampires were natural enemies, fighting over lands and their human livestock. Within the Agency, though, their kind often worked together.

To Colton's eyes, Rennick's supernatural qualities were obvious. The man's eyes caught the candle light more than they should. His wavy blond hair fell too perfectly around his cheekbones, and his pale skin didn't reflect the harsh conditions of living out on the frontier. He didn't look like a man who had grown up here under the hot sun and surrounded by sand. In fact, he didn't look like he'd worked a day in his life.

What disturbed Colton were the women huddled all around Rennick. The brunette behind him massaged his shoulders as he played. The blond woman gripped his arm and occasionally leaned over to glance at the other players. A woman with bright red hair sat backwards in a chair on Rennick's other side, with a cigarette hanging out of her mouth as she viciously grinned. Were they his bodyguards or lovers? Did they know what he was?

Colton leaned his back against the wall and watched the women in particular, planning his approach. He wanted to wait until they finished their game because he didn't want to draw too much suspicion. Then a large man at Rennick's table stood up. He was built like a person who spent most of his time in the mines, with powerful arms and a squared frame. As he got to his feet, he shoved back his chair so hard it slammed into the bar rail behind him and cracked. The loud noise quieted the room.

"No!" he cried in a drunken slur. "Not her!" He produced an old but well maintained Colt .45 in one hand and aimed it at Rennick's forehead. In the space of a few seconds, the mood of the room shifted.

The brunette woman behind Rennick screamed and flattened herself against the wall. The blond shot to her feet, and the redhead leaned her head back and cackled. The scream set off a panic. Shoved back chairs squeaked and glasses fell from the shaken tables, shattering on the floor. The cheerful piano music came to a dead stop, and the performers who had just entered on stage froze. The other poker players around Rennick's table stood and backed away with raised hands. Everyone in the room held their breath and fear held the air tight.

Colton clenched his fists against his own impulses. Fear had no scent, but the wolf inside was always eager for it. The muscles in his shoulders tensed and his body went rigid, preparing to pounce. He forced himself to breathe slowly and ignore the hunger pangs that hit him. It would be different if there were only a few terrified people nearby, but with so many, it was difficult to maintain control. He reached out and took hold of the back of a chair, digging his nails deep into the wood. The pain kept his mind focused.

For just a moment, Rennick glanced away from the gunman and caught Colton's eye. Recognition was there, acknowledgment, too, and perhaps just a tinge of fear. He recognized what Colton was. Colton hoped that was a good sign. Then Rennick turned to the gunman and was all smiles as he stared up at the man aiming a gun at his skull.

"Why must you always be such a sore loser, Sherman?" Rennick asked.

"She's the only one I have left, you cheat!" Sherman's arm wavered as he spoke. "She's my favorite!"

The redhead by Rennick giggled into her fist, trying to stay quiet.

Rennick gave a gruff sigh. "You can always find more horses. Besides, you're the one that offered her up." He placed a forearm on the table and leaned forward. "If you don't like the stakes, stay out of the game."

Sherman cocked his gun. "I had you! There's no way you could beat a full house twice in one night!"

"Look!" Rennick put his arms into the air and rolled back his sleeves to reveal his bare arms underneath. "I'm sorry luck hasn't been on your side today, but perhaps I can help with that." He reached into the pile of bills beside him on the table and placed a small stack in front of Sherman. The gunman blinked and reached for them.

"Ah-ah!" Rennick placed a hand over the bills with a sly grin. "Put the gun down."

Sherman hesitated, "But—"

Rennick snapped his fingers. "Come on now. Dallying just might change my mind."

With the huff of a child, Sherman obliged and put the gun on the table, then he reached for the bills. Rennick slid the gun to his side of the table with one hand and passed the bills to Sherman with the other.

"Alright then. Are we settled?" Rennick glanced around at his wary companions around the theater. "Come now, you all act like you've never seen a gun before! And where is that music?"

The piano started up again. The performers on stage continued with their skit. The tension in the room eased and the redhead starting laughing again, much to the annoyance of the other women. Suddenly, it was as if nothing had happened, as though Rennick hadn't nearly had his brains splattered all over the walls.

Colton pulled out his flask and took a sip, hoping the cheap whiskey would help take the edge off his nerves. As the fear dwindled, so did his symptoms, but his hands still shook. To anyone else he might look terrified, but that wasn't at all the case. The wolf in him fed on fear. Fear triggered its attention, and when it awoke, an unwanted transformation usually wasn't far off. Colton hated being near crowds. He never knew what would trigger him. He took another sip from his flask before pocketing it again.

"Come on!" Rennick smiled, organizing the remainder of his winnings. "I'm still in. Isn't anyone else?"

"Sorry, Rennick." A man with a thick bristled beard shook his head as he gathered his meager funds from the table. "I think I'm out for the night."

One by one, the players collected the few earnings they had and left. The blond woman told Rennick how wonderful he was and the brunette beamed at him. The redhead got to her feet, still shaking her head and laughing. He was fairly certain the blond and brunette were Rennick's lovers, but he had no idea about the redhead.

"Fine," Rennick muttered as he dumped his cash into a small satchel. He met Colton's gaze for just a moment before turning his attention back to the table. "Maybe I should retire for the evening." Reluctantly, he let Sherman take back his gun, but not before the brunette emptied out the bullets first. The three women escorted Rennick to a side door behind the poker table that looked like it led to the back halls of the theater.

Colton watched them. His new partner had one hell of an ego, but this might be the only chance he had to get Rennick's attention. He stepped past the first poker table, intent on talking to Rennick directly, but just as he got close to the door beyond the second table, the blond cut him off, her flaming red gown so close it grazed over his boots. Her flowery perfume nearly made him sneeze. She shook her head at him, and Colton was confused.

Rennick paused and looked Colton up and down. "You're here to see me, I presume?"

"Yes, about a business matter."

He smiled, "Of course it is. Follow me." He opened the door and stepped through. Colton started in behind him, but the brunette, a woman with eyes the color of a Texas sunset, glared at him.

"Ladies first," Colton muttered. He took a step back and held the door for the three ladies. He couldn't quite figure out why they were so obsessed with Rennick. Perhaps he paid them to stick around, or perhaps he had some kind of mind control over them. The blond glanced back at him and whispered something to the redhead, who cackled again. Colton frowned, but closed the door behind him as he stepped into the hall.

Compared to the main room, the hallway was eerily quiet. The voices and music were still there, but muffled and distant. Unlike the train station, the theater was built well. He wondered if it had been built with hay or sod to insulate the walls from the main room. If Rennick had built this place from the ground up, then this hallway had been clearly made for privacy.

The women walked ahead of Colton, determined to keep him separated from Rennick. Colton needed to get him alone so they could talk, but three nosy women around made everything more complicated. He couldn't bring up the Agency business in front of three humans. Rennick pulled out a large keyring and unlocked one of the doors, holding it open for them. After the women entered, Colton looked into the room and stopped short. It was a large bedroom with a bed against one wall. This wasn't a place to talk about business.

"What the hell is this?"

"My room, obviously," Rennick crooned. "You don't like it?"

Colton stepped toward him, blocking the doorway. He had tried to be patient, but Rennick was treating this like a joke. If they were going to be partners, then lines needed to be drawn. "I told you I had business to talk about. Is this where you conduct your business?"

"You mean this isn't the business you meant?" A smirk played at the corners of Rennick's lips. "I'm insulted! I thought you might like the ladies' company. They're very good at making guests feel at home."

Colton sighed. "Kick them out or we don't talk at all."

"Kick out my ladies? You *daft beast*."

Colton blinked.

"I always try to give your kind the benefit of the doubt, but I don't know why I even bother. At the end of the day, you're nothing more than a *rude cur*, aren't you?"

The slur caught Colton off guard. It was an old insult, one Colton hadn't heard since he was a child and first been turned. Shame forced him into a stunned silence. Rennick planted a hand on his chest and shoved him through the door. The push was hard enough Colton was knocked off his feet. He hit the wooden floorboards hard, and his lungs forgot for a moment how to breathe. Before he fully realized he was on the ground, a forearm pressed tightly against his throat.

Too late. Colton pulled at Rennick's arm. He should never have underestimated him. Each Agent was an expert killer; Rennick was no exception. In a matter of seconds, Colton had been brought to the ground at his mercy. He was definitely more than a simple card shark.

RENNICK WASN'T THE FIRST VAMPIRE COLTON had encountered. He had witnessed their frightening speed, but this was his first time on the receiving end of an attack. Laying on the ground with his throat burning and his eyes fixed on the ceiling fan above, Colton wondered how he could have missed the signs. Rennick hadn't known him from any other wolf on the street. He clearly had no idea who he was.

"Now that I have your full attention, we can talk," Rennick said, loosening his grip a tad. "Tell me where to find the leader of your little pack, and you might survive this night."

Colton tugged on the arm, giving him just enough space to speak. "I'm not in a pack. I'm from the Agency!" Despite Rennick's speed, Colton had him beat in strength. He almost had enough room to pull his head free.

"No, no." The vampire sighed. "I don't think you understand how this game works." With his free hand, Rennick revealed a dagger. "You know what this is, don't you? I'll bet your brothers and sisters do, too." The blade was simple and unembellished, but the handle made Colton loosen his grip. Made of silver, it had a wolf's silhouette carved into it. Colton let go. "That's a good boy."

As soon as Colton lowered his hands, the vampire's grip tightened again.

Rennick laughed. "Oh come now, the fact that you're still breathing means I haven't completely decided to kill you yet. Let's try again, shall we? Who is your leader?"

"No leader," Colton choked. "An Agent!"

Rennick laughed, "An Agent, really? Don't you think I would have been notified? You're not very imaginative, are you?"

"Breast pocket." Windpipe on fire now, it was all he could do to utter those two words. Stars danced around his vision, and he wasn't sure how long he could stay awake.

Rennick sighed; one of the women stepped forward to check Colton's pockets. Colton could barely see her, but her flowery scent was unmistakable. The blond in the red dress. Had the women been standing there the entire time? Did Rennick routinely kill in front of them? She reached around his flask and pulled out the letter Mr. Tep had given him days ago. She stood there for a moment, likely holding it up for Rennick to read.

Rennick's grip loosened, then released completely. Colton gasped painfully at precious air. It took a while to work up the energy to open his eyes again. Rennick stood over him with the letter in his hands.

"Well, crap. I guess I owe you an apology, Mr..." He looked at the letter again. "Fen. Fen? Are you Chinese or something?" Colton lay there trying to figure out if he could even talk let alone answer such a flippant question.

"I'll admit I don't usually pry, not in these parts at least. People can get downright defensive about family, you know?"

Colton croaked, "Jesus, if I say yes, will you shut up?"

Rennick gave a wide smile. He leaned down, took Colton's arm, and pulled him into a sitting position. Colton groaned, took the drink Rennick offered him, and knocked it back without asking any questions. His throat rebelled against the decision as the strong whiskey burned everything. He coughed into his elbow.

Rennick sat down on the floor beside him. They were sitting in the doorway to his bedroom. Colton had no idea where he'd gotten the whiskey from. "Feeling better?"

"You treat all your friends so well?"

"Only flea-bitten ones. Though you would be surprised. Some men enjoy when I play rough."

Colton blinked.

"I'll admit, I don't think I've ever seen a friendly wolf in these parts." He looked down at the letter in his hands. "Why didn't I get notified you were coming? I mean, it's a good thing I prefer to talk before I kill."

Rennick spoke quite casually about killing him, but Colton understood his perspective. Rennick was likely attacked by wolves on a regular basis. Being such a visible vampire in a small town was dangerous. He gave off all the signs of someone used to being hunted, from the slight fear Colton had sensed at the poker table, to the unexpected assault here in the bedroom. It made him realize just how on edge Rennick must be out here, especially for a lone vampire.

"I assume there's a wolf pack nearby?" Colton grunted.

Rennick got to his feet and stepped through a side door. "It's a small group, but damn persistent. For a while there, I was killing at least one a month!"

Once a month? That was more than just a passing interest. Those wolves were targeting him. It didn't make any sense, though, especially considering how many Rennick had probably killed. Most werewolves chose to live in a pack for the safety it promised. He had heard plenty of stories of wolves who had lost their lives to superstitious townsfolk or zealous hunters. The problem with a pack, though, was they ran the gambit from small, harmless communes to enormous, ruthless mafias. The fact Rennick had fended them off for so long was puzzling, especially considering most vampires would have fallen prey to them within a few months and Rennick looked to be flourishing.

"How do you manage it?"

"What, killing them?" He laughed. "I think you saw my methods. They're rather effective!"

"No, surviving on your own. I was told you built this place from the ground up. That takes more than just time, especially when you've angered a local pack."

Rennick was silent a moment. "I did nothing to anger them, just so you know. Ever since I arrived, they've been trailing me."

"Do they have a leader?"

"Does it matter? Even if I could kill the leader, they would just get a replacement and continue hunting me. Not that I wouldn't relish taking his head first." He sighed., "I'm looking forward to being relocated after this next assignment."

A shirt was tossed out and Colton arched his eyebrows.

It was odd for a man to start undressing in the next room without any warning, especially considering they just met, but this was the West. For all he knew, Rennick was the pinnacle of normal in these parts. That was when Colton noticed the three women that had been Rennick's companions were missing. Despite being distracted earlier, he should have heard them leave. "What happened to your friends?"

"Hmm?" Rennick sounded like he was muffled beneath clothing.

Colton got to his feet, planning to check the hallway. "Your lady friends?"

"Oh!" Rennick laughed, "You mean them?" He snapped his fingers and suddenly the three women appeared in the room, standing around a desk covered in papers, all wearing innocent smiles. What were they? A moment ago the room had been empty. Now they were approaching him. He could hear the billowing of their skirts as they moved, see they were breathing, and smell their perfume. No doors or mechanisms announced their arrival. As he studied each of them, a wave of uneasiness settled on him. It nagged at his senses. It felt familiar somehow, but he couldn't place why.

Creatures pulled from thin air. Spirits given form at the flick of a hand. At one time, it might have sounded like a bizarre magic show, but then realization dawned. These were Rennick's creations, his illusions.

Grady had taken him once to visit a girl living in a special orphanage in North Carolina. Her parents had been killed by a vampire hunter, and she had been taken in by the Agency. A full vampire, her room was completely boarded up against the daylight. Colton remembered her sitting on the edge of her bed amid candelabras, her dark hair long and limp around her frail features. She hadn't spoken a word since they had rescued her six months before, but she had a friend, a pet cat who meowed happily at her and nuzzled her hand regularly. Colton had spoken to the girl for a full thirty minutes and even petted and scratched the cat himself. Only later had Grady had explained the cat wasn't real. The girl had created it to have a friend after her parents had been slain. She might not be willing to talk, but the fact she created a friendly cat to keep her company was a sign she was healing slowly.

Colton stared at each of the three women, noticing now their similar smiles. They each had the same height, and they had similar dresses, just in different colors.

"You created them," he said.

"Absolutely." By the tone of his voice, Rennick was soaking up his reaction. A quick glance over, and he saw Rennick had poked his head out of the closet, exposing his bare shoulders, just to watch him squirm. "Do you like them?"

Colton stared at the women, gaze flicking between each of the people before him. They were illusions, not real people, but just as tangible. Grady's words came back to him, in that voice like a slow, patient storm. "A vampire's illusions are the breath of thought brought to life," he had said. "Just as powerful and just as deadly. Few can manage them, but be wary of those who can."

At the time, Colton had found it hard to imagine how a pet cat could be deadly, but now he understood. Only a handful of vampires could create them, and only the oldest bloodlines had the power to do it.

"The blond is especially delicious, don't you think?" Rennick gushed. "I saw that crimson dress in a Wells Fargo catalog a few weeks back and instantly thought of her." He paused and watched Colton while he drummed his fingers on the door frame. "Goodness, don't leave me in suspense now! What do you think?"

"I just... I've never seen them as people before. I hadn't realized how lifelike they could be."

Rennick shrugged. "They're good, but my father's were far better. He could make dozens of them."

A shudder went through Colton at the words. A vampire strong enough to create troops of followers at will, illusions that couldn't truly be destroyed, and who obeyed his every command. That kind of power was the stuff of legends. Even if Rennick's women were pale shades of his father's, they were still more impressive than the vampire child's cat. Rennick could create his own entourage whenever he wanted them. It made sense now why he was able to handle the city on his own, even with the interest of a nearby wolf pack. It also shed some light on how dangerous their assignment might be. Rennick was a powerful Agent.

"Your father must be very powerful if you inherited his skill," Colton said.

Rennick's amusement faded as he stepped out of the closet, pulling on a shirt. "I guess." He snapped again and the three women vanished as quickly as they had appeared. "Look, I need to make a few stops before we head out." He pulled a wide-brimmed hat on and stopped to adjust it in the mirror. "My place first to get some supplies, then to see Mary and let her know I'll be leaving, and then—"

"We don't even know where we need to go yet."

"Oh yes, and determine our assignment. I suppose Mr. Tep didn't give you very much to go on, did he?" Rennick sighed and proceeded to push Colton out the door. "I swear, for such a powerful group, you would think they could get their letters sent out to me on time."

Colton followed Rennick down the hallway and back into the theater. The smoky room made Colton cough for a while, which seemed to amuse Rennick. As they made their way through the room, Colton noticed how much more confident Rennick seemed compared to earlier. Without thinking Colton was a threat, he moved like the owner of the Crimson Theater should instead of as a shifty card shark. Again, Colton was surprised he hadn't picked up on Rennick's nerves earlier. It was something Grady always chastised him for: lacking perception in people.

They walked past the poker tables, full once again. Several anxious eyes looked up when he and Rennick passed them, as though his mere presence was enough to lighten their coin purses. Rennick assured them all he had no intention of joining their games, which lightened their moods. He stopped to chat with several men for a moment, so Colton moved ahead towards the main stage, grateful to avoid the bar this time.

Raucous laughter filled the main room. On stage, a man had partially covered himself with a checkered blanket and a woman ran around in circles screaming and beating Confederate soldiers with a picnic basket. The soldiers were trying to run past them to escape from gun blasts sounding in the distance, but the woman with the basket was causing them more trouble than the fake gunfire. Colton watched for a while, chuckling along with the audience every time she clocked a man in a gray uniform with a basket. He didn't even notice when Rennick had finished up, and approached beside him.

"Do you like it?"

Colton shrugged. "It's different."

Rennick rolled his eyes, "You were laughing just a moment ago. I saw you."

He shrugged, "It's not *that* funny."

Rennick pointed to the woman with the basket, "Would you believe me if I told you she writes most of our shows?"

"Really?"

Rennick nodded. "Everyone is always surprised. They ask me how I'm still in business," he said with a gleam in his eye. "These comedies are more popular than our dancing girls." When Rennick put an arm around his shoulders, Colton had to keep from flinching. His neck was still sore from getting pinned earlier. "Maybe once we're done, you'll get a chance to see the whole thing. I guarantee you'll find it better with a few drinks in you."

Colton pulled away from Rennick's arm with a sigh. "I doubt it."

Rennick smirked. "Fair enough." He led the way to the bat-wing doors, weaving in and out of the crowd, shaking hands, and occasionally mixing coins with handshakes to a few favored employees. Colton couldn't figure out if Rennick did it just to be seen as a generous owner, or if he was trying to impress Colton.

Once they reached the entrance, Colton leaned closer to Rennick to ask. "Is there going to be a problem with you just walking out?"

"It'll be fine. They're used to it by now." Rennick shouldered through the doors, but Colton paused. He turned back again toward the stage, scanning the crowd. He felt like they were being watched, but he couldn't spot anything unusual.

"Come on," Rennick called back to him. "My place is just a short walk."

CHAPTER 3

HOME SWEET HOME

EVERYTHING IN PERIDOT WAS JUST A SHORT WALK away, but the path wasn't always straightforward.

The general store was across the street, and the saloon called The Water Trough was beside that. Looking around at the people who lived here, Colton could see they didn't make much. Walking down Main Street, it was clear where most of their funds went. Past the shops and beyond the lights of the theater, the shanties began. The dark walls that loomed up on either side of the street in the distance etched black against the starry sky. It was odd to imagine most of the people who worked here lived in such rundown places.

Rennick turned away from the direction of the shanties and instead turned east along the railroad tracks. Once they were walking behind the buildings of Main Street, Colton thought they might be lost until he realized they were on a footpath. It was old, probably older than the tracks. After a few minutes of walking in silence, with no sound except the wind swirling up dirt and sand, Colton decided to ask the obvious.

"You don't live in town?"

Rennick chuckled, slowing his pace to walk beside Colton instead of leading the way. "No, there really isn't much to choose from."

"So why have a bedroom at the theater if you don't live there?"

Rennick glanced at him, his eyes catching the moonlight. "When I first got here, the inns were rather unacceptable, to be quite frank. I came here on assignment, one that only took me a few days to finish, and then I requested some leave time. It seemed like the perfect place for a theater. Peridot had so much potential! I setup a temporary home at the theater, making that the first section of the building that was completed. It took me a while to secure a real home for myself. Unfortunately there seems to have been a misunderstanding on how much leave time I wanted."

"So you've been waiting for another assignment from the Agency."

He nodded. "I've learned my lesson. Never take leave unless you plan to do it for at least a year. Otherwise, you're stuck."

The footpath took a sharp turn, and they were at the base of a hill, atop of which was a large homestead. The far side of the house was attached to a field that might have once held horses. It was so overgrown now with grass and weeds that without the fence, it would have looked separate from the property.

"Is all this yours?" Colton asked.

Rennick smiled. "Not the pasture, but the house is mine." He pulled out a large keyring and unbolted the front gate. Although clear just from his short visit to the Crimson Theater Rennick had money, seeing his grand home intimidated Colton. His father had worked on the railroad for most of his life, so Colton and his mom had never known money. The house's two stories might as well have made it a mansion, especially in a place like Peridot. It looked old, too, much older than any other building along Main Street. The front gate had a twin pair of Ss engraved into the wood, making it look more like a family legacy than something Rennick would own.

"It's great isn't it? I got a hell of a deal on the place." They walked up to the front door, and Rennick had to jingle the keys around to find the right one to let them in. He obviously hadn't been living here long, so Colton wondered if perhaps Rennick wasn't really the actual owner. He did have a taste for finery, and the homestead was likely the nicest home around; in fact, that might have been what caught Rennick's eye. The thought made Colton uneasy.

Rennick was already halfway up the stairs to the second floor by the time Colton stepped through the threshold.

"I'll just be a minute," Rennick said. Colton couldn't help but think that he was acting suspicious when Rennick disappeared around the landing.

Once his eyes adjusted to the darkness and to the moonlight that filtered in through the dirty windows, his unease deepened. Signs were everywhere Rennick didn't own the place; the wilted flowers in vases, the floral draperies, the dining table and chairs covered in sheets. Was Rennick squatting here? If so, what happened to the original owner? Colton rubbed the back of his neck as he remembered

Rennick's speed and strength. He could have slaughtered any hardworking family who used to live here. He hoped they hadn't had children.

Other than Rennick's creaking footsteps upstairs, the only sound was the ticking of a grandfather clock in the living room. Here, too, the furniture was covered, and the fireplace looked like it hadn't been used for some time. The mantle was covered in a thick layer of dust, save for a few bare, rectangular spots where picture frames must have once sat. He brushed his fingers over them. How long had Rennick lived here?

Colton wandered to the base of the stairs, wondering how he was going to approach Rennick about the details of the house, when a series of banging sounds overhead caught his attention. Was Rennick moving heavy furniture around, or was it something else? Colton pulled out his revolver and started up the stairs, stepping cautiously to keep from making any noise.

He had just put one foot on the landing when he heard "Hrk—!"

A shadow fell over the stairway in front of him, the final flight of steps that saddled up alongside the upstairs hall-way. Moonlight from one of the upstairs windows gave the figure a silhouette for a brief moment, but Colton couldn't tell if it was Rennick. Colton got on his toes and leaned up just enough to glimpse the second-floor hall. He caught the tail end of a boot disappearing into an open room.

Letting out a slow breath, he dropped down and put his back to the wall again. He double-checked his gun, made sure his Stetson hat was secure, then sprinted up the steps. He spun around the corner, down the hall, and stepped into the open room. A person lunged to reach cover behind a sofa, but wasn't quite fast enough. Colton fired, and the bullet hit the person's left shoulder. They had been in mid-air at the time, and the concussion spun them so that they landed on their side. The person didn't cry out or even groan. With his revolver still outstretched, Colton stepped into the room and started toward the intruder.

Gunfire erupted from the opposite side of the room and a bullet grazed Colton's left thigh. He fell to the ground, kneeling on his good leg. The shot hadn't come from the person he'd hit, but from a second person. He turned to see a large bed and a figure behind it, a black shadow hidden from the moonlight streaming in from the large windows. Colton had foolishly walked right into the middle of the room, and now he was crouched and vulnerable. It didn't matter if he hit or not, he needed to fire back.

The gun barrel emerged as the person prepared to fire again, but Colton rolled away and flattened down into the shadows. As the shadowy figure shot, Colton fired two shots back. When his opponent ducked behind the bed, Colton lunged behind the couch. His thigh burning, he crawled over to the person he had shot in the shoulder, gritting his teeth against the flaring pain in his leg. Even though the bullet had only grazed him, blood was pouring freely, and the scent clung to his nostrils.

He turned his attention to the person on the ground. A man in his mid to late thirties, but he was also a werewolf. Colton could tell by his scent. He was also in far worse shape. A heavy gash creased the side of his skull and his eyes were wide open; blood pooled around his head. Colton's mid-air bullet hadn't just spun him, it also had smashed his head into the sharp corner of a heavy wooden side table. It might have killed a man, but this was a werewolf. Already, Colton could see the bleeding from the man's head wound had slowed, and the gash was stitching closed piece by piece. In a few hours he would be fully healed and ravenous. These two weren't simple thieves or outlaws, they were trained to kill. And likely had been sent here to get rid of Rennick.

Colton leaned his head against the back of the couch. He thought of Rennick's words back at the theater, about how these wolves were regular attackers, and he cursed himself for not coming upstairs with him earlier. Normally, Rennick would probably be on edge and prepared for them, but Colton's presence had been a distraction. He wondered now if the scent of these two unknown wolves in the house had been the cause for his own unease downstairs.

"Where's Rennick?" Colton demanded, turning his attention to the assailant behind the bed.

"I've got him here," a man's gruff voice replied. Colton could only assume he was a werewolf, the same as his bloodied friend. His sense of smell was rather difficult to trust at the moment, between his own blood and the man bleeding out beside him. He could smell another scent, though, more pungent and obvious now he took the time to notice it: vampire blood.

"Show me."

Colton held his hat out on one side of the couch, then he leaned out from the other side to watch. Rennick was lifted up by his throat, his skin a pale blue in the moonlight, eyes lolling. Colton saw the flash of a gun just in time to duck, but the bullet went through his hat instead of him. It was a trick he'd used before. Out of habit, Colton hit the ground harder than he needed to, in order to give the impression he fell backwards. After hitting the floor, he quietly shifted to a crouch, ignoring the pain from his leg, and flattened himself against the back of the couch. He held his gun steady as the man approached. He would want to finish him off.

Unlike the one on the ground, this assailant was well trained. His footfalls made little noise on the old wooden floor. Colton waited until the man's gun came into view, followed by his shaking grip. They always approached with their gun extended, even though they couldn't yet see what they were aiming at. Colton shifted aside and fired at the man's wrist.

The man cried out, and the gun flew up wildly as he fired a hole into the ceiling. Colton got to his feet and fired again, this time at the man's forehead. Blood spurted out, his wide eyes rolled up, and he crumpled to the floor.

COLTON STOOD THERE, HIS HEART THUDDING IN his chest as he listened for any movement. He didn't want to be caught off guard again. He listened for footsteps, clothes rustling, panicked breathing; all he heard were shallow breaths coming from the far side of the bed. He reloaded his gun and approached his partner.

Rennick lay face down on the floor in his own blood. His hands were pinned behind his back in an upside-down prayer with his palms touching. A dagger had been stabbed clean through. His chest rose and fell with each breath, but otherwise he would have passed as a corpse.

Colton crouched down, hissing at the pain in his leg. It was healing, but slower than he wanted. "Rennick? Are you alright?"

Rennick groaned.

With his hands pinned together, it looked like some kind of ritual. Perhaps he was too quick to write off the group as some random wolf pack; perhaps it was a cult. It would explain why they were so intent on targeting Rennick. A vampire who wielded such powerful illusions might make a cult leader seem weak.

Colton gripped the blade's handle and pulled it free, gritting his teeth when Rennick cried out in pain. As he turned him over, panic set in. Rennick was trembling from head to toe and his face was tinged with gray, but something was wrong. A normal vampire would have started healing, even from such deep wounds. Instead, blood seeped steadily through his expensive shirt. Rennick was not a full vampire. He likely only had half or a quarter of the lineage, which meant bleeding out was a real danger.

"I had the whole thing under control," Rennick whispered. "Promise."

It was difficult now to imagine Rennick slaying an entire family just for their house. Yes, he had the strength to do it, but he just didn't seem the type. Even nearly dead, he still spouted bad jokes. "I thought you said you were a full vampire."

Rennick shook his head, dipping more of his hair into

the pooling blood. "I never said that. Don't put words in my mouth."

Colton pulled at Rennick's shirt, trying to find the source of the wound. A couple of stabbed hands shouldn't spill so much blood. He needed to keep him talking, though, just in case. "Interesting work they did with your hands. Is that normal for this group?"

"I don't know," Rennick said. "This is the first time they've gotten me. Effective though. I need my hands to... to create..." It took Colton a moment to realize he was referring to his illusions. For the first time, Colton considered how long this pack must have been trailing him. They not only knew where he lived, but they knew his strengths and his weaknesses. They knew how to act quickly and take him down.

Rennick's shirt had been torn to shreds, and a deep gash had been bitten out of his side. Werewolf bites were always distinctive, ranging anywhere from a sharp-toothed human-sized bite to an enormous wolf bite. The one who had bitten Rennick must have been partially transformed because it was too large for a human, but not big enough for a fully transformed werewolf. Blood poured from the wound, and Colton could see chunks of inner tissue beginning to spill out over the edges. Rennick was lucky to be conscious, though that jolt of pain to his hands might have pulled him back to reality. Rennick wouldn't last long like this, though; he needed to feed.

Colton sighed and glanced over the werewolves in the room. He might usually recommend them as blood sources, but werewolf blood was dangerous for vampires. He wasn't sure what it would do to a half vampire, either.

"Do you have any blood substitutes? Sent from the Agency?" Colton asked.

Rennick nodded. "Downstairs... kitchen."

In a moment, Colton turned, hurried down the steps and entered the massive kitchen. He thought they would be easy to find, but that was not at all the case. He flung open cabinets, looked around piles of dishes and glassware. Finally, he found them in the very back, near the oven. A few dusty cans with the Eye of Horus emblazoned on the front were the only indicators of the Agency. To people who might not know any better, they might look like canned meat or vegetables. Colton gathered all of them into his arms and hurried back upstairs.

He dumped them beside Rennick who didn't open his eyes. Extending his claws, he punctured holes in the top and snorted at the scent of processed chemicals trying to be blood. It probably was nowhere near actual blood for Rennick, but his body needed it to recover.

When Colton put the open can to Rennick's lips, the bloodlust kicked in, and Rennick took over the rest of the way. His eyes flew open and his pupils took on a dark, red glow. In a second, his fangs had extended and he clamped down on the edge of the can.

While Rennick drank, Colton watched the wound in his side stitch together. His exposed internal organs oozed blood like water from a sponge and slowly shifted and reformed. Layers of skin were pulled in again as his body reconstructed itself. Colton brought over another can and another, and his partner consumed them with ravenous speed. Finally, his torso was once again whole, save for a faint, glossy scar.

Rennick pulled away and shut his eyes. His cheeks flushed as though he had a fever. Colton got to his feet as Rennick regained himself. He had no idea how old the half vampire was, but he looked far younger than he probably should. His eyes looked a tad too big for his skull, giving him the odd appearance of a teenager rather than a man. His blond hair was streaked with blood, but even so, it kept that impossible sheen common to all vampires. Slowly, the rest of his skin lost its bluish tinge. His skin lacked even the smallest details that typically came with age, such as wrinkles or laugh lines. Watching him take on a typical human pallor only made Colton notice how inhuman he looked. It was rare to see vampires so close to death. It provided a glimpse at their true face without their human facade.

Rennick sat up, looking dazed. "I'm not a fan of canned blood, but I'll admit that feels much better. My head is spinning." He laughed. His eyes were still tinted a dark ruby color and his fangs hadn't disappeared.

"You look better," Colton said. He nodded to the bodies still lying by the end table. "There are a few cans left, do you want those, too?"

Rennick nodded slowly and blotted his stained lips on the back of his hand. He reached into a sheath on his side and produced his silver-handled blade, "We'll need to take care of them quickly before they recover. Want me to finish them off?"

Colton's eyes locked onto the handle and he stepped backwards.

Rennick rolled his eyes. "Why are you so spooked? You know it's not for you!"

"I know..." he muttered. He hated the way silver made

him tense, but it was an innate fear, an instinct that could never be controlled. At first, he was surprised the two werewolves hadn't noticed it, but then he saw the sheath on Rennick's belt. It was unusual, covering the entire dagger, not just the blade. Did he wear it to keep his weapon a secret? Or had he adorned that for Colton's sake?

He looked at the man closest to them. The gunshot to his head wouldn't kill him, any more than that head wound would kill his friend. Given a few days, they would be healthy. Already, Colton could spot the back of the bullet in his skull, getting pushed from the bone like a splinter from a finger. They would return to their pack and report what they learned. Then many more would come hunting, encouraged by the partial success. Of course, if they were killed now, the pack would still know something had happened, but they would be in the dark about the specifics. He and Rennick might still have the advantage for a few days.

Despite being unconscious, Colton wondered if some part of the fallen man was aware enough to know he was about to truly die. Shaking his head, he looked away. "You can finish them off."

Rennick's smile faded as he turned to the nearby werewolf. "I guess I can't blame you. I don't think I could finish off a vampire by taking their head off either. It's different killing a creature that isn't like you. Killing your own feels distasteful, doesn't it?"

Colton didn't respond.

Rennick flipped the dagger around in his palm with a practiced toss and pushed the handle into the gunshot wound on the werewolf's head. Even though the werewolf was completely unconscious, he still felt it coming. His eyes widened ever so slightly when the silver touched his blood, and a shudder coiled through him as true death arrived. Even with a bullet still lodged in his skull, even with his mind a scrambled mess, even after bleeding out on the floor, survival instinct remained. A primal fear every werewolf held. Colton shook, but he couldn't look away.

There was something horrifying but captivating about watching a werewolf die. He had seen it before, but repetition didn't make it any more bearable or lessen its impact. The blood at the site of infection first turned a silvery black and took its time spreading through the veins. It spread across the skin like a spider's web, and wherever it moved the body curled up on itself like those dried out mummies in Egypt. Colton could never tell if it was from the pain or the muscles being decimated. The werewolf's breathing grew labored as the silver etched its way down his neck to his chest and, finally, took hold of his heart. He gave a slight whimper as the tendrils exploded out to the rest of his body from there. It trailed up to either side of his skull and spread out over his face like the cracks in the earth that formed after a drought. His body turned the color of coal tinged with silver as the rest of his skin tainted. For a few moments, his eyes darted back and forth, a man trapped inside his dying body before the eyes, too, turned. The body caved in as the upper torso bent impossibly forward, landing and merging with the legs. It was like burning him alive without the mercy of a flame. In a few minutes, there would be no trace of him save for his clothes and a pile of ash.

Colton turned away and tightened his shaking hands to

fists. He hated hunting his own kind and murdering them with such torturous methods, but there was no other way to kill them. As much as he tried to tell himself he was saving countless human lives by destroying his brethren, somehow it never rang true. A hand landed on his shoulder and he turned. Rennick stood behind him. Other than his tattered shirt and the mass of blood still clinging to his hair, he looked perfectly healthy again. A stranger would think all that blood belonged to someone else.

"I'll take care of the other one. It'll take me a bit to clean up, though." The slight smile on his lips didn't quite reach his eyes. "Why don't you wait for me downstairs?"

Colton gave a bitter laugh that sounded more like a combustion of nerves. "You sure? I don't want you getting ambushed again."

"I've got this. No need for you to see it."

He wanted to protest, but he couldn't muster the strength. Behind Rennick, Colton spotted the pile of ash that used to be their enemy filling out the human clothes like a stuffed scarecrow.

"Fine," he said, and left.

CHAPTER 4

————

THE DISAPPEARANCES

ALTHOUGH RENNICK HAD ASKED HIM TO WAIT downstairs, Colton needed fresh air. He hurried down the steps past the covered furniture and pushed out the front door, gulping breaths of the crisp night air.

He still wasn't far enough away from those piles of clothes that used to be werewolves. So he kept walking, out through the tall, brown grass that grew over his knees. He strode out to the far end of the overgrown pasture, cutting a path through the grass, his boots crunching down the dry earth. Stars filled the enormous sky above. The wind swept through the surrounding field. Taking a deep breath, Colton tried to calm his nerves.

It wasn't the first werewolf he had watched be killed, but the image wouldn't leave him, and he hated himself for it. He couldn't forget the panic and terror in those eyes. His hands shook. Colton wished he smoked. He needed something to do with his hands, something to focus on. He drifted like a tumbleweed unable to control where the wind took it.

His fingers latched onto the metal flask in his pocket and he gulped down the alcohol within. There wasn't much left, but the burn felt good on his throat. It pulled him back into the moment and made him feel alive and present. He paced, drifting his hand over the sharp points of the grass, feeling the slightly painful leaves scrape his skin. He took another deep breath, and finally his hands stopped shaking. A large bat fluttered past, and he almost caught the scent of a flowering cactus.

Some days Colton wondered what his life would be like had he not joined the Agency. He liked to think he would be a lone wolf scratching out a quiet life somewhere on his own homestead, steering clear of any supernatural creatures that might come his way. Of course, after spending five years with the Agency, he knew that was an overly optimistic belief.

More people were moving out West and more of the bare land was being claimed. Hunters roamed the lands and lone wolves were easy targets. If they were lucky enough to avoid hunters, some rogue pack picked them up when life inevitably got difficult. Working for the Agency was tough, but it had some rewards. They did save lives, even though there was rarely any recognition, let alone thanks, from the people and beings they saved.

Grady had nearly been indoctrinated by a pack in his younger years before he joined the Agency. He spoke frequently of their brainwashing techniques, their abusive methods, and how only the lowest wolves would be sent on dangerous missions. The ones Colton had seen upstairs were probably fairly green, still trying to prove themselves to their leaders. Grady had been a talented fighter before getting picked up by a pack. He had gone in thinking there was safety in numbers, but realized quickly he was disposable. The frightening part was he had begun to believe it. The pack was targeted by an Agency effort to disband them, and Grady had been one of those rescued. He hadn't been in the pack very long, so they were able to reverse the effects. Colton wondered if the ones upstairs could have been rescued.

The Agency for the Betterment of Supernatural Creatures was a bit of a misnomer since half the cases they took were just as beneficial for humans as their supernatural neighbors. Though their agents were mostly powerful creatures and magic wielders, a few humans were scattered throughout. As for ownership, there was plenty of speculation. Some said it gained a solid investment from the US government during the Civil War when Lincoln recognized the agents were useful in helping the Union army. Others thought a handful of wealthy, magical socialites were the secret behind their deep pockets. After meeting Mr. Tep just a few days ago, Colton leaned toward the latter.

Rennick crossed the field to meet up with him. He had changed into a tan suit and carried a leather satchel. It was hard to believe he had nearly bled to death a few minutes ago.

"You clean up quick," Colton said with a nod.

"Thanks," Rennick said, holding out Colton's Stetson hat.

Colton blanched, shocked he had somehow forgotten it. He dragged a hand through his hair, chagrined, and took it back. "Thanks," he muttered as he placed it on his head.

"So, are you ready to head out?"

Colton sighed. "I suppose." He reached into his breast pocket and pulled out a folded sheet of paper. Straightening it to read the contents, he recognized the symbol of the Agency embellished in the top left corner: the letters ABSC with the eye of Horus underneath all contained within a wispy octagon of vines. "Mr. Tep told me about the disappearances."

"Oh, so just a few humans missing? That's not so bad! We break into wherever they're being held, kill whoever holds them, and set them free. Do you think it's the work of that werewolf pack?"

Colton shook his head. "No, I don't think it's going to be that easy. He mentioned some farm if I remember right."

Rennick laughed, "There's no farm in Peridot. Maybe they got the paperwork mixed up."

"I don't think so," Colton said. Rennick leaned over his shoulder to read the letter.

ABSC
Dispatch Office
ABSC Headquarters
Charlotte, North Carolina

Attn. Mr. Fen (WW-3):

We've been made aware of potential super-
        natural attacks at Davis Farm located
        near Peridot, Texas. The danger of the
        investigation has been labeled high, so
        we're assigning you a new partner,

Rennick Dalton (PV/I-3). Current
reports state the following:

2-3 Casualties
2 Missing (1 Male adult, 1 Female child)

> It is uncertain based on the reports whether
> these are supernatural or spectral in
> nature. Find out what is causing these
> disappearances and resolve it. Use any
> means necessary. Local registered
> members have been evacuated as a
> precaution.

Sincerely,
Mr. M. Tep
ABSC Director

Rennick's gaze met Colton's. "A little girl?" He hissed.

"I know." Colton folded up the letter.

"How old? Did he tell you that? You met with him in person, right? Surely he told you more about this. What do they mean supernatural or spectral?"

Colton sighed. "They only know limited information from the local registered members who were evacuated. It hasn't gotten to the point that humans really noticed, not out here anyway, but eventually they will. That's what they were afraid of. That's why they sent us out here."

Rennick shook his head. "Feels like we're always worried about humans getting scared. It's ridiculous."

"As for the spectral or supernatural, that's because they

haven't found any bodies. Nobody has seen anything. No one is demanding money. People just seem to disappear into thin air."

Rennick gave a nervous laugh as he twisted a finger around a lock of blond hair. "Great. So we honestly have no clue what we're up against. No bodies. That really doesn't sit well with me. And they evacuated any registered beings, which means they were afraid of them either getting targeted by the people or…"

When he trailed off, Colton finished the statement for him. "Or they could have been targeted by whatever is taking the humans. If that's the case, then probably some supernatural beings have been taken, too, and they just didn't tell us about it."

"Damn, I hate when they don't give us all the information. That's never a good sign."

Colton shrugged. "They probably didn't want to spook me into not coming, though it would take more than that to keep me away."

Rennick folded his arms. "We're both level three agents, which means we're not exactly new at this. If they redacted information about the assignment to us, the actual investigators, just because they thought we might run, that doesn't bode well."

They were silent a moment as the chilly wind swept through the tall grass, churning up the dry dust.

"Or maybe they're just being held captive by the werewolf pack," Colton said with a halfhearted smile.

Rennick gave a weak laugh. "At least we have some direction now, I suppose, even if I don't like where it's going. I need to take care of business before we start on this clearly dangerous mission."

"What kind of business?"

Rennick smiled. "I've been living here for almost a year now. I built the theater. I made this speck of a place profitable. People know my face better than their own kids. If I'm going to disappear and go on an assignment, I have to get things in order."

Colton shook his head. "Why did you even set roots down here?"

Rennick flung out his arms. "I don't know. Maybe I always wanted to start a little theater. Maybe I wanted to start a little business, just to prove that I could." He stared up at the starry sky. "Maybe I wanted to do something that people actually appreciated and recognized for once."

"Look, I didn't mean to—"

Rennick wasn't finished. "I couldn't ever get away with it on the east coast, but here? Nobody cares!" He shook his head. "I hire women to handle all levels, even bar tending. Back East, I'd get fined for that, but nobody bats an eye here. Nobody cares about the men or women I bring to my bedroom. They don't care about where I came from, all they care about is that I keep them entertained, I make them laugh, I give them the chance to make money, and I keep the spirits flowing." He swept a hand toward town. "People come to the middle of nowhere just to see the theater I built."

Colton put a hand on his partner's shoulder, and that seemed to pull him out of his rant. "Look, you don't have to do this. You can stay with your theater if you want."

Rennick gave a sad smile. "No, I knew it was short-lived

to begin with. I knew it couldn't last. Things like that just don't last for our kind, do they, Mr. Fen?"

Colton let the silence stretch for a moment as Rennick wiped at his eyes.

"My father was Mr. Fen. You can call me Colton. We're partners now, after all."

"Colton." Rennick said the name with a smile. "Yes, we are partners now, aren't we?" He headed toward the entrance to the pasture, back to the large gate that led down to Main Street.

Colton realized he was holding the folded up letter still in his hands. He slipped it into his breast pocket and hurried to follow Rennick.

"So, Davis Farm," he said, hoping to change the topic and give Rennick something else to concentrate on. "I thought you said there weren't any farms in Peridot?"

"There aren't," Rennick responded with more confidence. "That farmhouse is about fifty miles out, but the Davis family hasn't lived here for a long time. I didn't realize the building was even there still."

They stepped out of the large metal gate and Rennick locked up behind them. Afterward, he dangled the keyring in the air. "I just need to drop this off for safe keeping before we head out."

Colton eyed them. "Are those for the house or the theater?"

"Both."

MAIN STREET WAS MUCH EMPTIER THAN IT HAD been earlier. As they passed the Crimson Theater, all that remained were a handful of bleary-eyed patrons outside talking in low voices with friends. Through the bat-wing doors Colton could spot the empty tables now the place was cleaned up for the night. The red curtain was drawn across the stage. He assumed this was the place where Rennick would need to drop off his keys, but Rennick walked past his beloved theater and through the remainder of the few buildings that made up downtown Peridot.

Slowly, the buildings changed from large, well-kept shops to rows of cheap shanties. In one of the yards, a pack of mutts fought over a stolen scrap of meat; one even gave a warning growl as they passed. Downtown was a shadow of what it had been a few hours ago, but here there were a few places that still had oil lamps lit. These streets were dark and eerie. He caught a flicker of movement as a curious face disappeared from a darkened window pane and he thought of the wolves they had fought at Rennick's house.

They stopped at a shanty with a cheap wooden fence around the front. It was almost a beacon compared to the others from the many lanterns lit within. The walls weren't full of holes like the other shanties, and the door actually covered the entrance.

"Who lives here?" Colton asked.

"A dear friend of mine. Someone I really should talk to before we leave."

Rennick rapped on the front door, and Colton frowned at how the whole building seemed to shake with the motion. A woman with dark, unkempt hair cracked open the door, wearing an annoyed expression. She was clearly of Native American descent, but the strange part was she looked familiar. But that was impossible. Colton had been in Peridot for only hours.

Her annoyance melted quickly when she focused on his partner. "Rennick!"

"Hello, Mary," Rennick grinned. "You were brilliant this evening."

She pulled Rennick into an embrace. Colton realized where he had seen her before. On the stage at the Crimson Theater. The girl screaming and running in circles with a picnic basket. The actress who made the whole room guffaw with laughter. She still wore the makeup, though she had already exchanged her brightly colored stage dress for one with dull pink flowers and lace trim that had seen better days.

"I have a gift for you, dear!" Rennick whispered, pulling away. He reached into his pocket and fished out his keyring.

Her face scrunched up in confusion as he dropped it into her open palm. "But I don't understand..."

"It's my mother." Rennick sighed. "I'm afraid she's gotten worse."

Mary brought a hand to her mouth. "Oh no. Don't tell me you're going to go visit her. Not when the theater is doing so well!"

He sighed again. "I have to. I told you it might happen."

She moved her hand to her chest, swiping away some of the white face paint on her cheek and revealing her warm, bronze skin underneath. "We had that new play all planned out for this weekend too." Her eyes were glassy as she stared at him. Colton shifted his weight, really wishing he had stayed on the street. His movement caught Mary's eye, and she arched an eyebrow. "Who is this?"

"He's an old friend," Rennick said. "He's come to escort me back home."

Mary pursed her lips. Colton imagined she was pretty good at sniffing out bullshit since she made a living as an actress. Living in this dump likely heightened it. Up to this point, Colton assumed Rennick knew what he was doing. The skepticism in her eyes made him doubt.

"Odd that I've never seen him around before," Mary drummed her fingers on the frame. "Does he have a name?"

Colton made to answer, but Rennick answered for him.

"His name is Colton, and he just came to town. He was a childhood friend of mine. Just got into town a little while ago." He turned and gave a big, encouraging smile to Colton. It didn't improve his sincerity. "We went to school together."

Colton took a step forward to prevent Rennick from adding more lies to the pile. "Pleased to meet you, ma'am." He tipped his hat to her, but she looked suspicious.

"The pleasure's mine. If you are heading out of town, I'm sure the two of you would be happy to stop in and have a drink first?"

Rennick sighed. "I don't think we have the time to—"

She wrapped her hand around his wrist and hissed. "Unless you want me telling folks what you two really are."

Rennick gaped. All the confidence fell from him in an instant as she dragged him across the threshold.

Colton clenched his teeth. It was never good when a human found out about an agent. Not only was it dangerous for the agent, but it could also compromise the mission or even the Agency. He now wished Rennick hadn't decided to make this visit before they started on their assignment, but seeing as his partner was now being held captive more or less, it was too late for regrets.

With a short nod, he said, "I think we could take a few minutes to talk, ma'am."

"That's Miss Silva to you," she said, aiming a glare in his direction.

He tried to catch Rennick's eye as he followed the two inside, but his new partner looked dumbstruck. Their fight with the werewolves earlier had been a cakewalk compared to this.

MARY'S HOUSE WAS SMALL, BUT SURPRISINGLY roomy despite the ramshackle appearance from outside. The room they stepped into served as both a kitchen and a living room; through an open doorway he could see the edge of a small bed tucked into a corner. She pushed Rennick onto a rickety wooden chair next to a square dining table that had seen better days. He shrank down like a fearful puppy. Colton closed the door behind him and leaned against the wall, watching Mary pull glasses out to pour them each a drink.

"How long have you known?" Rennick's voice was small, for once matching his boyish appearance.

Mary smirked. "About half a year now, I'd say. Once I knew what to look for, it became obvious."

Colton didn't like where this was headed. A jilted lover

was prone to talk. If she told others and word spread, she could put other supernatural beings in danger, too. Word of mouth could spell disaster for any non-human who wanted to make a peaceful home here. All it took was a spark to start a blaze.

He decided to let his partner handle it. Clearly they were intimate, and the idea of getting caught up in a lover's spat didn't appeal. He took the glass she offered him with a polite smile, trying hard to ignore how she shoved it at him. He considered ducking outside, but Mary had a keen eye and would probably stop him as soon as he turned his back.

Mary was a tall woman with black hair that hung around her face. It was hard to tell what she looked like through the exaggerated stage makeup. He thought back to her on the stage earlier that evening, to her shrieking and waving the basket over her head. It was difficult to believe the woman who had made an entire room burst into laughter on stage was the same as the person before him. Her dingy dress hung awkwardly on her body. Too big for her, Colton couldn't help but notice the way it exposed far more cleavage than was considered decent. He couldn't decide if he found her attractive or terrifying.

Mary sat down at the dingy dining table beside Rennick and gave him a glass before downing her own drink in a single gulp. "At first, I thought I was jumping at shadows," she said. "But then I saw those women that always hang on you." Rennick tensed at the comment, and she pointed a finger at him over the glass. "Oh, yes, I've seen them all over town. At first, I thought you were parading them just to spite me."

Rennick took a tiny sip of his drink, but kept his eyes downcast. Colton applauded the man's perseverance.

"So I threw myself into my work of course, like any girl would." Mary said, "I practiced my lines, tightened up my footwork, and every night I came home and drowned my tears." She wiped at her mouth with the back of her hand. A sneer formed on her lips as she smeared more of the white muck from her face. "I did that far too long."

"I wasn't trying to upset you." Rennick's smile was genuine enough, but then he made the mistake of placing a hand on her shoulder.

Her eyes went wide as she shoved away his hand. "Get your goddamn hand off me."

Rennick blinked, then pulled back, and scooted his chair away from her. The legs squeaked loudly on the floorboards as he moved it back an inch.

"If you *ever* think of touching me again, you lying bastard..."

She didn't have to finish that line of thought. Rennick was cowering once again. She stared at him a full minute with eyes that would have made most men piss themselves.

"The men were the ultimate slap in the face, Ren." Mary poured herself another glass. "You brought so many of them by, showed them around, and even bought them drinks. Did you think I wouldn't figure it out?"

Rennick looked up at her curiously. "The men?"

"That's when I understood." She downed another glass.

Jesus, had Rennick killed off that many people? It was one thing if they threatened his life, but to kill a steady stream of innocent humans was straight up murder. The Agency had plenty of ways to provide blood, raw meat, or whatever special palette their agents needed, to prevent them from having to turn to humans for food. Rennick wasn't even a full vampire, so his thirst for blood ought to be much lower. Rennick looked thunderstruck.

He gaped at Mary, then turned to Colton. "I honestly don't have a clue what she's going on about. I would never—"

Mary slammed her hand on the table, making both men jump. "You goddamn liar!" She shot to her feet, still clutching the glass in her hand, and flung the remainder of her drink into Rennick's face.

"Mary!" He spluttered, pulling out a handkerchief. "This suit is expensive!"

"I don't give a damn!"

He dabbed desperately at his fresh suit as he got to his feet as well. Then he glowered at her. They were staring eye-to-eye now. Colton dropped a hand to his gun. It wasn't for Mary as much as for his new partner. Perhaps being out in the desert for so long had turned him hostile to humans. Perhaps he had gone rogue.

"Alright, Mary," Rennick shouted. "Out with it. What am I? What kind of horrible, disgusting monster am I?"

Mary faltered for the first time since they entered her home. She shook her head and took a step back. "Now, I never said you were a monster, Ren. I said you were a liar. Don't misquote me to your boyfriend over there."

Colton bristled. "What?"

"Oh, don't you even start with me, mister. I'll have a few words for you once I'm done with the yellow rat here!"

Rennick held up his hands, his face still dripping with

bourbon. "Wait, wait a minute. You're saying I slept with those men, aren't you?"

Her face flushed. "Don't you dare try to deny it! I spoke with a few and found out about it all. I know about what you get up to in your back room. You thought I wouldn't notice."

Colton sighed and his hand left his holster. This had nothing to do with Rennick's vampirism. He hadn't gone on some gruesome killing spree. He just had an unusual love life, and it had thrown Mary into a jealous rage. Rennick was visibly calmer, too, and he gave a grateful smile as he took her hand. This time she didn't recoil, though her eyes shone with tears. "You thought I'd left you for good, didn't you?"

"I didn't want to believe you'd rather have all those people instead of me. Why would you do that to me, Ren? Did you think I was too dumb to notice? Or that I wouldn't care?"

Rennick bit his lip. "I was afraid you would be angry, but I didn't realize you would be quite this—"

Mary shook her head. "I would've done anything for you, but that didn't make a damn difference, did it?"

Rennick put a hand on her arm and took a step closer. Then he wrapped an arm around her waist. "I know, and I'm sorry," he whispered.

She didn't resist him as he stared into her eyes. Rennick pulled her into an embrace and they kissed. It started tame enough, but then she gripped the back of Rennick's head and it became awkward. Colton felt out of place he was in the room. He wasn't sure how far this would go, but he didn't want to stick around to find out.

Colton cleared his throat, trying to avoid their eyes. "My apologies, but if we're hoping to see your mother on time." Colton emphasized the words as he stared at Rennick. "We need to be heading out soon."

He opened the door to step outside, then stopped. "Just for the record, Miss Silva, he is *not* my boyfriend. I'd appreciate it if you didn't spread any false rumors."

She was clearly confused, but Colton didn't care. Let Rennick enjoy his time with her if he wanted, but Colton wanted out of the place. The cool nighttime air filled his lungs as he closed the door behind him. The moon hung high overhead and dust blew down the road. His duster swayed behind him and he took his hat off to run fingers through his hair.

Rennick's love life was a damn mess, and he was glad he wasn't part of it.

Chapter 5

Mistakes and Heartache
Rennick

Rennick tried his best to keep from shaking. For a few minutes there, he feared Colton thought he'd been killing innocents. Having barely survived the two werewolves earlier, the idea of Colton turning his gun on him wasn't pleasant. All it would take were a few simple sentences, a few choice words, and suddenly that tentative bit of trust he and Colton had built up would be shattered. To hell with the fact Colton saved his life earlier. If innocent lives were involved, then the man would rush in with guns blazing, like a regular wolf in shining armor.

While Rennick admired Colton's dedication, seeing the man's hand stray to his gun nearly made Rennick lose it. He wanted to think Colton would check his facts a bit better before firing off shots, but somehow he doubted it. After all, if Rennick was going to be gunned down in such a petty way, he at least wanted to be guilty of whatever he was accused of doing.

His first mistake was bringing Colton along with him to see Mary. He should have known she would be suspicious, but Rennick was a busy man. How was he supposed to know what she was thinking? It wasn't as if he could read her thoughts. He hadn't anticipated she would find out about his lovers, or assume things about his illusions. He'd made quite a mess by not covering his tracks properly. To be honest, he had forgotten about her. It hadn't even occurred to him their occasional flings would make her feel so much affection for him. He hadn't expected her to be angry, nor known she'd been drowning her sorrows in drink.

Keeping up with his human toys was always such a chore. Normally, he would have fled town before allowing it to get this far. Once his flurry of relationships started overlapping, his leave was long overdue.

Mary hugged him tight. "Do you really have to go?"

"I'm afraid so, but hopefully I won't be gone long. I just want to be there with her. I hope you can understand."

She nodded, wiping at her eyes. "Can you tell me one thing, Ren? No lies this time, only the truth. Okay?"

"Absolutely. Anything for you."

Her face hardened at his words for some reason. She stepped away from him as a steady fury built in her gaze. "Did you ever love me?"

He smiled and reached out to cradle her chin, a bit surprised when she let him. "I came to see you first, didn't I?"

She nodded, her eyes searching. "That was sweet of you, but you're avoiding the question. Did you love me, or didn't you?"

Rennick sighed. "Of course!"

"Liar." She pulled away from him again and turned to stand in the doorway to her bedroom. Rennick stammered.

What had he done wrong? He'd said all the right words, used all his usual wiles. Why was she not folding into his arms?

"Mary…"

"I'll take care of the theater while you're gone, but I'll do it because I love it. Not you."

He winced. "I didn't mean to hurt you."

She turned, and her smile was genuine this time. "I know. To be honest, of all the things you've done, knowing that hurts the worst. You don't even know what you did to me, do you? I'm sure I'm not the only woman to feel this way, either. You don't know the hell you put us through." She shook her head, "It's just a game to you. You play with our feelings."

"No, that's not it at all." He wasn't sure what he was doing wrong, but anything he said only seemed to make things worse. "I never saw you as that."

She laughed, shoulders shaking under her faded, flowery dress. "Don't you ever stop? Maybe you've been lying for so long, you've actually started to believe it yourself."

Now she wasn't making any sense at all. He moved around the table toward her, but she held out her hand. "No, I don't want any more of you, Ren. You're not healthy for me. In fact, I think it'd be best if you just went ahead and left now."

Heat rose in his cheeks. "Don't do this, Mary. Don't treat me like this." This wasn't how it was supposed to end. She was supposed to believe him, to trust him, so he could leave and move on with his life. She was messing everything up. He felt guilty and even a touch ashamed, something he wasn't used to feeling. He didn't like it in the least.

"Get out of my house. Don't make me go fetch my guns, Ren."

"Damn it, Mary! You can't—you can't just leave me!"

She leaned against the archway of her bedroom door and folded her arms, "That's more like it. Not used to being the one dumped, I take it. It isn't a nice feeling. It hurts, doesn't it?"

He had never known her to be this vicious, this cruel, and it did hurt. It hurt more than he thought it possibly could. "This is not funny!"

"Oh, Ren." She sighed and walked closer, keeping the table and chairs between them. Her arms remained folded, too, as though she was afraid of what her hands would do if she didn't. "You're nothing more than a boy, aren't you? I get it now, and you know what? That's okay. The next time you come to town, look me up. Maybe then you'll be less of a child and more of an adult."

Rennick's jaw dropped as hot tears formed. How could she treat him like this? He was a celebrated theater owner. He was the golden child of Peridot. Everybody in the damn place loved him and yet, she had the gall to talk to him like this! He encouraged her talent at the theater, allowed her to put on shows, despite what people said behind closed doors. He gave her the chance to act, and was now even giving her the theater itself, but this was how she repaid him? His options were running out. There had to be something to try, something to say. She couldn't demolish him like this. He wouldn't allow it.

"The house." His voice wavered, knowing this was

Mary's true wish; her only desire in the whole damn world. As he whispered the words, a calm came over him. "It's yours, Mary. Take it."

She shuddered and her head dropped. "You would try that wound, wouldn't you? Just one last jab at me."

"No, I mean it. It's yours," he tried again. This one had to work. It was the last tool in his arsenal, the final card up his sleeve.

She looked up at him with tears streaming down her cheeks. "I hate you for that one. That was the worst." She took a deep breath, then added, "No, I don't want it. Maybe when you get back, you can find someone to sell it to."

Rennick couldn't believe what he was hearing. She wouldn't take the house? She loved that place more than the theater, or at least she used to. Had she lost her mind? What was wrong with her?

"But you can live there," he clarified. "You wanted it. I know you did. You can't be happy here. This place is—"

She came around the table and took his hand in both of hers, stroking them with her thumbs, a gesture of pity that made his stomach flip. She smiled as she shook her head. "No, Ren. I don't want it. You can offer it to me a million times, and my answer would be the same. I don't want it. I don't want anything of yours: not your money, not your house, not your horses, and not your clothes. You keep all of it. It won't win me over. You could offer me the world on the platter, and I would refuse it. I want you out of my life."

Rennick looked away, unable to meet her gaze any longer. He didn't know what to say. No one had ever refused him before, not like this. He always could dangle something over someone's head. It had always worked. So why was he failing so badly this time? Yes, he had planned to leave her, but it was supposed to be on his terms. He was supposed to be the one to initiate it, not her. He hurt, he felt shame, he felt raw inside, and he didn't know why.

Mary sighed and got on her toes to peck a kiss on his cheek. The warmth of her lips diffused his anger, but the pain soared as he realized he would never receive her sweet kisses again.

"Go, Ren," she said, her beautiful russet eyes staring into his, steady and determined. "Go see your Mamma, and don't forget to write me. I sure as hell hope your friend can keep an eye on you. Lord knows I can't."

Chapter 6

Playing Tricks

Colton stepped outside, already hearing snippets of Mary's raised voice. He really couldn't blame her. She seemed like she put a lot of faith in Rennick and depended on him to keep her job. Even though Colton was in no way involved in this, Rennick had still been lying to her. That made him uncomfortable. A part of him hoped he, too, wasn't making a mistake taking Rennick on as his new partner.

Eager to put distance between himself and Mary's house, he walked across the street. He really didn't want to listen in to their conversation. Hell, he didn't want to even know about it. He came here to do a job, not fret over the complicated livelihood of Rennick Dalton.

A cold breeze swept through the practically empty street, bringing sand and dirt with it. He couldn't smell the desert flowers out here, though, like he had at Rennick's home. All he smelled was dirt, piss, and a tinge of what might have been a dying animal. Colton took off his hat and beat it against his leg, knocking off some of the sand.

An impression in the dirt caught his attention. What looked like a child's footprints disappeared between a narrow alleyway between two of the shanties.

Probably nothing. He replaced his hat, unable to pull his gaze from the footprint. Could it belong to the missing girl? That was impossible. She had disappeared weeks ago. That print belonged to someone else. Another child who could just as easily become a victim, if they didn't catch whatever was responsible.

He closed his eyes, took a deep breath, and listened to the night air. Dogs were fighting down the street. Mary and Rennick were still talking. Someone was walking. Two more steps... A strange gait, almost lurching. He turned toward the narrow alleyway, noting all the shadowed buildings and not knowing what all might be lurking there.

These buildings were a perfect to hide. Some of them appeared abandoned, and some had crawl spaces underneath. If he wanted to capture children to take off into the night, this would be the perfect hunting ground. Colton stepped down the alleyway, hovering his hand over his gun. He heard Mr. Tep's voice in his head again. "It's precisely that attitude that will end up getting you killed."

It was true, and he knew that, but still Colton wanted to know. He needed to know. Waiting for Rennick would take too long. So he walked behind the pair of shanties. All these buildings were dark. All of them were quiet. They smelled of sun-bleached, decaying wood, not lived in homes. He paused and listened. The walking wasn't just two legs, he realized. It was as though someone was crawling.

Was someone injured? Struggling for help?

Colton pulled out his gun and hurried past the next building. These shanties were maze-like, and too many of them were abandoned. Too many empty husks just waiting for something to hide in them. He paused again to listen, but it was silent.

He felt like he was being watched. He looked around, gun at the ready, but he didn't see anything. There didn't seem to be anything alive in this wrecked section of Peridot, and it was alarming. His ears told him one thing, but the rest of his senses told him another.

"Colton, where did you go?"

Rennick. He must have finished his fight with Mary. Colton cursed inwardly. If he was the only agent on this assignment, he would have pursued whatever it was all night. But as Mr. Tep said, it very possibly could get him killed. That was, after all, why he had been given a partner.

With a snarl, he holstered his gun, turned around and walked back to Mary's home.

"There you are!" Rennick met him partway across the empty road. "What happened?"

"I thought I heard someone." Colton glanced over his shoulder. He still couldn't shake the feeling they were being watched.

"Should we investigate?"

Yes, he thought. *We should investigate every one of these buildings.*

But they were partners, and they had to investigate together for safety. "No, I don't think so. It could have been anything."

"The wind plays tricks out here. It has a mind of its own."

He nodded, knowing deep down it hadn't been the wind at all.

"I CAN'T BELIEVE SHE KICKED ME OUT." RENNICK spat.

"I know, I heard you," Colton grumbled. He really wasn't interested in what had happened, but that didn't keep Rennick from describing in minute detail every moment of his fight with Mary.

"After everything I've done for her! Absolutely ungrateful. Do you know where she would be without me? I've never been shown such disrespect. Oh, and did I tell you? She said I was nothing more than a boy. By god, if she knew how old I really was—"

"Quiet!" Colton snapped. They passed a huddle of men smoking near one of the shanties. He couldn't tell if they had heard Rennick's rant or not, but he didn't like the way they at them. He still couldn't shake the feeling he had when he heard that sound near Mary's home. Closer to town, he noticed more stragglers moving through the back streets. People going home after a late night of drinking, but they didn't know that something lurked in the shadows.

"Are you alright?" Rennick asked, keeping his voice low as they passed the smokers.

Colton shook his head. "It wasn't the wind. Something is out here and I'm not sure what."

Rennick glanced around, taking in the quiet shanties around them. "I wonder if it's related to Davis Farm."

"Probably."

He thought of Mary back in her home and the look of her thin walls. The thought something was lurking that close to her home made him uneasy.

"About Mary," Colton said as the lights of Peridot came into view. "You don't plan to come back once the assignment is over, do you?"

"No. I couldn't even if I wanted to. That's why I was going to set everything up before we left. But I can't exactly tell her that, can I?"

"No, you can't," he muttered.

"I offered her the house, and she turned it down. I don't know what to do. I've never been so rejected in my life."

He clenched his jaw. Mary shouldn't live in such squalor when Rennick had a large, vacant home. "I'm sure she'll manage," he muttered, more to convince himself.

"By the way, you were a bit too trigger-happy back there when Mary made it sound like I was slaughtering innocents. You always so ready to draw a gun on a partner?"

Colton shrugged. "You're fast. I figured I'd shoot first, then make a verdict."

"I really hope you're joking!"

"I wouldn't aim for your vitals," he said with a smile.

Rennick rolled his eyes.

"I wasn't actually going to shoot you for killing people. That's not my judgment to make. I was going to shoot you if you tried to hurt her."

"Oh, is that all? Don't I feel safer." Rennick gave a dry laugh.

Colton shook his head. Despite working together back

at Rennick's house they still had a lot of work ahead of them to really trust each other. Probably that was mostly on Colton's head. He didn't exactly have a good history of playing nice with others. He actually thought knowing that would reassure Rennick, but clearly it made him more agitated. So Colton decided to stay quiet for a while to keep from putting his foot into his mouth.

They walked in silence for a ways, listening to the sound of crickets in the distance and the crunching of their boots on the dirt road. Both the tavern and the theater had closed up for the evening, which meant it was quite late. Unlike the shanties they left behind, Colton saw no movement behind these blackened windows or along the narrow alleyways. He allowed himself to relax a little.

Rennick led them down another alleyway. Peridot was crisscrossed with them. They came to a smaller building set off from the main strip. Just above the open doorway was a hand-painted sign: Preston Holding Pens. It was one of the few lit buildings around. Inside, Colton spotted a bare desk and an assortment of bridles and saddles hung in a cluttered mess along the wall.

"What are we doing here?" he asked.

Rennick looked him up and down. "I don't know about you, but I'm not interested in walking fifty miles. We need transportation. I always keep a few horses on hand, just in case I need to leave town in a pinch."

"Fifty miles?" Colton whistled. "Davis Farm is that far out?"

Rennick nodded. He shook his arms out and cleared his throat, as though preparing to give a speech. He took the stairs up to the porch and knocked at the open door.

Colton had no idea how much it cost him to keep multiple horses here. When he had arrived at the train station earlier, he had spotted a few horses available for rent, though most of them looked too old and sickly to last long on any assignment, and certainly not for a fifty-mile ride.

From inside the house, an older man shuffled around the corner and donned his hat from where it hung on the wall alongside the gear. Wearing pair of overalls, he had no shirt, despite the cold. He yawned, as though he'd been asleep. Redness ringed his eyes, as though he either drank far too much, or never slept. He pushed his gray bangs out of his eyes and blinked at the two of them, as though not entirely sure they were real.

"How're you doing, Ben?" Rennick grinned.

Ben squinted for a moment and then began laughing. He came forward with more speed than Colton had expected and pulled Rennick into a bearish hug.

"Rennick! It's been a while, my boy! Why don't you come by to see me anymore?"

Rennick allowed himself to be hugged for a while before struggling to push away from the man.

"What can I say? The theater eats up all my time. You know that. I hate to bother you so late, but we're going to need a pair of horses for tonight." He nodded toward Colton at his side. "This is my good friend Colton."

Ben took Colton's hand and gave it a vigorous shake. Ben had far more strength in him than he looked, and Colton pondered if he had a bit of some supernatural element in his bloodline. When Ben eyed him up and down, Colton wondered if Ben mistook him for one of Rennick's many boyfriends. Fetching a pair of horses in the middle of the night probably added to the assumption.

"Always good to meet a friend of Rennick's. He's my boy, aren't you, Rennick?" he asked with a laugh and laid a heavy arm over Rennick's shoulders, shaking the man. It was supposed to be friendly, but Rennick couldn't hide his annoyance. "I'll be the first to admit that he's a little weird, even for a place like Peridot." Ben gave an infectious laugh despite Rennick's glare. "Oh don't get like that. Come on back and I'll get them saddled up." He dragged the back of his hand across his mouth to wipe off the signs of sleep before leading them around the back of the building. "Rennick keeps four horses here."

"My friend and I are going on a week's journey, but we'll be staying off the roads. I'll be taking Aidan, of course, but I'm not sure what horse you recommend for him."

"It's probably best if the horses aren't easily spooked," Colton added.

Ben chuckled and gave him a knowing glance. "I hear you. I think Tahoe should suit your needs. You two wait here and I'll be right back." Ben picked up some gloves from atop a pile of crates before heading into the barn.

Once Ben was out of earshot, Colton said, "He seems nice enough."

Rennick shrugged. "I suppose. I personally can't stand him, but he's paid to take care of the horses, not be my friend."

Colton shook his head. "That's the second person you've talked poorly about tonight. Here I thought you liked living here."

"It's probably best if you stop keeping count." Rennick

nodded toward the barn, "At least he's relatively sober tonight. Sometimes it's not worth the humiliation."

"Humiliation? That's a strong word, isn't it?"

"Trust me, it's not. One time he challenged me to a drinking contest. Wouldn't let me even go to the barn unless I beat him. It... didn't end well, at least not for me. I'm sure he got a kick out of it."

"You actually agreed to it? I'm surprised you didn't threaten to take your business elsewhere."

Rennick laughed and put his hands into his coat pockets. "That's a joke, isn't it? Where else would I go? Do you see many barns out here? See any advertisements for horses to rent?"

"I did, actually, near the train station—"

Rennick cut him off. "Yes, the train station. Those horses are brought in after being used up pulling wagons their whole lives. I wouldn't let any of them graze in the same field as Aidan."

Colton arched an eyebrow at him, "You're really protective of your horses, aren't you?"

"Around these parts, horses are more valuable than land. You can always find more land, but finding a good horse is nearly impossible."

They both drew quiet when Ben emerged from the barn. He led a horse on either hand, a copper-red chestnut with an excitable trot and a timid, sooty buckskin with dark patches down its head and along the flanks. They both looked strong and healthy, indeed, far different from the malnourished creatures he had seen for rent back at the train station.

"The stallion here is Aidan." Ben passed the reins of the

chestnut horse over to Rennick. His partner's sour demeanor changed almost instantly. Rennick wrapped his arms around Aidan's muzzle, whispering sweetly. Colton shook his head. He could criticize Ben and complain about Mary all day, but once his favorite steed was brought out, all that callousness fell to pieces.

"I'll be honest with you here, mister." Ben turned to Colton. "Aidan is definitely the faster of the two." He leaned in close and spoke in a whisper; Colton smelled the rank whiskey on his breath. He forced himself to stop breathing for a moment to keep from gagging. "But if you ask me, I'd rather have Tahoe at my side. Aidan's fast, but he's right cocky. What this girl lacks in speed, she makes up for with smarts, if you get me."

Colton nodded and took a big breath of clean air when Ben handed the reins over. He put his hand out for the mare to smell him. Her ears went down for a moment, and she stared at him with her large caramel eyes. Some horses were spooked by werewolves, but others didn't care at all. He was glad that Tahoe appeared to be the latter, but that might be due to Rennick's handling. She didn't even flinch when he reached up and stroked her muzzle, and he was pleased when she leaned into his palm.

"That's a good girl," Colton whispered.

"They're both beauties, aren't they?" Ben chuckled.

In less than an hour, Rennick had picked up supplies and they were heading out of Peridot. Since first stepping off the train, Colton was in high spirits. He was glad to be done with Peridot, at least for a while. He couldn't remember the last time it had taken him so long to start a mission. As the waxing moon hung high overhead, a tune came to his lips. He whistled into the night sky as they headed away from the buildings of town and into the desert, with the shadows of mountains in the distance to keep them company. If Davis Farm really was fifty miles away, they would be lucky to reach it by tomorrow night. But Colton never abided strict timetables, so he breathed in the moment. He took in the cold breeze, felt Tahoe's breaths beneath him, and set his gaze on the horizon. Whoever the kidnapper was, they had no idea who was heading their way.

PART TWO

DANGERS OF THE DESERT

Chapter 7

The Foolish Boy

They made good time at first, though occasional gunshots in the distance spooked the horses. The horses were smart enough to know gunshots were dangerous. It took some petting and cooing to get them to calm down. With all the rocky outcrops and vast open land, the shots could have come from anywhere. Colton couldn't make out how close they were despite his heightened senses.

The path had started out smooth, but once they reached an area not regularly traveled, the two horses had to step with caution to avoid the plentiful shrubs. The waxing moon provided plenty of light and the night sky was filled with stars. Mountains rose at their side, guiding them for as long as they were visible. Rennick's path had turned toward them. The shadows loomed over them as they rode closer until Colton could pick out a few nooks and crannies in the moonlight.

Rennick didn't say much. Ever since they had started their ride, the man had clearly been steeped in his thoughts. Despite their distance from Peridot, it seemed like his partner couldn't shake the place. Perhaps, with time to think on the back of a horse, whatever memories were chasing him could be forgotten. Regardless what plagued him, they had more pressing matters at hand.

A few hours after midnight, they slowed the horses. At first, they had taken a quicker pace to make up for lost time, but they would need to camp soon. Compounding that was the hazardous terrain. Pretty soon, Colton had felt Tahoe breathing hard beneath him, her tawny sides heaving with exertion. He pulled up next to Rennick. He looked almost as tired as his horse. Colton had forgotten that his partner had survived a serious wound before his argument with Mary and their visit to Ben. He was nodding forward and, based on the angle he leaned, it wasn't the first time he had fallen asleep while riding. As Colton drew up next to him, Rennick bolted upright.

"What's wrong?" he asked with half-lidded eyes.

"Nothing's wrong, but I think we should call it quits for the night."

He yawned. "Why? Think I can't keep going?"

Colton smiled. "I was thinking more of the horses, but that's a good point, too." Before Rennick could reply he added, "I think I saw a cave a ways back. Think that'd be good for the night?"

He nodded. "There should be a stream around here as well, if memory serves me. Maybe we can look for it come morning."

"Sounds like a plan."

They found the rock outcroppings Colton had spotted a ways back, and he hitched Tahoe to a nearby boulder. The cave looked abandoned from the outside, but he didn't trust it. Around these parts, a certain amount of paranoia was healthy. As Rennick dismounted, he tried to gauge whether he should bring him with him to check the place. Rennick was exhausted, but if anyone was inside, Colton might need the extra help.

"We should check it," Colton said. "I'm not in the mood for another ambush."

Rennick stretched, looking more awake now that he was off his horse. "I could send in a decoy."

Colton arched a brow.

Rennick grinned, then he looked down to Colton's side. Colton jumped at a tug on his coat. The horses were agitated, but Rennick laughed. Beside him stood a small boy, barefoot and wide-eyed. He wore a pair of dirty overalls with one strap that no longer fastened properly and a frayed straw hat. His face was covered in freckles and his eyes were a startling blue. He looked like a child who had never been shown a scrap of kindness. Colton could even smell the dirt on him.

He reminded himself the boy wasn't real, but it still made his skin crawl.

"I never knew you could jump so high!" Rennick exclaimed through his laughter.

Colton forced himself to take a deep breath. "Another illusion. I don't appreciate you using those things on me. How many of them do you have, anyway?"

Rennick wiped a tear from his eye. "Just enough to give you a start!"

Colton cleared his throat and gestured to the cave. "When you're ready."

"Okay, fine! Damn, it's just a little humor." After a moment, Rennick grew still and stared off.

The boy at Colton's side turned and walked straight into the dark cavern. Goosebumps crawled down Colton's back. Yes, it was an illusion, but the child didn't show a scrap of fear or hesitation on his face. It was eerie. A real person wouldn't act like that at all. He guessed Rennick didn't always give them personalities like his three ladies had. It was like watching a doll walk around without strings attached.

"You're so touchy," Rennick said.

Colton jumped again, much to his embarrassment. He thought Rennick would have to concentrate too much to be able to speak.

"Don't worry so much." Rennick grinned. "If there is anything living inside, the boy will find it." He turned to stare at the cliff wall beside them, his mind with the boy.

Colton crept up next to him, mindful to keep his voice low. "Can you hear what he hears?"

He gave a slow nod, but his gaze remained distant. "His sight is mine, too. Damn, it is rather dark in there. I should have given him a lantern." His eyes narrowed and Colton heard the striking of a match within the cave. "That's better, now what have we—"

Rennick stiffened.

"What is it?"

He bit his bottom lip and turned to Colton, seeming to break free from his connection completely. "We can't stay here."

"Why? What did you see?" Colton's eyes went to the

shadows within the cave, as though expecting the boy to be running toward them. Instead, he saw only darkness.

Rennick untethered and mounted Aidan, then spurred the horse into a gallop. Colton cursed and ran Tahoe. She seemed just as spooked as Rennick, trying to move away from the cave even while he unhitched her from the boulder. Colton glanced behind him, staring helplessly into the cavern. Something moved in the darkness, just out of sight. The shape of it began to emerge into the starlight, enormous and barely fitting within the gaping cavern, but Colton forced his gaze away from it. He didn't want to see it, didn't want the image of this impossible giant to sit in the back of his mind, haunting his dreams.

Part of his training with the Agency spoke of what they called *unexplainables*. These were entities or creatures that didn't have a name or a real classification. They were things that had been found, usually by agents or the accounts of rambling humans who had experienced them first-hand. Some theories thought they were old gods, worn and forgotten, but still lingering in the world, clawing out an existence. Others suspected they were merely sentient supernatural beings, no different from werewolves or vampires, but ones that ate off the human psyche. That was how the doctors had explained the rambling humans and the swathes of inexplicable destruction left in their wake.

The unexplainables were to be avoided at all costs and left alone. Allow them to live out their existence, the rules stated plainly, but most importantly, never look at or listen to one. That was how they climbed into the mind. That was how they feasted on the psyche.

Colton rallied against his instincts and turned away

from the cavern. He heaved himself up on Tahoe's back, but in his haste he must have accidentally hurt her, because she jerked hard and nearly unsaddled him. Bits of rock crumbled down the side of the mountain behind him, like the beginning of a rock slide.

It was emerging. Maybe from a deep slumber, maybe out of hunger or curiosity. But he sensed the cavern of the mountainside could barely contain it. Tahoe was breathing hard; she was scared, too. Colton focused on his horse, on this beautiful creature instead of the monstrosity behind him, looming closer. It was so difficult, though, to ignore his curiosity, to ignore that desire to know what it was. Tahoe didn't deserve that fate, though. She was innocent in all this. Hell, they had just met a few hours ago, and he wasn't about to let some monster they woke up hurt her. He righted himself in the saddle, then spoke calmly to her despite his pounding heartbeat. He aimed her toward where Rennick and Aidan were moving away quickly in the distance.

Colton could feel it watching them. Tahoe started off at a trot, but then increased speed as he urged her faster. Though left behind, Colton knew it was watching them. He felt its gaze in the goosebumps up and down his arms, in the tingling at the back of the skull, and in his sweaty palms. It was watching all of them. He felt bare and exposed there on the flat land with not even trees to protect him from its gaze. A part of him longed to look back, to see it standing in its terrifying full form illuminated by starlight, but he knew better. He knew what it was and what it would do to him. People out there still needed him. He urged Tahoe onward.

The cool night air swept the nervous sweat from his

brow, and only once they were a good distance away did he begin to relax. Rennick had slowed his pace ahead, but Colton still had to push Tahoe to catch up. They were pushing both horses far more than they should, but even though Colton no longer felt the urge to look behind him, he could still recall that barely visible entity shrouded in darkness within the recesses of the cave. Without a word, he came up beside Rennick.

They both let the horses slow to a walk so they could catch their breath. Rennick looked calmer, but the silence between them stretched. When they came upon a patch of land bare of shrubs, Colton decided to set up camp for the night. It wasn't as ideal as a cave, but he had no interest in finding another cave.

Dismounting, he looked around for a place to hitch Tahoe.

"There's no need. They'll stay with us," Rennick said, breaking the silence. "They've been well trained."

Reluctantly, Colton untacked Tahoe and placed a few blankets on her that Ben had tucked away in her saddlebags. The horses grazed on what little vegetation was available. Rennick gathered some kindling for a fire while Colton laid out the pair of bedrolls. Once the fire was going nice and hot, Colton pulled out a tin of canned meat and placed it next to the blaze to get it warm. Now he was near a source of warmth, he was keenly aware of how cold he'd become. Even with the fire going, it was going to be a long night.

"Are we going to talk about that thing back there?" Colton asked.

"I'd rather not."

Colton clenched his jaw. Clearly he was just as shaken as

Colton. He focused on cooking his canned meat. Rennick moved his bedroll closer to the fire and hunkered down beneath the blankets. Only his canned meat and the top of his blond head poked out.

"Are you hungry?" Colton asked, "I've got another can if you want it."

"No, thanks," came the muffled reply. "I ate earlier."

"Oh, yeah, you did kind of gorge yourself, didn't you?"

He hadn't meant for it to come out as harsh as it sounded, but Rennick didn't seem to care. Back in town, Colton had thought having a silent partner was better than one who complained all the time, but now he wasn't so certain. Colton laid down in his own bedroll, but looked up to see Rennick's eyes on him, gleaming from the light of the fire.

"I appreciate what you did back there, by the way," Rennick said.

"Back at your house? It wasn't a big deal. I'm sure you would've done the same for me."

Rennick didn't reply, and they were back to uncomfortable silence again. It was unnerving having Rennick's gaze locked onto him, steady like a cat's stare, unflinching and unblinking. It also reminded him too much of the unexplainable from the cave.

"I take it you haven't seen many silver deaths, have you?"

His words sent a chill up Colton's spine. He would rather not think of silver deaths, especially after the scare at the cave, but Rennick's steady gaze made him feel as though he was being tested. The fear he'd seen in that werewolf's eyes came back to him painfully clear. That unquestionable death, that certainty your life was about to be snuffed out simply terrified him. No silver death was ever the same, but the results never changed. "I've seen enough. I'd rather not see another."

Rennick relinquished his piercing gaze and turned back to the fire. Colton wasn't sure which version of his partner made him more uneasy: the gregarious kid or the sullen watcher. A wind swept over the grasses and Colton closed his eyes against the gritty sand. He shivered beneath his blankets and wished the fire would warm him faster.

As the gust passed, a question fell from his lips. "What did you see back there?"

Rennick's eyes drifted to him, then back to the fire, as though debating what he could or couldn't say. He was choosing his words, or perhaps his line, with caution. Colton wondered if the conversation was going to get shut down again, but the pause lingered. The fire crackled and a log popped, and the minute Rennick took to answer felt like ten.

"How old are you, Colton?" His voice didn't sound the same. It sounded weary and pained, as though its owner had seen far too much in the world. It was perhaps the exact opposite of how a card shark theater owner or even a broken-hearted Casanova should sound.

"Why does that matter?"

"Just tell me."

Colton sighed. "I'll be forty-three in a couple of weeks."

Rennick nodded, his eyes glued to the flickering fire. "This year I'm turning seventy-seven. I don't look it though, do I?" He arched his head out of his cocoon just to smirk. The cold be damned when it came to gloating.

Colton rolled his eyes. "No," he confessed. "To be honest, I figured you were just a stupid kid."

"Hmm, I won't contest that. I know you've probably been doing this Agency work longer than I have, but... have you ever seen something so terrible you want to blot it from your mind?"

Colton swallowed. Brief memories flitted through his mind trying to pull him back into them: a scream of pain, the smile of a man soaked head to toe in blood, and a night that had never seemed to end. Colton pushed away the thoughts and clenched his teeth. "You know what that sounds like, right?"

Rennick's eyes went wide as he clutched his blanket tight around him. "The psychic hunger of an unexplainable. Yes, I know. It certainly didn't want to be disturbed."

"I thought they were... you know, in deep oceans or walking between realms or something like that. Not here, near Peridot of all places."

Rennick laughed and turned to lie on his back. "This thing was old... very old. It knew the boy was a facade. It stared straight through it like it knew exactly who I was." His voice grew quieter. "I wasn't supposed to be there. I felt that."

"Damn." Colton groaned. "It got in your head then."

"Maybe? I don't know. I didn't hear any creepy commands or anything so obvious. None of that sort of thing; it was more like an emotion that came over me. Something that I felt that I knew wasn't my own emotion, if that makes any sense."

"It wanted you to leave."

"Yes, exactly. I felt like I was as small as that boy I

created, like I just walked in on a doctor in the middle of a complicated procedure, banging pots and pans and pretending to play along. I wasn't merely out-leagued, I was insignificant." He swallowed and his eyes went glassy. "It could destroy us both quite easily; we were insects to it."

Colton swallowed down the grit in his throat. "It wanted me to look at it."

Rennick glanced his way.

"I didn't. I knew better, but it wanted me to. It wanted me to see it. The cavern was falling apart as it came out, like it was too big for the cavern or maybe the cavern didn't really exist to begin with."

"In all my time," Rennick said in a hoarse whisper. "I never thought I would encounter one. I always thought they were fascinating, but now I never want to see one again."

The wind howled, the fire crackled, and Colton glanced over his shoulder to the shadows of the mountains. "Do you think it'll try to find us?"

"No, I think it wanted us off its property and we should both be glad we survived." Rennick snuggled deeper into his bedroll.

"Do you think we should report it?" Colton asked.

"There are plenty of things that live unperturbed in the wild corners of the world. The Agency knows about them, but can't really do anything. It's not all powerful, any more than we are. Every single agent has their weaknesses, but I don't think the unexplainables do. I think they're beyond weakness."

Colton shook his head. "If we did report it, it could be a warning for other agents, or for other supernatural entities that live in the area. It could prevent people from snooping around and stirring it up."

"Whatever it is and whatever it wants, I think it's best to leave it alone." Rennick shuddered. "I kind of wish I hadn't let the boy vanish in the cave. I don't know why, I just... I have a bad feeling like I left a shoe behind for it to find me."

Colton sighed and sat up to check on his can. It was warm enough to eat, and he was eager to change the subject. "If you want, I'll take the first watch. You could barely keep your eyes open earlier." Colton flicked his hand as a long black claw emerged from his index finger; he used it to pry open the lid. It was bland and tasteless, but at least it was warm, and he needed the meat to keep his strength up.

"It wanted you to see it. You didn't though, right?" Rennick asked.

He remembered the shape within the cavern just barely becoming visible in the starlight. The hairs stood up on his arms as he recalled the sound of the rocks tumbling down the mountainside as it emerged. "I didn't see it. I didn't see anything," Colton muttered as he licked his claw clean.

Rennick watched him for a moment before turning over. "That's disgusting, just so you know."

"Get some sleep." Colton growled. "I'll wake you in a few hours."

Colton curled down into his bedroll and listened to the nighttime sounds of the desert. The hours during his watch went by painfully slow. A serpent slid in the sand a ways away, a pack of insects were on the move a bit closer, and the wind whistled through the canyons. The noises of the night could be dangerous; listening too long could make him lose track of time. Sometimes, he forgot where he was or what he was supposed to be doing as he honed in on the different sounds. He imagined he could almost see the snake move through the sand, or feel the wind as it spiraled through the canyons. The temptation to slip into them was always present, especially when the mind grew quiet.

Late in the evening, a pack of coyotes yipped in the distance. Colton got to his feet and prodded at the fire; it was an excuse to hear them better, and their excitement was contagious. He had always found them kindred spirits, but a part of him envied them, too.

Ever since that night years ago when he decided to venture out alone into the darkness, careless of the full moon in the clear sky, he no longer had the luxury of such freedom. It had seemed like a good idea, using the light of the moon to guide him through the dense forest, but it was his undoing. The snow that decorated the trees was fresh and thick, the fluffy kind that made everything look like a fairy tale. With the bright moonlight, the woods were inviting. He had barely walked a mile when the werewolf pounced him.

A transformed wolf had more weight than it did in human form, something Colton learned quickly as several of his ribs snapped under the beast's weight. He remembered screaming from the pain as it bit his shoulder and took out a chunk of flesh and sinew. It tilted its head back and swallowed it down in a single gulp. It had smelled terrible, too, a putrid odor that made him want to gag even as he struggled to find leverage in the thick snow drift he was trapped in. Hot blood dripped down his shoulder and stained the white snow. The wolf took another bite and despite Colton's attempts to get away, the wolf was in no hurry, it knew its prey was trapped. Soon Colton was surrounded by his own blood. Exhausted, he could no longer muster the energy to pull away when the werewolf bent down for another taste. Realizing there was no escape, he resigned himself to death. That was when the hunters appeared.

There were three of them, but they weren't regular game hunters or even fur trappers. They had come to capture the beast, not to save Colton. They talked freely and openly in front of him, and Colton discovered they had followed the werewolf for much of the night, waiting for it to strike. A wolf would not quickly abandon a fresh kill, which had given the hunters the time they needed. Bait was necessary, but none of them were enthusiastic about throwing their own lives on the line. At twelve years old, Colton had done what they couldn't.

They didn't shoot the wolf. That was what surprised him as a child. They aimed their shotguns as they came close and tried to pull Colton away. Gradually they led the wolf in closer, so they could lasso its arms and eventually tie its muzzle. Once the beast was hogtied, they took their prize. Colton had been barely conscious, but he remembered the wolf's howls; it had made his ears ache. With a hand axe, they thwacked at its neck. The blade had been too dull to take it off in one slice. The transformed body would be sold in pieces to fill the needs of various buyers across the country. Some promised medical miracles with werewolf parts; others used them for display. The hunters had crates of ice ready for every part.

Then the hunters had looked to Colton. He was yet untransformed, but they knew that wouldn't last. His wounds were severe, but not to the point he would bleed to death, though Colton only knew that from their words. The hunters had two options: kill him or let him live and tell his tale. The only stroke of luck Colton had was he was a child. No one would purchase a boy's head to mount on their wall, even if it did belong to a werewolf. Perhaps one day when he was older, the hunters mused, he might go rogue and become a decoration himself. They must have debated for an hour. All the while, Colton felt the life draining out of him. He floated in and out of consciousness. Like a fever dream, he would wake occasionally and see the wolf in different levels of dismemberment, the snow and the hunters' boots stained with the beast's blood. They had discussed what to do with the foolish boy in the snow. It was just a casual discussion for a trio of merciless werewolf hunters.

While held by these hunters, Colton had learned an early lesson in the horror that still haunted him years later. The werewolf's head would be sold to a collector, "a nice mantelpiece above a cozy fire to scare little children". Precautions would be made to make sure the body wouldn't grow back and the wolf would remain a living ornament.

A silver death was preferable to an eternity of torture.

When his father picked him up at the local sheriff's office the next day, his wounds were nearly mended. He had been cleaned a bit, though Colton didn't know how or when. The sheriff and the officers barely spoke to him. Later he had learned the hunters had paid them off to keep quiet about everything. It must have been a hefty amount because they kept his secret. They had known what Colton was and how dangerous he would be one day. To them he had been a lost cause.

It took a full two years before Colton experienced his first change. He didn't know what it meant to go rogue as the hunters had said, but Colton was determined to keep the beast within him locked up. With his father's help, he barricaded himself in the shed during each full moon.

The nightmares never really faded, but Colton's understanding of his curse became clearer. He learned better how to control it, and how to make his body obey his will. He spent many years as a drifter, a gunman for hire, picking up whatever odd job would take him. One day the Agency found him. For the first time in his life, Colton had purpose and direction. He was accepted for what he was and given the tools to help others; but still, he wasn't truly free.

In the distance, the coyotes moved away until he could no longer hear their yips and cries. Colton sighed at the stars and moon above him. Weariness fell heavy over him. Rennick could take watch for a few hours.

It was dangerous when a man's thoughts exhausted him more than his work.

CHAPTER 8

SPIRITS TAKE YOU

"Come on, wake up!"

Colton groaned. Damn, but he was persistent. Would it kill him to let him let him sleep a little longer? A boot collided with Colton's side.

"Alright, alright." He moaned and turned over onto his back. The world was blinding and it took a few moments for his eyes to adjust. "What's the rush, anyway?"

Rennick towered over him with a bundle of blankets wrapped around him despite the heat of the blazing sun above. Colton had discarded his own blanket hours ago.

"Aren't you hot?"

Rennick gave a sad smile, "The sun and I don't get along very well. Without these, I'll burn faster than your nasty canned meat."

Colton yawned, stretched, and looked around the campsite. It never took long for the heat to return. The wind had calmed down since last night, but the sun was fully over the horizon. "You shouldn't have let me sleep so long."

"You're the one that woke me so close to dawn. You needed more sleep than that." Rennick rummaged in his bag and pulled out a long brown cloak. Quickly, he dropped his blanket and pulled on the much cooler looking cloak. Long enough to drape over his arms, plenty of extra fabric would cover his mouth as well.

"Sorry about that. Guess I got to thinking too much," Colton muttered as he gathered his things.

"It's a dangerous habit to have out here."

"Guess some habits are hard to break." Colton coughed, frowning at his dry throat and lips. He was glad Ben had provided them each with two full water skins. He had already nearly emptied the first one, though, and he'd rather not dip into the second unless there was an emergency. They needed to find a water source. Without one, the horses wouldn't last long. "Didn't you mention there was a stream out here?"

"Actually, I did a bit of scouting once it got to be daylight. It's a little out of the way, but we should still be able to make the farm by nightfall."

Colton saddled up Tahoe and pulled himself up. "Scouting doesn't sound much like watching over the campsite."

Rennick arched his eyebrows at him. "Neither does day-dreaming. We could always head straight to the farm if you're not thirsty."

"Can't you take a joke, kid?"

Rennick mounted his horse and led the way, swathed in his cloak with bits of his blond hair poking out on the sides. "I can, I just wasn't sure if you knew how to tell one." He halted Aidan, then turned and glared over his shoulder, "By the way, I'm not a kid. I am far older than you. Please try to remember that."

"Is that why you asked how old I was last night? So you could gloat?"

Rennick didn't reply.

RENNICK HAD BEEN RIGHT WHEN HE SAID THAT the stream was out of the way. Where before they had been traveling with the mountains always on their left, this time they headed straight toward them. As they got closer, the red and skeletal rock remnants that made up the mountains became more apparent. The crimson rock stood with gaping holes throughout, the combined artwork of wind, sand, and time. High above their heads, Colton could spot a few precarious perches that looked like they could break off and topple in a breath. Up ahead, Rennick slowed Aidan's gait so Colton could ride up beside him.

"I got to thinking this morning." Rennick's face shone with sweat beneath his layers of fabric. "The letter said that these attacks could be either supernatural or *spectral* in nature. Do you know what that means?"

"That we may not be able to see it."

Rennick nodded. "More than that. We might be dealing with ghosts."

Colton grunted and rolled his eyes.

"I suppose you're a skeptic, then?"

"Not entirely, I'm sure they do exist. Just seems like most of the time, it ends up being some charlatan pulling the strings. And I don't care what they say, those pictures of ectoplasm don't look real to me."

Rennick laughed. "Are you saying I'm a charlatan? I don't think I've ever been called that before."

"Your illusions are different. They're puppets, not some ghostly fluid getting vomited up by an attention seeker."

"I take it you've never fought spirits before then?"

"No, but I understand they're tricky." He thought back to his time at the Agency. They had given him nothing more than a pamphlet of information with some brief tips. He'd be damned if he could remember any of them now. If the Agency didn't put much importance on them, he didn't think he ought to either.

"I've only had to deal with one, and it was quite brief," Rennick said. "It wasn't on a mission or anything, and at the time I hadn't a clue what it was. I just ran." He gave a nervous chuckle at Colton's questioning gaze. "Don't look at me like that. Any sensible person would have done the same!"

Colton hoped running away wasn't Rennick's typical reaction to a dangerous situation. The man had leapt at the chance to leave Peridot, but Colton couldn't tell if that was due to the werewolf pack hunting him or his troubled love life. He suspected it was more the latter, even though the pack was far more dangerous. Then there had been his behavior at the cave last night. Rennick's first instinct had been to flee instead of fight, though that move was in line with common sense. You couldn't fight unexplainables.

Regardless, running away from danger seemed to be Rennick's talent, which wouldn't help with their assignment. Colton would have to keep an eye on him once they got to the farm. If they were dealing with ghosts, he didn't want to be abandoned on their assignment.

"Don't you want to hear the story?" Rennick asked with a mischievous grin.

Colton rolled his eyes. "Not really."

"Oh, you'll like it. Trust me, everyone does."

Colton said nothing, but for some reason Rennick took that as the cue to continue.

"I was working in Alabama at the time, years after the war, at a newly built theater called The Monarch. I was in the back room, reading through the latest script I was given. I forget what it was now, some play that had been written by one of the actors, I believe. I like to read them aloud when I first get one; it helps me get a feel for the piece. You know what I mean?"

Colton could feel his gaze on him, waiting for a response. "Sure," he said, though he didn't.

"I knew you were listening!" Undeniable glee filled Rennick's voice as he continued. "Anyway, I was really into it and started pacing around the room. Then the room went dark. It was as if every candle had been snuffed out in an instant. Did I mention I had like five of them lit? It happened quickly, too. Before you ask, it couldn't have been a breeze, either. That room had no windows and could get downright stuffy in the summer."

"I didn't say anything," Colton said.

"No, but you were thinking it," Rennick said with a smile. "The weird part was that they all were lit again in an instant. But it was strange. When I turned around, I could see the candles lit all around me, but the light didn't reach me. I was in some kind of shadowy cocoon. So I rubbed my eyes, but the darkness didn't leave. It was only when I stepped away from that spot that I was able to escape it. When I looked back into the corner where I had been standing, I realized the darkness was still there, hovering in front of me, only it wasn't just that."

He paused, as though choosing the best way to describe it, or perhaps how best not to show how it still affected him.

"I had to look at the edges to figure out what it was. There was a very obvious line where the shadow ended and the light began. It looked like the silhouette of a person, only taller. I stood there for what felt like minutes, me watching it, and it watching me right back."

Colton stared. "So you had been standing inside of a spirit?"

"Yes, that's what I sorted out later. I hadn't realized that it was colder there at the time, especially with my pulse raging like it was."

"So what did you do? Just gape at it?" he asked with a smile.

"I was terrified! If that happened now, I probably would have actually investigated it, but at the time I was completely new to this whole Agency thing. I was about to call out to one of the actresses in the next room. What was her name? She was a lovely girl with golden brown skin, had her hair pinned up perfectly around her face. She always wore a pair of worn-out red shoes that looked ghastly, but she was one of the best actresses in the entire theater. Anyway, she was in the next room, and when I opened my mouth to call to her, the shadow began to... expand."

Colton eyed him suspiciously.

"The entire room started going dark as the shadow

filled it." Rennick's eyes were wide as though he could still see it. "The shadow fell across me again, but this time the air went icy cold. I realized I couldn't breathe. All I could think at first was that it was swallowing me just like it swallowed the light. I thought it was trying to swallow my scream."

He looked down. Colton had to admit if this was an act, it was rather good.

"I guess I panicked. That was when I fled. I dropped the script and ran. They had to find a stand-in for me for the week because I refused to go back into that room. I refused to play that part. Something didn't want me to perform it, and I couldn't face that spirit again." He laughed. "I'm glad, too, because that play turned out to be awful."

Colton watched him in silence. He wasn't sure how he would react to something like that, something so removed from the physical world. If he had ever encountered a malicious shadow or spirit before, he had never noticed it. Maybe Colton wasn't as sensitive to those things, or perhaps they just avoided him. Either way, he was glad not to have been in his partner's shoes.

Rennick snapped his fingers. "Chloe, that was her name! She visited me every day that week to check on me. She was an absolute doll."

Colton frowned. "I guess you never figured out what really happened, then, since you didn't investigate."

"No, I suppose it's still a mystery. When I did finally go back weeks later, someone had stacked the pages from my script from that day. I must have flung them everywhere."

Colton grinned. "Had you been drinking?"

Rennick glared at him from beneath the fabric. "No more than normal."

"Ah. Then I'm sure you didn't imagine anything."

Rennick stared at him in silence for several moments until Colton couldn't hold back his laughter anymore.

"Here I am trying to be helpful. I don't know why I even bother. I thought you would find my experience useful!" Rennick urged Aidan on ahead. Over his shoulder, he called, "Don't blame me if the spirits take you by surprise."

The words only made Colton laugh harder. "It sounds like they took you by surprise."

Colton wiped at his eyes. It didn't take much to get his partner riled up, but in all honesty, what did Rennick expect him to think of such a story? Don't rehearse scripts for ghosts? The fact both of them had been called in for this mission meant taking down their target would be more dangerous than mere shadows in rehearsal rooms.

Colton smelled the water in the air before he heard it. Tahoe must have sensed it, too, because she quickened her pace without him having to ask. The stream itself wasn't particularly large, but the water moved quickly enough. Colton unsaddled Tahoe and allowed her to join Aidan in quenching their thirst. He crouched down at the edge, as well, and used the opportunity to refill his water skin. He took off his hat and splashed water along the top of his head, neck, and shoulders; his pulse quickened as the cold water hit his hot skin. "Damn, that feels good."

Rennick left his hood on and dunked his whole head into the water. He came up sputtering with a smile. "See? Worth the detour, I think."

"Definitely." He cupped a handful of water to his lips then froze. He smelled something on the wind, something that didn't belong to him, his partner, or the two horses. They had visitors—several in fact. He wiped off his hand and reached for his gun. He spun around just as three men emerged from the brush near one of the red rock formations. Two of them had pistols aimed at them.

The third had a shotgun trained on Colton. He said, "Drop the gun."

Colton let out a frustrated breath, but he tossed his gun on the bank away from the water.

"Hands up to the sky, both of you."

He and Rennick locked eyes. Three guns, two of them. They probably could take them, but it would be messy without weapons. He wasn't sure how much recovery time, if any, Rennick still needed from their fights with the pack members yesterday. It was a question he should have asked his partner earlier, and Colton cursed himself. Mr. Tep was right; he wasn't used to working with anyone. Now he was paying the price. If they worked together instead of Colton mocking him or being annoyed with him, they probably would have sorted that out already.

Fresh water was a commodity in any desert, and a perfect place to lay a trap. He had been so engrossed in Rennick's ridiculous ghost story he hadn't considered the obvious danger. He hadn't been paying attention. He knew better than that.

Colton raised his hands. "What do you want?"

Again, the man with the shotgun spoke. "The horses." Colton figured he was their leader, since his two comrades were so quiet. "We'll take whatever else you two have that's worth anything."

"That cloak looks nice," said the squat man, aiming his

pistol at Rennick's chest. His face was a pocketed mess, either from some gruesome gunfight or some survived disease. "You hiding money under that? Or something fancy?"

Rennick took a step backwards. Colton noticed now that the cloak was wet there was a fine embroidery on the edges, perhaps silk or something finer. It would have to be Rennick's expensive taste in clothing that got them noticed by the local thieves. Rennick had said he would burn faster than canned meat earlier, but that hadn't really given Colton any gauge. If Rennick lost his cloak, Colton wasn't sure if his partner would burst into flames or just get a sunburn, but he didn't intend to let it get that far.

When the man made a grab for the cloak, Colton ran at him. His intention was to body slam him away, but the leader was faster than he expected. A flurry of pain flared up his side as the shotgun blast peppered through his skin. His ears rang from the shot as it echoed throughout the canyon. Colton landed halfway in the stream, seeping blood into the water.

Too slow, he berated before falling unconscious.

CHAPTER 9

TRUMP CARD

RENNICK

RENNICK HAD SEEN SOME BALLSY MOVES IN HIS time, but never one with so little tact. While he appreciated Colton was willing to fling himself at bullets to protect him, was it really necessary? Both Aidan and Tahoe had taken off at the shotgun blast as Colton fell into the stream. The shorter man who had tried to grab at Rennick's cloak jumped as well, but the leader wasn't fazed.

"We'll take care of him." He aimed his shotgun at Rennick. "You go check on the horses, Jim."

The short man—apparently Jim—in front of Rennick pointed at the cloak. "But I saw it first!"

"You also made me put holes in his friend. Fetch those damn horses, or you'll be next."

Jim didn't protest, but Rennick saw the anger in his eyes. This group had pulled together out of necessity, which meant it wouldn't take much to cause a rift. The water downstream from Colton's body was already dark with blood. He didn't have much time to act. The other crony beside the leader was a tall man with sunken eyes who had likely drunk to the bottom of too many bottles.

The leader smiled at Rennick. "Let's try this again. Give it over, or you join your friend."

Rennick glanced over to the wall of the cliff. There was a large patch of shade not far from the bushes where the men had been hiding. From there, he might be able to gain the upper hand. It would require a bit of acting, but he did love any excuse to mix work and play.

"I tell you what," he blurted, careful to make himself sound terrified. "If you promise not to kill me, I can show you why we came out here."

The two men watched him in confusion. "Go on," the leader said.

"So, you won't shoot me?"

He relaxed his shotgun a little as the confidence worked into him. "Tell me what it is first, then I'll tell you whether you'll die alongside your friend or not."

Rennick swallowed. "There's a box buried out here. My brother, he left it when he was on the run last year. There's money in it."

That got their attention. "How much?"

Rennick stammered with tears in his eyes. "Almost a hundred."

Both of their assailants perked up.

"Find it."

Rennick nodded and walked back toward the shade.

"Are you sure about this? What if it's a trap?" That sounded like the tall man talking. It was amusing he had better instincts than his boss, though intelligence was rarely rewarded in these parts.

"It's worth the risk, and we outnumber him anyway."

Rennick stepped into the shade, aware the shotgun was aimed on him every step of the way. With relief, he felt the ten degree drop in temperature. His skin still felt uncomfortably warm, but nothing like it felt in the direct sunlight. He took his time removing the cloak and let it fall to the ground, then he started pacing while he examined the ground, as though looking for signs.

It didn't take long for the tall man to come forward for the cloak. He held the pistol at Rennick's head at each step, though. "Well, where is it?"

"I'm looking! Everything is moved around from what he said. Just give me a few moments."

With both weapons aimed at him, Rennick was limited in what he could do. He had incredible speed compared to these two, but that would only work for one of them. The other could still shoot him. The other one collecting the horses wouldn't be much longer, either. Summoning his illusions was also out of the question. It was difficult to focus with it being so damn hot. He thought it would be easier in the shade, but even though his skin didn't hurt as much, his head was swimming. Rennick had to hold out for his trump card.

"I don't trust him," the leader growled.

The tall man stepped in front of Rennick and kicked at the ground as though he thought the box of money would spring up from the sand. Rennick dragged a hand through his hair. It actually wasn't that difficult to play the role of nervous victim when two guns were aimed at his head. He was running out of time.

"There ain't nothing here but dirt!" The tall man

exclaimed, and then he fired his gun. Glancing at the stab of pain in his foot, he saw a burst of blood come up through the top of his boot. He fell to the ground, groping at the wound with both hands. Of all the places, why did he have to go for his foot? Now, he had even fewer options. What the hell was happening? Three idiot thieves ought to be easy to kill.

"Dammit, Will!" The leader strode forward and slammed the butt of his shotgun into the man's gut. "Did I tell you to shoot anything?"

The tall man doubled over. "No," he whimpered.

Rennick lay on his side now, clutching at his foot with tears in his eyes. He was trying to get the shoe off to wrap it in cloth or some kind of bandage, but he was shaking from head to bloody toe. Getting chewed on by a pair of werewolves was nothing to having a bullet lodged in a bone.

The leader pointed down at Rennick. "If he bleeds to death out here, how in hell are we going to find that money?"

In the stream, Rennick saw Colton push himself onto his knees. His partner moved slowly, as though in a daze. The two men nearest Rennick were too busy fighting to notice and in the distance, the third fellow was taking his time returning with Aidan and Tahoe. It was good the horses were so far off. Rennick didn't want them to get stuck in the middle of the bloodbath about to break out. Colton looked taller than before and blood dripped down his hands which were growing longer and more angular.

Rennick smiled. He had never had a werewolf fighting on his side before. Colton turned around slowly, hulking forward as his back elongated. His eyes had turned a dim yellow. This was going to be fun.

Colton took two long strides before buckling down to all fours and leaping into the air. The man, or rather the wolf, had incredible leg strength to jump so high. Now was the time to act. Ignoring the pain in his foot, Rennick got to his feet and took hold of the tall man's pistol arm from behind. Using the wall as leverage, he spun the man around and pushed him face first to the ground. His prey was too tall for Rennick to reach him when he was standing at full height but down here, his throat was exposed and vulnerable. Rennick knelt down beside him and pinned the man's gun arm behind his back. His fangs emerged from his gums with a slight bit of pain, and he sank them into his victim's sun-burned flesh. The copper taste of blood hit his tongue and spread like fire in his mouth; he drank deep.

With dilated eyes, he watched Colton lunge at the wide-eyed leader fumbling with aiming his shotgun at Rennick's head. Colton obviously was no longer aware of his actions. That was plain to Rennick just by watching his partner land on the leader. This was the wolf in control; he couldn't care less about what pain or abuse it caused.

Colton's feet landed on the man's shoulders with claws extended. Unfortunately, the weight was too much for the man's body to hold. Something cracked, and the man screamed as his body buckled. Something had broken, but Rennick couldn't tell if it was his legs or his spine. Regardless, Colton leaned in, his face now elongated with hunger. The leader was flailing his arms, trying to get hold of Colton to push him off, but Colton wrapped his long fingers around one of the arms and snapped it in two. The leader's screams reached a higher pitch as Colton then gorged himself.

Rennick felt the tall man's pulse slow. His victim wasn't quite dead, but he was weak enough not to move, and that was enough for now. He felt his foot stitch back together again. In the distance, the last man stood with wide eyes and a gaping mouth, a fool too lost in shock to realize he should flee. In his terror, he had even dropped the reins of the horses and they had wandered away from him. Rennick dropped his victim to the ground. The tall man's glassy eyes rolled slowly in their sockets as Rennick got to his feet.

He grinned. "Don't worry, I'll be back." He locked eyes with the short, terrified man in the distance; he suddenly realized the danger he was in and turned to run. Rennick leaned down to examine his foot. Amazing what a good feeding did for wounds; although his shoe wouldn't recover, his foot was completely healed, and the bullet was rattling around in his shoe. Beside him, Colton was busy feasting on the remains of the leader.

"Don't worry, I'll get the last one." He patted the wolf's shoulder. The wolf was sated and couldn't care less what Rennick did, as long as he didn't come between him and his food.

Rennick pulled his cloak on to shade himself from the sun. The feeding helped, but he still couldn't go waltzing around in direct sunlight, especially amid the sand reflecting the sunlight so well. Even though the short man had a head start, Rennick would easily overtake him.

The world around him became a blur as he ran; to others he probably looked like a darting shadow. In a few seconds, he outran the man who was still glancing over his shoulder when he should have been watching his footing. Rennick stopped in front of him. The poor sap ran headlong into him. Shaken, the man screamed up at him.

"Oh, it's too late for that," he cooed.

As Rennick sank his fangs in, he couldn't recall the last time he had fed so well in such a short period. Sure, Colton had a displeasing, sour disposition, but traveling with him meant he never went hungry.

Chapter 10

The Eyeless Grin

Colton sat down on the warm ground, taking in heavy breaths. His body tingled from head to toe, and he struggled to focus his thoughts. All he could think of was the blood in his mouth and the heat of the kill. He tried to remember the man walking towards him.

Oh, right. Rennick. His new partner. And they were somewhere in Texas.

Rennick's mouth and chin were smeared with blood, and he dragged a body behind him, the shape of which was blurry amid the bleached landscape. He shook his head to shake the dazed feeling brought on by the transformation. When he awoke from his blood rage, he had been devouring someone's innards with as much enthusiasm as a starving dog. He looked down at his hands. They were covered in blood, staining his sleeves up to the elbows. Colton concentrated on his breathing as his stomach churned. He was feeling better now, but he couldn't bring himself to look at what was left of his victim.

Rennick stopped in front of him a moment before

dropping the new corpse on top of the other remains. "That is... quite a mess," he said.

The ground around Colton's feet was splattered crimson. His vision finally came back to focus. Blood seeped across the dry sand, soaking down into the ground.

"You know, no one made you jump out in front of that shot," Rennick added.

Colton's voice was hoarse as he clenched his jaw. "Did you kill the other two?"

"They're dead enough." Rennick lowered himself down beside him and pulled off his hood in the safety of the shade. "I've come to a conclusion about your kind. Care to hear it?"

"Not really, but I'm sure you're going to tell me, anyway."

Rennick grinned and put an arm around his shoulder. "We only became partners yesterday, and already you know me so well!"

He laughed, but Colton didn't join him.

"Your kind are divided into two camps. The ones who adore killing. We know all about them. They'll just kill whatever gets in their way and tend to be ideal members of large packs. It's boring and unattractive, to say the least. Then there's your group. Wolves who serve a master or who are, in one way or another, devoted to someone or some cause."

Rennick cocked his head to the side as he wiped blood off his chin with a piece of someone else's clothing.

"The Agency loves you because you despise what you are. So you're easy to control. Unlike your brethren, you fight your natural instincts, and are therefore declared safer compared to other wolves. You're like a trained pet pooch who knows how to behave around house guests. You're still feral and quite dangerous, but you can be trusted to an extent."

Colton took a deep breath and stared up at the blue sky. "What's your point?"

"My point is that you're living up to your stereotype. Here you are, wallowing in self-pity and disgust because you ate a man. Even though it's part of your very nature."

"And you're not bothered by what you do? You're part of the Agency, too. If I'm a pet pooch, you're practically their pet cat." Colton said, surprised to see Rennick smiling.

"I don't know what you're talking about; I'm merely an employee. As long as I get the job done and I don't hurt any innocents along the way, why should I care about killing a few pathetic thieves? It's in my nature."

"They had lives," Colton murmured as he got to his feet. Talking about the deaths made him uneasy. If he thought too long about what was currently getting digested in his stomach, all of it might come back up, and that wouldn't look good to his new partner. He walked over to the stream and started scrubbing the blood off his arms.

He felt Rennick's gaze on his back for a long time before the man came over to clean off as well. "Are you going to be alright?"

He nodded, concentrating on the red flow of water moving downstream.

"Was this your first time... um, *slipping*?"

"No," he said, cupping water and splashing it onto his face. The cold made this far more bearable. "But it's never a good feeling to wake up and find yourself eating a man you were just talking to. It makes you feel…" His stomach rolled.

"Out of control?"

"Yes, but worse. It feels like betrayal. They never expect it, but hell, I rarely do, either."

Rennick snorted. "You are the proverbial wolf in sheep's clothing, but you really would rather be a sheep, wouldn't you?" He moved upstream to refill his water skin. "It wouldn't be the same, though. You would know what's out there, preying on you." Rennick cleaned the blood from his mouth and chin, his cheeks looking nearly rosy from feeding so much. He stood and sipped from his water skin, then turned to survey the bodies behind them. "I guess it is rather ghastly, though, isn't it?"

Colton nodded. Rennick stared at him for a long time before tying his cloak tighter and piling his first victim onto the pile of corpses. The man stared too much.

He scrubbed the remnants of the gang leader from his stubble. He looked down at his shirt, at the scattering of holes still streaked with blood. His wounds had healed and his body had even pushed out the shells, but his shirt was ruined. Between his transformation and the shotgun, the shirt was in tatters. He was lucky his pants were still usable. He pulled off the shirt, deciding his jacket would have to serve as his chief protection from the glaring sun. If they were lucky, there might be some provisions at the farm.

When he looked over, Rennick was examining his shoe. "I really liked these, too. Why do they always have to aim for my good things?"

"If you didn't dress like a wealthy theater owner, you wouldn't get robbed like one."

"And what? Wear rags like you?"

Colton ignored him. He tossed the remnants of his undershirt on the pile of corpses, choosing to look at Rennick instead of the bodies. "What do you think we should do with them?"

"Burn them, I suppose. I'd toss them in the stream, but I'm not fond of the idea. Blood is one thing, but corpses could contaminate it. We might need to make a stop here on the way back. Besides, it would be smart to mask how they died."

Colton nodded. "I agree. Though I'm sure plenty of bodies have floated downstream in these parts. A bonfire could attract attention."

"Only from other looters and bandits. I doubt there's much else in these canyons."

Except, of course, the monstrous thing they awoke in the cave last night. Colton thought about bringing it up, but decided against it. He was eager to leave this place.

They dug a trench around the bodies and placed bits of dried plants and tumbleweeds around the base to catch the flame. Within a matter of minutes the fire was blazing. It was a short walk for them to catch up with the two horses who had kept their distance from the attacks and the fire.

When Rennick adjusted their trail, they started off again. The sun wasn't quite at its highest point in the sky, but it was getting there. It would likely be late into the evening before they reached the farm house.

On the bright if disturbing side, at least they already had lunch.

COLTON SMELLED THE CORPSE LONG BEFORE THEY could see it. It was so rank he had to nestle his nose into his elbow to mask it. He had smelled dead bodies before, both animals and humans, but nothing with this pungency. The sun was in the process of setting and Colton pulled back on Tahoe's reins as he tried to block up his nostrils with his sleeve.

"What is it?" Rennick slowed Aidan beside him.

"Something dead, but worse." He moved his arm up to wipe the sand-encrusted tears from his eyes.

Rennick pursed his lips. "Close by?"

Colton nodded, unnerved Rennick and the horses didn't seem fazed by it at all. Werewolves had a good sense of smell, but it paled compared to a good bloodhound. It was usually only strong when he was fully transformed like during his near depletion of blood earlier. It shouldn't be bothering him so much. "Damn, it makes my eyes burn."

Rennick removed his hood once the sun began to set, and both of them were relieved the temperatures had started to fall. Even with his cloak and feeding so well, Rennick still looked badly sunburned. His skin was pink and wrinkled in places and Colton wondered how much worse it would have been if he didn't have the cloak.

"Maybe we can avoid it. I don't want us to get side-tracked, and we might still reach the farm before dark. We ought to be really close by now, but I don't see any sign of it." He eyed Colton with concern. "If it gets worse, let me know."

He nodded, but already he could tell his coat sleeve would be unable to fully mask it, especially since he had to hold Tahoe's reins at the same time. He wasn't acclimating to it either, which was strange. His vision blurred with tears and he thought he might gag, but firmly he held it in. "Damn." He groaned. "We must be nearly on top of it."

"Do you see that?" Rennick straightened and pointed over to a dip in the sand.

He shook his head. "Kid, I can't see anything."

"I'm pretty sure that's what you're smelling." Rennick dismounted and walked over to him. "This is ruining you, isn't it?"

He wiped at his eyes in frustration.

"Do you want me to help?"

"No, I'm fine," Colton lied. He hated asking for help, especially in front of a fellow agent like Rennick who might rib him for days because of it. At the same time, if they did come across bandits again, or anything worse, he would be useless.

Rennick folded his arms, a smile on his lips, insufferably patient. "Are you sure?"

"Look, if you want to be useful, give me a scrap of cloth or something."

Rennick's laughter made him bristle.

"Some cloth! Something long enough to tie around my face."

Finally, his laughter ceased. "Do I look like a tailor to you?"

If Colton could see better, he'd throttle the man.

"Surely, you've got something. A spare shirt, a neck tie, something... quit being an ass."

Rennick laughed again. "Such a temper! Hang on a moment, if you're capable of being civilized for a moment." He pulled a bag off of Aidan and rummaged through it. "I have blue, yellow, or pink. Pick one."

"I knew you had to have something," Colton grumbled. "Yellow, I guess."

"For a man blubbering over some dried up corpse, you sure are a smug bastard." Rennick picked up a long yellow strip of fabric and Colton reached for it, not really able to identify it because his eyes were so blurry. Rennick held it away from him.

"Hang on a moment! Let me soak it first. It'll help." He balled it up in his hand and pulled out his own water skin.

"I don't care." Colton sighed. "Whatever works at this point. This is terrible."

Rennick carefully poured water onto the balled up scarf. Colton dismounted and allowed his partner to wrap the cloth around his head so it covered his nose. Rennick must have kept some mixture of herbs either in his water skin or his bag because the scarf smelled strong and almost spicy. He couldn't quite recognize the scent. It was strong enough it almost overwhelmed the putrid smell. Colton reached around and grabbed a tail of the scarf and used it to dab at his eyes, grateful to be able to see again.

"Thank you," he said, his voice muffled. "I promise I've never reacted to a corpse like this before."

His partner looked him over. "Does the water help?"

"It does. Thanks. What's in it?"

"Mostly mint," he added with a smile. "I get tired of tasting where my water came from."

To his credit, Rennick didn't mock him once, even though Colton knew he looked ridiculous. Instead Rennick led him over to where he had spotted the body. Most of the corpse was covered in sand, but the head was still visible. The face and eyes were sunken, and the thin skin that remained was stretched taut from the heat, giving them a very skeletal appearance. There was really no way to tell how long they had been there; the desert preserved a body like a piece of jerky. The sand had covered them from about the shoulders down, but even still, it was easy to see their clothing was little more than tatters. The eyeless person grinned up at them with yellowed teeth in the diminishing sunlight, guarding their secrets.

"There's no telling what they died of," Rennick whispered. "I would guess dehydration and with merely a day's ride away from water, too. Quite a shame."

Colton nodded. "What's even stranger is that the body is still here. I've seen plenty of buzzards pick a corpse clean that's been dead for a lot less time. It doesn't look like anything has really come near here."

"Maybe they're smelling the same thing you are."

"Hmm." He turned back to Aidan and Tahoe behind them. They were even nosing in the sand, looking for brush. "I don't know, the horses don't seem to mind it much."

"Perhaps it's not meant for them. Maybe it's specifically meant for your kind." Rennick cocked his head to the side. "Do you think that pack back at Peridot might use this sort of thing? As a boundary for their territory, or something silly like that?"

"I don't think so. I admit I've not been around many werewolf packs before, but I've never smelled something this rank. I usually try to stay away from them."

Rennick laughed. "You and me both. Maybe someone just likes their jerky extra crispy."

"That's disgusting." He ignored Rennick's continued laughter as he crouched. Dragging his hands over the sand, he pushed it away from the edges of the body, unearthing pieces of it carefully. He unearthed a small black mass only lightly covered by the sand. At first, he thought it was a scrap of clothing, but then he saw teeth marks on the protrusion. He pushed away more sand and leaned down closer to see the tooth marks clearer. Bone. As black as if it had been dipped in oil. He excavated further, and Rennick crouched down beside him.

"What is that?" he asked.

Colton didn't respond. He dug down carefully, not wanting to damage the body and not wanting to touch it either because of the smell. More bony protrusions emerged. It was a thumb and four fingers, blackened from time out in the sun, but the end of each finger lacked any skin. "Have you seen anything like this before?"

Rennick stared at it, all humor lost. His eyes were wide. "Never."

His partner dug out the rest of the hand, then used his foot to move the limb to the side so they could look at all the fingers. Every single one of them was lacking skin at the tip and had teeth marks on the bone. They had been gnawed on.

"I don't know of any werewolf that eats like that, do you?" Colton asked.

Rennick shook his head. "I don't know of any scavenger that eats like that. Surely, that happened after death, right?"

He shook his head, "I have no clue. Maybe they were trying to dig out of something."

Rennick shuddered. "No, I do not like where this is going. Let's get away from this place."

Colton eyed him with concern. "What if this has something to do with our case?" Rennick turned toward the horses, but didn't respond. "If it is, then we ought to investigate this."

His partner then glanced over his shoulder. "Our orders were to investigate Davis Farm, not the dried up corpse hidden somewhere in the desert that smells so bad it's clearly designed to keep werewolves away."

He got to his feet with a frown. "You think it's that simple?"

"Do you have an explanation? I'd be happy to ask the corpse, but I don't think they're in the mood to talk right now."

They stared at each other in silence. Colton felt in his bones it was somehow related to their assignment, but he couldn't explain why. He had no proof, and Rennick was right; it was affecting him the worst. He rolled his shoulders and broke their conflict with a sigh.

"You're right, we should probably get moving. The sun's almost set."

Rennick turned back to the horses and mounted Aidan again. "Look, I know you want to investigate, but neither one of us knows what we're looking for. For all we know, they could have been a victim from that unexplainable we found the other day."

Colton shivered at the word as he put his hands onto Tahoe's side, wrapping the reins in his hand. "Don't talk about that thing right now, okay? Let's focus on one threat at a time."

"Okay then." Rennick circled Aidan around so they were side by side as Colton pulled himself up onto Tahoe's back. "Focusing on one threat, our orders said the killer might be spectral, like a ghost, right? Spirits can't do that to people. They're intangible; they don't gnaw a person's fingertips off for fun."

"You don't know that," Colton said with a smile. "They could."

Rennick glared at him. "I've done research on the spiritual world, unlike you. I haven't come across any record of that happening before."

"Look, I may not have done research, but I read the same orders you did." The two of them turned their horses back to the trail. "They don't know what's responsible, and they guessed that it could be spectral or supernatural. That means it could be either."

"What's your point?"

"It means nobody knows what we're dealing with here," Colton said.

They both glanced over to the corpse stuck in the sand. Now that its fingers were visible, it gave it the appearance they were beckoning to them.

Colton lowered his voice. "For all we know, it could be a ghost that gnaws on fingers."

"I guess you're right." Rennick shook himself. "I don't like that you're right, but you are."

They grew silent as they rode past the corpse, more out of nerves than respect. Colton stared down into the sunken eye sockets, noting how the ground dipped around it.

"Why do you think the body was left here?" Colton asked.

Rennick shook his head. "I don't know. That's another piece that bothers me. We're in the middle of nowhere. This isn't wolf territory, but maybe it's marking someone else's land."

Colton clenched his teeth. A chill went down his spine despite the lingering heat of the sun. "Maybe it's like the impaled bodies that Vlad Tepes put outside of his castle walls. Maybe it's supposed to scare away intruders."

His partner gave a nervous laugh. "If we weren't on orders to investigate, I'll be honest, it would have worked on me. Any sane person wouldn't want to be anywhere near a thing like that."

He nodded in agreement, wondering how long it would take the sand to bury the body for good, or if whatever put it there would let the sand ever fully take it.

Part Three

A Forgotten Farm

CHAPTER 11

LIVING THINGS

COLTON WASN'T SURE WHY THEY CALLED THIS wreck a farm. He was pretty sure nothing edible ever grew in the sand surrounding the weather-beaten, decrepit building at the base of a hill. The wood had bleached and warped from ages of sitting in the baking sun being ravaged by the nightly wind and sand. A few of the wall boards had fallen long ago, leaving gaps in strange places where creatures would be able to crawl inside. The forgotten boards lay in various states of decay around the base of the house.

Nature had reclaimed her wares, much as she tried to do with the grinning corpse in the sand.

As they drew nearer to the building, Tahoe slowed. She drew up next to Aidan until they were side by side, then they both stopped completely. Colton and Rennick exchanged a look, but despite their gentle urges, neither horse would move forward.

"Just another bad omen," Colton grumbled. "I don't get it, they had no problems with the corpse we passed. And it smelled godawful. Suddenly we come up on a building that looks like it's barely standing, and they freeze up."

Rennick didn't respond. He merely stroked Aidan's neck, his brow furrowed. Colton felt like there was supposed to be a pattern to it all, something that should stick out, that would explain everything, but the more bizarre situations they encountered, the more his concern grew.

Despite being a werewolf, he didn't consider himself a superstitious man. His father had been. When he wasn't breaking his back building the railroads for wealthy investors, he came home with strict demands. He wanted the windows kept open as much as possible to bring in good luck, even when it was freezing outside. No cleaning was permitted on the lunar new year, even if it was filthy. He refused to trim his toenails at night for fear of inviting ghosts. Colton hated the little superstitions at the time, but now he wondered if there was some truth in them. Hadn't his father given some warning about entering a house that had been abandoned for too long? Maybe there was some kernel of truth to his wariness.

Colton shook himself back to the present. "Have these two ever acted like this before?"

"No, they're usually better than this." Rennick stroked Aidan's mane. "Come now, won't you please move for Daddy?" The two horses nuzzled each other for a moment, but made no move forward.

Colton sighed. "I guess we'll have to walk from here on out." He dismounted and Rennick did the same. Instead of reaching for his saddlebags though, Rennick pulled Aidan in close, stroking the horse's muzzle.

"You better not abandon us here! If you do, mark my words there will be no more apples for you later! You understand me?" Aidan pawed awkwardly at the ground, prompting Rennick to wrap his arms around the stallion's neck. "I know, I'm sorry. I didn't mean it. We get back, you can have all the apples you want."

Colton shook his head and turned to Tahoe. He stroked her flank before heading down toward the remains of the farmhouse. Now he took a moment to pause, he realized his senses were screaming at him, too. Maybe the horses were onto something. The horses could go wherever they wanted. He didn't want to put them in more danger than they already were. He called for Rennick without turning. "You coming?"

"Yes, yes. I had to let him know that I'd be back. He gets so worried sometimes."

Up close, the building was in worse shape than he thought. Part of the roof had collapsed, after the walls beneath it had finally buckled, separating the house into two sections. He peeked in through the front door frame, which was missing a door. That entryway went straight into what looked like the kitchen. That room ought to connect to the long section of the house. To the right of the kitchen was the collapsed room, but there was a much smaller section beyond that. He wasn't sure if that area would even be accessible.

He pulled out his gun as he stepped inside. The crunch of grit under his boots echoed throughout the room. He saw no movement and no obvious signs of life. There was a place where the pantry once stood, and in the middle of the room was a large table. It looked like it was in better shape than the rest of the entire building. He moved in closer to examine it.

It was in surprisingly good shape, but long scratches extended down the length of the tabletop. Otherwise a thick layer of dust and sand lay over most of the table. "I think I found something."

Rennick had his own gun out and had been backing him up, but at Colton's words he holstered it and approached. "What is it?"

"I get the impression someone's been here more recently than the farmers who owned this place."

Rennick dragged his fingertips over the scratches. "They could have been made by a human. Do you think the disappearances might not be supernatural after all?"

"It's possible, but we shouldn't rule out anything yet. Just keep your gun handy."

He nodded and looked down to the floor with growing concern.

"Do you know what bothers me more?" Rennick said. "I don't see any sign of animals. This place has taken a beating, but it would still be shade from the wind and the sun. Why don't they use it? I don't see bird nests, snake skins, or even rodent droppings. It's odd."

Colton stayed silent. It was another piece of the puzzle, but he had no idea what it was supposed to mean.

Rennick walked along the walls. "I'm telling you: living things attract other living things."

Living things. Perhaps that was it. Nothing came close to the building, and no scavengers went near the body. There weren't even flies around it. He thought of the horses refusing to approach. He recalled reading about how hallowed ground was supposed to be protected from dark entities. This place seemed to be the exact opposite of that. Or was it merely a coincidence? He considered Rennick and himself to be dark creatures; anything that feasted on humans had to be inherently dark. Was that why they were allowed to approach the farm? If it prevented living things from going near it, did that in turn mean he and Rennick were not in fact fully alive?

He shook his head to clear his thoughts. Going down that path was dangerous, especially when they were in an unsafe place. If they were allowed to come near the farm, it probably meant whatever controlled this land wanted them near. Either way, they needed to be careful. They needed to stick together and not get separated.

"I'll be right back," Rennick said. Colton looked up as he darted out the door.

"Wait, what? Come back here!"

When Rennick poked his head back inside again, Colton realized how desperate he must have sounded. "What is it? I said I'll be right back."

He clenched his teeth. "I don't think we should split up. We should search this place together."

Rennick leaned against the door frame. "Look, I understand your concerns, but we're quickly losing daylight. You and I may both work quite well at night, but if there was a group waiting at the other end of the building waiting to ambush us, they would probably wait until nightfall. Personally, I would go one step farther. I would wait until after we had made camp, started taking watches. That's when any group is most vulnerable."

"Great, I'm glad you gave them good instructions if

they're listening," he said through clenched teeth. "Why can't you just follow what I say?"

"Because you're wrong, of course. Did you forget we also have a missing little girl somewhere, too? What if she's tied up back there, dying of thirst or starvation? I promise, I'll be right back. Quit worrying so much."

He didn't like it, but Rennick had a point. Recalling the kidnapped victims renewed the urgency of the situation. There was a missing man, too, who Colton had entirely forgotten about. This end of the building was open and easy to access, a wonderful place to draw in prey. The other end didn't even have a doorway to get inside. It was more likely a place to keep hostages rather than a place to plan a group ambush.

"Alright, but be quick."

"Don't worry! I have a walking army with me, remember?"

"It's not exactly an army," he grumbled after Rennick left the room. "More like a dance troupe."

CHAPTER 12

BREAKING IN

RENNICK

EVERYTHING ABOUT THE PLACE MADE RENNICK uneasy, from the fallen wooden boards, to the collapsed roof, to the missing front door. It wasn't so much his concern for hostages that made him want to break away to check out the other end of the house, it was more his desire to be done with the place altogether. He also wasn't too keen to have Colton's eye on him everywhere he went. Or having to follow the wolf's orders all the time. The man wasn't always right, despite what he might think.

When Rennick stepped outside, he realized that the farm wasn't just uncomfortable, it made him queasy. It was as though his inner ear was off and he couldn't stand up straight. Even when he forced himself to stand still, he felt like he was still moving.

The farmhouse as a whole was completely unappealing. He didn't like looking at it from the outside, and being inside of it only made the uneasiness worse. He theorized he wasn't the only one affected by it, either. When he had opted to split up and cover more ground, Colton had clearly panicked. At any other time it would have been funny, but being inside the farmhouse sapped away all humor. No, despite Colton's concerns, it was best to investigate quickly so they could make camp before it got pitch dark. Rennick didn't like the idea of sleeping within sight of the place. If they were done quickly enough, maybe they could ride off a good ways first. He doubted he would sleep easy, regardless.

The sun was nearly set in the distance with only a few determined rays streaking out over the ocean of sand. The stars glittered overhead, filling the sky for another cloudless night, and the temperature was steadily dropping. With the roof of the farmhouse collapsed in the middle, the building looked angry somehow, as though it blamed the entire world for its unfortunate state of disrepair and was going to have several words to say on the topic if it could ever figure out how to speak. The back end of the building was in a far better state than the middle, though, and there were two sets of windows that remained fully intact along the walls.

Rennick checked around the outside first, searching for any sign a human had been here, but there was nothing. No footprints, no buried utensils, no forgotten tools. Nothing. He even took a few moments to shuffle his feet around the base, just to make sure sand hadn't hidden anything from view. It was as if no one had ever lived in the farmhouse and it had simply sprung up, fully formed, from the sand.

He sighed, placed his hands on his hips, and looked to the windows. "I didn't want to have to do this, but it looks like there's no alternative."

He holstered his gun and bent to peer through one of

the windows, cupping his hands around his eyes to see. Darkness. Not even the outline of furniture.

He frowned. That couldn't be right. There were still a few rays of sunlight that should have shown something inside, especially with his own excellent night vision. He stepped back and took a closer look at the window. He looked along the frame and noticed a small crack of light along the edge. Someone had pushed something up to block the view from the outside. Clearly whoever did it hadn't wanted anyone to see inside. He tried to look between the small gap, but it was no good. When he tried the next window, he found a large piece of black cloth had been draped over it from the inside, which was not at all suspicious.

"Wonderful." He put a hand to his jaw, considering his options. Whoever had blocked these up had been trying to keep other people from looking in, or didn't want much sunlight entering the room. That meant there might be hostages or even vampires inside. He had heard of full-fledged vampires forced to do something similar in a pinch, and the list of missing people could easily indicate they had a vampire on their hands. Out here, it could prey on vagrants and the curious, possibly snatching a rodent or two if it got near enough. It would also explain the were-wolf repellent grinning corpse they had encountered.

Rennick went back to the first window and took a moment to steady himself, then bashed his elbow through the glass. Going through the glass wasn't painful. His coat was made of a sturdy leather and prevented the shards from cutting him. Striking the piece of furniture, on the other hand, did; and Rennick instantly knew it was made of sterner stuff than wood.

He bit his tongue to keep from yelping in pain, and gently pulled his arm free, shaking it out as the pain and numbness pulsed down his forearm. "Ow, ow, ow!" he hissed, rubbing at it pathetically. He waited to see if Colton was going to come running out to check up on him, but he didn't.

"It's alright, Colton," he muttered. "There's no need to panic, just making some renovations."

Perhaps Colton was so deep into his observations of a dusty, wooden table he didn't have time to respond. More than likely, he was too busy brooding again to care about a little broken glass. Or he was being rude.

Once the pain in his arm had died down some, Rennick pushed free the rest of the shards of glass and finally reached in to deal with the blockade. The feel of cold metal surprised him as he pushed against it; the weight was substantial. He had to shove it in bursts, finally making a gap big enough to slip through. Colton probably wouldn't have been able to make it, he had a bigger frame than Rennick, but Colton would have probably been able to move the metal monstrosity with far less effort, or perhaps even punch through it. More than once, Rennick considered getting his partner to help, but decided it wasn't worth the inevitable jeering.

He began hacking as soon as his feet touched the ground inside. The air was full of dust that clung to the back of his throat. His theory of a vampire living in this mess began to fade. Undead or not, he doubted anything could live in such a filthy room. Heaps of paper were scattered about, no longer housed in the giant metal bookshelf he had moved to enter the room. The papers were in various states of decomposition, and many of the pages had curled in on themselves, browning in the steady heat. He had to step through them as he moved throughout the room. The other window he had seen also looked in on the room, and he couldn't repress a chuckle as he examined it. Behind the black fabric covering the window were long pieces of painted wood. Each piece was nailed in on all sides of the window, at least four in all. There was no way he would have had the strength to break through. Colton had the claws after all, not him, and although he could have created helpers to get through it, he wanted to save his strength for when he truly needed them. He had learned a long time ago not to waste his abilities on simple menial chores. That was a sure way to find himself exhausted and vulnerable.

He looked around the room a bit longer, noting the daylight leaving as the sun set in the distance. His vision wasn't his concern as much as his safety. Darkness brought out all sorts of beings: ethereal, supernatural, and everything in between. He turned back to the window he had entered and prepared to slip through the gap he had made earlier, but the window was blocked. The gap he had created was gone, and somehow, the bookshelf had been pushed back into place to close off his exit.

Suddenly, the idea of splitting up seemed like a really bad idea.

"What the hell?" Rennick muttered, the fear in his voice echoed back at him off the bare walls and decomposing mounds of paper. He put his fingers along the edge of the bookshelf and tried to pull it backward, but this time the thing wouldn't budge. He pulled so hard his fingers blanched, but it didn't move an inch.

But when he looked up, he gasped. The window was completely intact. Like it had never been shattered. Like he had never crawled inside. It was back to its original state, down to the grimy dust that clung to the glass and the cobwebs lining the inside.

"That's not possible!" he cried, reaching out to put a fingertip against the glass. He brought it back to his face, looking at the dust covering it. His heart lodged in his throat and his stomach clenched as panic took hold.

He spotted cuts that dug into the side of the metal bookcase. Long, deep grooves extended down the sides. They were eerily similar to the markings Colton had found on the kitchen table. The bastard was right. They should have never split up. But Rennick had been cocky, and certainly not for the first time.

His heartbeat pounded in his temples as he spun to the opposite window. He jumped up to grip one of the wooden boards in an attempt to pull it down, but the nails held it fast. Like they were secured into stone instead of decaying wood. Even with his full weight, the board wouldn't bend.

Everything else in the damn house was falling apart, yet somehow this room was plugged up like a fort.

He landed unsteadily on the papers and had to take a few steps back to regain his balance. His inner ear spun, making the queasiness rise and fall. "That's impossible. It can't be real, it must be an illusion." He swallowed; his throat dry. He tried the bookshelf one final time, but it wouldn't budge. "How did you do it?" He cried, all his pride leaving him. He banged his fist against the wall instead. "How did you move this thing without me noticing it? Or even hearing it?"

Rennick felt something sharp dig into his leg, just above his ankle. With a cry, he stumbled to his knees. At the center of the room, the mounds of decayed papers had toppled aside. Beneath them, a trapdoor had been lifted. From the gap emerged a hand that gripped his leg. Tiny claw-like nails dug into his flesh. He glimpsed her face in the shadows: a young girl. She might have been an adorable scamp once, but that wasn't the case, anymore. Her hair was long and splayed around her head like she had passed through a storm, and her arm was deathly pale. Her face was a mixture of dirt and bruises, mixed together so she almost looked like a corpse. She stared at him with piercing, pale blue eyes, one arm holding the trapdoor up, and the other holding onto his leg.

He forced a smile despite the pain. So this was the missing child. Yes, she was violent, but there was no telling what horrors she'd had to endure. The letter never said how long she had been missing after all. Strange things could happen to the mind when it was pushed to its limits.

It took a moment for him to control his breathing so he could actually speak. "Hello there, child. Are you... hurt?"

She didn't move, but he thought he felt her grip tighten. A trickle of his own blood slipped down into his shoe.

"Are you hiding down here? Can you show me the way out, perhaps?"

The girl shuddered for a moment, then let out a high-pitched shriek that made his ears throb. She scrambled so quickly out of the opening Rennick wasn't able to even pull his gun free. Her clawed hands ripped across his chest, his legs, his face. Before he knew it, his fangs had emerged. His vampiric instinct told him to fight back. No, he had to keep control, he had to think, not rely on animal panic. He tried to scramble away from her, but she skittered after him, tearing at his skin. Eventually, he couldn't hold back his instincts any longer. He lunged at her, clamping his fangs onto her throat and drinking deeply.

A terrible, putrid taste landed on his tongue. He gagged, reeling back from her. "What are you?" he hissed. He fell, landing hard against the wall and settling down in the decayed papers. They stuck to his bloodied legs like leaves. He couldn't see. Something was wrong with the blood, with the girl, with this place. Something was wrong with her, and he had tasted it. He bent over and spit up a good amount of the black gunk that made up the girl's blood onto the floor. His body was on fire, the world was spinning, and he was breathing so fast he thought he would hyperventilate.

He curled up into a ball in the corner of the room, his cheek pressed against the cold metal of the bookshelf. The girl opened the trapdoor completely and now stood over him. She was only a fraction of his height, but she seemed impossibly tall to Rennick's dazed mind. "What are you?" he whimpered again.

The girl with the mussed hair stood calmly and watched him with fierce, pale blue eyes. As the world faded from view, she stalked towards him, her filthy pants dragging and snagging on debris as she came closer. Her throat was still spilling black sludge from the two puncture wounds Rennick had made, but it poured out in clumps, making a thick trail down the side of the girl's dingy white shirt. Rennick shuddered and finally lost consciousness.

CHAPTER 13

DEAD ENDS

COLTON LISTENED TO RENNICK MOVE AWAY FROM the front entrance and toward the other end of the building. It was disturbing how quickly the place fell silent. It didn't take long before he had lost all sound of Rennick, even though he was so near. If he had any suspicions of the place having wildlife inhabitants, the silence proved otherwise. All he could hear was the wood creak under his footsteps and his own breathing in the still, dusty air.

He couldn't quite figure out what made him feel uneasy about the farmhouse, but Rennick didn't seem bothered by it. In fact he seemed to be attacking their mission with enthusiasm while Colton wallowed in uncertainty. If he was going to be honest with himself, Colton hadn't felt right since spotting the corpse earlier. It had put a dangerous omen on their mission, and he couldn't seem to shake it.

He pulled off his hat and dragged fingers through his sweaty hair. He needed to focus. Peoples' lives were at stake and he needed to be a professional. Replacing his hat, he pulled out his gun and headed toward the back hallway. It was connected to the kitchen and connected to several rooms, but it was littered with debris. It gave a small glimpse at whoever was foolish enough to build the place. A pile of wood rotted against the wall; some upgrade that never got started left forever unfinished. Where pieces of the walls in the kitchen had crumbled from age, long streaks of dwindling sunlight streamed down the shadowy hall, spotlighting the dust particles that hung there.

Colton's heart was racing, but he couldn't really place why. He could hear the steady beat in his temples and his palms were sweating. He had to stop to wipe the perspiration from his gun hand before continuing. Nothing was here, the place quieter than a tomb, so why was he so on edge? There was no logical reason for it.

Two doors led off the hallway, an unusual choice for such a simple construction. Most of the farmhouses he had seen were much more basic with perhaps three rooms total: living, kitchen, and bedroom with *maybe* an outhouse. This place had at least five rooms, assuming the collapsed area counted as a single room. Only large, expensive farmhouses boasted anything so complex, and usually they had enough land to help pay for such a hefty price tag. Judging by the quality of the land, Colton doubted this place had even been finished before it was abandoned. The owner was probably not from the area. He either bought the land without looking at it first and didn't know what he was purchasing, or he was an idealist who thought he could turn the area into something useful. The place had been doomed from the start: there was no convenient water supply, the land was barely habitable, and there wasn't even shade to protect the crops from burning to a crisp. What had possessed the fool to take on such a task?

All the doors on the hallway were intact, which made sense since they were more protected from the elements. They also had the benefit of not being on the outer wall of the building, so the weight of the roof wasn't as drastic. That had probably led to the partial collapse at the center of the farmhouse.

Colton stopped before entering the hallway. The proportions were off. The walls on either side didn't have the same height, though that could have been due to a lack of planning on the builder's part. Plenty of these places had a piecemeal construction, and were sometimes erected by men who hadn't lifted a hammer in their lives.

He turned to the first door to his left and gripped the handle. The dirt and dust from years of disuse made him doubt he would find anything useful inside, but he checked anyway. The door creaked open, then stuck from the sagging door frame. Colton had to shoulder his way inside. Sand sprinkled onto his hat from atop the frame. The room was dark. The walls were still keeping out the light, so it took a moment for his eyes to adjust.

In the center was a large bed, or at least the frame of a bed. The head and foot boards were crudely shaped pine, but the sideboards could barely be recognized, they had aged so poorly. The bed frame sagged in the middle from the pressure, leaning both ends of the bed toward the middle, and gave the appearance its last occupant had been an enormous fellow.

Colton crept into the room, noting the thick layer of sand on the floor, and the equally thick layer of dust along the wooden bed frame. He could see no signs of footprints or any other tracks, and although many places would have made a perfect home for a rodent, again there was no trace of one. Nobody had been in here for years.

In the corner of the room was a pile of papers, about a foot tall. They no longer really appeared to be papers, but more of a paper mash, rectangular in shape. He stooped over it and peered at the scrawled letters on the top page. He couldn't read anything on it, but it looked like some official document based on the scrawl. He tried to pick up the single page to see if the ones underneath were any more legible, but the corner broke off in his fingertips. What little writing he could make out on the next page was even more illegible, having partially fused with the papers beneath it.

He sighed. The investigation was turning into an enormous dead end so far. He hoped Rennick was having better luck.

Colton went across the hall, wondering what they would do should this place turn out to be abandoned. If their quarry was using the place as a stopover, then staking it out overnight might be a better alternative. If that led nowhere, then there was the possibility that the Agency had been misinformed. It could be a different building. Hell, it could be a different town altogether. Procedure would mean they would have to ride back to Peridot, go to the telegram office, and notify the Agency of the miscommunication. Then wait there to receive further orders. Maybe they would even put them in touch with the informant who gave them the lead to begin with.

Colton stopped himself from stepping headlong into the next room. Before he realized it, he had taken hold of the next door knob and turned it. He looked down into his palm with wide eyes. Shiny metal glinted up at him. This knob had no dust or sand on it. He rubbed his thumb against it to reassure himself what he saw was true. He aimed his gun forward as he pushed open the door. It swung gracefully on well-oiled hinges, and Colton was met with another empty room. He checked left and right, looking in each of the corners to make sure some attacker wasn't waiting for him. Then he spied a pair of double doors on the floor at the far end of the room, the kind that typically lead down to a basement or cellar. Why was the entrance to the cellar in a bedroom? Underground entrances were usually on the outside, not indoors where snakes or insects could get inside. Not unless there was something to hide.

The floor was clean here. There wasn't a speck of dust or sand on anything. It was as if this room had been specifically made for the underground entrance. Thinking of that made Colton's skin crawl. There was no telling who or what he would find waiting inside. He crept up to the wooden doors and gave a curious tug. A chain rattled on the other side, keeping the door locked. Before moving forward, he needed to regroup. He needed to show Rennick what he had found.

COLTON COULDN'T SUPPRESS A SMILE AS HE headed out of the farmhouse. They had him. He could almost guarantee they would find the bodies of the victims, and possibly the missing little girl as well, behind those doors. The sun had disappeared under the horizon, and the chill night air was coming in quick.

He headed toward the back of the building. "Rennick! I found something. It looks like we're heading underground." He turned the corner, but there was no one.

"Rennick?" He looked around at the endless hills. No tracks led away from the house. He cursed. Perhaps Rennick had gone to wait with the horses. He turned to head back to the front of the building when something on the ground caught his eye. He squatted and had to angle his head just right to see it again. A piece of glass. He picked it up out of the sand, surprised at its size. It felt grimy, but it wasn't just from the sand. He could clearly feel cobwebs or spider webs on it as well.

He turned it over in his hands. The window above it was whole. He tried to look inside, but a piece of furniture blocked his view. Dust on the window indicated it had been here for some time, but perhaps it had been broken at one point. That didn't explain the cobwebs on it though, and that made Colton anxious. He knew, of course, the glass could have been laying in the sand unnoticed for ages. If it had come from the broken window at some point, with as little rain as this area got, it was likely the cobwebs would get baked onto the glass in the heat. He rubbed at the shard again, trying to ignore the uneasiness that filled him, and headed back toward the horses.

He pulled off the yellow scarf Rennick had given him and wrapped the shard in it before sliding it into his pocket. It was hard to spot glass, especially in mere starlight, but he was still surprised Rennick hadn't picked it up earlier. Had he even explored that area at all?

Maybe Rennick had run for it. Colton's mouth went dry at the thought. Fear and disappointment crept into his veins.

"Rennick!" he called, unable to keep the anger from seeping into his voice. Rennick wasn't answering him. Why should he? He was probably long gone. Colton walked around the perimeter of the house, but saw no trace of his partner.

Of course Rennick wouldn't be here. His anger increased with every step. He should have been suspicious about the way Rennick demanded to make all the arrangements before heading out and the eagerness he had to leave Peridot; he had planned to leave for good. Colton made his way back to the horses and walked up, placing a hand on Aidan's flank. Both of them were so much more loyal than their master. Both horses stood out in the dark, fully trusting Colton and Rennick would return for them.

Colton paused stroking Aidan's neck. Would Rennick have left without his horse? Even if everything else was an act, his affection for Aidan had looked real. Colton opened the saddlebags Aidan was carrying and narrowed his eyes. If Rennick had abandoned him, he'd left behind two good outfits and, more importantly, his cloak. He wouldn't get far come daybreak without that. There was the possibility Rennick had a stash buried somewhere around here, but the more Colton thought of it, the more unlikely it seemed. There were plenty of better opportunities to bolt than waiting until they reached the farmhouse.

The cold was seeping through his layers of clothes.

Strong winds had started again and Colton wished he had packed another shirt. His coat alone wasn't going to keep him warm if he stayed outside. He considered taking one of Rennick's, but was fairly certain it wouldn't fit. Rennick had a much smaller build, not to mention his taste was gaudy as hell. Colton turned back to the farmhouse.

If he went underground to find the bodies likely stowed there, he could run into a good deal of trouble. Not only could it be a trap, but it might be a waste if there was nothing down there. If he went into the cellar and got trapped somehow, he wasn't sure how long it would take him to get out. He didn't like the thought of their horses being strapped up to the place either, though he doubted either of the horses would get close enough to the building to let him tie them.

Then there was Rennick. Colton didn't really think his partner had tucked tail and run, but maybe he had taken on a lead without asking for help. Now he was in trouble and Colton was at a crossroads.

There were two or more missing people hidden somewhere. They could be trapped in that cellar. Colton was almost certain it was a human they were facing now, though that did little to make him feel more comfortable. Of all the creatures they were trained to take down in the Agency, humans seemed to cause the most trouble and be the most resourceful. Werewolves, vampires, wendigo, even mummies usually had a motivation. Humans were unpredictable and may not have any obvious rhyme or reason for their actions. Those were the difficult ones to catch and the most depraved.

He gave a heavy sigh. "Looks like I'm going in, you

two." Colton pulled the packs off the horses and dropped them just inside the kitchen. If there was trouble or the horses couldn't wait any longer, he hoped they could fend for themselves. If he tied them up at the farm house, they would not only attract unwanted attention, but if he was gone too long, both of them could die. At least they should know how to reach the stream.

Tahoe flattened her ears back as Colton removed her bags.

"If we don't come back, you two need to go home. Don't wait up for us," he whispered, stroking Tahoe's muzzle. She whinnied in response and Aidan pawed at the ground. "I know, I don't like it either. But I don't know what's going to happen to me. Hell, I don't know what's happened to Rennick either. You two need to stay safe. This is no place for a pair of beauties like you."

He squared his shoulders and headed back to the farm house. He had to place a hand on his hat to keep it from blowing away in the cold wind. He didn't turn back to the horses, not wanting to give them hope he would be returning. Because he had no idea if they would be.

The farmhouse was still dark, but somehow it felt like it waited for him.

PART FOUR

THE DESCENT

CHAPTER 14

THE TUNNEL

COLTON TOOK HIS TIME SORTING THROUGH supplies to make sure he had the essentials. The more he thought about going underground alone, the more items he wanted to bring with him. Closed spaces always made him uncomfortable. He wanted to be prepared. The last thing he did was verify his supply of bullets. Werewolf strength and senses would only do so much. Sometimes, it took a steady hand, too.

Once satisfied, he turned toward the dark hall. The starlight outside coming in through the gaps in the walls only gave so much light. A human would have to fumble about, but as a werewolf he could make out more since he still had some light. It did take his eyes a moment to adjust. He took a drink from his hip flask, allowing the whiskey to burn his senses awake, then he took up his gun again. Cautiously, he approached the bedroom door where he had seen the underground hatch, turned the handle, and stepped inside.

He froze. The room was just as clean as before, but the

hatch was open. The person who had opened still stood on the wooden steps that led underground. Blue eyes stared back at him with a disturbing lack of surprise. It was the boy Rennick had created at the cave. An illusion, but one that still sent a shiver down his spine. Every detail was the same from his bare feet to the single broken suspender of his overalls. Even his freckles were in the same places. In the seconds it took Colton to recover from his shock, the boy ducked down into the tunnel.

"Wait a minute!" Colton called.

With an unsettling smile, the boy pulled the hatch doors closed behind him.

"Stop!" Colton cried as he lunged across the room. The deadbolt locked on the other side and the chain rattled as someone dropped it back into place. He pulled at the handle with a growl and heard the slapping of bare feet as the boy ran deeper into the passage.

The boy was playing a prank on him. Or rather, Rennick was. Colton was not amused with this game. He kicked at the door and it rattled on its hinges. "Come on, you bastard, let me in!"

He listened, hoping to hear sounds of his partner, but all he could hear was the boy's bare feet running into the distance. A shiver went down his spine. Exactly how big was the underground cavern? And why was Rennick hiding down there? It had to be Rennick, nobody else could make that little boy. Finally, the sound of the boy's feet disappeared completely. He was only an illusion, though. It wouldn't surprise him if Rennick was mimicking the noise just to freak out Colton while he huddled in a corner wearing a smug grin.

He clenched his fists. "This is not a game. We have a lead here. Quit playing around!"

He grabbed hold of the handle again, braced his feet upon the frame, and yanked as hard as he could. The wooden door bulged and groaned under his grip. He gave a final pull, and the handle wrenched from the wood. Colton reeled back and managed to avoid colliding with the warped bed frame. The handle slipped from his fingers, flew through the air from the momentum of his arm, and landed with a loud clatter on the floorboards behind him. He stood for a moment just staring at the misshapen metal with alarm.

Whatever game Rennick was playing, the racket it was causing would certainly attract someone's attention. It was bad enough they were talking and walking around the building, but that ruckus had to have ruined any element of surprise they had left.

"Fine," he sighed. "I guess there's no need for silence anymore."

He reached into the hole left in the door from the handle's removal and yanked the wooden door off its hinges. He threw it on the ground, surprised at the dust cloud that came off of it. Had there been dust on it when the boy had closed the doors? He couldn't remember, but at the moment, he was too annoyed to give it much thought. He was too focused on his childish partner and their elusive target. Colton pitied whichever one he came across first.

He looked down into the cellar, expecting to see a storage room or at the very least some shelves or crates, instead a long, dirt tunnel stretched into pitch darkness.

Looking down into that gaping emptiness made the hair stand up on the back of his arms. He couldn't continue until he had some light. As good as his eyesight was in limited starlight, underground he would be completely blind. He needed something to use as a torch. He glanced to either side of the steps, for some reason expecting Rennick to be hiding there, waiting for him to come down; but there was no place to hide.

A prickle of worry formed at the base of his spine, but he ignored it. He turned around and picked up one of the warped wooden planks from the hallway. Sand slid down its sides as he raised it, enough to take it down to half the width he thought it had. He put his foot on the middle and used both hands to snap off a sizable end. It wouldn't be the lightest torch in the world, but it would work. He pulled out the yellow scarf from his pocket and discarded the glass shard he had wrapped in it. He then went to Rennick's pack and pulled out the other scarves as well. The fabric was thick but pliant enough. He wrapped all three scarves around the jagged end of the wood. He pulled a wide-mouthed bottle from his own pouch filled with oil and propped the makeshift torch vertically in it. It would need to soak for a few minutes to stay lit down there.

Of course, getting the damn thing lit would be problematic. He needed a strong, steady flame, which meant building a fire. It would attract the attention of anyone outside. But he didn't have a choice.

He gathered enough dry grasses to make a small fire, then set to work getting it to light. He dug out a ditch near the front door and pulled out his flint and steel. The wind made it difficult to start a flame. He had to stop every few minutes to wipe the sand from his eyes, but eventually it caught. When the flames had grown to a decent height, and he no longer had to protect it from the wind, he fetched his torch. It had soaked up a good amount of the oil, dripping slightly as he lifted it from the bottle. He pocketed the bottle with the remaining oil before lighting his torch outside. As soon as it was lit with a strong flame, he kicked out the ground fire.

Only the starlight remained. Colton looked around at the vast emptiness and listened to the wind. No coyotes were out tonight, at least not close enough to hear, but he caught the scent of melons. He smiled. There had to be a saguaro cactus out there somewhere in the distance. Somehow, it survived close enough to this cursed place to be picked up by the wind. That gave him a small scrap of courage. He would need it to face that passage.

With the torch in one hand and his gun in the other, Colton returned to the bedroom. Queasiness hit him as he took the steps down into the dark underground corridor. Something about this whole setup seemed wrong, but then again, if it was easy, he wouldn't have been called in. His boots met with soft earth as he descended the tunnel into darkness.

IT DIDN'T TAKE LONG FOR THE LITTLE MOONLIGHT down through the hatch entrance to disappear behind him. The tunnel sloped endlessly downward. The walls were solid dirt, the same as the ground. He could have stood in the center and put his hands flat against both of the walls they were so close, but he hugged one wall, always at his back, to be sure of his surroundings. He tried not to think about how far underground he had traveled or about how many tons of dirt lay between him and the surface. Instead he tried to figure out why the tunnel was there to begin with.

Could the target have dug it out himself? Doubtful. It would have taken a team of men weeks, maybe even months, to dig out such a distance. The walls felt so smooth, though, it was as if a large boulder had been pushed through the opening in order to make the path, compressing the dirt against the walls.

The more disconcerting fact was there were no support beams, no pillars, nothing to account for how the tunnel was held up. Thinking how badly the farmhouse had been constructed, Colton hoped this tunnel was better quality.

The air had been dipping colder as he moved away from the heat of the building. That much at least made sense to him, but then he began to feel warm breezes. Like something big was breathing hot air into the tunnel from ahead. He paused for a moment, his hands shaking as he tried to identify it. The breeze would come and go. There was no real pattern to it. Mustering up his nerve, he forged ahead, ever downward and ever onward.

At one point, he wondered if the tunnel would even end, or maybe it went on like this until he popped through at the center of the world. He shuddered, just then noticing his torch was dying.

He would have to put it out in order to add more oil and relight it. Otherwise, the fire would start eating the handle of the torch. Of course, that required being alone in the darkness, not that he had seen anything other than dirt for the past half hour or so, but that knowledge did nothing to appease his nerves.

Colton felt like he was being watched. He knew that feeling well. It made his skin crawl and his trigger finger itch. He looked back up the tunnel then down it again. Nothing. Nobody was here to watch him. So, why did the hairs stand up on the back of his neck?

Regardless, if he waited too long to relight, he would have no torch left. So, he crouched down and pulled out the bottle of remaining oil. He would need to keep some bit of flame burning to relight the new torch, so he holstered his gun and pulled on one of his gloves with his teeth. Then he pulled off a piece of one of the scarves slowly burning and dropped it to the ground. Even through his leather gloves the pain was still fierce. It took a moment for his fingers to heal as he stomped out the torch.

Darkness rushed in. The only small scrap of light came from the piece of scarf at his feet. Colton's pulse quickened. With shaking hands he propped the torch upside down in the bottle of oil. Then came the worst part: waiting.

He stared back and forth, up and down, the tunnel, straining to hear any trace of movement. There had been no sign of Rennick, no sign of anything down here. But if he was being watched, this would be the time to strike. He had to resist the urge to make any noise, to fidget, to hum, or anything that might distract his senses. Though the urge was strong. He should have been counting, making sure the torch had plenty of time to soak up more oil, but he'd forgotten to start.

After he felt it had been soaking for long enough, he pulled out the torch and propped it head up against the wall while he closed up the jar of oil. His hands trembled, and the lid was slippery; every time he lost his grip his heart skipped a beat.

The tiny bit of flame on the ground was growing dimmer, and he didn't have the time to waste on this stupid jar, but he knew the risk. If he accidentally dropped it and caught himself on fire, he would be in a lot worse trouble. Caution demanded he take his time. Finally, he put away the oil and wiped his hands down on his jacket. He snatched the torch again and held it close to the tiny flame, trying not to suffocate it. His hands trembled, sweat from his brow made it hard to see, and the darkness was suffocating. The confinement in the narrow underground tunnel was getting to him, and everything felt like it took too long.

The flame didn't spread as quickly this time. He hadn't soaked it as long as it needed. It caught the torch, finally, and ever so slowly grew brighter, pushing away the darkness. His heart still thundered in his chest, but he could breathe easier.

He stood up and nearly bumped heads with the blue-eyed boy. He was so close, Colton could have counted the threads in his overalls.

CHAPTER 15

LOST IN THE DARKNESS

COLTON CRIED OUT AND TOPPLED BACKWARDS IN a manner very unlike an agent. If Mr. Tep could have seen him in that moment, he probably would've have been fired on the spot. He shot a hand out to catch himself only to put it into the scarf with the tiny flame he had left on the ground. He screamed, and this time fell flat on his rear with a thud.

The boy stared at him with such intensity Colton blinked with shock. He hadn't heard him walking, but then again, he was an illusion. So he wouldn't hear him, would he?

It took him a few moments to get to his feet. The boy, who had been crouched down, mimicked him, standing up straight with the same speed, not once blinking his big, blue eyes.

"Where are you, Rennick?" Colton asked, feeling a twinge of fear at the base of his spine.

The boy looked at the torch Colton had dropped on the ground, then looked back up at him.

He shook his head. "What the hell does that mean? Do you want the torch?"

The boy shook his head.

"You want me to…" He almost dared not to say it. "Put it out?"

Again, the boy shook his head.

He swallowed. "You want me to come with you."

This time the boy only stared. It would be so much easier if it would speak. Maybe then Colton wouldn't feel so damn crazy. He crouched down and collected his torch, keeping an eye on the boy the entire time. He half expected to be rushed or attacked, but the boy didn't make a move.

Rennick's illusions were usually far more active. The women at the theater talked and laughed. He was certain they could interact with people as well. This one, though, was very different from the others. Was that merely because Rennick enjoyed portraying the boy as having the personality of a rock? It didn't feel like his partner's style.

"Alright," Colton said. "Lead the way."

The boy turned and walked downhill. His footsteps didn't make the slightest sound, like a ghost. For several minutes, they walked in silence. In the distance, a dim light appeared. Very faint, it flickered like candlelight, but the sight filled Colton with relief. It was a foolish feeling really, because something told him this boy wasn't leading him anywhere good, but he couldn't help it. He'd had enough of this claustrophobic tunnel with its cold, stifling darkness. The light got brighter as they moved closer, and the boy turned around to face him, maintaining his gait downhill.

"I wasn't expecting you to make it this far," the boy said. His voice was deep and raspy; it sounded more like an old man than a child. Colton realized then Rennick wasn't holding the strings for this illusion. Somehow, something was forcing him to do this. That was why the boy's behavior was off. Colton's hands began to shake again.

"I watched you pass by my guardian." The child smiled, and Colton tensed. "But don't fool yourself about the house. I let you come down here. If I didn't want you to come down, I wouldn't have let you."

He nodded slowly. "I appreciate that. I'll admit that's quite a feat to get Rennick's illusion to behave like that."

"To me, it's child's play. The real fun will come soon. Don't be in such a hurry, Mr. Fen."

A chill went down Colton's spine. Who was this person, and how the hell did they know his name? He tried his best to not show his surprise.

The boy gave a deep laugh. "I know much about you. I know where you come from and I know why you're here. Your mission is quite hopeless, though. You can't stop us now."

Colton swallowed, yearning for a swig of his whiskey but knowing better than to try. It was trying to frighten him, to intimidate him. He had to focus, instead, on analyzing it because there was no telling how much Colton had given away from his own fear and shock already.

"You sound like you know a lot about me, but I don't even know your name."

The boy smiled at him. "I have been called many names. Do you know what an Iya is, Mr. Fen?"

He shook his head.

"The Sioux believe it is the personification of evil, bringing disease as it kills. Of course people have many names for things they don't understand, don't they? I prefer to be called Kaga. I was given that name once, and I'm rather fond of it."

The echoes within the tunnel only amplified the inhuman qualities of Kaga's voice. It no longer sounded human anymore. The Agency had failed to mention he would have to deal with the personification of evil in his duties. He was pretty certain he would have noticed that small print on the contract. Murderers, thieves, unexplainables, the supernatural, or all of those combined he could usually handle, but this was an entirely different level of threat. Colton had never been a man prone to turning yellow, but this thing at his side, that somehow had hold of Rennick, that spoke to him like a man, that smiled and leered and bragged about bringing disease and death wherever it went; this thing made him want to turn tail and run back to the surface.

The only thing that gave him the courage to continue was knowing Rennick had to still be alive. Somewhere down here in this underground tunnel, his partner was trapped and being used to create this false illusion. Colton clenched his jaw. As much as Rennick had unnerved him over the last couple of days, Colton couldn't bring himself to abandon him.

The boy led him around the corner, walking backwards with his sick smile, reveling in Colton's fear. When Colton turned the corner, he had to squint against the amount of light. They had entered a chamber far larger than the tunnel. It could have been the size of half the farmhouse. At the far end of the room an immense fireplace was giving off waves of heat; Colton had felt it even before the boy had appeared at his side. Already he felt the sweat forming on his brow and back, but as he stared at the black smoke that shot up from the flames, he found himself questioning his sanity once again.

How was a fireplace even working this far underground? There shouldn't be enough air down here to keep the blaze fueled, and he was certain the black smoke would have attracted attention above ground, but his senses told him otherwise. Wouldn't he and Rennick have spotted the plume of smoke up top from the farmhouse, or had they traveled that far from it? Nothing in this place seemed to make any sense. The more Colton tried to untangle it, the more uncertain he became. The boy stepped aside and pointed toward the hearth, his eyes fixed on Colton. With a shaky breath, he walked forward.

The silhouette of a man stood in front of the fireplace, leaning a hand against the dirt wall. The alcove for the fire was so large it would have taken three stacked men to reach the top of it. Inside the logs were as big as a cow. Colton didn't know of any trees around these parts even close to that size. He moved closer, taking his time so his eyes could adjust to the much brighter light. He could make out the color of the man's outfit now and recognized the blond hair.

"Rennick?"

The man's shoulders shook as if in laughter and Colton placed a hand on the butt of his gun. He was having a hard time telling what was real and what wasn't anymore, and the words that Kaga had said earlier, about being the personification of evil, resonated with him. Was he being tested? Was this all another sick game? A thousand questions swam around in his mind, but instead of allowing confusion to take him, he tried to remain calm. He needed to analyze everything first before making a move he might regret.

"It's a beautiful fire, isn't it?" Rennick said. "So very warm."

Colton's gaze swept up and down the man, trying to determine if this was really his partner or not but, like the boy, every detail was perfect. His shoe still had a hole in it from the assault at the stream. "That's funny," Colton said. "You were pretty sick of the heat earlier today."

Rennick crossed his arms and turned toward him. Claw marks crisscrossed down from his neck to his stomach, and his face was puckered with deep, raw gouges. None of them had begun to heal as they should have, which immediately had Colton concerned. All the blood he could spot was dried, but it looked like Rennick had bled extensively. Trails of it went down his pant legs and blotched his shoes. He looked like a walking corpse.

"What happened to you?" he asked.

Rennick shrugged, his lips curling into a smile; a bit of blood oozed out from a wound on his cheek. "I guess you could say I had a bit of an accident." That was when Colton noticed his eyes. They were solid black. The blood that covered his partner wasn't actually blood, it was too dark to be. With the firelight behind him, Colton had thought it was merely a trick of the light. Now he was close enough to see it all had the same color as his eyes.

"Rennick..." He took a step closer.

"It was a terrible idea taking this job, did you know that?" He smirked, "Oh, of course you do. I suppose it's a bit late regrets, but it really is amusing that we thought this was going to be a simple assignment. I suppose he gave you his name, right?" He looked to the illusion still standing at the entrance to the tunnel.

"You mean whatever is controlling your boy? He said his name was Kaga."

A shudder swept through his partner. Rennick stared at the child for a long moment, then nodded and turned back to Colton. "You know I don't want to do this, right?"

"Then don't. It doesn't have to be complicated, Rennick. If you don't want to do something, you just don't do it. It isn't hard."

Rennick smiled. "I'm afraid you're wrong."

IT WAS THE SECOND TIME THAT RENNICK'S SPEED took him by surprise. His partner lunged toward him, a blur of movement. Colton took a step back, but it was too late. Rennick had hold of his left arm. His partner was far more skilled than he'd let on. His startling speed spoke to the power of his vampiric heritage. In an instant, Colton knew he was at a clear disadvantage. Just as he shifted his weight to pull his arm free, Rennick spun around. He felt the pressure build until his forearm snapped in two.

Screaming, Colton fell to one knee. Waves of pain and nausea enveloped him. Arm bent at an odd angle, the bones clearly not lining up, he wondered if he might pass out.

Rennick leaned in close with expressionless eyes and

whispered, "I don't want to have to do this, but he's giving me no choice."

Everything was quaking, but Colton forced himself to stand up. His only chance of getting out of this alive was somehow breaking Kaga's control over Rennick. "You always have a choice," he insisted through clenched teeth. "What's the point of all your speed and your illusions if you let someone else pull your strings?"

Rennick shifted his weight back, pulling Colton's useless arm with him. White hot pain flooded through him and Colton whimpered. The world darkened for a moment as stars danced in the corners of his vision. Then Rennick jabbed sharply at his stomach. He doubled over at the fresh pain. Struggling to breathe again, he realized with a touch of terror he had never really seen his partner fight. Back at the theater, Rennick had held back more than Colton had even imagined. It didn't matter what tiny percentage of vampire blood Rennick did possess, the little he had was more powerful than any full-blooded vampire Colton had encountered. Warmth spread out from his midsection. In a matter of seconds, Rennick had given him a broken arm and some major internal bleeding. Even with his rejuvenation, which as a werewolf he probably relied on too much, Colton was keenly aware of the precious seconds that would slow him down. Time was on Rennick's side.

Somehow Colton had fallen to his knees during the assault and Rennick's breath was hot on the back of his ear. "I'm sorry."

This was it, this was the finishing blow. His cocky, childish partner who he had nearly written off as not knowing a thing about how to fight, had wiped the floor with him in an instant. What had Colton done? He hadn't fought back once and had even tried to talk him out of it, but that had only led to more pain. Did he survive the vicious werewolf assault years ago and go through all the training with Grady to die in such a humiliating fight? Rennick mocked him for being too softhearted, for having a bleeding heart. Was he a coward for not fighting back? If so, what was he afraid of? Hurting Rennick?

Colton clenched his fists.

If his partner was so good at dishing out pain, then he could stand to take some himself. Those werewolves at Rennick's house hadn't realized how lucky they had been to catch him off guard, but those were just novices. Colton was a professional. He could take a hit and not be taken out. He had trained for years, been shot more times than he could count, and considered himself a detective and a protector. Rennick didn't need his protection. Not by a long shot. He had walked in here planning to grab Rennick and get the hell out, request reinforcements, and take a more strategic route. He needed to change his strategy, and quickly, before shock and fear got him killed.

More than that, he needed to realize a hard truth: Rennick might already be beyond saving.

That one hurt more than he thought it would. More than his broken arm and wounded pride.

Rennick tossed Colton's hat to the side. Colton made his decision before Rennick could possibly hit him and paralyze him.

Just as the air moved, signaling the coming strike, Colton ducked and rolled backwards, throwing his partner off balance.

Rennick gasped.

Colton felt the pinpricks of pain at the tips of his fingers as his black claws extended on his remaining good arm. Black blood splattered when Colton slashed at Rennick's exposed side, ripping through the fabric and tearing off long strips of flesh. Rennick cried out and flung himself to the side, but Colton was glad for the space. Every second was another moment his body could try to heal itself.

He got to his feet, extending the claws on his broken arm as well. He could feel the bone stitching back together again. It wasn't usable yet for an assault, but Rennick might not know that. Size and intimidation were Colton's friends at the moment. His stomach still ached, but already it, too, was healing. As much as he had despised gorging himself on that bandit earlier, his rejuvenation was boosted because of it.

Rennick looked down at his side with a strange detachment, as though it was someone else's wound and not his own. "I liked that shirt."

"He's infected your mind," Colton said. "Surely you can see that."

Before he finished speaking, Rennick charged. Colton was prepared this time, though. He dodged aside, but Rennick was quick to stay after him. Colton kept dodging, but couldn't avoid him forever. If he wanted to really fight him, he would have to fully transform, but that came with a whole host of other problems. It would mean allowing the wolf to take over, and to be honest, the wolf frightened him more than Rennick's vicious speed ever could. It saw no difference between friend and prey. It could tear his partner to shreds.

He didn't have long to make up his mind before the wolf chose for him. The injuries, his adrenaline, and fighting in hand to hand combat was luring the beast out. Fur sprouted along the backs of his arms and hands. His teeth grew longer and his jaw pushed forward into a lupine shape. Soon he was battling himself along with Rennick.

"Struggling?" Rennick asked. Then he started pressing his advantage.

Colton gained height as his shins stretched and his palms morphed into paws. Already, he was finding it difficult to keep his balance on two legs, and the scent of fear on Rennick only made it worse. It wasn't just fear, it was terror. Rennick was telling the truth when he said he didn't want to do this. Kaga was urging Rennick into his own grave. Before, Colton had suspected Rennick planned to subdue him, but now he wasn't so certain. It seemed Kaga planned for Colton to devour his own partner instead. Or maybe the fight between the two of them was just fun for him.

The battle had shifted. Rennick was losing ground quickly now. Colton had pushed him toward the massive fireplace and Rennick was getting sloppy. Something would have to give. He wasn't sure if his friend's wounds were overwhelming him or if it was fear, but his movements had slowed. His attacks weren't making contact as often, while Colton's claws were shredding his arms. Rennick's speed was also his enemy. He was wearing down, unable to avoid Colton's attacks. When he finally tried to run, away from the fireplace, Colton made his move, or rather the wolf did.

He lunged forward, jaws wide, as Rennick desperately tried to avoid him. He had little room to move, though, especially with Colton blocking his way. Colton wrapped his jaws around Rennick's arm. Something inside of him hesitated. If he dared to bite him, to taste Rennick's flesh, he wouldn't be able to stop. The taste of a fresh kill would overwhelm him, and the wolf would own the show. He didn't want to watch his partner get disemboweled. He had more self control than that, and he had more faith in his own humanity. He froze instead of clamping his teeth down on Rennick's exposed arm.

Colton could have ended the fight then, but he didn't. He allowed Rennick to slip past him and stood there, a hulking, partially transformed monster gaping at its prey. He breathed in the heat waves of the fire before him, wrapping his mind around what nearly happened. Again, his pause gave Rennick just the moment he needed.

A hiss of pain and the perfume of seared flesh, was all the warning Colton had before hot embers were tossed into Colton's eyes. Colton was too slow to sidestep it. He wasn't adjusted to his partially transformed body. The focus he'd had was lost. In the midst of grappling with his own identity, his limbs had become uncoordinated. He was in a great deal of pain from this partial transformation, and his body was bulky. Then came the pain of the embers tossed in his eyes.

Colton howled and shuffled backwards, stumbling against one of the cold earthen walls. He shook his head and tried to pull out the remaining embers, but he'd forgotten his hands were no longer dexterous. Instead, long claws rake across his snout. The movement burned the embers even further into his eyes and he let out another agonized scream. He rolled on the floor and dragged his face against the wall before finally collapsing in exhaustion. His eyes burned and his body morphed back into its normal shape. His limbs felt raw from the partial transformation and his many wounds still ached. His eyes were swollen and seared shut; his vision gone. The pain was so sharp and his body so exhausted, he had to fight against losing consciousness.

"Rennick?" he whispered, but his voice was nearly unrecognizable. "Rennick, are you still here?"

Perhaps in his fury he had torn the man to pieces. He wasn't sure how long he had been howling in pain and scratching at his eyes. He imagined feeling his way around the cavern only to find a bloody mess of cloth and flesh in a corner. He thought maybe the boy was still there some-where, but he was a creation of Rennick's, too. He would be alone and blind down here, trapped underground and lost in the darkness.

He swallowed down the panic trying to take hold of him at that thought. He would rather be killed here than be subjected to such a dark fate. Then he realized even if Rennick was alive, he might have simply left him here. Kaga might have sent him on another task, some other bloody deed, and Colton would still be trapped alone down here.

"Rennick!" he called out again, his voice breaking.

A familiar perfume wafted past, and hands pulled him to his feet. Another pair of hands supported his shoulders. Then he heard the ruffling of petticoats. Rennick's other illusions. He had almost forgotten there were others besides the boy. All Colton could do was hang limp in their grips, but he couldn't suppress a smile.

"I was afraid I had killed you," Colton said.

"No, not quite." Rennick sounded weak, breathless.

Colton may have been blind and his body worn and beaten, but something inside lifted when he heard Rennick's voice. Even if his partner was still controlled by Kaga and he himself might end up a dead man, it gave Colton great satisfaction to know he hadn't killed Rennick. It gave him a strange sort of peace and clarity. At least, he thought, he could die here with a mostly clear conscience to know he hadn't lost complete control.

"I'm glad," Colton whispered. "Your ladies, will they kill me now?"

"They could, but they won't. Not yet. If he wanted you dead, you would be. They're here to keep you from collapsing." He gave a wet cough. "You know, I never imagined you would give me so much trouble."

Colton shook his head. "I could say the same."

When he felt the women shifting, Colton tensed, wishing he could see what was happening. He thought he could hear light footsteps approach, too light to be Rennick's. Then something heavy struck his temple and he fell unconscious.

CHAPTER 16

A Heathen and a Demon

COLTON THOUGHT HE KNEW WHAT DEATH smelled like. He had killed more than he would like to admit: humans, animals, and everything in between. He had seen the piled carcasses of cattle after a drought. He had witnessed floods that cut down whole herds, where the ground had been soaked through with decay and the air was so thick with flies that even with a cloth held over your nose, you couldn't get within twenty feet. What assaulted his nostrils now was ten times worse.

It was old death mixed with new corpses and Colton groaned as all the levels of decay permeated his lungs and taste buds. He pushed down the urge to hurl and calmed himself enough to figure out his surroundings. His first instinct was to open his eyes, which was far more painful than he expected. His eyes felt like they were covered in coarse sandpaper and regardless of whether they were opened or closed, he couldn't see much.

He didn't think he was completely blind; he could still see shades of light amid all the surrounding darkness, not that he was anything close to a doctor. His eyeballs felt crusted over like a layer of charred meat on top of an over-cooked sirloin, and already he felt his tear ducts working futilely. No more of that. Best to keep them closed to prevent any further damage. It took a few moments to calm himself again and allow the pain to recede.

He was bound. A thick, scratchy rope had been tied around his wrists and another wound around each of his legs. Even if he could get free, he wasn't sure where he was.

He tried to concentrate on any scent he could catch, hoping it would give him some clue, but the smell of death hung so heavy in the air it clouded anything else. Panic threatened, tangling its icy fingers around his heart. Groping around in the darkness inside of some torture chamber was more terrifying than the pain of his eyes. It made him reluctant to try to escape, even though he knew once his captor returned, he probably wouldn't last long. He was lucky to still be alive at all.

Gritting his teeth, Colton opened his eyes again against the crusts of his eyeball and eyelid rubbing together. One of the layers shifted slightly, changing the limited light and darkness that he could see. It gave him just enough hope to keep at it. Working through the pain, he blinked again and again, until the layer of gunk covering his eyes finally fell off. That had been painful, but now looking around he could make out more shades of light and dark. It wasn't perfect, and his eyes were still wet and raw, but at least he was closer to being able to see.

Slowly, his sense of smell grew accustomed to the rot, and Colton smelled something else. Moist dirt. They must be still underground. He dragged his foot around and scented what he could. The dirt here had a different smell from where he'd fought with Rennick. The earth had been tougher there, not giving easily under pressure. Here though, the earth was still soft and malleable. He might not be as deep underground as before, and that gave him a small comfort.

Straining his eyes, his vision slowly improved. He looked around for anything identifiable. The roof of the cave stretched above, but strange shadows hung down from it. They were spaced apart in the large cavern, but for the life of him he couldn't identify what they were. They hung in different shapes and sizes. With the smell, though, it didn't take much to imagine what was up there.

Something moved toward him, and judging by the way the lights and darks danced across the swinging arms and moving legs, it was definitely human. It was too tall to be the figment of the boy, and it was missing the bell-shaped skirts the three ladies had worn in the bar.

"Rennick?" Even though he tried to keep his voice down, his baritone still reverberated off the cavern walls. The place was bigger than he thought.

The man slowed his gait. "Hello, friend. Glad to see you're coming around."

Colton chuckled. "After the beating you gave me, I don't think you're allowed to call me a friend anymore."

Relief washed over him at hearing Rennick's voice. Even if Rennick was now his enemy, the icy panic relinquished its hold. If Rennick was still alive, he thought, there might be a chance for him, too.

Rennick was silent, and Colton wished he could see his expression. The shadows that danced across his face made

Colton feel like he was talking to a doll. Rennick turned, distracted by something in the distance.

"He's coming," he whispered.

Colton couldn't tell if that was fear or reverence in his voice. A scraping sound echoed through the cavern like the dry scales of a snake dragging against a rock. He looked around to spot it, his gaze settled on a strange round form crawling toward him.

Colton trembled. "What is it?"

"Kaga." Rennick's voice dripped with obvious admiration this time. "He wanted to speak with you."

So this was the being who had captured Rennick and lured Colton into a trap? The creature that had somehow spoken through Rennick's illusion. Colton tried to focus, to keep himself from shaking as Kaga approached. He could hear the labored wheezing of a creature quite unused to movement. When something cold and wet touched his arm, Colton bristled, pulling against the ropes that kept him bound. Kaga gave a cruel laugh.

"You know, I've had many interesting creatures in my collection. Humans of every shape and size, several vampires, of course, and even a pair of baby dragons. But somehow I have never had the pleasure of having my very own detective werewolf." Kaga said the words as though referring to a character in a children's book. Several icy digits slid down Colton's cheek, rather sharp like dull razors. He could feel the moisture they left behind like a slug trail.

It took a moment for Colton to find the nerve to speak. "Is that why you captured us? To add to your collection?"

"Yes, and no." Kaga moved around in front of him, and

Colton could see for the first time the full shape of the creature. The head and upper body looked like fleshy bulges, and its belly fell to the ground and dragged across the cavern floor until it tapered to a stunted tail. Weird projections stuck up along his sides as though he was being ferried along with the oars of a ship instead of walking. "I doubt you can see it now, Mr. Fen, but you have the privilege of being in my impressive collection room. I keep my trophies here until I tire of them."

The creature leaned forward and trailed fingers along Colton's scalp and down a few strands of hair. The labored breathing was almost directly in Colton's face now, and he had to hold his breath to avoid the smell.

"Soon enough, you will join it. Now that you are here, it is merely a matter of time."

It stepped back and Colton gulped down a breath. "A matter of time before what? Before you finally put me out of my misery?"

Kaga laughed, "Misery? Oh my naïve little pup, you don't know the meaning of the word. I will show you what misery means, and you will beg me to end you before I am finished."

"So you mean to torture me? If you expect me to talk, it won't happen. If you know who we are, then you should know that the Agency never gives us much information beyond our current assignment."

"I care not for your knowledge. I want to see your descent. I want to watch as your mind unravels and your body falls apart. When starvation sets in, I want to watch you devour yourself in your madness. Then I will know that you are ready to join us."

Kaga dragged a claw down his temple and Colton flinched at the pain. Blood trickled down the side of his face.

"You will be more of a challenge to tame than your friend was. Your body is made to resist, which is why I must focus on your mind. That is, after all, the weakness of your kind."

He shook his head free of Kaga's claws. "Some of us don't possess such a weakness."

"Hmm." Kaga gave a low chuckle. "Your arrogance is delicious. I am curious to see how long you do last. I've tamed plenty of werewolves, but never one that was also an agent for ABSC. I'm sure you'll give me quite the challenge, even if you don't meet my expectations. Regardless of how long it takes, I will still break you."

He had to admit Kaga made a good point. What chance did he have of breaking free when his senses were shot and his only ally was now a puppet? Even if more agents were sent to investigate the situation, Kaga could easily kill them. He got the impression he and Rennick had been monitored before their arrival. Kaga said he had allowed the two of them to get close. He could be bluffing, but Colton couldn't be sure of that. As much as he tried to keep up this bravado, the mask was slipping and his courage wavering. How could he pretend to have the upper hand when he was so powerless?

"Do you know what I am, Mr. Fen?"

The question took Colton so off guard, it took him a moment to formulate an answer. "One hell of an ugly monster."

"Oh, please, I expected a more creative answer! I doubt

you are a God-fearing man, but I would expect even a heathen to recognize a demon when he saw one."

His limbs went cold. "A demon?"

"Yes. I've not always been so. In fact, I was a man once, a very long time ago. I didn't realize what I was at first. I didn't understand why the Lord didn't take me into his arms, like I had always been taught. Then I realized what He in His great wisdom had given me: a new calling. Just as Lucifer was cast out of heaven, I was denied entry to Heaven for my many crimes in life. I was the sinner in life, and I was lost in death." Kaga paced, raking dry scales against the stone.

Kaga hissed in a simmering rage.

"It was horrible to realize that the Lord had turned his back on me. To realize that the Creator I dedicated my entire life to serving had abandoned me when I needed him most. I spent years trying to unravel his intent, to understand the new purpose he had given me."

He paused, and then his voice became a harsh whisper. "Tell me, Mr. Fen, what makes God great?"

Colton's mouth went dry. "I don't know."

Kaga gave a giddy laugh. "Of course you wouldn't. He smote you for your sins a long time ago, didn't he?"

He flinched.

"God is great not because of his followers or his words. His infinite war against all evil makes Him great. That was what he needed of me. He needed me to do what he could not. He must have seen that spark of cruelty in me at some point. I thirsted for bloodshed in life, and he must have known what I was capable of in death. So I did his bidding as well as I could. I tortured men, women, and children. I drove pious priests mad, and I slaughtered hundreds. I made civilizations disappear overnight. I stole children in their sleep."

A cold shiver jolted through Colton. He forced a meager smile, "You speak of driving me mad, but it sounds like you lost it a long time ago." Kaga turned toward him but didn't say more, so Colton continued. "Perhaps your god never wanted you to become this grotesque thing. Maybe you're simply doing what you always wanted to do. Maybe it's just an excuse for you to hurt—"

Something lashed out and struck him across his mouth. It sounded like a whip, but a sharp barb on the end dug into his skin as it dragged across his face.

He cried out from the searing pain.

"How entertaining! A werewolf, of all beasts, trying to teach me about godliness. One of the most unclean and bloodthirsty creatures in the entire world. It would be laughable if you weren't so arrogant. Death will come for you soon enough, little pup. Don't hasten so to greet it. I see in you nothing more than a desperate animal caught in a trap. I will tear your mind to shreds and let you pick up the pieces just so I can shatter it all over again."

The demon snickered and this time his voice dropped to a threatening murmur.

"How does that nursery rhyme go? The one they tell children so that they know how to kill a werewolf should they ever come across one? *Death only greets a werewolf in her finest silver gown.*"

Kaga gripped Colton's chin with cold, slimy fingers. This time he couldn't shake the creature away. "No, perhaps death is too good for you, little pup. I think I'll keep you. You will be mine for eternity. Can you imagine that? Can your little mind even perceive of so much time?"

Colton held his tongue. He had pushed Kaga too far, and now he would have to pay for it.

Kaga laughed. "I can imagine. Maybe one day I might even illicit a thank you from those lips."

Tears rolled down Colton's cheeks. His body trembled against the rope bindings. He was grateful when Rennick stepped forward.

"What should I do with him, master?"

Kaga was silent a moment before answering. "He needs to be cowed. This one has quite a tongue on him. Normally, I might leave you here to starve, Mr. Fen, but no. I think you need more. To destroy the mind, you must start with the body. We shall skin him."

CHAPTER 17

———————

A TRAINED DOG

"WE SHALL SKIN HIM."

Colton's heartbeat thudded in his ears as the words sank in.

He knew he had pushed Kaga too far, but he hadn't expected such a leap. The pain would be excruciating. Worse yet, it wouldn't kill him. He would be living when Rennick was done with him, alive enough to experience the agony of his skin growing back. The ground tilted beneath his feet and Colton would have stumbled to the ground if he wasn't tied in place. Kaga and Rennick were still talking, but he didn't hear them. He looked up at the blurry, hanging masses above them and wondered what—or who —they were. If they had been werewolves, there was a good chance they might still be alive, too.

The only reason Colton didn't pass out was because Kaga had his disgusting fingers digging into his chin. Never before had he wished to let go of himself, to slip into unconsciousness and escape the waking world. He was bound and mostly blind; his partner, the closest he had to a friend for thousands of miles, was going to torture him; and if the Agency ever did look for their two missing agents, Colton was certain they would find little. Kaga had been doing this for far longer than anyone could have suspected. Pain blossomed in his chin when Kaga finally retracted his claws and forced Colton's attention back to his surroundings.

"The mere mention of it sends his mind into a panic," Kaga spoke almost gleefully. "Already his mental foundation is crumbling beneath him. The rest of it will topple down soon enough. Once we have utterly demolished any sense of reason he maintains, then he will join us. He won't have a choice at that point." Kaga's hot breath fanned Colton's face. "Does this talk terrify you, Mr. Fen?"

The single thread of dignity he had left prevented Colton from saying yes, admitting his own defeat. That small bit of pride was all he could cling to, so Colton gripped it with both hands.

"You may fight it now, but you will learn the futility of it. Eventually you will realize, as they all do, that you deserve it. You deserve the punishment, Mr. Fen, and you know it."

Kaga scratched his way across the rocks and left them. Shaking from head to toe, Colton thought of the trio of bandits at the river and the two werewolves back at the theater; there was a kernel of truth to Kaga's words. Kaga had intentionally planted it, but that didn't stop it from eating at him.

Colton had killed many people over the years, even his own kind, and he had written them off as deserving it. They had been harming innocents, he would say, and he was simply protecting those that couldn't protect themselves.

The guilt ate at him; Kaga had seen it clearly and used it against him.

He glanced over to where the foggy shape of his friend stood motionless where Kaga had left him, like a trained dog. It sickened him to see Rennick so demeaned. The man was much more of a free spirit, unusual yes, but quite comfortable in his skin. He didn't suffer from the same guilt that lingered with Colton, and watching him obey orders against his nature pained Colton.

"What do you think?" he asked, not even sure his friend could answer if he wanted to. "Do I deserve this?"

Rennick shrugged. "I don't have a clue, but you obviously think you do. That's really all that matters, don't you think?"

He shook his head. Even under Kaga's control, Rennick could still get under his skin. It was as though he was hardwired to be able to piss him off anywhere, anytime. Something about the way Rennick said it implied that Colton was being a fool.

"And what about you? Do you deserve this?"

Rennick pulled out a long, thin shape that must have been a knife. "No, not at all. I deserve to be surrounded by admirers and naïve saps with deep pockets, not trapped down here by my master. But I don't have a choice here, do I?"

"Are you saying I do?"

He shrugged. "You might. Either way, you're going to be in a world of pain in a few moments." Seeing the blade in Rennick's hands helped Colton focus. Then he realized the painful truth: Rennick was his only way out of this. He was *their* only way out. With that realization, Colton examined what they had to work with.

His partner was controlled, but he still had his own personality, his own voice. That meant some part of him wasn't controlled by Kaga. He had some form of his mind still.

There could be some chance, even a small one, Colton could reach that part of him. There had to be some way to get through, some words or some memory that might cut through the manipulation.

"Rennick," Colton whispered when Rennick leaned forward and pushed back the cuff of Colton's sleeve. "You do know who I am, right?"

His partner was silent. He tried again.

"You must remember who you are, don't you?"

Rennick chortled. "Who I am? I know precisely who I am." He stepped back and cleared his throat, as though presenting on a stage. "I am a master illusionist and an accomplished ABSC agent, a born and raised half vampire of the Dalton clan. I am also a renowned actor." He gave an exaggerated bow.

Then he pulled out a ribbon and tied back his blond hair. It gave Colton a few more seconds and a small bit of hope. If his partner was suddenly concerned about his appearance, then he had to be reaching something.

"As for what my master wants me to do with you, I can tell you simply enough. He wants me to drain you near death, so that you're easier to skin. He doesn't want me to get harmed in the process, which I greatly appreciate. Each day, I'll drain you down so you can't shift and try to bite my head off. It'll also slow down the healing process, which means more pain, more torture... you get the idea."

"You don't have any problems with it, then?"

When Rennick shook his head, Colton sighed. This was going to be more difficult than expected. His partner had a strong personality, an ego, and even stated he didn't deserve such treatment. The man was a pompous ass, yet somehow, the demon had put him under his thumb in hardly any time at all. How had Kaga done it? How had it claimed his mind?

Colton tensed when his partner took hold of his arm. "So you're just going to slice my wrists and let all my precious blood spill out on the ground? Seems a bit wasteful."

His partner cocked his head to the side. "You're delirious if you think I'd deter even slightly from my orders."

Colton shrugged. "I guess that's a good point. I mean, it would be dangerous, right? I mean, you're not a full vampire after all. You wouldn't be able to handle my blood, though you clearly need it. I know how bad I beat you up earlier."

Rennick placed the knife against Colton's wrist, preparing to slice him open, but then he froze. "Of course, I could handle it! He just told me to use the knife is all."

"And why do you think a clever demon like Kaga would want that, hmm? Even he knows you wouldn't be able to handle it. Stop fooling yourself."

Rennick flung the knife to the ground with a flourish. "That is not at all the case!" He fidgeted for a moment before proclaiming, "I'll drain you myself." He paused.

"But... I'll take a small taste first, just to test it. I suppose I might as well, since it's just going to be wasted otherwise."

He snatched Colton's arm. He was still quite strong despite their battle earlier. It was as if the fight had merely been an exercise, though Colton clearly recalled his partner being slashed up and badly wounded even before the fight. How was Rennick even standing at this point?

Twin pin-pricks pierced his wrist when Rennick latched on. For a moment it felt like a match flared up against his skin before the vampiric bite parted him from his senses. Like the numbing agent of a mosquito, it quickly filled his entire body. His body went limp, his head foggy and detached. The world around him no longer felt important.

For most people it probably felt like being drunk, but for Colton it made him delirious. Not only did he no longer care about his limbs growing cold, but he fancied he enjoyed it. The thought of being drained by Rennick actually sounded kind of fun. He allowed his mind to drift as his partner pulled his blood from his veins. He was so lost in the deadly current he barely noticed Rennick pull off of him and double over in pain.

CHAPTER 18

A FADING LIGHT

COLTON BLACKED OUT ONCE RENNICK REMOVED his fangs. When he came around, Rennick lay on the ground. Even without clear sight, Colton could tell he was convulsing. Cries caught in the man's throat and his limbs thrashed against the ground. He winced. A pungent odor came, one that he recognized. It was the black ooze that had covered Rennick's wounds during their battle earlier. This time it was potent. The stench was so strong Colton turned his head away from Rennick. Though still reeling from Rennick's bite, slowly his body was recovering, and the wolf in him was angry.

He wasn't sure how much Rennick drank from him, but it was not a sip. If he transformed fully, he might get free, but Rennick could be killed. Colton took a deep breath, trying to calm the wolf down to keep himself from transforming, but it didn't work. The heat began in his chest, always where the transformation started, where his blood burned the hottest. A chill went down his arms and his fur started to sprout. He clenched his jaw against it. His teeth grew sharp and the familiar taste of copper filled his mouth. Flares of pain shot up and down his spine. He shook his head, willing his limbs to go lax against the ropes, willing himself to focus on his breathing and calm his mind.

It was difficult taming a beast that lived in your own skin. Newly bitten werewolves could never control it and might never learn the skill. It had taken him nearly two decades to get it right. Even still, he struggled. It was like learning to prevent an angry volcano from erupting.

Grady had told him the wolf couldn't claw its way out of a calm mind and a quieted body. Anger fed it. Control was key. The wolf stepped in when control was lost, when its existence was threatened. The wolf was a self-centered survivalist that would claw through stone if it had to, in order to live. Control enabled werewolves to be agents. Control allowed them to survive. Kaga was right about one thing, though, the mind was his weak point.

A werewolf with a weak mind could get severely injured and, in the panic, transform and devour family and friends. Control was the compromise between physical pain and emotional heartache.

Colton took a deep breath as the fur retreated into his arms. The spasms in his spine ceased, and his teeth changed back. His body was dead weight against the ropes and he hung there for a few minutes as sweat poured off of him, giving the wolf time to go back to sleep. Every muscle in his body ached and a throbbing headache had formed just behind his eyes. He looked down at his feet. Rennick wasn't moving.

"Rennick," he croaked.

Still no movement. His concern grew. Vampire and

werewolf blood were innately incompatible, preventing cross infection. It also meant it was a painful poison if one ingested the other. Luckily for him, Rennick hadn't known how Colton's blood would affect him. In human homeopathy, werewolf blood was used to purge illnesses and cure diseases. The saliva was infectious. If Rennick had been a full, young vampire, it probably would have killed him. As it was, Colton hoped as a partial, it would help clear gthe man's senses. He hadn't realized how much Rennick would drink from him, though the wolf never had good timing.

"Rennick," he whispered, his vocal chords still not quite back to normal. His body had been ready to kill earlier, and it wasn't fully back to being tame yet. His throat contorted and he twisted his neck side to side as tendons and muscle shifted painfully back into place. His mouth was dry and the ropes against his wrists and legs felt more painful and scratchy than before. The headache was now reverberating through his entire skull. He tried again.

"Wake up, kid. Don't leave me alone like this."

Rennick took a deep breath. His chest rose, but it was still several moments before he finally groaned.

"Don't call me kid." His voice was raw.

"Just stay with me," Colton urged. "Keep talking to me."

Rennick gave a weak laugh. "I can't believe I did that. I can't believe you convinced me to do that." He shook his head and spat. "Yuck!"

Colton smirked. "I told you it was a bad idea."

"I know. No need to rub it in." He sat up and sheathed his dagger. "No wonder he wanted me to use the knife.

How did I drink this stuff?" He spit again, his face twisted in clear disgust.

Scanning the far end of the cavern, Colton looked and listened for any sign of movement. He wished he could see better. Surely Kaga must have heard Rennick's screams. The walls amplified even the slightest noise. How could he not have heard it? If he did know, then why wasn't he here already? Maybe it was difficult for him to move. If that was the case, they didn't have much time.

Rennick grabbed Colton's exposed arm as he pulled himself up to his feet. Colton could tell he felt far too cold to be human.

"Sorry," Rennick said. "I just feel so strange..."

"You need to feed. It doesn't matter if it's human food or blood, but your body needs to recover." Colton could spot the dark lacerations on Rennick's face. He guessed they were wounds that hadn't healed. "He nearly killed you, didn't he?"

Rennick laughed. "Your blood nearly finished me off."

"Can you hurry up and cut me loose? We need to go."

His partner fingered the ropes as though just now noticing them. "I can try."

He fumbled with removing the dagger from his sheath, then had to lean against Colton to keep from falling over. His breathing was labored and for a moment, Colton was afraid he was going to put the silver handle against his skin he was so shaky.

"Take your time. Don't push yourself."

"You're joking, right? It's a little late for that." He had to use both hands on Colton's arm to lower himself to the ground, then he cut on the rope at Colton's feet. "I'm not keen to stick around either, but I won't get very far on my own. Not like this. I can see why he wanted me to beat the crap out of you earlier. Normally, these would be easy for you to break, right?"

"Don't worry about that right now," he urged. The longer it took, the more nervous he became. The silence of the cavern got to him. All he heard was them. Kaga had to know what was going on, but the fact he hadn't shown made him nervous.

Rennick used Colton to get to his feet again, then cut at his wrists. "Stop pulling! You're tied to stone here. You're not going anywhere with these on."

Colton growled.

"Besides, you'll need your arms free. I can barely walk, and I'm not doing all this work for you to waltz out of here without me."

"I didn't mean that. I wasn't going to leave you here, I just hate not knowing what he's planning."

Rennick glanced up to him. "You mean that? Even after I kicked your ass?"

He rolled his eyes. "You didn't kick my ass. You were told to kick my ass."

"Yeah, but... I still won, right?"

Colton ignored him. He could banter with the man later. The ropes snapped and blood rushed into his arms again. His legs hadn't felt so bad, but his arms had been tied tight. He wrung them out, hating the tingling sensation.

Rennick held onto him and sheathed his knife again. "I'm sorry, it's ridiculous how weak I am right now."

"It's okay. Come on, we'll get out of here together." He

slipped an arm around Rennick and shifted his weight so that his partner was leaning against him. Rennick smelled like the black gunk and he was covered in something sticky like molasses. Doing his best to ignore the smell, he kept moving. He hauled Rennick up into his arms and started walking.

"Whoa, hold up!"

Colton froze.

Rennick gripped his shirt with trembling hands. "You better let me give orders on where to walk, 'cause you nearly careened us into a pit."

Colton frowned, looking down at the shadows not far from his feet. "I can't *see*."

"That is obvious."

He grunted and turned around. "You must be feeling better if you've got jokes."

"I've always got jokes. It's how I cope. Let me lead, okay? You can trust me for that, can't you?"

He sighed. All he could think about was Mr. Tep talking about how he needed to be able to work with his partner. At the time, he thought that included camping out on the range together, not relying on him to keep them both from plummeting to their deaths. Mr. Tep was right: he wasn't ready for this kind of teamwork. Hell, he wasn't ready for any of this. He had a hard enough time trusting anyone, let alone a partner he had only met a day or two ago.

Rennick studied him. "Is this really so much to ask of you?"

"Fine." Colton snarled. "Do you know how to get out of here?"

Rennick nodded. "We're closer to Peridot than you might think."

They walked uphill, downhill, and down a twisted path. Finally, they reached a dark place, a tunnel he assumed, similar to the one he had used to come down here.

Coming to a stop in front of it, his old claustrophobia landed on him like the hand of an old, unwanted friend. He didn't want to climb into that tunnel, especially not without his sight, and especially not having to trust Rennick to be his eyes. He pulled an arm loose to wipe the sweat off his brow.

"Do tunnels bother you?" Rennick asked, his head lolling to the side. He seemed to be fighting to stay conscious. Colton wondered if it was due to the blood loss, if his body was using up resources to heal, or it was some remnant of Kaga's control. Either way, he needed him to stay awake, especially now.

"I hate being underground."

Rennick chuckled. "Then this must really be rough for you."

"Yes, it is. Thanks for pointing that out." He shifted Rennick's weight and headed in, even though his instincts screamed against it. "You know, I could just leave you here if you want."

"No, that's fine." Rennick shook his head. "It's not exactly my kind of place."

They headed further into the tunnel and his heart thundered in his chest as it grew darker. As they turned a corner, a spot of light was visible in the distance. He squinted, trying to figure out what it was.

"Is that a torch?"

"It sure is." Rennick sighed. "Get me closer and I'll bring it with us."

Colton did as asked. When Rennick took hold of it, Colton couldn't see how it was affixed to the wall, but he could hear the sound of wood scraping on metal. He narrowed his eyes. "Why would a demon like Kaga need torches?"

"There's more than just Kaga down here," Rennick said as he brought the torch forward. "I was brought down by one of his little helpers."

Little helpers. Colton didn't like the sound of that. He pushed that unease aside and focused on the task at hand. "Don't burn us with that," he muttered. "Do you think it will last until we reach the surface?"

"Not a clue, but I sure do hope so! I really don't want to be stuck in a dark tunnel with only a werewolf with me. I hear they're dangerous."

Colton grunted in annoyance.

Rennick led them further into the tunnel. The torches that had been sparse before were soon gone, and Colton was grateful that Rennick had thought to grab one. As the path led upward, Colton searched the darkness beyond the firelight for any other source of light. Behind them, he heard the scrape of what could have been a footfall.

He paused. "Did you hear that?"

"Yes, and trust me when I say it's best to keep moving." Rennick urged him forward despite his exhaustion.

Colton lowered his voice. "Did you see something?"

"Not yet, but I don't want to. Please don't stop."

Colton agreed with that. They walked in silence down the seemingly infinite tunnel. He heard another scrape behind them. This time he knew it was a footstep, and Colton picked up the pace. Rennick was shaking in his arms. He hoped he would stay awake until they reached the surface.

It didn't help that he couldn't see. The longer the tunnel stretched, the longer the darkness remained, and the fainter the torch flame burned. Then he spotted it, beyond the torchlight, white light. Not another damn torch, but daylight. He moved quicker, eyes on the exit, ignoring the sweat dripping down his back. His partner didn't complain and gripped onto Colton's shirt.

Finally, they emerged. He breathed in the hot, dusty air, so grateful to feel sunlight, to no longer be trapped underground. He shifted Rennick's weight and realized with growing dismay where they were. His vision was slightly better now than it had been below ground. They stood on the very outskirts of Peridot, outside of what he guessed was one of the dilapidated shanties, and probably just a few buildings down from Mary Silva's home.

Part Five

Surfacing

CHAPTER 19

BLIND AND BROKEN

COLTON SQUINTED AROUND AT THE BLURRY buildings around him. The scent of sun-bleached wood told him more about his location than his eyes could.

"There's no way we walked fifty miles underground," he muttered. When Rennick didn't respond, he realized with alarm he had no idea which direction to go. "Which way?"

His partner put his arm up to shield his eyes. He was breathing hard. In the bright daylight Colton could vaguely see the black gunk that streaked his face. Rennick finally spoke. "Give me a moment. It's too damn bright out here."

Colton looked behind them into the tunnel they had come from. It looked like a normal cave entrance from out here. When the wind shifted, though, he caught the slight scent of rot wafting up from the tunnel.

He frowned. Had the smell been that strong when they were below, or was there carrion somewhere nearby? Then he remembered the scraping sounds of footsteps they had heard below. What if something had followed them up?

"Pull it together, kid," he growled into Rennick's ear. "I don't think we're alone up here. We need to find some shade."

"Alright." Rennick sighed and dropped the dim torch to the sand. He swayed back and forth as he looked around. Colton shifted the man's weight in his arms. His muscles were burning, but he didn't want to drop him.

"Don't pass on me. I need your eyes still."

"Go straight," Rennick whispered.

Rennick's voice guided him through the back alleys, and wound around the run down and abandoned parts of Peridot. Colton hadn't realized how many buildings were hidden away back here. Following Rennick's instructions, he twisted them around corners, took sharp turns, and shuffled beside buildings that with his blurry vision seemed to lean farther than they should. Or maybe that was just how they were built.

He had thought this town was only recently setup, so it surprised him that there were so many shanties already. It made him realize how little he knew about Peridot and reminded him he was still just a visitor.

Finally, Rennick settled on one of the abandoned buildings, though Colton suspected his friend was simply getting worn down by the glaring sun. His face looked pinker than before and that probably wasn't a good sign.

It didn't take perfect vision to tell the place was in far worse condition than Mary's place had been. It smelled sour and grimy, like something had gone bad a long time ago. At least it had a place where Rennick could lie down.

He went to put Rennick down in a corner of the room.

"Whoa, hang on a moment." Rennick groaned.

"There's gross… debris on the floor there. Can you knock that aside?"

That wasn't just debris. Flies were all over it and it smelled godawful. But Colton bared his teeth and did as asked, kicking something surprisingly light into a far corner. Flies flew everywhere, and he shook his head as they swarmed the air.

"What the hell are you on about? Debris," he snorted. "That was a corpse."

Rennick grunted an uncommitted sound.

"You're not a very honest pair of eyes." Colton smirked. He expected to hear some quip or at least a protest, but Rennick's silence wasn't a good sign. He laid Rennick down on the now clean spot.

"You need food," Colton said. "We both do."

Though Rennick was breathing hard still, he said, "That's an understatement. I'm so thirsty."

"This is your city. Is there anyone here we can trust?" They couldn't just walk up to some random person on the street and ask them for a bite to eat. If Rennick was as weak as he seemed, he was probably as pale as a corpse. Colton could only imagine how monstrous he himself looked. If either of them were outed, it could lead to a silver bullet in his skull and to Rennick losing his head.

"Not really, but I have an idea." Rennick messed with something in his pocket. He pulled out what must have been a cloth bag, but he had a hard time getting into it since everything on him was sticky. "Here, hold out your hand." He placed a few coins into Colton's palm, his skin icy cold despite the intense heat. "You'll need a disguise first."

Colton nodded, hoping his partner would have something simple in mind. Of course when it came to clothing, nothing was ever simple with him.

Rennick pushed himself up to his knees and had Colton squat down in front of him. He looked over Colton's hair and shirt with an air of disgust.

"Is it that bad?"

"Oh, yes. You look worse than the flea-bitten mutts around here and trust me, that's says something. We'll have to start from scratch."

Rennick gave orders and Colton followed them, fetching whatever he needed. Wooden pieces, disgusting fabric he had to tear off from Rennick's supposed junk pile, and a few other items Colton tried hard not to identify. All of it smelled awful.

"Are you really planning on doing something with this? 'Cause if you can I will be impressed."

"It's a shame you won't be able to appreciate it, not until we get some food in you at least, but I promise you: no one will recognize you when I'm done. I've done just about every theater job there is." He cleared his throat. "Take everything off first. You're covered in blood and who knows what else. You look like you've been sleeping underground."

Colton chuckled. "You're going to wrap me in rags that were on a corpse, and you're concerned with how I look?"

Rennick glared at him. "Look, there's a difference between being a drifter who's wandered into town and a thief who's come to cause trouble. Right now, you're more on the thief side. Your clothes look nice, like they've been stolen, especially for someone as obviously unwell as you are. A corpse's clothes, however, are free game. A drifter would rather steal from a dead man than a living one. Need I continue?"

Colton gave a frustrated huff. "But I'm blind! Doesn't that make a difference?"

"Absolutely! A blind drifter has even fewer options, especially if he has no one to care for him. Oh, don't look at me like that. You'll do just fine. Trust me a little, won't you? On the bright side, I don't think anyone is going to mess with you."

Grudgingly, Colton allowed his partner to dress him. He could imagine Rennick doing this with one of his pet actors, dressing them in something flamboyant, shiny, fluffy, or some other nonsense. Rennick was using grotesque rags instead of those fine materials, but still Colton didn't like being in the same shoes as so many of his pet people. It made him uneasy. He wasn't anyone's pet any more than he wanted to be ogled. He was kind of glad he couldn't read his partner's expression very well due to his eyes.

For his part though, Rennick was a complete professional. It made the very unusual situation much easier. Perhaps Rennick was trying to be respectful, or maybe he was simply exhausted; either way, Colton appreciated it. They had both been through a lot together. In that moment, Colton was unexpectedly glad Rennick was his partner.

Rennick crawled over to the corpse Colton had kicked aside and started pulling off pieces. It looked like a coat and a shirt were literally yanked off the dead man. The coat came off easy enough, but the shirt took more work.

"You don't think he's one of our casualties, do you?

One of the people we're here to find?" Colton asked, watching Rennick work.

"It's possible, but neither of us are in any condition to continue this investigation until we're fully recovered."

He nodded, trying to breathe as little as possible.

Rennick shook loose what could have been scorpions from the shirt before bringing it over to slide over Colton's head and cover his bare chest. His skin crawled as the sleeves of the shirt fell down over his arms. Rennick pulled the coat over next. It had no sleeves, but at least he didn't have to shake anything off it. Honestly, it felt more like a sack filled with holes that Rennick had torn in places, making it more of a cloak. Then Rennick pulled out a dusty hood and slipped it over Colton's head, pulling it down almost to his nose.

"Please." Colton gagged. "I don't want to smell this thing any more than I have to."

"You'll want it," Rennick assured him. "That hood is going to keep you from being seen. Keep this down, or your eyes will give away what you are. You're very wolfish at the moment." He got to his feet and made his way over to a different corner of the room, moving slowly as though he might collapse at any moment. His burst of adrenaline from putting together the disguise was beginning to fade. He dragged his boot around along the floor before reaching down and rubbing his hands in the mess.

"What are you doing?"

Rennick came back and raised up his hands. "Dirtying you up." He proceeded to rub both hands all over Colton's face before he could raise any protest. It wasn't just dirt he felt being rubbed into his skin, it was ash from a firepit. If

Colton was gagging earlier, he barely wanted to breathe now; he couldn't help but sputter as the grime made its way into his mouth.

"What the hell!"

Rennick gave a weak laugh. "They'll never recognize you now."

"No kidding!" he spat. "Now I look like a mad man."

Rennick tried to lower back onto his shady spot on the floor, but collapsed part-way. When Colton took a step forward, Rennick waved him back. "I'm fine, I'm fine. Just getting dizzy is all."

His own discomfort seemed petty compared to Rennick's. His partner was not even a full vampire and had been pushed to his physical limits. Given what little they had available, he should be happy Rennick was able to put together anything for him. "Just relax." Colton said, "I'll go find some food. Don't move around too much until I—"

"Wait, that's not—"

Slam!

Pain burst around his nose and forehead as Colton walked face first into the wall.

"What the hell." He groaned and rubbed his grimy face.

"That was the door. You need to open it to get through it."

Colton stared at it. He had thought it already open based on how much light he could see, but now, up close, he saw it was only broken boards vaguely making a door.

Rennick chuckled behind him. "You need a walking stick, my friend. Take this piece of wood."

He took a long stick from Rennick so old and worn he

had to hold it with care to prevent splinters. "Is this all we've got?"

As he lowered himself to the floor, Rennick's nod was barely perceptible to Colton's struggling eyesight.

"You sure you'll be alright while I'm gone? I'm not too thrilled about leaving you so close."

He didn't need to say Kaga's name. He could just imagine the snake-like creature making its way through the tunnel and up to town, just so it could get hold of its weakened servant once again. Or send something worse.

"Somehow, I don't think he'll come up right away, not while there's daylight at least," Rennick said. "That gives us a few hours."

Colton thought of the smell of rot he'd caught near the entrance to the cave. "You're guessing. That thing doesn't care if it's daylight or night."

Rennick chuckled. "Sure, but I have to be a little optimistic. I think it's around noon or maybe three, so you should have some time. I'm sorry... it's too bright for me to look outside."

Putting together the disguise had taken its toll on his partner's very limited energy. Once again, Colton kicked himself for all the mistakes that had led them to this point. They shouldn't have split up at Davis farmhouse, he shouldn't have allowed himself to be blinded, and he shouldn't have given Rennick such a beating. His partner had such a big mouth, though, it was hard to remember sometimes he was more human than him.

Chapter 20

Salvation

COLTON STEPPED OUT INTO THE HEAT OF THE DAY and instantly regretted the layers of fabric. Gritty bits of sand blew into his face and clung to his stubble. He gripped his walking stick and started forward. Before, he felt like his vision had improved, but now it was worse than before. He had never realized how much he relied on his eyesight; already he could tell it was going to be a long trip to reach the grocer on Main Street. For the first few minutes, he ran into at least five buildings. So he slowed his pace and tried to take his time, but that was only the start of his worries. Random debris became an obstacle course: an old fence post sticking out of the ground, a random rusty bucket left in the sun, even a belt and leather strip that might have once belonged to a harness. Everything was a tripping hazard. That's when he realized he was holding the walking stick too high.

By the time he got the hang of it, he was tired, annoyed, and even more bruised. He wanted to hurry, but the walking stick forced him to be slow. He knew he had seen blind men moving faster than this, so it hurt his pride to realize how reliant he was on his vision.

He thought he was nearing Main Street when his stomach growled; the pain that clenched hold of his insides forced him to double forward. He held his aching stomach until the pain passed, but it wasn't a good sign. The longer he went without food, the more likely the wolf would emerge, always determined to survive. Rennick might have looked more like a corpse than Colton, but he probably still would have been the better choice, had he not been so weak. Self-control down underground was easier. There had been hardly any people down there; the hunger hadn't hit him like this.

The worse the pain became, the more likely he would change, and there would be little Colton could do to stop it. Even the most seasoned werewolves couldn't prevent a blood rage brought on by hunger.

It must have taken nearly an hour to make the ten-minute walk downtown, and the closer he got, the more his hunger grew. Various scents descended upon him like a landslide, from the old scent of alcohol at the bars, to the horse manure that lined the street. It was much busier than it had been the night before, and Colton was hyper-aware of every person who sidestepped him, every child who nearly ran into him, and every annoyed comment from behind as he walked at a snail's pace.

His senses were in overdrive. Everything was taken in with such intensity it was almost surreal. Was this merely due to his hunger? He wasn't sure. He had never allowed himself to get to this point of starvation before.

Then he caught the scent of freshly cooked steak from

the bar across the street. Heaven help him. He could hold his own against angry passersby, wilting vampires, and even a demon; but the smell of a well-cooked steak pulled him apart at the seams.

His stomach clenched again and he broke out into a sweat. The tips of his fingers burned, his claws, just beneath the surface of his skin, eager to be set free. His teeth began to extend, and that familiar ripple of pain went down his back. Colton lunged towards the wall of a storefront, nearly tripping over someone in a rocking chair. The world lurched under his feet, but the hot wood against his cheek helped him to focus.

"Move along," the old man in the chair growled. "We've got no need for your kind here." He was getting to his feet, and Colton heard something heavy and metal drag across the wooden porch. Something pushed against his shoulder, and it took all of Colton's strength to keep from lashing out. "Last thing I want is dead weight on the doorstep."

Colton forced himself to move, though his body was going rigid. He needed to focus; he needed to remember his breathing. He stumbled down the steps and into a narrow alleyway beside the building. He had to get away from them; he didn't have a choice. He had to get away from the crowds, away from the scents, and away from the feel of humans all around him. What had he been thinking coming here so weak? The wolf inside of him would eat the entire city if he let it.

His fingertips grazed the hot roundness of a barrel, and he settled down behind a stack of them onto the hot sand. He wasn't sure what had been stored in the barrels before, but they now reeked of sour alcohol. He breathed in the scent, grateful for anything that would wash away the steak from his memory. Slowly, his body became his again, and his head cleared. The makeshift cloak Rennick had thrown together for him was soaked through with sweat, but the breeze helped.

Leaning back his head, Colton looked up at the sky. It looked just as blurry as everything else. Eating was the only way he would be able to see again, and he had to keep from transforming. He dropped a hand down into his pocket and felt the coins.

How was he supposed to do it?

Everything would have been so much easier if he wasn't a werewolf. He could walk into town and buy food. He looked sick and badly injured, but nobody cared when money was on the table.

"Here we thought there was going to be a show."

Colton jumped and climbed to his feet. He held out the walking stick, turned in circles, and strained his ears. Several pairs of boots crunched on the sand; he was being surrounded. He'd been so distracted he hadn't noticed their approach. Two were coming up on either side of him, and a third was moving in behind him. He caught the scent of dried blood on them, but another smell was more familiar.

"You're with the pack, aren't you?" Colton asked.

"Would you look at this guy?" Another voice sounded almost directly beside him. Colton spun, the walking stick aimed out. "Do you really think you're going to hurt us with that?" The wolf was right, of course. Hell, Colton didn't have the slightest idea how well this piece of wood would stand up in a fight, but he had nothing else. He probably had three guns aimed at him at the moment.

Pulling his own gun would leave him open to attack. Not that he could see anything to shoot.

"For a minute there, we thought you were going to start tearing up the town!" The first one chuckled as he walked closer, one leg heavier in the sand than the other. He had a slight limp. Perhaps he ought to target that one first. "We were hoping for some good sport. It's a shame you chickened out on us."

"What do you want?" Colton tried to keep his voice steady, but wasn't sure if it was worth it. He was hopelessly outmatched. They must have caught his scent and knew he wasn't one of them. He and Rennick had overlooked much in this plan. Neither of them had considered the pack being active in the middle of the day.

"You and your little leech killed our friends," the man with the limp said. He had a lower pitch to his voice. He was transforming, which meant his two friends wouldn't be far behind. They meant to make short work of him. Even so, Colton wasn't about to be taken out without a fight. He extended his claws and gripped his stick with both hands.

"You and your friends shouldn't pick fights they can't win," Colton said. Damn, that sounded so arrogant it could have passed for one of Rennick's lines.

The group didn't seem to appreciate his humor. With a growl, one of them pulled the walking stick out his grip. That didn't take long. He hadn't even realized they had gotten so close. This wasn't going to be pretty.

Another one grabbed his arms and tried to pin them behind him, but Colton readjusted his weight and tossed them into the barrels. The scent of rancid alcohol filled his nostrils and he snorted.

Someone rushed him, an arm held out. He spotted the dim outline of claws coming toward his face. Pulling back just in time, he felt them graze his nose.

A punch to the gut took him by surprise. It came from the man with the limp. Of course the fists that came down on his shoulders were also a surprise, but by then there was little he could do.

His face hit the hot sand hard and blood filled his mouth. If he planned to fight these three, he needed to transform. But if he did, he was so hungry he would attack more than just them. A weight came down on his back and his arms were yanked up behind him. Someone grabbed his chin and pulled it up. A man crouched down in front of him, the shadow of a smile on his lips.

"You will be our message to the Agency. This city belongs to us, kin slayer, and your head will serve as a warning. Maybe we'll send them a picture."

The other two laughed. The man in front of him pulled a knife from his boot and held it to Colton's neck. What a pathetic way to die. He thought of Mr. Tep sliding open the letter in his fancy office with some expensive letter opener. He thought of the frown on his face and the anger in his eyes.

It wouldn't only be Colton's death either, it would mean Rennick's, too. The outrage made him spit blood into the man's face. He hoped it would give him the chance to turn things around, but then a second weight came down on his back. The other two had him pinned. He couldn't break free of both of them.

One grabbed the back of his head and slammed his face

into the ground. The blade drew blood as it slid against his throat. He cried out but only tasted sand.

Then gunshots blanketed the air.

WHEN THE GUNSHOTS RANG OUT, ALL CHAOS broke loose.

The people pinning Colton fell aside to the ground. The knife at his throat dropped, and suddenly the thick smell of blood enveloped him. Overwhelmed, Colton could no longer control the wolf. Hunger pangs tore through him as his claws extended; his teeth grew sharp and he fell upon the scent. Digging into the fresh meat, he gorged himself. His mind went blank and he only dimly heard the sound of a gun getting reloaded. Then his mind came back into focus, along with his eyesight.

The blurry, red mass beneath him, who Colton had just disemboweled, turned into a partially transformed werewolf with a gunshot to his chest. He looked down to his beastly hands tipped with long, black claws and covered in blood. He staggered backwards, his head spinning, but something cold and metallic bit into the back of his head.

"Not so fast," a woman's voice hissed behind him. "Arms in the air, and get against the wall."

He knew what a gun muzzle felt like. The voice was familiar but he couldn't place it. "Do we know each other?" He grunted.

"Turn around!"

Mind still reeling, his body still shook from the adrenaline rush. Parts of his bloody feast still dripped from his chin. But he did as he was told and turned to face the faded wooden wall of one of the shops.

"I should have known you were a wolf, Mr. Fen. I should have guessed that the first time I laid eyes on you. I suppose I was just too upset to notice."

Colton cleared his throat, "Do we know each other, miss?"

Silence. He prepared for the gun to go off, praying endlessly that a silver plug wouldn't dance through his brain. The bullets she had used on the others weren't silver, he knew, because he would have smelled it. However, she had reloaded the gun.

"You ought to know me. Turn around and let me take a better look at you."

He sighed, already knowing how he probably looked with the bloody mess from his victim mixed with Rennick's makeshift disguise. He turned slowly, and upon seeing each other they both gasped in surprise.

"Oh god..." She gagged.

"Miss Silva!" Colton forgot himself for a moment and dropped his arms in absolute humiliation. He wiped at his face and chin. "I am so sorry you had to see this."

She clapped a hand over her mouth and looked slightly green. She held the gun steady though.

He took a step forward, "Let me explain, please? Just put the gun down."

She tittered a nervous, high-pitched laugh and a wide smile fell over her lips. "Why the hell are you afraid of this little thing, anyway?" She lifted the pistol only slightly. It was a well-made gun, and one she handled with ease. "It's not like it'll do you any harm. I guess it didn't do much to them either, did it? I mean, if you wanted to kill me you probably would have done it already and..." She looked down at the surrounding bodies, and Colton noted the body he had feasted on already looking more whole than before. "Oh, God, they're going to kill me when they wake up, aren't they?"

"Maybe not. Stick with me and they should leave you alone."

She shifted her weight, but kept the gun steady. "And Ren? What did you do with him?" Her voice went small. "You ate him, didn't you?"

He winced.

"Can you at least tell me where you left his body?"

"I didn't eat him." He sighed. "He's injured, but before you start firing shots, I didn't do it. In fact, if I don't get him some food soon, he'll keel over any minute."

She nodded and took a deep breath. She glanced down to the three men at their feet, as though she was ticking away how much time she had to live. "Mr. Fen, if that really is your name..." She put away the gun on her hip holster attached on the outside of her dress and moved a stray bit of hair out of her eyes with a shaky hand. "Not to be blunt, but why the hell should I listen to you?"

"Look at it this way. If you come with me, yes, there's the chance I could attack you, but you already know these three will come hunting you once they wake up." She didn't look quite convinced, so he added, "Besides, if Rennick finds out I sicced three blood-crazed werewolves on you, I don't think he'll ever forgive me. Especially seeing as how I caused it to happen."

Mary gave a small smile and nodded. Her hand hung over the butt of the gun in its holster even as she stepped around the bodies. At one point, Colton offered his hand to assist her, but she flatly ignored it.

"He needs food," Colton whispered as they walked down the alley. "Any kind of food. He's been starved for days."

"And you want me to help, is that it?"

"I didn't say—"

"And you don't have to," she spat. "Look, Ren may be an idiot, but he's my idiot, and you better not have him dead in some creek out in the middle of nowhere."

Colton blinked. "Why the hell would he be in a creek?"

"I don't care who you think you are, but there's no way you're getting anything from anybody looking like that." She frowned and looked him up and down.

"Oh..." He rubbed his bloody hands together.

Mary shook her head. "You have just about as much sense as Ren does, you know that, Colt? Get back there, steal some clothes, and clean yourself up. You start walking around like that, people are going to think you're diseased."

"Did you just call me Colt?"

She stared at him with a cocked eyebrow until he turned around and walked back to the bodies. He didn't think it was possible for anyone to be more annoying than Rennick, but Mary Silva was very quickly proving him wrong.

Chapter 21

Turning Heads

Colton dragged his hands down the clean shirt. It was a little tight on him, but it was the only one not covered in blood and gore. The pants he got from another werewolf were a better fit. Finally, he picked up a hat and dusted off the sand. He smiled. A Stetson, it only had a few drops of blood on it. Mary was an excellent shot. He placed it on his head, glad to have a hat again.

Mary was in the alleyway with her back to him, clearly anxious.

"I'm clean now," he said, coming up behind her.

She turned and looked him up and down for a moment before adding, "I see that."

He reached into his pocket and pulled out the small bag of gold coins.

Her eyes went wide. "Is that all from Rennick?"

"I may have picked up a few from our werewolf friends back there, too."

She nodded and put out her hand. "Give me the bag. I'll head into the grocer and see what I can find."

He had a twinge of panic. "You don't want me to come with you?"

"Probably not a good idea. No offense, Colt, but you've got blood under your nails still. They may turn some heads."

He looked down at his hands. He had cleaned them off on spare clothing as well as he could, but clearly it hadn't been perfect.

COLTON PACED FOR MORE THAN AN HOUR BEFORE Mary returned from the grocer. She carried a large crate of food and shoved it into Colton's arms as soon as she reached him.

"I was thinking," she said while Colton readjusted his arms around the crate. "Rennick gave this to me months ago, and I don't think I've ever taken it off." She tugged at something on her neck. Colton caught the scent of something that put a shiver down his spine: silver. "It was the first gift he gave me."

He hadn't noticed it before, but now he couldn't take his eyes off it. It was a simple design, a chain with a silver oval locket that probably contained tiny photos or silhouettes within.

"It's empty," she added. "But Ren and I always planned to go to the state fair and get our silhouettes taken." She sighed. "Back when we were together, I guess."

He nodded. "You planning on using it on the three werewolves we left back there?"

"Would it actually work?"

He exhaled. "Sure. I guess you've never killed a werewolf before." He hadn't meant for the bitterness to enter his voice.

She shook her head and pulled off the necklace. "Here. Can you do it?" She held out the chain to him. The silver locket hung a foot away from him. Taking a large step back, he clenched his jaw.

"Please, don't..." he whispered.

"Oh, sorry." She pulled it back. "It would hurt you, too, wouldn't it?"

He nodded. "Is the chain silver, too, or just the locket?"

Mary shrugged. "I have no idea. Ren didn't really tell me any details about where he got it, and I never thought to ask."

"Then it's probably best if you handle it. Come on, I'll talk you through it."

The three wolves lay where they left them, though now in various states of dress. They, however, were also nearly fully healed. There was no time to delay. Colton put aside the crate of food and joined Mary as she walked between them. They started with the ones who were lightly wounded, the ones closest to waking.

They moved quickly. Colton gave instruction on where to place the locket, and Mary moved between them with finesse. When they reached the last one, the man with the limp who had taken the brunt of Colton's rage, Mary looked back at the other two wolves who were slowly turning color. Horror and fascination crossed her features as their bodies transformed to ash.

"My god," she whispered. "They're falling to pieces. Colton, I—"

He didn't let her finish. He put a hand on her shoulder to pull her attention back. "This is the last one. Go ahead and finish him."

Her hands were shaking now. "I don't know, Colt, this doesn't seem right."

He lowered his voice. "Look, Mary, if we don't do this, he'll wake up soon. And when he does, he's going to be angry. And hungry."

"Yes, but I'll be with you and Ren, won't I? They won't bother me if—"

He shook his head. "They'll be so hungry, they'll kill anyone. Eat anything."

She turned toward Main Street behind them. A woman with a child walked past them, a basket filled with food from the grocer in her hand. "You mean they'll attack anyone?"

"They won't care if they're old, young, healthy, or not. To them, all of those people will look like food."

She studied Colton intensely, though he wasn't sure why. Perhaps she didn't believe him. Perhaps she saw him as merely some heartless killer. Or maybe she remembered he was one of them.

He stepped back finally, unable to maintain her gaze. "You would have killed them earlier with that gun, wouldn't you?"

"Yes," she whispered.

"Then how is this any different?"

She pursed her lips. "It seems... cowardly."

That was a word he hadn't expected her to use.

Barbaric, cruel, messy, yes, but cowardly? That had never even occurred to him. That seemed to be the very least of his worries when it came to turning wolves into piles of ash. Cowardly was the perfect word for it, though. It summed up precisely why he hated doing it, finishing off werewolves who, even in deep unconsciousness, realized what was happening to them. They couldn't fight back, they couldn't protect themselves, they were vulnerable.

He wasn't sure what to say. It was unfair he had to convince her to do it, especially when he could barely stomach the job. "Fine, do what you want, but if you turn your back, you'll have innocent lives on your hands."

"The way you say that, it sounds like it's happened before."

He froze and stared at her for a moment, his lecture deflating. He turned down the alleyway and picked up the crate, waiting patiently for her to join him. "If you're going to do it, do it. We don't have all day to waste." He glanced back to see Mary crouch beside the man with the limp and press the locket against his wound. The other two had already fallen to ash, like disproportionate scarecrows crumpled in on themselves.

Mary was replacing the locket around her throat when she joined up with him. They didn't speak as they joined the commotion of people along the storefronts. Colton was surprised Mary's gunfire hadn't caught any attention, but this was Peridot. Maybe gunfire wasn't so unusual.

At least, if anyone did venture to the alley in an hour or so, all they would find would be a few scraps of clothes. Sure, it looked like a bloody mess, but no body would be found.

"You're taking me to him, aren't you?" Mary asked.

"To Rennick? I will, but I can already tell you that he won't be happy to see you. Not in the shape he's in."

She straightened the shawl around her shoulders as they stepped around a horse and buggy. "And why not? He's always in the mood to see me, Colt. Maybe you're the one he won't want to see."

He smirked, pleased to see Mary wasn't too broken up about that business in the back alley. "There are things about Rennick that you don't know, and I'm not sure he wants to share it with you."

She laughed. "That's Rennick, always taking and never sharing." Her eyes went wide as a realization struck her. "Oh, God, he better not be a werewolf, too! I'll kill him if he is." She paused as the weight of her words settled in. She caught Colton's eye. "I'm sorry. That's not what I meant."

"No, that's not it. Just keep your voice down," he said, noting the curious glances.

She blinked at him, looked around, then fell silent. He could see her mind working, churning away at the few pieces of information she'd been given. Only when they reached the more desolate shanties did she finally voice her thoughts.

"I never knew there were so many werewolves in Peridot. I thought they would be in other towns, you know, near the big cities or out in the middle of nowhere. Not here where everybody and his brother carries guns. Not where it's so easy to get found out." She adjusted the edges of her shawl and distanced herself a bit from him. "Now I'll be questioning every single bandit raid I hear about. Every time I see some louse get hung, I'll wonder if it's really a wolf. Hanging doesn't kill you all though, does it?"

"No, ma'am." He tried to avoid her gaze. She was treating him more as a curiosity instead of a person, and he wondered if this was how folks in freak shows felt. Not once had he tried to attack her, but that didn't change the way she spoke about him and his kind. They were compared to raiders and louses, barely above the lowest parts of society. As frustrating as it was to hear, though, he had grown used to it over the years. Mary's opinions weren't unique. He had long ago come to terms with the fact he would always be seen through a lens of distrust and distaste. Although he liked to think Rennick had an easier time of it, being half human, lately it seemed more of a hindrance for him. He was just human enough to be able to mingle freely, but the vampire in him would always be a weakness.

Colton led Mary through the multitude of buildings, insisting they both keep their guns visible ready as they walked. He wasn't sure if he should beware of thieves or more of Kaga's followers. Shadows skittered away behind a lopsided shack. A head disappeared behind cracked windows. Many eyes stayed on them as they moved. He was surprised he hadn't been attacked earlier with his walking stick, but the three wolves following him into town might have prevented thieves from approaching.

Peridot had many complicated layers, and he was only just beginning to understand them.

As they approached the shanty he and Rennick had used as cover, Colton realized just how disgusting the place was. He had smelled the human waste and the undeniable scent of decay earlier, but seeing it in the daylight with his full vision was somehow worse. Mary pulled a faded handkerchief out of her bag and covered her mouth and nose. Colton had no luxury.

As they drew closer, Rennick's scent grew stronger. His true scent was masked, of course, by the overpowering poison that still clung to him. Food was the priority at this point, but bathing was definitely on the list. Colton was about to enter the doorway when Mary took his arm.

"Is this where you're staying?" She brought the handkerchief down and stared at the shack, mouth agape. Mary might not have been dressed in the latest fashions or done up in stage makeup, but seeing her against the backdrop of derelict buildings, the air reminiscent of alcohol and piss, made Colton realize just how out of place she was here.

"I know it's not pretty," he whispered. "But it's the best we have right now. Rennick was pretty bad off and this was as far as we could get." Her entire countenance changed from revulsion to determination in the blink of an eye.

"Is that you, Colton?" Rennick's voice was weak, but he was still conscious.

A feeling of relief washed over Colton. He had half expected his partner to be dead when he returned. It had taken him such a long time just to reach town, it surprised him not only was Rennick alive, but awake.

Mary pushed her way past and darted inside, heedless of a giant spider web over her head in the archway of the door or the insects that scuttled away from her shoes.

With a grimace, Colton followed her inside.

CHAPTER 22

A Rough Hewn Emerald

THE AIR IN THE ROOM WAS THICK WITH DUST. As the sun crept closer to the horizon, orange beams of light streaked across the old, warped floorboards and broken furniture. Colton was glad he hadn't been able to see when they first found this place.

The ceiling was webbed from end to end and in the diminishing light, he could see the spiders skittering back and forth in irritation at the three trespassers. Colton couldn't help but hunch as he stepped inside. In the corner were the remains of the corpse Rennick had filched his clothes from and Colton shuddered at the sight. Mary crouched down next to Rennick, trailed fingers through his hair, and wrapped an arm around his shoulders.

"You're late," Rennick whispered, pale eyes moving between the two of them.

Mary glared up at Colton. "Why didn't you tell me he was this bad?"

"I told you he needed help." He put the crate of

groceries down near the door, unwilling to put them too far inside the room.

He pulled out an apple and handed it to Rennick. Blood would put him on his feet faster, but that wasn't an option. Rennick ate absently, sniffing up and down Mary's hand as he chewed.

"You smell good..."

"We need to get him to a doctor, not pass out fruit!" Mary said.

"Trust me," Colton said. "Food will do him more good than some butcher with a knife."

"Can we at least get him out of here?"

"Let him get a little strength up, and I promise you we'll leave as quick as we can."

She glared daggers at him. "This isn't the best place for a snack, Colt!"

From outside came a noise that made every hair on his neck stand up. Bare feet hitting the ground.

In a few long strides, he crossed the room and held up a finger. Mary stared up at him, gaping but silent.

The noise came again. Somebody was running quick. Like a child's footsteps. The first thought that came to him was Rennick's illusion, the young boy in the overalls. But his partner had no strength to create them. Colton glanced to Rennick. He was still slowly chewing through his apple, as though trying to remember how to eat again. He couldn't have made an illusion if he could barely feed himself.

The room felt eerie and still. Strain as he might, he couldn't hear any further footsteps. That made him uneasy. Mary got to her feet. She must have heard the noise as well, because her hand went straight for her revolver.

"Not expecting any visitors, are you?" she whispered.

He shook his head.

"Any idea who it is?"

"It sounds like a child," he said. "But somehow that doesn't feel right. But I doubt they're friendly." He shook his head and turned his gaze back to Mary. "Do you think you can shoot straight if you carry the crate?"

"Not a clue, but I'll be damned if I'm staying here. What about Ren?"

"I can carry him."

She arched an eyebrow at him, but Colton ignored it. More footsteps caught his attention. The child, or whatever it was, was circling the building. Behind it now, it moved toward the entrance he and Rennick had first entered, the side closer to the tunnel. Keeping his eyes locked on that entrance, Colton picked up Rennick and slung him over his shoulder.

Rennick groaned, but he didn't complain; he probably didn't have the strength.

With his free hand, Colton drew his pistol. Mary picked up the crate with difficulty, but finally situated it against her hip and pulled out her own pistol with her free hand.

"You ready?" he asked.

"Whenever you are." Her voice was filled with more steel than fear. Something about her determination fueled his own resolve.

"Stay close."

She nodded, and they moved toward the door closer to town. Each footstep creaked on the old floorboards. If Kaga wanted to find them, Colton was certain he could without much trouble. Rennick was right, though, Colton and Mary had arrived far too late. It was nearly sunset; the long shadows from late afternoon had perhaps urged Kaga out of hiding. If this was one of Kaga's minions, then it might have the unnatural strength and endurance Rennick had when he was possessed.

Progress was painstaking, but they moved slowly and left the shack, careful to check all the corners as they made their way toward Main Street again.

Once a good distance away, Colton looked back at the shack. A pale, waifish child slipped into the building. It was a girl, probably no older than eight or so. She was so emaciated she could have been mistaken for a ghoul. She was also fast, far too fast, and too quiet for a normal child.

If he had seen her the night they first stepped foot into Peridot, he would have probably mistaken her for a ghost. He glimpsed her face in a second, and then a moment later, she was gone just as quick, but her grisly appearance seared into his mind. She was covered in the same sticky gunk as Rennick. It streaked down her thin body as though someone had dribbled oil over her. Even at this distance, Colton could tell she had been in that state for far longer. Her clothes hung on her as though she was nothing more than a set of bones, and her lips had pulled away to reveal black gums and yellowed teeth.

Whatever Kaga had done to her had twisted her into something almost beyond recognition, a tortured puppet much like Rennick had been. Colton wondered if, perhaps, beneath the wretch she had become, she was still a small, terrified child locked inside her own mind. The thought made him want to leave Rennick and Mary to fend for themselves and run back to... do what?

Rennick had to drink Colton's blood to save him from a similar fate. That was out of the question for a small human child. She was human, not a vampire. Then there was the option he hated: putting her out of her misery. The worst option. If she was conscious and aware beneath gunk, could he bring himself kill her? The honest truth was he wasn't sure.

When Colton was confident they had gotten far enough away from the shack, he holstered his gun and switched Rennick to the opposite shoulder. His partner groaned in opposition, but remained boneless and dazed. Mary followed his example and put her pistol away as well, finally giving voice to her thoughts.

"What the hell was that thing?"

The slight waver in her voice made him realize how terrified she was. She was pale and her hands were shaking as she adjusted the crate of groceries. "You saw it?" he asked.

"You're damn right I did!" Mary turned to lead the way as she messed with something in her pocket. "I don't know if I'll be able to sleep again knowing that thing is so close by."

"That thing was a child," he growled.

She peered at him through her mussed black hair that had fallen into her face. Then she turned away to step through a gate. Colton froze. Was this her house? He looked over his shoulder, thinking how quick and quiet the girl had been. He understood better why Mary was so frightened.

She pulled the key free from her pocket, unlocked the

front door, and slammed her hip against it until it finally opened. The hinges gave a moan before finally letting them inside. But then she pointed with her elbow toward her bedroom.

"Just lay him down in there for now."

Colton nodded, though he didn't need the direction. Her home was small enough to see all the ins and outs of it from the front door, but he did appreciate her direction. Even if she and Rennick had been lovers, he wouldn't have felt right laying Rennick down in any woman's bed without her consent.

Mary put the crate of groceries down on the dining table. "What does he need?"

Colton rummaged through the crate and pulled out as much fruit as he could carry, then placed them all next to Rennick on the bed. Though he was only partially conscious, the smell of more food seemed to rouse him. Without a word, he started in on the fruit. His eyes were half lidded, but he moved at inhuman speeds. Clearly, the food earlier had helped. Colton took a few steps back toward the main room. Mary watched from the doorway to the bedroom, her face a mixture of curiosity and confusion.

"What is he?"

"Not human," Colton whispered.

"Any fool with two eyes could see that. I've seen corpses with more color. And he eats so fast."

"He's a vampire, or at least partly." He tensed when her jaw dropped.

"Does that mean one of his parents was a blood drinker?"

"That's right. Though I don't think he'd be too happy about you calling his father that."

"I'm sure he's upset if his mother is so ill still."

Colton stared at her for a long moment before realization dawned on him. "Mary... I don't know if he would want me to tell you this or not, but none of that was true."

Her face changed from shock to anger in a flash, but Colton continued.

"We're investigators. We were trying to find out why people were going missing in town, and we got into more trouble than we expected."

Her shock and anger softened. She looked into the room at Rennick, who had already eaten a good chunk of the food. When she tried to enter the bedroom though, Colton put an arm out to stop her.

"Not yet. Not until he's able to talk again. There's still a chance he'll confuse you with food." She looked like she was about to argue, but then she caught Rennick's eyes.

Rennick had frozen with one hand in the pile of food, and was watching them closely. Both of his eyes gleamed bright red and iridescent in the shadowed room. Mary took a step back and finally turned away.

"You know I've been with him for over half a year." She moved over to her small, grimy mirror and pinned back the loose strands of her hair. "It's amazing how you think you know a man. You feel like you're close. You can really talk to him. Then you find out his big, ugly secret, and you wonder how could you miss something like that."

Colton watched her in silence. He wasn't sure if there was anything that he could say or do that might comfort her.

Her eyes were glassy. "Why didn't he ever tell me?"

For a moment, Colton thought about telling her what he believed was the truth: how humans didn't like anything that wasn't like them; the dangers of superstitions, especially the ones out west; how Rennick probably feared what Mary might do if she found out the truth. It didn't take much to put together an angry mob.

But Mary didn't need to hear that. She needed support, not harsh words. So he decided to stick with the basic facts. "Folks like us don't usually like to talk about being monsters."

Her reflection smiled at him, distorted in the tiny mirror. "Shoot, I've seen plenty of men far crueler than you, Mr. Fen."

Colton laughed and took off his Stetson and hung it on a peg. The hat had once been white, but now it was covered in dirt and dusted with spider webs. The blotches of blood on the rim stood out bright red against the grime. There was no telling how many owners the hat had known, but Colton knew where the blood came from. Remembering the werewolves collapsing into dust dropped his mood.

He frowned. "I think you forget, ma'am, that I was eating a man earlier."

Her smile flickered in the mirror for just a moment as she studied him. Finally, she turned to look at him square, her face no longer disfigured in the glass.

He was struck by her beauty. Her black hair was piled high, some spilled over the back of her neck like a carefully coordinated waterfall, accenting her neck and collar bones. Her face was smudged with the dust and dirt from the day, and made her bronze skin gleam in the dim light. Her shoulders still had bits of webbing from the shack, but a certain strength and confidence in her couldn't be hidden. She wasn't attempting to be beautiful, but it followed her all the same: in her stern eyes, in the determination in her jaw, and in the understanding of her smile.

Something pulled at him inside as he stared at her, barely wanting to breathe. He remembered how she had looked after her show at the theater, face caked with make-up to hide her features on stage. Without it, he actually got to see her instead of her persona. It was strange he hadn't noticed her beauty earlier, though neither the bloody alleyway or the insect-ridden shack had been particularly good for appreciating it.

Mary's loveliness was more rough-hewn, like an uncut emerald plucked from the ground and still adorned in the earth that birthed it. She wasn't a woman who belonged on a stage; she was more suited for a fight or a shooting match than life as a poorly paid actress.

She arched an eyebrow. "Are you alright, Colt? Maybe you need to be the one lying down."

"I'm fine." He averted his eyes, dragged a hand through his sweaty hair, and willed his heart to slow down.

"You sure?" She smirked. "I'm sure I could fit you next to Ren. He's so scrawny I could probably fit the both of you."

He didn't respond and instead focused his eyes out the window.

What in the world was happening to him?

CHAPTER 23

PUNISHMENT

AFTER GORGING HIMSELF ON FRUIT, UNCOOKED cuts of meat, and one raw potato, Rennick finally fell asleep. It took a full hour for him to wake, but for Colton it felt more like five.

He was uncomfortable. Somehow, Mary had shifted something inside of him, pulled something that hadn't been pulled in a long time, and he wasn't sure what to do. He had known women in his life, but he had never felt his insides tense because of a woman before. These feelings were more appropriate for a boy rather than a man in his forties.

He could barely look at her without falling into a dumb stare, so resorted to staring out the window instead. The child they had seen could find them here, he'd told her, and he'd certainly meant it, but she was annoyingly perceptive. He had a hunch she knew what was wrong with him, but she didn't say a word about it. She was an actress, he reminded himself, and probably had a penchant for seeing through lies.

Mary took up some of the wrapped pork they had purchased at the grocer's. "You hungry?"

He kept his eyes glued outside and grunted a response. He was afraid of the fool he might become if he stared into her eyes again. Outside, the shadows had grown long and were beginning to fade into the blackness of night. Lanterns were being lit and travelers were quickly identified by the flare of their cigarettes. He tried to stay alert and kept his eyes and ears open for any sign of the pale girl, but the night was quiet. He must have dozed off at one point, because he jumped when Mary barely touched his hand.

"Calm down!" She laughed. "I thought you wouldn't mind lighting some candles since it's getting dark."

He nodded and caught the delicious aroma that filled the room. His stomach growled and Mary's smile grew wide behind the rim of a glass of whiskey.

"Well, somebody's hungry. It sounds like Ren's beginning to rouse, too." When she squeezed his shoulder, heat rose up into his cheeks. He got to his feet just as Rennick shuffled through the doorway from the bedroom, almost as pale as his white shirt. His blond hair hung in limp ringlets around his shoulders as though it was as bereft of cheerfulness as he was.

He caught Colton's eye and shrugged. "What can I say? I smelled bacon."

Colton helped him to a chair in the main room, marveling how weak he still was. If Colton had been injured this much, all it took was a decent meal to get him back to normal. For Rennick, it was apparently more complicated. For the first time since they met, Colton actually appreciated being a werewolf.

He went throughout the room and lit candles. He hadn't realized how many Mary had until he was given the task to light them all. It was probably due to her late nights at the theater.

Despite Rennick's obvious weakness, he didn't let it bother him. Colton would have been panicked, but Rennick acted like it was nothing worse than stubbing his toe or cutting his thumb. He was even dressed in one of Mary's white blouses that was obviously too small for him. The sleeves were too short and it couldn't even button up the front, but he wore it with as much zeal as any of his specialty suits.

Mary's brightened at seeing him. "I was making some for Colton, but I'm glad to see you're hungry again, Ren. I was hoping you would come around before I finished up."

Colton felt a tiny pinprick of jealousy take hold. He didn't like the way she appreciated Rennick's company so much, but he pushed aside the feeling.

Rennick waved a hand. "You shouldn't have troubled yourself. I would have been fine." His voice sounded confident enough, but his eyes were hollow. It was lucky they had reached him when they did, because Colton doubted Rennick would have lasted much longer out in that shack on his own. Considering how quick the girl had appeared after they had arrived, they had probably saved his life.

Mary brought over a plate of bacon sandwiches that might have fed five giant men instead of the two stragglers who sat around her living room. Then she grabbed three glasses that were mostly clean and fetched some water from a satchel hung by the door. She poured herself a second glass of whiskey as well. Once they were all seated, she picked up her glass and clinked it against each of theirs. "To surviving one hell of an evening!"

After several minutes of silence, during which Colton devoured one sandwich and began on a second, Mary spoke up. "So, Ren, apparently your friend is a werewolf." Rennick nearly choked on a bite and Colton couldn't help but chuckle. "I thought it was awful strange that such a good friend of mine would forget to mention such an important detail."

He gaped at Colton, then at Mary, "I'm sorry, I just—"

"And what about your dear old mum. How is she doing?"

Rennick merely blinked at her this time; struck dumb by the flurry of questions.

Mary laughed. "I'm just trying to keep you on your toes. Don't mind me."

Rennick gave a half-smile and looked to Colton for support. Colton cleared his throat. "She, um, walked up during a very unfortunate event in town earlier."

She snorted. "Unfortunate isn't precisely what I would've called it. More like disgusting."

"I was starving," Colton said.

"He was chowing down on a fellow werewolf. I've never seen anyone eat like that, well, except maybe you, Ren."

Colton felt his heart throbbing in his temples. Was that really how she saw him? Was he nothing more than a cannibalistic dog to her? "I was blind." He sputtered, "They came out of nowhere—"

"I was trying to take a shortcut to the grocer, and when I turned the corner they were about to slit his throat! I shot them all, of course, but then he lunged at one of them." She stood up to show Rennick precisely how it happened. "Then Colton crouched down with the man, and the next thing I know, the poor man had this giant hole in his belly. Ren, honey, you would not believe all the blood!"

Rennick was saying something, but Colton couldn't hear him anymore. All he could hear was Mary's voice. He dug his fingers into the wood of the chair. "It wasn't like that." He shook his head, but his entire body was shaking with him. Rennick stood up, but Colton barely paid it any mind. His partner was saying something, but his voice was distant, and Mary was on a roll, her description only broken by occasional bouts of laughter.

"There he was, just drenched in the man's blood and what does he say to me? He says, do we know each other? He's eating a man, but is still determined to be a proper gentleman! How in the world was I supposed to act, Ren? I figured I was a dead woman for sure—"

A loud snap rent the air as the arm of Colton's chair broke off. The room went silent as both pairs of eyes turned to him. He got to his feet and muttered some sorry excuse before he pushed his way out the front door.

The night air felt icy against his skin. What had he possibly seen in that woman? Had he really thought her beautiful a few hours ago? Oh, she might look nice, but it was a facade like everything else about her. She was a cruel, spiteful woman, who relished in breaking him apart. Perhaps that had been her goal all along. She ensnared him like a trapper and then tore him to pieces.

He tossed away the arm of the chair he'd broken off, then he turned and stormed down the street until he was several buildings away from Mary's house. Many of the houses were deserted, the only people around either tucked tight in their homes or still enjoying the night downtown. Colton sat down against an old, rotted fence post, and leaned his head back against it.

He had forgotten his hat in *that woman's* house, he lamented. He couldn't refer to her as Mary anymore in his mind; she had fallen so far from that name he barely wanted to admit she existed. His hand ached from tearing the chair arm free, but he couldn't care less.

His anger wasn't just about her. He knew it, even if it hurt to admit. It was his own failure. The entire mission was an absolute waste so far, and there was no way to fix it. He had never failed an objective before, but he knew what steps he had to take. Tomorrow morning, he would head into town and send a telegram back to the Agency, back to Mr. Tep, and inform them of the trouble. The mission would require a much larger group of specialists, members who were better at working together, preferably ones without connections in town. As long as they didn't know of a Mary Silva, they would probably pull it off just fine.

Kaga's words came back to him suddenly, in that disturbing, cruel voice: *You deserve the punishment, Mr. Fen, and you know it.*

A shiver went through him, partly from the night air, but partly from the memory of its breath against his neck. He thought of the man he had eaten at the river, and of the werewolf he devoured, too, as Mary had just so joyously recalled.

He didn't like to think about the lives he had taken. He didn't want to remember the faces of the men and women he had killed and eaten against his will, but Mary made him remember. With gruesome amusement, she made him recall what he had done, reopening the painful guilt all over again. She made him look at himself from a human's perspective, and the more he looked, the more he wondered if the demon was right.

CHAPTER 24

A WOLF IN A TRAP

ABOVE HIS HEAD, THE STARS MADE THEIR LAZY path across the vast sky. Colton wasn't sure how long he lay there, lost in his thoughts, but his anger cooled. The sound of hooves hitting the sand broke him from his reverie, and he glanced down the road to see a chestnut mare approaching.

"Tahoe?" he whispered. The horse's ears perked up, and she trotted a bit faster toward him. Colton was on his feet in a matter of seconds and he put his hand out to her. She seemed nervous at first, but once she knew who he was, she relaxed and let him stroke her side. She was also alone. "Aidan abandoned you, did he?"

She looked thinner since the last time he'd seen her, when was that? Only a day ago? Two days? He had no way of knowing how much time had passed since Rennick knocked him out and he awoke in Kaga's cavern. He should have asked Rennick, though Mary might have been a better choice, seeing as how she hadn't lost time like he and his partner had. Colton patted Tahoe's flank as he turned back to Mary's house.

Most of the other homes had turned out their lights for the evening, but Mary's house was still lit. She and Rennick were probably getting reacquainted again, and the thought created a familiar tightness in his chest. Colton sighed. Leaving in a rage meant it was more difficult to go back, and the night air was getting cold. There would be curious looks, demands for explanations, and an abundance of questions he didn't feel like answering.

Gripping a bit of Tahoe's mane, he walked the horse back to Mary's place. Along the way he picked up a half-full feeding bag hooked over the edge of one of the few remaining fence posts and gave it to the mare. It was probably stale, but Tahoe didn't seem to care. Colton decided he wasn't going to report their mission as a failure. Not yet at least. The more he thought on it, the more he realized they deserved vengeance on Kaga, whether he was a demon or not. Last time, they didn't know what they were getting into and Kaga had used that to his advantage. Next time, things would be a little different.

Inside, he could see Rennick and Mary sitting around the table chatting. He must have told her some kind of joke because she was caught up in laughter. Colton tried to tap into the anger he'd felt earlier when he looked at her, tried to replace his attraction with disgust, but that anger was gone. Like it or not, Mary had a hold of him like a wolf snared in a trap, and he hated himself for it.

Getting Mary involved in this mission might have compromised him, and if she insisted on returning with them, back into the tunnels to fight the demon, he knew she would distract him. His concern for her would outweigh his own safety, possibly putting the entire mission in jeopardy.

He would have to convince her to stay. Mary wouldn't like it, but he would rather deal with her fury than see her in any kind of pain. The very thought of it cut him keener than Mary's cruel joke earlier. Perhaps Rennick would help him. She might be more willing to listen if she had to deal with both of them. Rennick would understand his concern, too, or at least he hoped he could.

Colton put a hand to his head to remove his hat, only to realize he'd left it inside. He exchanged a sour look with Tahoe before heading up the front steps and rapping at the door. He was caught off guard when Rennick answered, his eyes clear and his color fully restored. The food had done wonders to restore him.

Colton cleared his throat. "I just need to say something to Mary is all."

Rennick stepped out of the threshold, forcing Colton to step back, and pulled the door closed behind him. "I think we need to have a chat, actually."

Something in Rennick's voice sounded like admonition, but Colton was in no mood for speeches. "No, really, I need to speak with her."

"I disagree. I think if you go in there right now, one of you is going to say something you'll regret. Not that you don't deserve it." He smiled at Colton's shock. "Actually I would fully endorse it." Rennick wrapped what he could of the thin white blouse around himself.

"You think I deserved that? She mocked me for being a werewolf. She mocked me for almost starving and having to hold back from eating the whole Main Street. I can't change what I am."

"No, but you can accept it. Her words hurt you, but what did you expect? She's a human. I'm sure you were pretty shook the first time you saw a werewolf attack. You eat people for a living. Sometimes I do, too. She's allowed to make light of it. She's scared and a little drunk. The whole situation clearly upset her."

Colton frowned and went down the steps. Behind him, Rennick gasped.

"Tahoe?" He bolted past Colton, which only put the poor mare on edge. "Sorry, dear, sorry." He stroked her flank. "I'm just glad to see you made it! You really are clever, aren't you? A bit of a survivor, really."

Colton wasn't listening. Rennick, for once, was right. As much as Colton hated admitting it, to most people he was a monster. Mary's amusement was probably her way of dealing with the shock of it. Strangely enough, he thought of the play he had seen at the Crimson Theater, the one Mary had written. She had turned a bloody battle into a humorous escapade, and the crowd loved it. Surely, many in the audience had known victims of the war, or had even been in battle, but the humor made it easier to swallow, took the sting out of the wound. Mary had taken it too far with her mocking earlier, but she probably hadn't intended to hurt him.

Colton deflated. He had overreacted, probably destroying the remnants of anything he might have had with her. He turned back to the front of the house and tried to see Mary through the window. She hadn't looked angry at the time, but the way Rennick spoke, perhaps she was now. He tried to catch her eye, but she stood with her back to him, pouring herself a drink. Rennick slipped an arm around Colton's elbow and eased him out to the main road again.

"Is she angry?" Colton asked, worried now about other potential repercussions from his violent outburst. "She doesn't look angry."

"No, not now, but she was."

Slowly that cold sludge of guilt crept into Colton's stomach as the words sunk in. Mary had gotten them food, allowed them to stay at her home to recover, and she had saved his life from a group of werewolves; like a child he had stormed out. What right did he have to call Rennick a kid when he threw such childish fits?

"I didn't mean her any harm," he said.

Rennick shuddered as a cold wind whipped sand down the street. "I know you didn't, but don't think I missed the way you've been looking at her either."

Colton blinked, "You saw that?"

"As clear as those stars. She saw it, too, by the way."

He swallowed, wondering when his mouth went dry. "What did she say about it? Anything?" He groaned and shook his head. "Hell, I don't even know what I'm talking about. That woman pisses me off one minute, and then I feel like an ass the next."

Rennick watched him closely. "She does seem to have you wrapped around her finger. I'm not jealous or anything, if that's what you're so worried about."

He gave a nervous laugh. "I didn't think you would be. Not with the fight you two had. She can't come with us, you know, even if she wants to. She'll get in the way."

That devious grin returned as Rennick arched his eyebrows. "Is that the reason?"

"She doesn't understand what she's up against, and she'll probably get herself hurt."

Rennick's gaze was piercing. "I think you're fooling yourself if you believe that. Let's be honest. We both know what the real reason is, Colton. You don't think you can control yourself around her."

He didn't like the way his partner smiled when he said it, clearly taking an inordinate amount of glee in his observation. He gave a heavy sigh. "Let's just pretend for the moment that you're right. What about it?"

"You are so very entertaining!"

Colton couldn't look at him.

"Perhaps instead of preventing her from coming with us, which will be a challenging feat I can assure you, maybe you should try not to be so distracted?"

"You make that sound easy."

"I'll tell you what: I'll try to help convince her to stay, but I'm not making any promises."

"You two planning on letting this poor horse freeze to death?" Mary stepped past them carrying some thick blankets that she piled onto Tahoe's back. Colton and Rennick stepped apart, neither of them meeting her gaze when she turned on them.

"So, it sounds like you two are conspiring against me out here." She folded her arms. "Do I get any word in this, or are you two going to make the decisions for me?"

He and Rennick exchanged looks before Colton stepped forward. "We're only worried about your safety."

Rennick stepped away from him with a sigh.

"You boys may not think I'm cut out for this line of work, but I'm involved now. The question is will you two be at my side when I go chase down that girl, or do I strike out on my own?"

"It's not just that girl, Mary. It's more dangerous than you think!" After a glance at his partner, Colton added, "Rennick and I don't think you quite understand what we're dealing with here."

Rennick tossed up his hands up. "Oh, don't drag me into this!"

Mary laughed. "And you boys do?" She lifted a cigarette from pocket, lit and took a drag as she glared at each of them. "Seems to me you two are just as lost as I am. Or is it normal to be going around town blind and searching for scraps of food? That wasn't part of some grand scheme, was it?"

She just had to bring it up again, didn't she? Colton felt the anger build up inside again. "This isn't a game!" Behind him Rennick groaned. "This isn't some shooting gallery where you'll get an award for firing off your father's gun. You saw what we had to do with those werewolves. It'll be more like that: messy and dangerous. To be honest, I don't know if I like the idea of having to protect you down there."

"Protect me? I saved you earlier, you jerk! You would have ended up dinner and Ren would be dead right now!"

"We're not fighting werewolves or creepy kids!" Colton took a step forward and took Mary's hand. Her eyes were fierce, but she didn't pull away. "I'm talking about the creature that lives underground. He nearly killed us both, and I'm sure he's responsible for that poor little girl, too. What we're going up against would kill you on the spot without hesitation. This demon collects things, and for some reason it wants the two of us alive. I don't think it would be so forgiving to—"

"A human?" She snapped. "Just because I don't have sharp claws and fangs doesn't mean I'm not dangerous. I'm a hell of a shot, you know."

"Mary, that's not it." Colton's pulse raced. Even if he did work up the nerve to tell her how he felt, she would probably think he was lying just to get her to stay put. Rennick was right, he never should have argued with her earlier. "This demon is nothing like—"

"Wait a minute," Rennick whispered. "Come inside. I've got an idea, but we can't talk about it out here." He pushed past the two of them. "You mention demons in a place like this and all hell breaks loose."

PART SIX

———————

THE DEMON

CHAPTER 25

EVIL SPIRITS

RENNICK CLOSED THE FRONT DOOR AND PULLED the thin curtains over the windows. They sat down around the table in Mary's living room, Colton stuck with the same seat as before. The arm of the chair had been completely ripped off, leaving the back of it bent and barely attached, which made the four legs lopsided. He had rendered it almost unusable, but he settled down in it, anyway, reluctant to draw attention to his earlier outburst.

"So I'm guessing you have some kind of plan?" Colton asked.

"I never said it was a plan," Rennick clarified. "Don't get ahead of me. It's just a thought I had. Colton, you called Kaga a demon earlier."

"Wait," Mary said. "Is Kaga its name?"

"That's what it called itself." Colton sat back in his creaky seat. "It wanted to skin me and turn me into one of its brain dead minions." He chuckled at the deadpan expression Rennick gave him. "I'm sorry, but that's what you were. In my book, that makes Kaga a demon or, as my old man would say, an evil spirit."

"Trust me, there are plenty of things that could fit that description. Demons aren't the only sadistic creatures in the world."

"The child we saw," Mary asked with a flick of ash into her empty whiskey glass, "was that the demon?"

"The child," Rennick drummed his fingers on the table. "You saw a child? When did this happen?"

Mary glanced at Colton. "When we pulled you out of that disgusting shack with all the spiders." She shook the cigarette between her fingers. "It looked like a child, or at least it had the frame of one. I know it wasn't alive, though. I'm certain of that."

"There's no telling if she was alive or not," Colton muttered. "She could still be alive and just trapped in that body. Kind of like how Rennick was."

"So, it was a little *girl*? Are you sure about that?" The intensity in Rennick's eyes made Colton uneasy. He could smell the fear on him.

"I couldn't tell for certain." Mary rubbed at her arm. "It looked like some kind of child, but moved more like a spirit."

Colton shook his head. "I'm sorry, Mary, I saw the same thing you did. It was obviously a little girl. We were too far back to say for certain if she was alive or a ghost."

She glanced to him with a cool expression, and he liked the way her eyes caught the candlelight in her frustration. Wait, where the hell had that come from? Was he actually trying to make her angry just to get her attention? Heat rose to his cheeks.

"It was a ghost, Ren," Mary stated. "She was as pale as a white horse and with teeth as long as a coyote's. I've seen plenty of dead bodies in my time. Trust me, she was very dead."

"She wasn't a ghost!" Colton growled, knocking his elbow into the table and rattling the glassware.

"And how the hell would you know?" She pushed her chair back and got to her feet. "How many ghosts have you seen, Colt?"

Rennick groaned and placed a hand on his forehead. "That's enough! As far as I can tell, neither one of you can figure out what you saw."

Mary stammered, "But, Ren, I know what I saw!"

He put out his hands. "I know you do. I believe you. In fact, I believe the both of you." His eyes were hollow. "I think I'm familiar with what you both saw."

They both went silent. A pit form in Colton's gut. Mary's eyes went wide and she settled back down in her chair.

Rennick drank from a glass of water before continuing. "I don't think we're dealing with a demon at all."

The pit in Colton's gut grew. "What do you mean?"

"It's dismissive to call it a demon. Yes, it skins people. Yes, it is dangerous and cruel, and it takes pleasure from causing others pain. It likes to collect people, for some odd reason. It even forces its minions to attack people, but does that make it the spawn of hell? To be honest, I don't think so. I've heard of living, breathing people who have done worse. So why should we believe Kaga?"

Colton considered it a moment. "What about its body? How do you explain that?"

"So you saw it?" Mary asked, her eyes narrowed. "You didn't look like you could see anything when I found you."

"I saw enough of it. Kaga didn't move like a person. He didn't move like he had two legs even."

Mary blinked.

Rennick cleared his throat, looking down at the table. "His body isn't exactly a true body. It's more like a mismatch of things. It's kind of hard to explain, but I'm pretty sure a real demon would be a bit more functional. He couldn't exactly chase us down on his own. His minions could. He collects people to recruit to do his bidding. Like he almost did to me."

The room was silent for a moment. Outside, the wind hit the thin walls of the building. Mary took another pull on her cigarette and Rennick got up and refilled his water. Talking about this made Colton's skin crawl. He was fortunate to have escaped. He wondered how many vampires and werewolves Kaga had taken control of in the past.

As Rennick settled back in his seat, Mary spoke in a quiet tone. "My father told me of a man who was a collector. He lived out in the middle of the woods in an old shack. He would visit graves and dig up people, and bring them home with him. He preferred the company of dead women over living ones. The corpses were his only friends. He dressed them, gave them plates of food, even played the piano for them." She knocked the ash into her whiskey glass, her hand shaking. "He did all that on his own without any sort of minions, and he had two legs. He was no demon, merely a sick man." She gave a brief smile to Colton.

"What did they do to him?" Colton asked.

"They hung him at the gallows the very day they learned of it." She pursed her lips and let out a shaky breath. "He didn't even realize there was anything wrong either. Can you believe that? How do you get to a point like that and not realize..." Neither Colton nor Rennick spoke as she stared down at her drink. "If Kaga isn't a demon, then what do you think he is, Ren?"

"I think Colton had it partially right." He gave Colton a smirk. "Kaga isn't an evil spirit, just a spirit." Rennick leaned back in his chair and crossed his arms over his chest. "He's just your regular old ghost who's gained too much power. Granted, it takes years to get to that point, maybe even a century, to build up that kind of strength, to nurture that much hatred; but he must have found a way. I've only ever heard rumors about that kind of poltergeist."

"Polter-what?" Mary asked.

Rennick leaned forward again, drumming his fingers on the table edge. "Poltergeists are spirits that have gained so much strength that they can interact with living people. Usually it's something minor, like tossing plates or opening doors, but Kaga is different. Somehow, he found a way to control people, to make them do things they wouldn't normally do."

"That's what happened to that little girl," Colton whispered. "She's just like those dead women that Mary mentioned, only she isn't completely dead yet." Mary looked at him, a sad expression on her face. "I'm telling you, she's under his control."

Rennick chuckled. "Hell, that's what happened to me. When I drank from that little girl, she broke everything. My whole body hurt, and suddenly I was trapped in a nightmare. It was even worse when I realized I couldn't control my body. It was still mine, but someone else was pulling the strings. I couldn't even take a piss if I wanted to. The more I tried to fight back, the more painful Kaga made it."

"So you saw the little girl before?" Colton asked.

Rennick nodded.

Colton sighed. "I don't know how he was able to push you so far. You shouldn't have physically been able to take as much abuse as you did."

His partner sipped at his glass again as a slow grin spread across his face. "I definitely suffered because of it. Though you have to admit I beat the ever-loving hell out of you."

Colton scoffed. "With a ghost's help you mean. On your own you never could have taken me down."

"Whatever helps you sleep at night."

"So what's the plan then?" Mary asked, amusement slipping into her voice. "You two going to sit around and arm wrestle all night? No offense, but I don't think that will help much with Kaga."

Colton licked his lips, thinking back to that hole in the ground, back to Kaga's voice. A chill went down his spine at the memory before he spoke. "There was something else about Kaga, something I can't quite put my finger on. We spoke for longer than I would've liked." He paused, trying to put his observations into words. "Let's say Kaga is a ghost. That means he was once a man. When he was alive, I think he was a very religious man. Somehow, I think that's linked with why he has that hatred you mentioned, Rennick. I accused him of choosing his path on purpose, not because his god wanted him to, but because he wanted an excuse to torture people. That really pissed him off." He rubbed at the stubble on his chin. "That might be something we could use. A vulnerability we can exploit. You think that's an angle we can take?"

Rennick tapped his fingers on the table. "I'm not sure how that would work. He's enamored with himself, with taking on this demonic persona. I think it might be dangerous to challenge him like you did." Rennick's gaze was distant as he stared up at the ceiling. "I remember being in Kaga's chambers. It was in one of the back tunnels. That cavern is honeycombed with them. I looked up at one of the walls, and he had a man hanging upside down from a hook. The belly was flayed open; he must have been there for some time." His eyes went glassy. "It was horrible." His voice broke, and it took him a moment to continue. "I wanted to run, to scream, to look away, but I couldn't. I couldn't do anything except stare at it. I suppose because Kaga wanted me to see it. He wanted me to know what he was capable of."

Colton pointed a finger at him. "He wanted you to believe that there was no escaping him. He wanted to convince you that he was a demon."

Mary shuddered and put out her cigarette in her whiskey glass, then stood to fetch more water.

Rennick put his elbows on the table, seemingly pulling himself away from the memory. "My point is that if we attack that core belief of his, we may end up shooting ourselves in the foot. It could anger him." He shook his head, his blond hair falling around his face. "I think we'll need something more devious down there." His hands trembled against the tabletop.

Colton leaned forward across the table and put a hand on Rennick's arm. "Are you sure you can go back down there? I think you got the worst of it."

His partner's eyes were red. His shaky hands turned to loose fists and he gave a nervous smile. "Of course! I'm looking forward to giving him a few nightmares in return. Personally, I think I deserve the first hit." He chuckled, but his smile faded when Mary sat down again.

Colton sat back in his chair as a silence fell upon them. Rennick stared at Mary a long moment before he reached across the table and pried her fingers from around her glass of water, instead entwining her fingers with his.

When he spoke, his voice was soft. "Mary, we're dealing with something we don't completely understand here, like you pointed out earlier. This will probably be exceptionally dangerous. You saw what happened to the two of us when we went in without any idea what we were up against."

She started to reply, but Rennick squeezed her hand and continued.

"I don't want you to feel like you have to do this just to prove something. If you want to help, simply for the sake of helping, then I'm behind you all the way. But if you're doing this to prove something, I promise it's not worth it. You've already proved you're a more than capable markswoman. Please don't put your life on the line for something so silly as pride."

Colton expected her to have some snide remark. Hell, that's what she would have done if he'd said those words. Instead, she gave Rennick the warmest, sweetest expression Colton had ever seen from her. "Thanks, Ren." She picked up his hand and planted a kiss on it, her eyes never leaving his.

The heat in Colton's chest expanded and the room suddenly felt uncomfortably warm. He wanted Mary to look at him like that.

"Kaga nearly killed you," she whispered. "He's been murdering my neighbors and enslaving children. Now, if you think I'm the kind of woman that is happy to sit idly by and allow cruelty like that to continue, then you must have mistaken me for a gentlewoman. I won't back out now, Ren, no matter how many horror stories you tell me."

She planted another kiss on Rennick's knuckles with those delicate lips. Then she reached over and took Colton's hand. With her fingers soft against his tough palm, his heart raced. The warmth in his chest spread up to his cheeks and down to his groin.

"You, too, Colton," she said. "I may not agree with you all the time, but that doesn't mean I want to see you hurt either."

She squeezed his hand. He wished she would place her lips on his knuckles, too, but she didn't.

"I don't want you hurt either," he said, unable to meet her eyes and hoping she couldn't see his red cheeks.

CHAPTER 26

TOO RICH

TEPID SOAPY WATER SPILLED DOWN OVER HIS shoulders and Colton sighed with relief. He sat in a large bucket, and the night wind was cool against his skin as he used a wash cloth to remove all the blood and dirt from his skin. Goosebumps rose up and down his arms from the desert wind, but he didn't mind. It was good to be clean.

He dripped water over his head, letting it slip behind his ears and settle in his beard. Washing off the grime for the day eased off the horrors of Kaga's cavern, the guilt from the werewolf attack downtown, and the disgusting disguise he had been forced to wear.

He took a deep breath and caught the sweet smell of cacti nearby. Surrounded with a few privacy walls, he stared up at the waxing moon hanging high in the sky. He used to find it comforting to look up and see it in the sky, back before he was bitten.

"You almost done?" Rennick's voice came from the back door of Mary's house.

Colton chuckled. "Yeah, almost." He got to his feet and

dried off. He got first dibs on the water only because Rennick was covered in that sticky substance from Kaga. He stepped out and pulled on his undergarments. They weren't the cleanest, but they weren't ruined like the rest of his clothes.

Tomorrow, he would have to go into town to pick up some real clothes.

"The tub's all yours."

Rennick stepped into the small space, a towel wrapped around his waist. "Ooh, it's a little brisk out here, isn't it?" He had already cleaned up his face and hands, but his hair was a gross mess along with his neck and upper arms.

"It's still worth it," Colton said, pulling on his undershirt.

Rennick looked him up and down before turning to the tub. "Thanks for saving my life today. I'm glad you're my partner."

"Despite what I say sometimes, the feeling is mutual." Colton put a hand on Rennick's shoulder. Rennick arched his eyebrows. "I'll see you in a few."

"I won't be long. It's way too cold out here for a luxurious bath."

THEY TOOK TURNS SLEEPING, KEEPING WATCH IN shifts. Mary insisted on taking the longest watch, half the night. He and Rennick had opposed it at first, but Mary won them over with logic. As the least injured and the most rested of the three, she would have a better chance of spotting anything unusual. As much as Colton wanted to argue, even he had to admit she made good points.

Colton settled down on Mary's bed. It was a cheap frame with hay for its filling, but it was better than sleeping on the floor. He was grateful she let them use it. She had also cleaned it up after Rennick slept on it earlier. He didn't want to smell that gunk from Kaga while he slept. The memory of it clung to his nostrils despite the bath.

Rennick came from his bath, toweling out his curly blonde hair. "I'm going to be a frizzy mess tomorrow, but at least I'm clean," he said.

"I still don't know if Mary should take the longest watch. She says she's well rested, but she's only a human," Colton grumbled. "She needs more rest than either of us."

"I know." Rennick yawned, crawling up on the bed closer to the wall. "But she does have a point. You look as exhausted as I feel." He chuckled. "If we had to face Kaga tonight, you and I would be liabilities."

Colton grunted, folded up his grimy clothes, and placed them on his boots. Hopefully, it would prevent any scorpions or snakes from crawling inside. "I still don't know why he didn't follow us here. He could have. And that may still be his plan."

"Don't think about it for now, won't you? I'm tired. You're tired. We can't plan anything more until we sleep. For all we know, Kaga is getting his forty winks as well."

That made him laugh. "I guess you're right. Though sleeping is going to be difficult. This bed is too small."

"You're not wrong," Rennick scooted back so that his back was flush with the wall. "But I'm so tired I could probably sleep in a chair if I had to."

"That might not be a bad idea," Colton said.

"That was a joke!" Rennick turned over, facing the wall. "I promise I don't bite. Er, not while I'm asleep at least. Seriously, though, just get some rest. We'll need to work together to finish this."

Colton leaned down and blew out the candle beside their shoes before climbing into bed. It was not at all comfortable and he felt like he took up way too much space. The bed frame was too short, so his shins hung off the bottom edge. Despite that, the rest of him was grateful to be in a bed.

He hadn't had the fortune of sleeping above the ground in weeks, and his joints thanked him for it. Behind him, Rennick squirmed and shifted. Finally, though, his partner stilled.

Rennick was a strange man with weird quirks and a plethora of problems, but Colton was grateful to have him at his side. Without him, he wouldn't have survived this ordeal, and he knew it.

Colton listened to the wind whistle down the street outside and the sound of sand grazing against the wooden walls. He thought of the haunted little girl and the werewolf he had gutted in town. He thought of the raspy voice of Kaga and the smell of his rotten collection of carcasses.

Rennick sat up with a jolt. Colton's eyes snapped open, and he reached down beneath the bed where he'd stored his guns for the night.

"What is it? What's wrong?"

"Grabbing a blanket. It's cold," Rennick muttered, pulling a large woolen blanket up and covering both of them before hunkering down again. He had to shift a bit to get comfortable again.

"Thanks," Colton muttered, shifting his legs under the blanket. He hadn't even realized he was shivering, and he grabbed the blanket up to his chin.

"No problem." Rennick yawned. "I was cold; figured you must be, too."

"No, I mean, thanks for your help. With everything."

"Oh, right." Rennick turned his head and glanced back at him.

Colton considered dropping it. It would be easy not to answer and let the unspoken question drift off, but no. This wasn't something he could just ignore. He didn't usually ask for help or say thanks, but then again, he owed his life to Rennick several times over. The realization weighed on him more than he expected. "You've had to save my hide more often than I would like lately. You helped us figure out where to go, got us horses. Hell, you even gave me money to buy food."

Rennick snickered. "We're even then, I suppose. I might be no better off than that little girl without you. Hell, we might both have been turned into Kaga's puppets. I guess we do make a pretty good team, don't we?"

He grinned back at his partner. "We didn't die from our mistakes, so I guess that's a good step." Outside, the wind quieted down. The waxing moon shed its light over the clear night sky and sleep finally settled on his shoulders.

COLTON WOKE TO THE SUN SHINING IN HIS EYES from a crack between the threadbare curtains. He groaned and shifted to his back to escape it, only to roll on top of Rennick.

There was a flailing of limbs and much unintelligible cursing before Rennick squeezed out, "Get off me!"

Colton sat up and turned to Rennick grumbling behind him. His eyes went wide.

"We're at Mary's, remember?"

The situation slowly came back to him and Colton rubbed his eyes. "She was supposed to wake me. We were going to trade out for the watch overnight."

Rennick put his arms over his head and arched his back. "I guess she decided against it."

"Mary?" Colton called out with a croak.

"Right here." She entered the room with a smirk on her lips. She had cleaned up from last night and wore a long skirt that came down to her ankles. Her hair was done up in braids and piled atop her head. For a moment, Colton was struck dumb by her beauty. "Did you two sleep alright?"

"Well enough." Colton grunted and swung his legs over the edge of the bed.

Rennick sat up behind him with a loud yawn. "I slept great, actually. What about you, my dear? Did you get any sleep?"

She pulled a strand of hair into a bobby pin. "I passed out sometime near dawn. You two were sound asleep, and I just couldn't wake you."

"Imagine that. I guess Colton makes a good bed buddy. Except when he nearly crushes you when he wakes up." Rennick laughed.

Colton ignored him. "How long were we out?"

"It's nearly noon now. I went out earlier and got you two some decent clothes." She winked at Rennick. He had worn another of Mary's blouses. He must have pulled it on after his bath last night, though Colton hadn't noticed. "I had to guess for your size, Colt. I'm going to get breakfast started. You boys don't take too long." She went back into the next room, pushing a curtain closed behind her to close off their room.

Colton beamed a bit because she had referred to him by that silly nickname. He hadn't liked it at first but, somehow, it had grown on him, kind of like Mary. He looked to the end of the bed. Two piles of clothes were neatly folded and lay on top of their boots.

He glanced to Rennick, and gave a laugh. "It sounds like the lady is used to having to dress you."

He was surprised to see the plain excitement on his partner's face. Apparently, all it took to catch his eye was a fresh set of clothes. "Sometimes, but Mary has excellent taste." Rennick gave a knowing look. "Perhaps if you showed a bit more gratitude, you might have a better chance with her." He pulled off Mary's blouse. "A man can never have enough clothes."

"I don't think that's how that saying goes." He shook his head.

He turned to his clothes stack. He dressed himself slowly, partially because he was still stiff from everything yesterday, but also because the fabric was surprisingly nice. Mary did have good taste when it came to clothing. She had picked out a black frock coat made of linen, matching pants, and a plain cotton shirt. Colton couldn't remember the last time he'd had a full new outfit. Even when he'd visited Mr. Tep, it was in a suit he'd had to darn several times. This suit was a little too big in places, but it allowed him to move freely in it, which he appreciated. Overall, it was surprisingly comfortable. He had no idea where she had gotten the money for it, but he would have to remember to pay her back.

"What do you think?" Rennick asked.

Rennick's coat was a slate gray in comparison to Colton's solid black, it also had two additional flap pockets on the front and a bit more detail along the seams. Mary had probably gone out with the intention of picking up an outfit for Rennick; Colton's was merely an afterthought. But he was happy with that. At least he was an afterthought.

"It looks good," Colton said. "I'll admit, this is nicer than the clothes I normally wear."

"You look good in it!" Rennick smiled as he adjusted his sleeves.

Colton nodded. "Thanks."

"Did you see there are matching hats as well?"

Admittedly, that made Colton excited. The outfits were nice, but they didn't compare with a well-made hat. They were both Stetson hats, like the one he had lost down in Kaga's cave. Colton held the hat in his hands for a long minute, noticing how soft the fabric felt and how new it looked.

A problem nagged at him. It felt wrong. It felt like it belonged to some high-class banker rather than an agent, the equivalent of a hired gun.

"What's the matter now?" Rennick asked, though he had mirth in his voice.

"It feels... too nice, doesn't it? It's too high quality. Won't we attract too much attention dressing like this?"

"Really? I saw that hat you got yesterday. I'm assuming from those werewolves? It smelled awful. You know that. You have a better sense of smell than I do."

Colton grimaced. "Yeah, you're right about that."

"You think that awful old hat is somehow less suspicious? Any store you walk in is going to remember you by your smell alone. It's just disgusting."

"You're right."

Rennick nodded. "If you're hoping to get people to run away from you more which, correct me if I'm wrong, but I don't think you do, then it's perfect."

Colton held out his palms. "I get the point."

"But this one? Now this looks sharp." He took the new black hat out of Colton's hands and slid it down on his head.

The fit was nice, but Colton just couldn't shake the odd feeling. "It still feels like a hat I would see on a paper pusher or a politician, not me. It's too clean."

Rennick blinked, then laughed so hard he wiped away a tear. "If it's grime you're looking for, I'm sure we'll find some soon. Don't worry."

Colton couldn't keep his hands off of it, though. It was difficult getting used to a brand new hat on his head, one that had never been broken in before. Come to think of it, he couldn't recall ever owning a new hat. Even the first one his dad gave him years ago was second hand. All of his hats had always known a head before his, but he liked to think it added personality. A hat should have a story; this one felt like a blank slate. It felt rich and it felt valuable, especially since Mary had given it to him. He had never cared about whether he might lose a hat before, but now he did.

Rennick directed him out into the living room before Colton could change his mind.

CHAPTER 27

BITS AND PIECES

MARY MADE A POT OF HOT WATER WITH SOME herbs thrown in for taste and cooked up a few slices of pork. It made a decent enough meal, especially since they were going underground. Colton poured some water for them while Rennick grabbed a piece of pork.

"Sorry we slept so long," Colton said with a glance to Mary. "You must be exhausted."

"I'm actually just fine," she said. "To be honest, I was surprised we didn't have any trouble last night. The worst I saw was a drunk pass out across the street."

Colton shook his head. "That's two nights in a row that Kaga hasn't taken the opportunity and attacked us. He's waiting for something and I don't like it."

He sat down with his drink, eyeing the odd herbal mixture Mary had concocted. He was reluctant at first. Drinking something so hot seemed counter-intuitive to the heat of the day, but she was right; they needed the liquids. He took a small sip and marveled how it soothed his throat.

He hadn't realized how much the wind and sand had gotten to him.

"He must know we fled his chamber," Rennick added between mouthfuls of food. "If that little girl saw you, then he knows we're still in town."

"He also knows we're on a mission for ABSC. He seemed really interested in that when he was questioning me."

Mary brought out a plate of fruit consisting of apples and a few berries. She took the cup of hot water Colton offered with a smile and her gaze lingered a little longer than normal. Colton shifted in his lopsided seat.

"There's no telling what he's planning." Rennick grabbed a handful of blackberries. "Kaga didn't give me any details or let anything slip. All I could tell was that he had clearly lost his mind."

"He's a ghost." Colton grabbed some pork and an apple. "I don't think he has a mind to lose."

Rennick shook his fork at him. "Maybe he's the exception. He's been doing this for a while. Long enough to have corpses hanging from the ceiling like holiday decorations. If anybody has lost his noggin, it's that guy."

"Ew," Mary muttered as she grabbed a plate. "I'm assuming his decorations were dead, right? Please tell me none of them were alive. Or in between like that child we saw."

Colton caught her eye. Now it was his turn to smile. "So you don't think she's a ghost?"

Mary smirked. "You're never going to let that go, are you?"

He beamed at her. "Not anytime soon."

"If that girl was alive," Rennick said with a frown. "There might be others hanging from his canopy. Ones I didn't see. I wasn't exactly allowed to go poking around in those hidden tunnels, hunting for fellow possessed folks."

"More trapped minions. More people stuck under Kaga's thumb for who knows how long." Colton shook his head. "Damn. We don't even know the numbers we're up against. It could be dozens. Hundreds."

Mary pursed her lips. "I don't care what we're dealing with to be frank. If it attacks us, I'm shooting it." She cut up her food. "Sorry, Colt. I know that may irk you."

He gave a heavy sigh. "I understand. Though, I still don't like it."

Rennick turned to Colton while sipping on his herbal water. "You know, I was thinking about what you said last night. You said he struck you as the religious sort—before he died. Clearly, that religion has twisted him in death. Maybe we can try to turn that around on him somehow."

"Turn it around? What do you mean?"

"Kaga thinks he's a demon. He's not. We can all generally agree on that. But he believes that he's a demon so much that he's built this image of himself in his mind. He uses it to justify his horrendous actions. So I ask you both: what destroys a demon?"

"An angel," Mary whispered. "If either of you know one, please let me know. We'll drop them a line at the telegram office."

"Sure!" Colton laughed. "I wish it was that easy. I'm pretty sure ABSC would've let us know if they had an angel on staff."

"No, no, no. That's not what I'm talking about." Rennick sighed and tried again. "We may not be anything as noble as an angel, but we will be going down there to fight him, regardless."

Colton mulled over a bite of apple. "So you're saying... we'll be acting like angels. Since we're opposing him, we're acting like an angel would. Am I following you right?" Colton asked.

With a noncommittal grunt, Rennick turned to Mary. "You get what I'm talking about, don't you?"

Mary spoke with a toothpick between her teeth. "Maybe. You're saying that simply going down there to stop him, by fighting him, we're enforcing his belief that he's a demon, right?"

Rennick nodded. "We're feeding into his belief that he's evil and we're good."

She scrunched up her face. "So... the plan is that we shouldn't fight him and feed into that belief? I'm confused, Ren."

He groaned and dropped his head into his hands. "This really isn't that complicated, you two! We pretend like it's all an act! We feed into his expectations of us and use that to our advantage. We play up the fact that we're too weak. We'll pretend to be nearly defeated, hobbling around, screaming, you know, that sort of thing. He'll let his guard down. That's when we strike!"

Mary and Colton stared at him in silence.

Colton gave a nervous laugh. "First of all, you're assuming I can act. I guarantee we'll run into trouble." He sipped his water. "If that's our only plan, then we're in a lot of trouble. Especially that last part about striking when his guard is down. When does that happen exactly? I'm pretty sure his guard is never down."

Mary laughed, spilling some water from her cup.

"He's not a real demon," Rennick insisted. "He's a ghost. He's a poltergeist, something that is actually quite easy to destroy if you know how. There are rituals for this sort of thing. They're old methods, but they're still effective."

"But you said he's been doing this a long time, right?" Colton asked. "How do we know somebody else hasn't tried that on him before? How do we know it will actually work? I get the impression he's had a lot of enemies over the years."

Rennick pushed his plate away and sat back. "I'm not hearing any better plans. Do either of you have a better idea? I say, if he wants to play mind games with us, we play them right back on him."

"Could we get help?" Mary asked. "What about those werewolves in town the other day? You mentioned they were in a pack, right? Maybe we could convince the others in the pack to help."

Colton let out a whistle of air. "I don't think they'll be interested, Mary. We've killed a good chunk of their pack over the last few days. I'm pretty sure they'd rather shoot us than work with us."

"I get that, but this is their town, too, right?" She said, "Shouldn't they be given the opportunity to help defend it?"

"For all we know, they're helping him kidnap people," Rennick said.

Colton grimaced. "I had that thought, too."

She asked, "But why?"

Rennick shrugged. "I don't know why anybody would want to help a ghost kill people. I'm thinking of all those corpses I saw while I was down there, though, especially the hanging ones. They were skinned, flayed... that takes both precision and practice. Kaga didn't have that precision on his own. His movements aren't so careful. Which means somebody has been helping him."

"I can't help but think of how many minions he might have down there." Colton grunted.

Rennick said, "I got the impression he was using the hanging bodies to scare off anything that might get too curious, but I'm not sure how he cut them up to begin with. Not with his own limbs, that's for certain." He tapped his fingers on the table, "Maybe he possesses people like he did to me."

Colton nodded. "That's how he was going to have you skin me, remember?"

Rennick gave him a thin-lipped nod. "I'd rather not, to be honest."

"What about that little girl?" Colton asked, "He's making her do that, too, isn't he? Forcing her to torture people like that."

Rennick sighed. "If he's trying to be some sort of demon, I doubt she'd be spared that gruesome task."

Mary shuddered and crossed her arms, "So, how do we keep ourselves from getting possessed? I don't want to go down there to help you two and end up... like that."

"Oh, that part's easy." Rennick sat back in his chair and

sipped at his cup. "Don't drink anything that looks like black oil. I made that mistake by drinking from that little girl. I don't know what it is, but it is definitely not blood."

Colton couldn't help recalling he and Rennick battling in the firelight and seeing all the black gunk covering his partner from head to toe. Rennick was being nice by referring to it as oil. To him it had looked more like sludge, something that spewed out of some noxious sewer. When Rennick had vomited up the blood he drank from Colton, it had been full of that stuff. It didn't look like it should even exist in this world.

"So, don't eat something unless you know what it is." Mary smiled. "I think I can remember that."

"That's of course assuming that it's the only way he can control people, yes." Rennick sipped at his water, then froze. "Just a moment, I have a thought."

He stood and darted back into the bedroom to fetch his old pants that still had the black goop covering it. He folded it over. A large glob was visible on one of the pant legs and he held it out. "Mary, can you see this?"

She blinked at him, "Um, yes."

He rolled his eyes, "No, not the pants. What's on them?"

She smiled, "Dirt? Is this a joke?"

He gestured to Colton. "She didn't mention it yesterday, not once. Here, don't touch it, but..." He brought it closer to her. This time she studied it more carefully, her brows furrowing. "You don't see the black tar, do you? It's all over these pants."

She shook her head. "No, but I take it you can."

"We both can," Colton added, realizing how Kaga and his minions were able to move about town without anyone suspecting. "I bet you can't even smell it can you? Smells worse than a puddle of fresh piss to me."

She sniffed it, careful to keep her distance. "All I smell is dirt and sweat," she gave a weak smile. "You know, how Ren normally smells."

Rennick chuckled. "Thanks, Mary." He left to return the pants and then came back. "It does confirm my suspicions. I'll bet none of his puppets realized they were even eating the stuff, they probably did it accidentally."

"This is normal for you guys, though, right?" Mary's voice had a tinge of fear to it now, and Colton couldn't blame her. Knowing Kaga could control a person without them ever suspecting was terrifying. "I mean, you've dealt with something like this before, haven't you?"

Colton let out a shaky breath and exchanged a glance with Rennick. Slowly, the shock fell over Mary's face.

"We're not amateurs, if that's what you're asking," he said, fumbling, "It's just that..."

"Spirits are kind of tricky," Rennick said. "Even weak ones require coordination. It's more a game of strategy than strength. You have to make sure it's in the right position to be banished. It also takes a lot of time to prepare. You create a binding circle to keep it still, then you recite the incantation to destroy it. All three of us will have to stay inside the circle until the ritual is complete. It's not easy. Normally I would say we create the binding ring here and lure him out, but I don't think he'll fall for that. Why come himself when he can send one of his minions?"

"The thing is…" Colton pulled off his fancy hat and dragged a hand through his hair damp, freshly clean hair. It had been ages since he could do that. "From what I've read, you don't really fight them, it's all a matter of keeping your head straight. We have to do more than just believe we can defeat this thing, we have to *know* that we can. You have to be focused and clear-headed. Otherwise we could have some trouble."

"What kind of trouble?" she asked, looking between each of them.

Both men fell silent. Colton was no expert, but the warnings he'd read in the pamphlet he received on spiritual entities clearly stated the repercussions for failing to bind a spirit were never good. If it failed, they would be lucky to survive Kaga's wrath. Angry spirits were known to trail and torment those who had targeted it until death, making all of their lives a living hell. After all, Kaga had plenty of time to wait. The living, on the other hand, were always running out of time.

"Let's just say it's not pretty," Rennick added with a nervous little laugh before rushing to continue. "The ritual isn't complicated, but most of the trouble comes from keeping the spirit in place long enough until it's banished. That is the most dangerous part, distracting it so that the ritual can be finished. With a spirit like Kaga, that's sure to be tough."

Mary nodded, clearly trying to wrap her mind around it all. "You mentioned he doesn't have a real body, right? What is he made of then? How does he get around? I'm assuming he's not walking around in his old corpse, right?"

Colton sat back and glanced to his partner. "I'll let you handle this one."

Rennick drummed his fingers on the table. "He's made of... people, animals, whatever he's killed, or found dead, I imagine. He puts together bits and pieces of whatever he finds that's useful. Since he's determined to be a demon, it's mostly from corpses. Very rotted corpses." He cocked his head to the side. "Though, that could give us an advantage." He looked at Colton. "It takes work to control his own makeshift body. He controls his minions with that gunk, but other than that he may be more limited in what he can do."

"So it might not be able to fight us?" Mary asked, her fear replaced with a tentative smile. "I'm just trying to figure this all out. You're both way more experienced at this than I am. Even if we're all out of our depth on this."

"Look at it this way..." Colton reached over to touch her arm. Mary, to his silent joy, didn't push him away. "The only way a spirit like Kaga can interact with the physical world, our world, is if he believes he can. He has to have an incredible amount of confidence in himself just to do the tiniest little action. That means Kaga is probably overflowing with confidence. And that can be taken away from him."

"It'll be tough to shake that arrogance, too," Rennick added. "If we work together, we might be able to blindside him."

"So we'll play bait." Mary arched her eyebrows. "Ren, are you volunteering?"

"To be fair..." Rennick grinned. "I think it's obvious I'm the most experienced at banishing spirits. I've read a few books on the matter, so compared to you all, I'm a genius on the matter. Since I'll be busy destroying him, I'll volunteer *not* to be the bait, thanks."

Colton glanced to Mary. He figured she was going to try to volunteer herself next and, already, he was prepared to oppose her. It would practically be suicide for her. He couldn't allow it. His broken chair groaned as he leaned back and waited.

Mary glanced to him, then looked down at the table. Probably preparing herself for the argument that would ensue. "I think Colton would be best for the job."

"I don't think—" Colton stopped. "Wait. What?"

"What?" She shrugged. "You're clearly tougher than I am. To be honest, I don't fancy standing face-to-face with even a pretend demon."

He was dumbstruck, but Rennick laughed, clapping his hands. "Excellent! I think that's a perfect idea. I can do the binding circle, and Mary, you can cover us both. You have the best aim."

"I can do that. Not a problem."

Colton just stared at her. How could she volunteer him to be bait, and even argue he would be better at it? He was going to do it, of course, but it was different when she volunteered him instead. It would have been better if she had just offered, then she could have at least given him the ability to be chivalrous.

"Colton?" Rennick asked, "You good with this plan?"

"I guess." He grunted and downed the rest of his hot drink. Already, it had grown tepid. "It would be nice if I didn't get volunteered for it."

"What?" Her eyes went wide. "I didn't *volunteer* you,

Colton, I simply suggested it. You're more than welcome to sit out, if you're so bothered by it."

"I was going to do it anyway." Colton sighed. "But that's not the point."

Mary pursed her lips, "Maybe you should have taken the initiative and said something instead of making me speak for you."

"I didn't do that."

Rennick pushed back his chair with an obnoxious squeak. "We're back to this then, are we?"

Colton laid his hands on the table. "I would prefer it if you allowed me to make up my own mind next time, is all."

Mary rose to her feet. "If I did that, we would be here all day!"

Rennick laughed so hard he clutched at his stomach. Two angry glares didn't faze him. "Honestly, I think everything would be better off if you two just kissed already."

"Stay out of this, Ren!" Mary snapped. "And Colt, while you're complaining about having to be bait, I'll make sure that nothing gets close to Ren while he creates that circle... ritual... binding thing." With a huff she gestured to him. "I think you'll do just fine being bait. You seem to be quite good at getting yourself screwed over, at least."

Colton's jaw dropped and Rennick fell into peels of laughter.

She stuck out her chin and gave Colton a small smile before she cleared the glasses from the table. Colton tried to muscle up some sort of retort, but his mind was completely distracted. The look she'd given him was hardly one of malice or anger. In fact, if he wasn't mistaken, she had outwardly flirted with him just now.

He closed his mouth and tried to ignore Rennick's unending laughter. He had to reel in his thundering heartbeat, and confusion flowing through him. He couldn't figure out whether he wanted to scream at her or kiss her; the result left him momentarily paralyzed.

He had to admit she knew how to get under his skin.

CHAPTER 28

One Hell of a Shot

All three of them moved wordlessly throughout Mary's house, moving between the kitchen and the dining table. A pile of items lay upon the table and Mary kept bringing more.

Colton appreciated her efforts. Putting together supplies was difficult. They would be underground for a long time, though none of them knew precisely how long it would take to flush Kaga out of hiding. Considering the multiple tunnels Rennick had mentioned, this was one of the more pressing problems for Colton, and something he had trouble talking about with the others.

Dealing with Kaga and his child minion was secondary to having to be deep underground and dealing with those damn tunnels. Each time he thought back to traveling through that tunnel on his own in absolute darkness, his hands shook and his mouth went dry. Worse still, Mary was going to be with him. He really didn't want to look like a fool in front of her. He had already embarrassed himself once. He didn't want to do it again.

Mary seemed to have completely different concerns. She was paranoid about running out of ammunition, so insisted on carrying extras in the pockets of her skirts. She looked like she had rocks weighing her down.

"You know, Mary," Rennick said with a smirk. "I won't lose track of you with all the noise you make from those extra cartridges. Honestly, don't you think it's a little overkill?"

She bounced on her toes, then set another cartridge of bullets into a pocket. "Sorry, Ren. After hearing what this Kaga did to you two? I don't think overkill is possible."

She turned to work with a lantern she was trying to figure out how to bring. Rennick pulled the strap of a large, leather bag over his shoulder.

"Speaking of overkill," Colton muttered as he stepped up beside his partner. The bag looked packed full, and he frowned at the amount of weight the two planned to carry. "Do you have to bring so much? What the heck do you have in there?"

"A backup plan." Rennick flashed a toothy smile and patted the bag.

Colton arched an eyebrow. "I didn't realize we had one of those."

"We do now." His partner turned to him with absolute seriousness. He glanced over to Mary, then lowered his voice. "This is in case all else fails, my friend. I really hope we don't have to use it."

He didn't often see his partner so grave and hadn't expected it. Pursing his lips, he nodded. He wasn't sure what Rennick had in mind, but they all understood how dangerous it would be if Kaga won. They couldn't let that happen.

"Let's hope it doesn't come to that," Colton muttered. He turned to gather his Stetson hat before they headed out the door, then paused. "Think you got room in there for something extra?"

Rennick laughed. "I don't know. It better be small. It's pretty full already."

"I'm just thinking. If this goes like we're hoping it will —you know, without your backup plan—I may need a few things once we're out."

"Oh?" Rennick cocked his head to the side. "Like what? A change of pants from soiling yourself?" Suddenly, he was all humor again and here, Colton was trying to be serious.

"You know," Colton hissed. "After being bait?"

Rennick clapped him on the back. Colton bristled. Mary glanced their way and heat rose to his cheeks.

"What are you whispering? Spit it out, already!"

He took Rennick by the arm and pulled him close. "I may be pretty damn hungry if we survive this. I don't want to put you or her in danger."

Rennick blinked at him for a moment and tried to wrench his arm free, then his eyes went wide and he froze. "Oh, right. If you get bad off, then..."

"Exactly. Remember the creek?" The thought alone made him shiver, and he hoped Rennick couldn't tell. "I'll eat whatever I can find, be it a vampire, a corpse, or a human. I had Mary pick up a couple cans of meat at the grocer yesterday. I left the others at that damn farm. It shouldn't take much to hold me off if I get to that point. If that doesn't stop me, then..." He swallowed the dry pit in his throat and his voice trembled. Breaking eye contact, he looked away.

"Are you bringing your dagger?" he asked.

Rennick's voice trembled. "I wasn't planning on it, but I will if you think I should."

He nodded.

Rennick grabbed the scabbard from his supplies and tied it around his leg. "I know what you're asking me to do, and I won't do it. I'm not going to kill you if you turn wolf on us. I would simply lead you to where you couldn't harm anyone."

"Look, you're not helping. I'm not joking about this. If I get that bad, I don't what to hurt either of you."

His partner leveled him with a cool gaze. "I'm not joking, either." He slid the blade into the scabbard. "And I promise you won't hurt either of us. Maybe a few jerks that could do with being killed off. Trust me, Peridot is full of those. But I'll make sure your... *feeding* is kept discreet if that's what you're worried about."

Colton stared at him. "I don't want to hurt anyone. Even your personal enemies."

"Um, we won't have a choice. If you transform, I'm looking for whoever I can find to sate that wolfish hunger of yours." He patted Colton's stomach with a smile.

"I'm relying on you to make a judgment call about who lives or dies."

Rennick chuckled and shook his head. "You worry too much. Trust me a little, won't you?"

Colton frowned, reminded of Mr. Tep telling him how he needed to learn to trust people more. That meeting in his clean office and the smell of wood polish felt like years ago.

His partner patted his arm, "Honestly, you really are wound tight. You need to relax more."

"How the hell am I supposed to relax when we're going down to face a demon?" Colton growled.

Rennick's eyes narrowed and his brown eyes flashed in a beam of light through the window. "He's not a real demon, Colton. Don't feed his ego. It's all a facade."

He went quiet.

He knew Rennick was right. They had all discussed as much, but Colton couldn't help but worry. He knew what it felt like being at Kaga's mercy and he wasn't looking forward to facing him again, demon or not.

Rennick stuffed two cans of meat into his satchel, somehow finding a way to tie it closed again. "Since I'm bringing these," he said with a huff, "you have to promise me something." Rennick turned to pull on the pack again. "Don't let him in."

Colton knitted together his brows. "What the hell is that supposed to mean?"

Rennick met his gaze. "If Kaga finds a way to turn you, to control you, then Mary's and my chances grow slim. For a lack of a better word, you're our shield. You can take hits that would kill either of us."

He bared his teeth. "I hate that you're right."

"He's also got his eyes on you," Rennick said. "You're the one that got away. He's controlled me once, and it's possible..." He took a deep breath. "It's possible he could take hold of me again."

Colton put a hand on Rennick's shoulder. "My blood

broke the spell last time. If it happens again, I'm right here. Now that I know how to battle it, I promise I won't let him keep you. He treated me like an oddity, so there's a chance he might not be able to control werewolves without a lot of work. I don't think he can slip into my mind as easily as he did you."

Rennick frowned as he adjusted the straps on his pack. "I sure hope you're right about that. Otherwise this will be a short, one-way trip."

THE SHADOWS WERE LONG WHEN THE TRIO stepped out into the quiet street. The heat of the day was at its highest and most people were off in the mines or inside one of the downtown shops, finding ways to escape the heat.

He looked where Tahoe had been tacked the night before, but Rennick had already returned her to Ben's stable so she could recover. She had already done enough to help them and was due to rest. Colton worried about Aidan, wondering if he was wandering the desert still trying to find his way home, or if something had happened to him.

An older boy walked past with wide brown eyes, eyeing them curiously. He met Colton's gaze, gasped, then hurried down the road. Colton couldn't blame him. They were an intimidating sight.

He wiped at the sweat on his upper lip. He wasn't as sensitive to the sun as Rennick, but he wasn't crazy about being baked either. Rennick had been forced to use a blanket since his cloak had been lost in Kaga's cavern, and it wasn't nearly as effective. He was squinting constantly without a hood to use as shade.

"Where to?" Rennick asked.

"The girl was back this way," Colton muttered and took the lead.

In the daylight, the shacks on this end of Peridot looked far worse than they had the evening before. Many were full of holes that might have been shotgun blasts, and few had working doors, or even shutters. Everything was bleached from the relentless sun and sand had engulfed a few of the structures. The wind wasn't that strong, but still Colton felt the gritty taste of sand in his mouth. It was impossible to avoid it.

They reached the shack where he had spotted the girl lurking the day before, each with their gun drawn. Colton stopped at the entrance. The little girl had made a mess of the place. Debris that had been piled in the corners of the room lay strewn across the floor. The dried up corpse, whose clothes Rennick had used to disguise Colton, had disappeared. Probably taken to be added to Kaga's collection before they could even investigate it. The thick layers of spider webs along the ceiling had been disrupted in large swathes. There was also the strong scent of the black gunk that had infected Rennick, and blotches of it were scattered throughout the room.

"Are we going inside, or are we going to stand out here till I melt?" Rennick groaned.

Colton went first, cautious where he stepped. "Stay away from the walls, Mary. I can see the sludge the girl left on them. I was hoping I'd see something that might tell us what she was up to."

Rennick pushed past Mary into the cool shade and pulled out a handkerchief, wiping the sweat from his brow. "And why in the world can't we do that from inside?" He froze as he caught sight of the ceiling. His eyes went wide. "Oh ew, are those... spiders?"

Colton chuckled. "Oh yes. There's a bunch of them, too."

"I-I don't remember these being here. Were they here before? When I helped you dress?"

Mary smiled at him. "You really were out of it, weren't you, Ren?" She sidestepped a large black spider hanging directly in front of her face. Colton stared at her. He had seen plenty of people shriek and shy away from far smaller insects. Mary didn't though. She brushed aside the webbing as though it was cotton candy.

Rennick nearly walked chin-first into the spider Mary had avoided and gave a meek little whimper before stepping around it. "You know, maybe being outside wasn't so bad after all."

"You're free to go back and melt if you want," Colton said. "I've no idea what's around the back of this building, though."

Rennick clenched his jaw, but remained quiet as they made their way through the shack. Close to the rear entrance, Colton looked up into the mass of webbing on the ceiling again and noticed another pocket that exposed the wooden ceiling. He put up his hand to it and dragged his fingers across the tiny black marks.

"What is it?" Mary whispered, pushing webbing out of the way to be able to look at it.

"Scratches," Colton whispered. "Like the ones we found at Davis Farm. Is it from her fingers? How the hell did she get up there?"

Rennick dabbed at his forehead. "I really hope she wasn't crawling around up there." He shuddered. "Why would she do that?"

"More importantly, how?" Mary asked. "Seems more like something a wraith would do than a child. Sorry, Colt."

He scratched his chin. If the kid was possessed by Kaga, she should still be limited by what she could do as a human, much like Rennick had been limited in what he could do. They could be pushed to their limits, but they were still restrained within those limits. Little girls shouldn't be able to crawl across ceilings or walls any more than Rennick could have punched a hole through a wall. "I don't know how she did it, but something was crawling around up there."

"What if it wasn't the little girl?" Mary asked.

"Another of Kaga's, you mean?" Rennick asked with a grimace.

"Exactly. Maybe it was another of Kaga's puppets," she said.

"There were other missing persons," Colton muttered to himself. "Damn, who were they? From the letter, remember?" He turned to Rennick, "I remember the girl. She was listed as missing. There were others though."

"I think she was the only one missing," Rennick said. "A few casualties, but no information on the bodies. They must not have been in very good condition if Mr. Tep didn't mention them. If the girl was as decomposed as you said—"

"She wasn't rotting." Colton growled. "She looked emaciated and nearly dead, but she wasn't dead yet. If we can get her back, we might have a chance at saving her."

"That's a foolish risk, Colt," Mary said. "We're going to have our hands full with Kaga. Nobody has time to waste on some lost child who nearly killed Ren. It's better if we count our losses now, else we might regret it later."

"If I'd done that, Rennick wouldn't be here right now."

Mary winced and turned away. "I'm sorry, I didn't mean..." She took a breath. "Alright, we try to help the child if we can, but we stick to the plan. You two are the experts here, right? Shouldn't you be the ones leading me?"

Rennick smirked. "I think he just did." He wrapped a hand around Mary's arm. She squeezed his hand against her side with an affectionate gleam in her eye.

Colton turned away. He needed to focus on the mission, not get distracted by his emotions. "The tunnel isn't far from here. It goes straight down into his—" Colton turned to see Rennick and Mary locked in an embrace. He glanced away quickly and tried not to pay attention to their voices as they whispered to each other.

His heart dropped at the sight, though. He thought they were separated, but here they were locked in a lovers' embrace. Heat rose to his cheeks. Jealousy ate within. Thoughts like these were poisonous for any mission. He need to bottle them up tight.

"It's so close to town," Mary whispered. She had appeared at his side without him even knowing. That's how damn distracted he was already.

He nodded. "Unfortunately. He'll know we're coming, just like he knew we left."

"You think he's waiting for us?" She stared at him. "Why?"

"Something tells me he's looking forward to our return." Colton clenched his jaw. "He's had a full day to prepare, just like we did."

"It's like a dance," Rennick added with a smile on his lips. "He wants us to try to stop him. That way, when he crushes us, it proves just how terribly evil he is."

"I've heard of thinking like your enemy." Mary shook her head. "But you two take it to new levels."

WHEN HE AND RENNICK HAD ESCAPED KAGA'S tunnel last time, Colton hadn't paid much attention to his surroundings, much less the building they emerged from; he had been too focused on simply getting out alive. From the outside, the shanty looked just as rundown and ugly as any of the other close-knit buildings; the walls looked like one good wind might topple them. Nothing distinguished it from its neighbors and nothing signified it as the entrance to a demon's cavern, but the inside told a different story.

The door had long ago fallen off, leaving the inside open to the elements. There had once been furniture and some semblance of a living area, but time had transformed everything into hulking, misshapen mummies. Colton's attention was drawn most to the cavernous hole in the center of the room. The edges looked like a few insects had tried to call it home, but even they didn't have the nerve to delve much deeper. The tunnel went down at an angle then turned, preventing him from looking farther in, but it meant the daylight wouldn't reach very far, either. Mary crouched down, lighting the lantern she'd brought. Colton took a deep breath then stepped down into the tunnel.

"You know, I can see just fine," Rennick muttered. The nervousness of his voice betrayed the confidence of his words. "Even in the darkest tunnels I can probably see better than either of you. Any shred of light or glint of metal lets me see like it's candlelight." He swallowed hard before following Colton down. Then he turned to put a hand out to help Mary.

"Good to know." She ignored his help and leapt down into the pit. As she jumped, her dress flew up. Colton glimpsed riding trousers beneath her dress instead of the expected petticoats. He turned away quickly, embarrassed on her behalf. He felt bad for her. The heat was bad enough without having to wear two layers of clothes.

With a grunt, Colton stepped around them to take the lead. Rennick could take up the rear. He started down the tunnel. Mary held the lantern at her side, carrying her pistol in the other.

Colton's heart skipped a beat when he turned the corner, met by the dark, empty path ahead. The tiny flame in Mary's lantern looked small and helpless compared to the immensity of the darkness ahead of them. He cleared his throat before he spoke. "Do you remember how far it was last time, Rennick?"

Rennick laughed. "You're kidding, right? I couldn't even walk!"

Colton tried to smile and Mary gave a nervous chuckle. Their anxious humor was a testament to their nerves.

They walked for a ways, long enough for the glint of sunlight behind them to be entirely blocked out. They walked for what felt like hours, but was probably only a fraction of that. The path before them continued sloping downwards.

Colton was fine at first, but the longer the tunnel stretched, the more his old claustrophobia whispered to him like an unwanted friend. It was the third time he had been surrounded in pitch black darkness since his arrival in Peridot. He liked to think he had gotten used to it, but he hated every moment of it. The smell of the dry dirt all around them clung to the back of his throat. The path they took angled down, so he knew the further they went the more ground stood above their heads. The worse thought, though, was realizing, if the tunnel did cave in, his friends would die and his body would continue to try to regenerate over and over again.

His legs weakened, and he paused against the dirt wall. His hands shook as he pulled out a cloth, wiping the sweat off his brow and neck. Mary took the cue and sat down on the ground, placing the lantern to the side. Their little bubble of light was so very tenuous compared to the emptiness ahead and behind.

"It just keeps going and going," she whispered.

Rennick sat down beside her. "It's always downward, too. Like we're being eaten alive."

"I know…" Colton closed his eyes and tried to calm himself. His pulse was racing and his palms were slick with sweat. He was beginning to look forward to reaching Kaga's cavern, simply to be free of this suffocation. It was getting hard to even breathe.

"You alright?" He opened his eyes to Mary standing before him, her face a dancing mixture of shadows and light. Her warm, brown eyes glowed almost a golden color in the candlelight.

"I'm trying to be," he admitted. "Being below ground like this, it... gets to me."

Rennick nodded. "Don't worry, I don't think it'll be much farther. I can smell the bodies from here."

When Rennick mentioned it, Colton caught the scent as well. He must have been so distracted to miss them. "You're right," he whispered. Stretching his senses, he could not only smell the corpses, but he could hear something as well. Something ahead of them was moving, but even when it was quiet, he still couldn't quite make it out. Was it scraping? Footsteps?

"What I'm more worried about is what will happen when we get down there." Mary tightened her braid, then froze when Colton put up his hand. Rennick sprung to his feet and hurried to Colton's side.

"Do you hear something?" Rennick whispered.

"Yes, it's faint." Now the others went silent, Colton caught it again. This time, he was able to identify it: breathing. Whatever it was was trying very hard not to be heard, and if Colton could barely hear it, that meant it was skilled, indeed. "I hear it breathing. Be ready."

"Kaga?" He heard steel instead of the fear he expected in Mary's voice.

"No, I doubt Kaga could be quiet even if he wanted to be. This is different," he whispered, recalling the noise the sluggish monster had made when he had been without sight.

"Kaga is merely a spirit, though. He wouldn't need to breathe. I mean, that's considering our theories are right." The doubt in Rennick's voice caused a pit in Colton's stomach. If Rennick's theories were wrong, they were in way worse trouble.

"Mary, stay behind us," Colton hissed. "Keep the light up."

"Way ahead of you." She picked up the lantern and turned up the flame to give them a bit more light. With her other hand, she retrieved her pistol again.

They stepped carefully with their weapons drawn. It was difficult to see past the ring of light made by the lantern, but both he and Rennick could make out the figure ahead of them.

"Don't move," Colton called to the dark shape further down the tunnel, just outside of the candlelight. "Step slowly, and come into the light with your arms above your head." It was definitely a person. They were tall and leaned against the wall as though exhausted. Slowly, as though inebriated, they pushed away from the wall. accompanied by a sick squishing noise. The figure stumbled a bit before standing straight, then raised their arms above their head and came toward them.

With each step, they came closer to falling. Colton wasn't sure what he would do if they fell dead on the ground. The light spilled over one bare foot covered in sores and blisters. Their pants had once belonged to a gentleman, but were torn now at the knees, which were similarly scarred, bruised and covered in dirt. They were terribly emaciated; Colton was amazed they could move at all.

Wearing a tattered shirt grayed and stained with blood, the man moved fully into the light, revealing the sunken horror of his face. Large, soulless eyes fit into two shadowed eye sockets and a scraggly beard stuck out at all angles from his blistered chin.

Colton at first assumed his lips were pulled back from his teeth forming a grimace, but that wasn't quite right. His teeth gleamed yellow in the lantern light. His gums were such a dark color he couldn't tell if they were real. His lips had been completely eaten off.

Looking at him, Colton was hit with an icy punch to his gut.

The emaciated man gripped the wall of the tunnel as he almost toppled again and Colton's gaze was drawn to his fingers. Covered in blood, the fingers' nails were almost worn off. Red trails of blood lingered on the wall when the man straightened and walked toward them again.

"Kaaaaaag…" The man's voice was barely audible. Colton realized if he had been mad enough to eat off his own lips, he might have done the same to his tongue as well. He stepped to the side to put himself between this ghoulish man and Mary.

He wasn't sure what to do, so decided to say the first thing that came to mind. "Take it easy, we'll get you help. Whatever Kaga has done to you, we can stop it."

A shudder traveled through the man and his large, watery eyes lolled about in their sockets like wet cue balls. He stared at each of them, his Adam's apple bobbing up and down as he tried to speak. "...khrrr..." he uttered and a drip of saliva spilled from his lipless jaws.

"Hey Colton?" Rennick whispered, "I don't think he cares."

"You're one of the folks that was missing, right?" Mary asked. "Are you from Peridot?"

The man dropped his arms limply to his sides, as though his muscles simply gave out from the strain. His head slid up and down with a nod.

"Alright then," Colton muttered. Whoever he was, the man could understand them. Even if his mind was nearly gone, he could respond. It gave Colton a small flare of hope. He relaxed his stance. "Come with us, and we'll get you some help."

The man stared at him for a moment, then hunkered down to the ground in a crouch. His pant legs stretched over his legs, revealing their stick thin outlines. His bony knees stuck up on either side of his head, but he stared at them with disturbing intensity.

"Don't be frightened. We won't hurt you," Colton whispered. "Come with us and Kaga won't be able to touch you again."

Rennick took a step forward. Of the three of them, Rennick could probably sympathize the most. He knew what it was like to watch helplessly trapped inside his body. Underneath his hideous shell, the man was perhaps confused and maybe a little crazy from starvation. Who wouldn't be?

None of them were prepared when the man leapt.

He jumped to the ceiling with incredible speed, and with a bizarre dexterity. He clung to the rocky ceiling with the bloody stubs of his fingers, and did the same with his bloody toes. As he scurried across the dirt ceiling, black blood dripped down, either from his pant legs or some other wound. Colton jolted back for fear of it hitting his face. He pulled out his gun and fired a shot. The man leapt to the side and avoided it easily. He was impossibly fast. Unfortunately, the bullet hit a large rock instead, ricocheting straight for Rennick. His partner cried out in pain.

The crawling man stopped dead in his tracks and turned his head almost impossibly backwards to look at Rennick. With a series of leaps, he turned and dropped in front of him. Rennick was now face-to-face with the gaping, tongueless mouth of the man dripping with Kaga's black poison. He tried to shove it back and shoot, but the creature dug bony fingers into his shoulders. It was as if it had found the strength of a mountain lion. Keeping its grip tight, the creature picked up its legs like a gymnast and kicked hard into Rennick's chest.

Rennick fell backwards, hitting the ground hard enough to knock his gun out of his hand. The emaciated man was on top of him in an instant, digging fingers into Rennick's arms.

The clatter of the metal pistol brought Colton back to his senses. He rushed forward and wrapped his arms around the creature's waist. Even his strength couldn't wrench it free, but he was at least able to keep its bite at bay. Slowly, Rennick worked on fingertips that still dug like metal pikes into his arms, but the creature had no intention of moving. The howling growl it made before it tried to bite a chunk out of Rennick's face didn't sound like anything a human could make.

"Hold him still!" Mary cried, trying to get a good shot. Colton moved his hold upward along the creature's torso. Beneath the thin layer of clothing he could feel each rib as the creature wiggled in his grip. With a grunt, he pulled the creature's arms up and back so that it was forced to relinquish Rennick. As soon as Rennick started dragging himself away, the creature flailed again and a high-pitched cry erupted from its fragile body. Colton couldn't hold it still for very long.

"Shoot it!" he cried just as the creature planted its feet. Would it lunge again, or maybe find a way to flip Colton onto his back? It shouldn't be so powerful! Where the hell was it getting so much strength?

He braced himself as the creature's head turned toward him, a complete ninety degrees to the side. It flung the remains of its grimy hair into his face. Colton had to keep from gagging as the black gunk, which covered the creature from head to toe, splattered against his face and just under his nose. One bulbous eye locked onto him, and Colton realized they had been played for fools. There was malice in that horrible gaze. No trace of fear, curiosity, pity, or anything that might have meant there was a person inside to save; just hunger and rage.

A shot fired. Colton flinched and braced for another ricochet to go astray. The scent of human blood hit his nostrils, mixing into a disgusting combination with the black gunk. The creature in his arms went rigid for an instant before falling still. Colton wouldn't let go. He didn't dare release it until Mary came over and put another shot into its skull. The body didn't even twitch.

Colton dropped the creature to the ground and wiped down his face before taking a deep breath.

Rennick sat on the ground beside the man, staring at him with wide eyes. He was panting, but gave a crooked grin at Colton. "I didn't see that one coming!"

"That was too close."

Colton shook his head and held a hand out to Rennick. As he pulled him to his feet, he noticed the gun in his hand. He must have grabbed it after it was knocked away. "Was that shot you?"

"No." Rennick chuckled. "Mary is fortunately a far better shot than you are."

He frowned and turned to see Mary grinning at him.

"That was one hell of a shot," he admitted, wiping the black gunk from his clothes.

"I know." She laughed.

"Are you okay, Rennick?"

"Yeah," he said and lifted up his jacket to show that the wound on his side was already healing. "I moved, so it didn't get me direct, but it still grazed me. I guess the fresh blood triggered it. Made it... hungry."

"Like a predator." Colton crouched down next to the man's body. Both of Mary's bullets were embedded in the creature's skull, no more than a centimeter apart. He glanced up to Mary standing over him still grinning.

Colton nudged the body again with his boot. A large puddle of black ooze and brilliant red blood pooled around its cranium. He looked dead, but even fifty bullets in the man's head wouldn't stop Colton's skin from crawling.

"Should we do something to make sure he's dead?" he asked.

"I don't think he'll be climbing walls again, if that's what you're concerned about," Rennick said.

"I just worry that Kaga might find a way to use him still."

"A corpse is a corpse, my friend."

"Kaga is made of corpses, remember?"

They went silent for a moment. Mary pushed past them and put a third bullet into its skull. The noise reverberated up and down the tunnel like a rolling drum. "Third time's the charm. Does that help, Colt?"

"Thanks." Colton gave her a nod, then turned to Rennick. "Wait a minute. Why the hell didn't you conjure up your illusions, kid? That would've been an ideal time for it, or do you just like being a damsel in distress?"

Rennick's face went blank and then slowly contorted to chagrin. "What are you talking about? What illusions?" He glanced to Mary, then gave Colton a wide-eyed look, begging him to play along.

"Really? You're okay with her knowing you have to drink blood, but not about the illusions?" He shook his head, even more entertained as Rennick glared at him. "You may as well tell her now before we go in. We'll need all the extra firepower we can muster soon enough, and that includes your illusions. I'm sure you would have brought them out once we reached Kaga, right? You do know how dangerous this is."

Rennick squirmed, flicking his gaze between the two of them.

"What's he talking about, Ren?" Mary swept a strand of hair behind an ear and leveled a concerned look at him. There was more than concern in her voice, though. It was clear to both of them Rennick was hiding something from her, and Colton couldn't figure out why.

Rennick tried to keep his cool for a few minutes, but finally spoke. Colton expected an apology, but instead Rennick turned his venom onto him. "Why? Why do you insist on referring to me as a child? You know for a fact that I am the elder of either one of you. Honestly, do you know how much more experienced I am?" He gave a suave smile to Mary, who looked bewildered.

"If you don't want to be treated like a kid, stop acting like one," Colton muttered. They were this close to the cavern, but for some reason, Rennick decided it was the best time to throw another bravado moment. He couldn't wrap his head around it. Maybe he was afraid of dying before he could properly humiliate himself. Colton was half a minute away from laying him out and dragging his unconscious body back to the surface.

"I do *not* act like a child! Why does everyone say that?" Rennick was shaking, and Colton was starting to wonder if perhaps he really was as upset as he seemed.

Mary stepped forward and placed a hand on his shoulder. "Ren, calm down. It's not important."

He stared at her, quaking before her but apparently unable to turn away. "Mary..."

"It's alright," she whispered as she rubbed his arm. By the look on Rennick's face you would think she was hurting him. "We're just having a bit of fun with you. There's no need to take it personally. Right, Colt? You don't mean it, do you?"

He sighed. "No, I don't."

Rennick closed his eyes and hung his head low. "Mary, I

am so sorry." He put his hand out and waved it. The three ladies in ball gowns stepped out of the shadows, each of them gorgeous without a speck of dirt on them. They looked so prim and elegant in the ugly tunnel, especially with the body of the dead man beside them, that they could have stepped from a dream.

Mary had her gun raised so fast she could have shot the three of them in the blink of an eye. "Who are you? Where the hell did you come from?"

Rennick bit his lip. "I made them. They're not real, see?" He waved his hand again and the blonde woman disappeared as silently as she had emerged.

Mary gasped, still keeping her gun raised and aiming back and forth between the two remaining girls. "They're not real? What do you mean?" Then she froze and her aim faltered. Her eyes went wide, and she stood up straighter. "I know these women."

Rennick fidgeted at Mary's side, looking like he wanted to curl up and disappear like his illusions.

"They're always with you when we're playing poker," she whispered. Then her eyes turned to steel as she spun, aiming her pistol this time at Rennick. "You cheat!" she cried.

He put his arms into the air with slow reluctance, already admitting defeat.

"You had those three looking at cards, didn't you? I bet you have some way of communicating with them? Hand signals, perhaps?"

"Yes, I can see through their eyes." His voice broke, and he had to clear his throat.

"You little thief! You stole everything! My money, my

sweet little colts, my—" Her voice dropped as full realization kicked in. "You stole my home. My father's home!"

"It was only temporary. I never intended to stay here so long." Rennick's hands were trembling as he backed away against the wall. "I was going to give everything back after I left!"

Mary took another step forward and placed the barrel directly to Rennick's forehead. "How dare you!"

As much as Colton didn't want to get involved, he really didn't need his partner's brains splattered all over the wall. He approached Mary with slow steps and a calm voice. "Looks like this little weasel robbed you blind."

"Oh, he did. Mark my word, he'll pay, too!"

Rennick winced. "See what you've done? She's going to kill me!"

Colton placed a hand on her shoulder, feeling her muscles tense. "You know, we need him alive if he's going to help us with the ritual."

Her eyes narrowed. "Then it looks like that old demon is going to have to wait, isn't he?"

He gave her shoulder a squeeze. "We need him, Mary. He's the only one who knows how to destroy it. I agree he deserves it, but we can't worry about it now." He gave a hard look at Rennick. "When we get up top, though, that's a different story."

Rennick's eyes went wide. "But Colt—"

He put a finger up to his lips and Rennick went silent.

Mary stood as still as a statue, still pressing the gun barrel hard to Rennick's forehead. "You know, Colt, I hate it when you start spouting truths like that." She lowered her pistol; Rennick relaxed a little.

"I wouldn't be much of a partner if I didn't stick my neck out for him occasionally."

"I know you have to, but I don't think he deserves you as a partner." She gave him a small smile before picking up the lantern on the ground. "Come on, boys, we have a demon to kill."

Mary started forward while Rennick and Colton stared after her.

He whistled and shook his head. "Your girl, she's…" He licked his parched lips, trying to find the right word.

"I think deadly is the word you're looking for," Rennick hissed. "And frightening, I'll give her that one, too."

He finally gave a short nod. "I was going to say beautiful."

Rennick chuckled. "She is that. Though she wasn't aiming a gun at your head just now, was she? Trust me when I say it's different when that happens."

He nodded, patting Rennick's arm. "Somehow, I'm pretty sure she would still be beautiful. Did you really cheat to get her house and her horses? Aidan and Tahoe were hers originally, weren't they?"

Rennick huffed and spoke in a low voice. "Despite what she says, I'm not entirely to blame for all that business. She's the one that put her own family home on the table; nobody forced her into it. I even told her it was a bad idea, but as you can tell, she's a hard woman to dissuade."

"She does like to live dangerously, doesn't she?"

Mary turned around, a hand on her hip. "Are you boys going to linger in the shadows and talk about me behind my back, or are we here to deal with a demon?"

Colton couldn't help but admire the sparkle in her eye as he and Rennick hurried to catch up.

PART SEVEN

MONSTERS AND HEROES

CHAPTER 29

THE RITUAL

THE CAVERN WAS MASSIVE, BUT IT WASN'T AS dark as Colton had expected. Torches hung along the walls, but he hadn't a clue who had lit them. A few of them were perched on low-hanging stalactites, and it didn't take much to imagine the man from the tunnel leaping up there without any fear of falling. The ground was not only uneven, but filled with trenches and gullies, all with jagged edges. From here, he spotted several black pits that probably fell for miles. He was glad Rennick had guided him earlier. It could have gotten ugly.

Then he spotted the chains hung between several stalactites. The heavy duty kind used in railroads and shipyards about as wide as his arm. He took a few steps forward, trying to make sense of one of the shapes hanging from one. The chain ended in a large, nasty hook plunged through an unidentifiable corpse. All he could tell from its shape was it was far too large to be a person. It could have passed for a bull when it was alive, but the limbs and head had been removed, leaving only the torso behind. Insects swarmed it; he was glad he had grown mostly accustomed to the smell of death down here. The chain was pinned with a piton to the top of the cavern. Could the man they killed earlier have had the strength to drive it in from such an odd angle? Colton didn't think so, but the fact *something* had that ability sent a tremor tearing through him.

He broke his gaze from the gruesome visage and turned to his partner. "Where do you think he is?"

Rennick pointed down to a tunnel at the base of the opposite wall, all the way on the other end of the cavern.

"Alright." He wiped at the sweat on his lip. "So you're going to make the ritual symbols around the edges, right?"

His partner nodded. "When I finish the ritual, he'll be destroyed, and he'll lose any influence he might have over his little pets."

Colton turned to Mary, who had already pulled out her pistols. "And you *will* cover him, won't you?"

"I suppose so." She sighed, ignoring Rennick's wide-eyed glance. "Though if you're distracting Kaga, I don't see why I have to babysit Rennick. Other than those bodies, this place looks empty."

Colton stole another look at the heavy piton holding up the bull's torso. "I think we might have to deal with more than just Kaga down here. There may be something more powerful than the man from the tunnel."

She eyed the walls. "If that's the case, we're vulnerable out here. Look at all the holes in this place. There are plenty of places they could be hiding."

His mouth went dry. He had been so focused on the hanging corpse, he hadn't even considered the terrain.

Muttering, Rennick crouched to pull out his supplies. "I'd better get started then."

At the other end of the cavern, a flat platform of rock in the center of the cavern led to the entrance of the large tunnel Rennick had indicated. "I'll head to the mouth of his tunnel while you two get things set up. Maybe I can give some kind of warning if he shows."

"Wait," Mary said. "Don't get too close to it. Keep your distance if you can. Make him come to you. We'll have a better aim that way, and if anything happens, we can cover you."

It was a smart move that, once again, Colton hadn't considered. His normal, admittedly dangerous, tactic of rushing in would be suicide here. Normally, he tried to attract fire in his direction because he could take it, but that wouldn't work here. Like Rennick had said, if Kaga got hold of him, the other two would be done for.

"That's a good point," Rennick said as he pushed his blond hair out of his eyes. "If we're lucky and he doesn't notice us." He shrugged. "Maybe he won't even show."

Colton sighed and shook his head.

"What?" Rennick protested. "He might not even be here right now. If so, we might be able to finish preparing the ritual before he shows up. Then we just lure him out into the opening and catch him!"

"With all the shots we fired back there? I don't think we're that lucky," Mary added.

"We can't depend on luck, not here," Colton said. "Keep your voices down, and try not to shoot unless you have to. We may have gotten lucky, and he didn't hear any of the shots in the tunnel—"

Mary laughed.

"—but if not, we can guarantee they'll hear it down here."

Rennick stood up with a piece of circular metal in one hand that reminded Colton of the rim on a barrel. In the other hand, he held a fistful of white chalk. He turned and walked along the wall, stepping carefully on the uneven ground.

Colton faced the tunnel on the far end, planning his path over. A cool hand slipped into his. Mary was watching him, her face etched with concern. "Be careful, won't you? Don't do anything stupid."

"I'll try." He smiled, hoping he could at least alleviate her fears. There was no cure for his own.

She gave a warm smile and nodded before letting go. A heat rose in his chest. He would fight a thousand Kagas for that smile to be aimed at him again. Already, he knew if anything happened to Mary, he would drop everything to help her. He also knew that was a liability, but it was too late for regrets. She turned and followed Rennick, holding her skirt just high enough to keep from tripping, and giving him a glimpse of the men's pants underneath.

Colton waited until she caught up with Rennick before making his way down to the flat platform. The ground was more patchy than he had noticed the last time he was here. Of course, he had been blind then. Gaps between the rocks were frequent, and he had to leap across several dark, endless chasms to reach the center platform. No wonder Rennick had been slow at getting the two of them out before. Traversing this alone was difficult enough; he couldn't imagine trying to lead a blind man through it.

When he reached the center, he couldn't help but notice the heavy bodies hanging high above his head, or the occasional sound of a squeaking chain. He could tell now, although the large torso of what was likely a bull had caught his attention first, many of the bodies were human. A few still wore remnants of clothes. Heads and limbs were missing, the same as the bull. He scoured the ceiling for any sign of movement, but everything was still.

Higher up and to the side, he saw Rennick and Mary making their way along the wall. Rennick was using the metal rim to trace a circle, then chalking in arcane symbols, and speaking incantations. Mary faced Colton, but she wasn't looking at him; she, too, was scanning for movement.

He set aside his concern, needing to focus. They could take care of themselves. He turned his attention to the darkened tunnel entrance. It was at least twice the size of the tunnel they had traveled through earlier. He hadn't a clue what Kaga even looked like. He knew the voice, the scent, and he even knew the sound of his movement, but he hoped he could recognize him. Staring into the darkness, he listened to his own quick breaths in the awful air. It was eerily still and impossibly quiet. Occasionally, a drop of water fell from one of the stalactites. All he could hear were the footfalls of his friends and the buzzing of flies high overhead.

He reached out with all of his senses, trying to pick up any movement. Although the air was still, it also felt thick and electric, like a lightning storm was approaching. The hairs of his arms were standing up and his body was thrumming, but he couldn't explain it away as nerves. It was more than that. It was a familiar sensation, one he hadn't consciously been aware of the last time he was down here. Was this what spiritual energy felt like? He tried to think back to that stupid pamphlet on it from training, but the description had been bland: *An inexplicable feeling of anxiety and fear*. That wasn't quite right, though. It was too simplistic. Spiritual energy, it seemed, felt like walking into a trap.

A trap that now made perfect sense. Kaga had plenty of time to prepare, so why would he place a single man in the tunnel as his only defense? Was he that pompous? Colton wiped off the sweat from his lip before taking up his guns again.

He had been doing this job for less than five years, a mere pittance compared to some of the older agents he had met. His trainer, Grady, had been doing it for twenty. Grady's motto had always been never get comfortable. Complacency, he often said, was the number one cause of death for agents in the field. Lack of attentiveness was a death knell. He had trained Colton to use every ability he had. Even the ones that didn't always make sense.

Most didn't pay attention to the warning signals their bodies sounded off, so they were easier prey. Listening was difficult. It required a calm mind and a calm body. So, despite his fear, Colton calmed himself. He took deep breaths while still keeping his eyes glued on the tunnel. He forced his body to relax, and he concentrated. Rennick and Mary were leaping over another gap up above. There was the sound of chalk on stone. But there was something else, too. Something moving, occasionally knocking bits of gravel. They were not alone.

"Watch out!" Mary shouted from above.

Something slammed into the small of Colton's back and pushed him to his knees.

CHAPTER 30

PUPPETS

COLTON'S HAND SLAMMED INTO THE ROCKY ground as he fell and he had to grip tighter to his pistol to keep from losing it. On instinct, he rolled to the side just as something scraped the stone where he had been. He climbed to his feet and turned to see his assailant. It took a moment for him to recognize the little girl he had spotted briefly the previous evening. She was a mess of black hair and pale skin. Within the torchlight, shadows flickered across her face. Mary was right; she looked dead.

Her cheeks were hollow and her nest of hair was knotted with grass, blood, and even spider webs. He could even make out wet clumps that must have been more of the black gunk that had possessed Rennick. Her lips were gone, likely from her own doing if the man from the tunnel was any indication, and her teeth were a mix of blacks and browns. She snarled at him and charged. Colton used her momentum to fling her to the side. The girl regained her balance quickly and turned back to him with murder in her eyes.

He put away his pistol.

"What are you doing?" Mary called out. She was still watching from her perch beside Rennick. Aggravation filled her voice, but he ignored it. Instead, he focused on the little girl in front of him. The child's fingers were bloody, but he fingernails were still attached. Her elbows and knees were rubbed raw from crawling around on stone like a wild animal. He had been hesitant to put away his weapon at first, but then he had glimpsed her eyes behind the trails of dark hair. A piercing grayish blue, he couldn't help but think of the pack of coyotes he had heard that first night after they had left Peridot.

Any resolve he had to kill her melted with those eyes.

She uttered another growl, but this time he didn't dodge her assault. Instead, he planted his feet and unraveled a rope from his belt. She was fast, which meant he had to improvise. He had set up the hondo for his lasso earlier, but he hadn't expected to need it for the girl. He kept her at a distance until he was ready. When he swirled the rope over his head in a large lazy loop, she stared at it, captivated. The distraction didn't last very long, but Colton got the time he needed to gain momentum.

When she came at him again, he flung the rope, and it fell around her waist. When he stepped aside, momentum tightened the loop. He moved closer to her one step at a time as she struggled. If she had been in her right mind, it would've probably taken her under a minute to get out, but the way she shook and pulled at it only made the binding tighter. Her mind was gone.

He wound the excess rope under his elbow and around his hand so both of his arms would be free. She tried to dart, but the rope wouldn't let her. He knelt and grabbed both of her forearms in his hands. Her bones felt tiny and fragile beneath his grip. She tried to bite at him, but he stayed behind her. He moved the girl's two arms to one hand while he unraveled the spare rope.

A gunshot sounded, so loud that Colton jumped. He looked for Rennick, finding him in another corner of the cavern, scribbling on a wall. Mary guarded him, and let off another shot. Two men, both looking more like corpses than human, were moving closer to them. One held a large knife, and the other was a werewolf. He was partially transformed and rapidly turning into his full form. Colton's heart sank. If Kaga had a fully transformed werewolf on his side, Mary and Rennick didn't stand much of a chance.

Three ladies in ball gowns appeared around the wolf, each with a pair of pistols. The wolf lunged for the blond only an instant after she was summoned, and flung her aside. The redhead fired a shot straight through its skull, and the wolf crumpled like paper to the floor. Colton blinked. Were those women using silver rounds? If so, that meant Rennick could create a weapon to destroy any werewolf on the fly. What a terrifying thought.

Pain in his left hand made Colton look down. The girl's teeth had sunk into the skin between his thumb and forefinger. Blood oozed out and spilled along her lips. He pulled away his hand with a grunt. Black hair obscured her face as she bit madly at the air. Her mind was already gone. There might not be any coming back from it.

With caution, he tied her arms behind her, making sure the loops around her waist and legs were tight. She wiggled in place, but she couldn't get out of his knots. Good, maybe she would survive this after all.

He pulled out a knife from his belt, cut off the excess rope, and hooked it onto his belt. His hand was already healing from her bite. He didn't know if there were any other children in this mess, but if there were, he intended to do the same for them. A woman's shriek snapped his attention back upstairs. Three fully transformed werewolves towered over Rennick and Mary. When had three appeared? They also had at least ten scurrying people crawling across the side of the cavern, leaping between stalactites, using the wolves as cover.

One of Rennick's ladies, the dark-haired one, had been snatched from her siblings and shoved against the wall. The wolf tore out a huge chunk of her shoulder, blood smearing across the wall as she tried to fight back. Colton still couldn't wrap his mind around how the demon had possessed werewolves. The blond shot through the wolf's skull, but the other two wolves were moving closer.

Colton panicked at first, then he remembered they were merely illusions, not real people. But how would that impact Rennick? Their anatomy was realistic enough, at least from this distance. He hadn't even realized the illusions could bleed.

After a moment, he spotted Rennick leaning against the wall behind Mary. He clutched his head as though someone had struck him. So much for the illusions being truly invincible.

Colton cursed. He was supposed to be a distraction, but his friends were about to be slaughtered. He should have asked Rennick what happened when one of his illusions got killed. They should have discussed what to do if they got surrounded, but they didn't think there would be so many. None of them had expected it.

The plan needed to change. He leaped off the center platform and rushed across the rocky terrain, boots slipping on the loose stones that littered the cavern. He pushed past the two werewolves, one of which was now making a meal of the blond illusion. At least they were distracted.

Mary caught his eye as he rushed past, but she didn't let up on the gunfire. He reached Rennick in the back corner. His partner was holding the side of his head and his eyes were wide. He looked to be in pain, but Colton couldn't see any wound.

"Give me your dagger," Colton said.

Rennick shuddered, but then pulled the dagger out of its casing. He flipped it over in his hand and gave it to him blade-first. "Be careful with it," he said with a weary expression. "Don't let it touch you."

He nodded and narrowed his eyes. "Are you alright?"

A shriek from behind was cut short, and Rennick let out a groan. He clutched his skull with both hands and looked ready to fall to his knees. Colton put a hand on his shoulder, but that only seemed to make him angry.

"Don't worry about me, just get rid of them," Rennick hissed. "I'm finished with the inscriptions. We need to get down to where you were. Clear us a path."

He nodded. He had to trust Rennick was being honest. That losing his illusions left and right wasn't tearing apart his mind. If Rennick didn't think it was important enough to tell him the details, Colton had to trust he was right. They had to work as a team. He couldn't leave Mary alone for long, especially with only a single illusion left and two werewolves bearing down on her.

He turned just in time to see Mary dispatch another possessed man. This one didn't have any fingers left and had been creeping closer, keeping low to the ground. The last remaining werewolf was behind him, bounding forward, its muzzle wet with an illusion's blood. The last of Rennick's illusions kept trying to shoot the wolf, but he dodged the shots with ease. He was bigger than the others, probably older, too, before he had been corrupted by Kaga.

The large wolf grabbed the redhead who was the last of her sisters, and wrapped a large, clawed hand around her throat. His fingers easily met at the back of her neck. He gave a quick squeeze before he flung her over the edge and down into a chasm. Colton saw a flash of petticoats before her scream was cut short. From behind, he heard Rennick grunt as though he'd taken a hard blow. He had to hope he was still standing.

Mary hurried to Colton's side as she reloaded. "They keep coming. The more we kill, the more that appear."

"If we wanted to get Kaga's attention, I think we've done that, at least. I'll take care of shaggy." He held up the dagger, and understanding flitted across her face.

"Colt, be careful. If you let it touch you—"

"I know." He nodded, trying not to let his panic rise. "Get Rennick down to the center platform. He won't make it on his own. I'll join you soon. Just keep them away from him. Can you do that?"

"Will do. Stay safe, Colt." She hurried off behind him toward Rennick.

The large wolf stood in front of Colton with fangs

bared. He was definitely bigger than Colton was when he transformed. He reached up to wipe the sweat off his lip. This wasn't going to be easy.

The smell of Kaga's black tar was fresh on this wolf. It was almost overpowering compared to the others. It dripped from the werewolf's fur as though he'd been dipped in ink. Everywhere he stepped he left a trail of the black, slippery mess. His shoulder bled crimson. Likely a shot Mary had intended for his skull. She had far better aim than Rennick's illusions, and they had been good enough to take out most of the werewolves that had cornered them here.

Colton tightened his grip on the dagger, feeling the steel bite into his flesh. The pain was sharp, but embedding it slightly into his skin would keep his grip on the sharp end of the blade and away from the deadly hilt.

The werewolf arched backward and howled, a long moaning sound that echoed worse than the gunfire. He was calling in reinforcements. Colton winced at the noise, but moved in, hoping to catch him while he was distracted. In a few quick steps, he lunged for the wolf's bloody shoulder wound, extending the blade's handle forward, but the wolf knew his game. It cut its howl short and bounded backwards, dodging the blade. With a large paw, it nearly mauled Colton's face. He dodged away just in time.

"Alright." He huffed. "If that's how we're going to play."

He loosened the lasso on his belt. The wolf's black eyes darted down to the hand with the rope and a snarl emerged from his black slicked teeth. The bristling fur on the back of its neck was the only indication Colton had before the wolf leapt forward. He jumped backwards, but even though he missed the wolf's crushing weight, its long arms still snagged him. Its black nails hooked into his calves and Colton cried out. The wolf stared into his eyes as it crawled forward, digging another set of claws into his thigh. Colton groaned; the wolf's eyes narrowed.

The pain was what it wanted. It no longer suffered from hunger or any of the other normal troubles. Pain was what it fed on now.

As the wolf moved forward again and its claws dug deeper, Colton bit back a groan. It didn't like that. The wolf snarled and leaned its head near his face, its muzzle so close he could smell the putrid scent of its breath: a mixture of old meat and black gunk. When it finally went to take a bite out of his neck, Colton made his move. He spun to the side, grunting as the claws in his thigh dragged through his muscle and skin. In the same fluid motion, he brought the butt of the dagger up to the wolf's shoulder wound. The hilt was an inch away when much to his surprise, the wolf released him and scrambled out of the way.

"Damn!" Colton cried.

With one large, clawed hand, it grabbed hold of Colton's forearm bearing the dagger. It gave a deep, reverberating growl and forced the dagger into the sky, like showing off a prize. The wolf had played him just as he had played it. He had anticipated his move. That meant there was more to this wolf than the mindless actions of Kaga's other victims. He had a mind, and with it, the ability to strategize, possibly just as well as when he had been alive.

"I admit it, you're good," Colton muttered as the wolf squeezed his arm. The pain increased tenfold. He guessed that the wolf was attempting to break his arm, or tear off the limb. Colton had to move quickly. Since the wolf was no longer pinning him, he pushed up to his feet, grabbed the wolf's arm for leverage and flung himself up onto the crouching wolf's shoulders. It certainly hadn't expected that!

With a flurry of claws and snarls, it reached up and tried to throw him off with its free hand. It wasn't about to let go of Colton's arm, which still gripped the knife, but it had a bad angle now.

He dropped down, keeping his legs together, and landed at the base of the wolf's long, bushy tail. He hit with his boots right at the coccyx, where the spine extended outward, with as much force as he could muster. The wolf howled in pain and his free arm scratched long slices into Colton's back. Searing pain tore through him, but he stood fast.

The wolf spun, trying to drag him against the stone wall. But its claws were still dug into Colton's arm and it was still a difficult angle. He clung tight to the wolf's long hair and jumped up, landing on the base of its spine again. The bones crunched beneath his heels and the wolf howled in pain. Its tail was now bent at an odd angle. Finally, the wolf let go of Colton's arm.

"Sorry, pal." Colton plunged the hilt of the dagger into the bloody shoulder wound left by Mary's bullet, digging it around the gaping hole before pulling it free and dismounting the wolf's back.

It clawed at the wound with frightened whimpers. Already it had turned a smoky gray with the poison. Colton turned away. It was bad enough taking down such a good fighter, but having to watch his body melt away from the silver was too gruesome. He flung the blood off of the hilt of the dagger as the wolf howled in pain, already growing weaker.

Colton looked down at the center platform. Rennick was back to back with Mary, and their guns were blazing. Kaga's puppets surrounded them. Colton started down with the blade of the knife still digging into his palm. The pain wouldn't last forever though, and that knowledge helped him ignore it. The claw wounds in his back and legs were already healing. Mary and Rennick were fighting off a hoard of eight wall crawlers who had to be terribly quick to avoid Mary's aim. They were likely the reinforcements the wolf had called in, and Colton kicked himself for letting it summon them.

As a whole, they had grossly underestimated Kaga's minions, but he hoped that Rennick really was ready to start the ritual. If not, Colton wasn't sure they would see daylight again.

Chapter 31

Word Games

By the time Colton reached the center of the room, half of the attackers had been dropped, but four more still remained. His friends were in the center of a ring of corpses, standing back to back. Mary reloaded, but Rennick's shots were off. He hit a leg here, an arm there, another in the stomach. All it did was slow them, not drop them. What the hell was he doing? Perhaps losing his illusions in such a gruesome manner was too much for him to handle.

Once he was close enough, Colton fired a bullet into a woman's head who was crawling too close to Mary. The woman clutched wildly at her skull for a moment before collapsing. Colton stepped over her and fired another shot at a man closing in on Rennick. He was limping from one of Rennick's stray bullets, but he ought to be downed.

"What the hell are you doing?" he growled.

Rennick's gun arm was shaking so bad it was a wonder he was able to shoot at all. "I'm sorry," he whispered.

Abruptly, he dropped his gun arm and put a hand to his head. He was paler than he had been earlier, too. "I don't know what's wrong. I feel... off for some reason."

Mary dispatched the remaining creatures and, like a well-oiled machine, moved to reload despite the empty cavern. "You can say that again, Ren. I didn't realize I'd be the one carrying this fight. Who knew you were such a terrible shot?" She was smiling, but the smile faded as she got a better look at him. "You do look bad. Are you okay?"

"I don't know." Rennick stumbled outside of the ring of bodies at their feet and leaned against a large boulder. "I feel weak... ill or something. It's odd. I've never felt sick before."

"Maybe you didn't fully recover from being Kaga's minion," Colton whispered, his mind racing with what that could entail. If Rennick was never fully released from Kaga's hold, he could still not be fully in control of his actions, another one of Kaga's many puppets. With the addition of his illusions being slain above, it might be enough pressure to let Kaga gain control of him once again.

"Don't look at me like that," Rennick said. "I was fine earlier. I don't think that's it."

Mary holstered one of her guns, but she kept the other ready as she scanned above and around them. "It was something upstairs wasn't it? You started moving slower. I thought it was part of that ritual."

"Did something attack you up there?" Colton asked.

"Nothing attacked me, but every time I put up an insignia it felt like something leeched from me. Controlling the girls became more and more difficult. Then they started dropping. I should have been able to take all of them on without help." He sighed in disgust. "I'm lucky you came, Mary."

She smiled, the firelight from a torch flickering across her face. "You keep flattering me like that, Ren, and I may just forgive you for stealing my house."

He chuckled, pointing a lazy finger at her. "I'm going to remember that. If we get out of here, that is." His voice wavered.

"We'll get out of here," Colton said. "Don't start talking like that. The ritual is ready; we just need Kaga."

Rennick slumped down against the boulder and closed his eyes.

"Ren," Mary asked as she crouched down beside him. "Is it normal for it to drain you like this?"

"I don't know," he said with a half-smile. "I've only ever read about them. This is the first one I've done."

Mary and Colton exchanged worried glances. Normally, Colton would berate him for failing to mention the detail earlier, but if it was their only chance at destroying Kaga, what choice did they have? Surely, Rennick had realized that, too, but it was too late for that now. He turned around the room, scanning the cavern walls for anything else that might try to take them by surprise. Colton spotted the tunnel entrance they had come through earlier.

"What the hell?" He pointed up to where the entrance used to be. The wall looked completely solid now, as though the tunnel had never existed. "Where the hell did it go?"

Mary gasped and Rennick climbed to his feet.

"When could he have done that?" Mary asked. "We haven't even seen him."

"He has ways of moving things around without our knowledge." Rennick shook his head as the others turned to him. "Kaga did that to me with a window the other day, too. That's how he caught me. One minute the window was broken, and the next it was repaired, as though I had never gone through it."

"Can ghosts do that?" Mary asked.

Colton scoffed. "Looks like they can now. Add that to the list of surprises on Kaga's list. I didn't think he had werewolves under his control, but I was off on that one, too."

"He's played us," Mary stated flatly. "We've walked right into his hands."

"Indeed you have." The sickeningly sweet voice of Kaga echoed down from the tunnel before them. Slowly, the creature pulled itself into view. Colton had only glimpsed Kaga's shadowy shape before, having to guess what the demon looked like. In full sight, he was more disturbing than anything Colton could have imagined.

Rolls of tissue made up the chest and belly that fell down to the ground and made the dry scratching noise that accompanied his movement. The angled projections stuck out from the sides of his body at first reminded Colton of the legs of an ant, but now he could look at them, he recognized them as bones. Human leg bones, a couple of animal bones, even the frail bones of a cat. They moved asynchronously, jutting out from the pink mangled tissue that made up the bulk of his body like candles embedded on a birthday cake. He had no arms except for the appendages Colton could see, but his face was even more grotesque.

Kaga might have at one point known what a demon's face ought to look like, but his view of it had been tainted by years, possibly decades, even centuries of living this hellish existence. A few parts might have passed as a traditional demon, such as the bull horns poking through the top of his cranium. The face, however, was impossibly deformed. Bits of flesh and tissue tried to form a forehead, cheeks, and a gaping hole made up its mouth. Kaga had used a series of rusty nails as teeth in whatever shape and size he could find. The nose consisted of two small holes just above the larger one for the mouth, and the eyes... The eyes would haunt Colton for the rest of his life, however brief that might be.

Having two eyes alone wasn't enough for Kaga, he had to have six. Some of the eyes might have once been human, but were yellowed and decayed. One of the fresher ones looked to have been from a bull or cow, and two looked like the small eyes of children. There was no order to their placement across its face, just apparently wherever Kaga felt they would appear the most sinister. As disgusting as Kaga was, Colton saw now how Rennick had come to the conclusion that he had once been human. Kaga had the mix-matched appearance of a creature emulating a horror, not quite knowing what he was mimicking. It gave Colton an odd sense of relief to know he wasn't a real demon. Surely, a real one wouldn't have such a sloppy, uneven appearance.

"My goodness, you have been busy." Kaga's many eyes moved in different directions around the cavern. His mouth curved up into a smile and the nails of his teeth bit into the thick tissue of his mouth. He didn't have to move his mouth to speak, his voice simply emerged. Colton thought back to the little boy, Rennick's illusion, who had spoken to him in the tunnels. Kaga projected his voice through an illusion, so it was probably just as easy for him to project it through this heap of flesh.

Mary gave a strange mix of a gasp and a scream and backed away. Colton glanced to his partner. Rennick's eyes were hard and he gave Colton a disturbing smile. Clearly, his partner had a crazy idea in mind, but Colton hadn't a clue what it might be. Then he remembered his role: he was supposed to be the distraction. He needed to get its attention, even though that was the last thing he wanted to do. Somehow, he found his voice to speak.

"Your puppet victims didn't last long," Colton said and stepped out ahead of Rennick and Mary.

"My *victims*?" Kaga's long laugh echoed along the walls of the cavern.

He didn't care one bit about the lives he had destroyed. To him they were merely parts, the fabric needed to make his macabre body. Only a few feet away from them was the ring of bodies Mary and Rennick had finished off moments before. Beyond that, the little girl Colton had tied up squirmed against her bonds like a wild animal. Looking at her snarling and trying to bite at her ropes, a terrible rage filled him.

Kaga was no demon, regardless of how he tried. He was nothing more than a pathetic copycat trying to be something he could never hope to be. He was a twisted and disgusting man who had been somehow left to his own devices after his body died. His obsession to be some intangible force of evil consumed him. Of course, he had to have been a human once. A real demon wouldn't need the conviction of others to prove its evil. A spineless, self-conscious, doubtful human would, though. Now here they were surrounded by death and waste. So many lives had been lost, and what for? The whim of a mad ghost.

"I imagine you know now why I allowed you to come," Kaga crooned. "Even demons long for fun once in a while. Killing people all day can get so boring. You have no idea."

"Why the charade?" Colton asked, "Why even let us go to begin with?"

"To give you hope, of course! How miserable your deaths would have been. You were two broken animals, brought down with hardly a finger from me. A little pushing, a little prodding, perhaps, but little more than that. You lived up to my expectations, though, and came back to me. I knew you would."

Colton clenched a fist. "And the people you tortured? You did it for fun, I suppose?"

"My dear Mr. Fen, I can see how it could be difficult for such a simple wolf like you to understand. These people"—he looked around the room at the piles of bodies—"they need something to fear, something to fight against, someone to terrify them when they close their eyes at night. That is what I do, what I provide. It is as necessary to this world as the very houses of God. Surely a cursed beast like you should know that."

"Necessary?" Rennick narrowed his eyes, "Those people you controlled, how exactly did they need you? How could they possibly tell their children stories about you at night? Did they spread the word of how to properly fear you? Did they worship you like some unholy deity? No, of course not. You wouldn't let them. Why would you want that, when you could have them here as your slaves? You didn't want stories of your ill deeds. You're fooling yourself if you think you did this for some higher purpose. You just wanted to see the fear and pain in their eyes. You tortured and abused them until they were all used up. All due to your silly pride. You aren't a demon, Kaga. To call you that would be an insult to any real demons that might exist."

An anxious twitching went through Kaga's bony limbs like the shivering of a tree branch in the wind.

"Anyone can claim to be a demon," Colton said, staring straight into a pair of Kaga's eyes. "I think you relished torture even when you were alive, didn't you? This whole charade of following a higher power is just an excuse for your sadism."

Rennick gave Colton a warning look, as though he was treading too close to the edge.

All six of Kaga's eyes were focused on him now, and Colton felt a shiver go down his spine.

"That is not the case," Kaga said. "God has given me a new purpose, a new place. Why else would he force me to remain here? He has given me the strength to do these things. The ability to control and to punish. When they beg for God's mercy, I refuse it for him."

"What gives you that right?" Colton asked. "Who says that you have any right to kill them? Just because you're confused doesn't mean you can take it out on anyone."

When Rennick sucked in a breath, Colton gave him a curious look. He must have said something he shouldn't have, though he wasn't sure what that could have been. Rennick kept glancing his way, to warn him, but Colton wasn't sure where the line was. This was what they wanted him to do after all, to distract Kaga.

Kaga smiled and his misshapen mouth curved upwards unequally, the nails digging into the flabby flesh of his lips.

"My simplistic little wolf." Kaga chuckled. "You and I are rather alike, wouldn't you say?"

Colton faltered. "What?"

"You don't have to kill in order to survive, do you? Yet you do it. You do it without guilt and without much hesitation." Kaga broke out into a low laugh. "You don't even limit yourself to humans like I do. You kill your own kind."

A heaviness came upon him under Kaga's words. He thought of the werewolf he had finished off just a few moments ago, an older, stronger, and more seasoned wolf. He thought of the trio from the pack he and Mary had killed in the back alley. Then he remembered the gang of thieves he and Rennick had murdered near the stream. His heart sank and his body trembled. He knew Kaga was merely twisting his emotions into a knot, but despite that, the truth resonated deep inside. As much as Kaga twisted words, the little truth there felt like a hot iron in his gut.

Colton knew his own weaknesses. Hell, Rennick had even pointed it out to him beside the stream that day. He had always hated what he was, but Kaga must have seen it, too. The demon knew just what words to say to slip the knife in and tear at his core. Kaga had a very good point. When pushed into a corner, when bled near to death, when starvation gnawed at his belly, Colton's high grounded morals were quick to decay.

He could talk about how much he hated what he was, but did that change anything? Did that prevent him from slaughtering thieves just because they pumped a shot into him? Colton had literally jumped in front of it, too, as Rennick pointed out. Had he wanted to get hit? Deep down, did he really want to give in to that animal impulse and tear those poor fools to shreds? A hand came down on Colton's shoulder, and then Rennick stepped in front.

"That's a rather low blow," Rennick said in a snide tone. "I don't think I've ever heard such a blatant lie, and you could say I'm a bit of a connoisseur of lies. If anything, Colton is your very opposite, you pathetic, cruel, little man. You look at his body count and assume you must have something in common, but you don't."

Colton stared at him in utter bewilderment. Rennick was defending him? He thought his partner could barely stand him. Yet, here he was taking down a self-proclaimed demon as though he were speaking to a theater patron.

Rennick took Colton's chin in his hand. "First of all, you see this face? This is one handsome man. I'm sorry, Colton, but it's true. Now I don't know where you got the idea of what a demon looks like but..." He gestured to Kaga's mismatched face. "But you're really off the mark! You don't exactly look terrifying to me, just sloppy. Lazy, even."

He put a hand across Colton's shoulders, leaned in and tapped a hand on Colton's chest. Colton didn't have a clue how to react.

"Second of all, you make it sound as though my friend here loves to kill. I think anyone who has killed at his side before would be quick to point out how much he hates what he is. I mean absolutely loathes it. With such a passion that I'm pretty sure if we let him"—Rennick leaned forward and put his hand beside his mouth as though telling a secret—"he'd run off and go live under a rock somewhere. And every time he even thought about killing someone or transforming into a werewolf or even look at a good pair of legs, *BAM*! He tortures himself for it." He slapped a hand against his back. "That's simply how he is!"

Kaga was silent and all eyes focused closely on Rennick now. He might be stunned, but it was hard to tell with a nonexistent face. That was what made Colton realize Rennick was right. He was exaggerating, of course, and taking some dangerous liberties, but in the end he was right.

Rennick turned his back on Kaga and began to pace. It was such a simple motion, but it changed everything. Colton no longer felt like they were staring down some hideous beast they couldn't possibly hope to defeat, but a frightened man with far too much power. That was something Colton had done plenty of times before. For the first time since Kaga appeared, he felt like they actually stood a chance.

"While you sit down here in your ugly cave and get your kicks off on torturing people, my self-proclaimed martyr over here is wallowing in self pity." Rennick's eyes narrowed, "In fact, I bet you haven't felt a shred of pity your entire life *or* death. Don't you think so, Colton?"

He caught the gleam in Rennick's eye and couldn't say how incredibly grateful he felt. He nodded, knowing full well, now, this wasn't just his partner coming to his rescue, but Rennick was trying to anger Kaga into action.

"I don't think he knows the meaning of the word pity." Colton smiled.

"I was a man of God!" Kaga's cry echoed throughout the cavern. "I was given a new life, a new purpose! He showed me how it was to be done, and I've excelled at his order. I've proven myself to him in ways that you simple beasts could not fathom." His eyes moved between the two men before settling between them. His gaping mouth shifted into that terrible grin.

"What about you, my dear?" Kaga hissed through his rusted metal teeth.

"I-I don't know," Mary whispered. Colton gave out a shaky breath as his confidence faltered. From her voice alone, he could tell she was overwhelmed. He hadn't heard that fear from her the entire time they had traveled underground, but when confronted with Kaga's grotesque face, now it surfaced.

He glanced over to her and the terror on her face made his heart sink. Kaga would never be able to ignore such fear. He wasn't sure where Rennick planned to go with this, but he hoped he got there soon. If Rennick was just bluffing, and as a card shark that was completely plausible, they were doomed. Try as he might, though, Colton couldn't read a damn thing on his partner's face.

"Do I look like a demon to you, my child?" Kaga whispered.

"Not quite," she whispered, her voice wavering.

Rennick openly stared at her now, despair clear across his face. Any hopes Colton had in Rennick's plot faded quickly.

"Mary..." Rennick whispered, but it was too late. She

had already shown she was the weakest of their group, and made herself an easy target.

Mary's voice was so small she almost sounded like a child. "The demons I imagined never looked like you. They were..." Her voice caught and her glassy eyes were wide. "They were different."

Kaga's laughter emerged again as he looked up toward the ceiling of the cavern. "Different. I can be different."

CHAPTER 32

JUDGMENT

COLTON HEARD THE CHAINS RATTLE ABOVE AND instinct kicked in. He lunged for Mary, wrapped his arms around her, and pulled her out of the way. A loud crash sounded as they fell to the ground, arms and legs splayed together.

Three large carcasses had landed, surrounded by the thick metal chain that had hung them. One of them was the bull's torso, but the other two were human. Unlike the bull, the human bodies were more or less whole. Their skin was gone, but everything else was accounted for. Their faces were contorted into fleshy, grinning skulls. Flies buzzed around them, not at all fazed by the drop. The smell made him want to gag.

Mary got to her feet. "What is he doing?"

"I imagine he's trying to be creative," Rennick muttered, rushing over to help Colton to his feet.

The bull's carcass split down the center, ripping with the wet snap of tearing muscle and bone. Half of it flew toward Kaga, the tissue twisting and contorting to mold to his needs. An upper arm first, then a lower arm to match, wrapping the two parts together with strips of the flesh bound so tight they could have been rope. The other half of the bull flew next, creating a second fleshy arm to match. The chain was next. It skewered Kaga straight through his bulbous body and wrapped around each of the limbs like ivy around a tree branch.

One of the human arms was next, and it snapped in four places in mid-air. It took hardly any effort on Kaga's part. A bone was no more difficult to break than a twig. The arm continued to snap until Kaga had made two pincer like hands out of the single limb. He attached these to his newly created arms. Kaga was smiling.

This was his whole purpose. This was the reason Kaga hadn't killed them before, and why he had allowed them to return. They were his petrified audience, and once he was done putting on this act, they would no longer be needed. He would then turn his full fury on them trapped so deep underground there would be no escape.

Colton moved closer to Rennick, never letting his gaze drop from Kaga's display. "We're dead, aren't we," he whispered.

He didn't know why he was even asking. He knew the answer already, but he had to know Rennick was out of options, too. He had to know if it was truly hopeless. He had to be certain if these would be their last minutes alive.

Rennick gave a mischievous smile. "Didn't I tell you I had a backup plan?"

Colton blanched. "That's right, you did, didn't you?"

"Explosives."

Colton stared at him. "So that means we're definitely dead, then."

"Not exactly, but we'll need to make a run for it soon. I want you to grab Mary. I'll catch up with you."

"What are you talking about? We don't have anywhere to run to. He blocked up the entrance, and I'm not about to go running through the tunnel of horrors he came from."

"Don't argue with me on this," he said, his voice lowering. "Just keep him busy. I need time to finish the ritual."

"If you say so," Colton said.

Kaga finished constructing his new limbs. The spidery legs picked up his sluggish girth, and he scuttled closer to them, bringing with him a cloud of flies. Colton stepped in front of Mary when Kaga's head loomed in close.

"Is this more like what your were taught to fear as a child, my dear? Is *this* a demon from your nightmares?" When his voice boomed into their minds, Colton reached back to take Mary's hand in his. Her fingers felt icy. He turned his attention to Kaga.

Guns were going to be rather useless against a monster that already had a chain going through his body. They would only be good for a distraction at best. Since Kaga's entire body was made up of dead parts, how could Colton possibly do any damage to it?

Kaga's eyes shifted between them. "Do you really think you can protect her?"

It was a simple enough question, but it meant Kaga's show was far from over. He wouldn't just kill them; he was planning something worse.

"If you want her, you'll have to go through me," Colton said.

Mary punched his shoulder. "No!"

Kaga reared up on his skeletal legs. "Excellent! This will be great fun!" He stretched out a fleshy arm. At first, Colton thought he was going to strike him, but then he spotted the chain in the air. It had unwrapped from Kaga's other arm and curved backward like a snake. Before Colton could fully understand what Kaga was trying to do, the chain extended out and whipped around Mary's body. In a panic she fired a shot before her arm was pinned to her side. Her scream pulled Colton free from his stupor.

"Mary!" he cried and lunged at her even as the chain picked her up off the ground. Colton gripped tight to the chains and he was also hoisted into the air with her.

Kaga brought them both up to his hideous gaze. "Oh, I was hoping you would join us." Kaga hissed. "She is lovely. Perhaps I'll flay her alive like I did the others. You had best fight for her, little werewolf."

Kaga's laughter made Colton's blood boil. He extended his claws out on his free hand and looked at the chain wrapped around Mary's body. He didn't know what good it would do to cut them off of her. Kaga could just pick them up again and use them as projectiles or something. Hell, he didn't even know if his claws could cut chains.

"Best be careful." Kaga growled. Abruptly, they moved and the sudden jolt made him dizzy. "You might want to think that through more."

Colton looked down to see Kaga was holding them over one of the deep, endless chasms that littered the cavern. His eyes went wide and he glanced at Mary. Tears rolled down her cheeks.

"Damn it, Rennick!" he cried, "do something!" He turned to look back toward the center of the cavern; Rennick didn't appear to be listening. Instead, he was rummaging through that stupid bag he'd brought with him. Rennick looked up with wide, fearful eyes. Why hadn't he rigged the explosives earlier? It was too late to do it now. Wasn't he supposed to at least be working on the ritual?

Mary screamed so loud it made his eardrums hurt.

"Calm down!" Colton yelled. "We'll figure a way out of this."

Kaga laughed, and Mary cocked her head to the side and whispered, "On my order, cut the chain." Her eyes flashed down to the long piece of chain that extended from her to Kaga's grotesque body.

"What? But—" He looked down at the chasm beneath their feet. "We won't survive that."

From his peripheral vision, Rennick's movement caught Colton's eye. He glanced over to see Rennick had pulled something from his bag. It looked like a knife, but the blade was as dark as coal.

"Colton," Mary hissed, and he turned back to her. She gave him the most deadly, nerve-shattering glare Colton had ever seen. Then, in a flash, the look was gone, and she was screaming again, at such a pitch he was certain he would soon be deaf.

That look stayed with him, though. Hell, it might just be emblazoned on his nightmares. Mary, he realized, was putting on a show of her own, and her acting skills were far better than anything Colton had expected. It also meant he needed to play along and not direct attention over to his partner. Colton was still in charge of distraction, and it looked like Mary had joined him. His fingers shook as he started pulling on her chains.

He tried to keep an eye on Rennick who looked to be in the midst of the most bizarre ritual he had ever seen. Both of Rennick's hands were covered in blood, but without looking too closely, Colton couldn't tell where the blood had come from. Kaga's laughter rose as Colton and Mary swung from one side of the cavern to another, forcing Colton to hold on or fall. He thought he might puke if it kept up, but Mary was in hysterics. She was sobbing, screaming, pleading, and struggling so much Colton would have been just as taken as Kaga by her performance.

Another chain shot up from Kaga. This one aimed for Colton. It wrapped around his free arm and pulled his hand behind his back.

Colton let out a cry as it pulled just hard enough to hurt, then he felt the metal wrap around his other wrist as well. He needed that arm. He was using it hang on to Mary, otherwise he was going to fall into the pit. The chain pulled harder, but unless he dug his claws into Mary's shoulder, he wouldn't hold on for long.

"Put your legs around me," Mary cried. "Quick!"

A flush went up his cheeks, but he did as Mary asked. He wrapped his legs tight around her waist to keep from falling. They were now face to face in a position that would have had most women blushing, but Mary was focused.

He winced and gave a strained, "Sorry."

She smiled at him.

Colton vaguely noticed Rennick crouched in the distance, planting two bloody palms down on the ground. A breeze erupted and spread across the cavern, as though an enormous door had been opened. Everything shook, and a few stalactites fell from above.

Colton looked back at Mary. "Did he just cause an earthquake?"

She shook her head.

Kaga's laughter ended. His grotesque smile faded, and it took a moment for the bony legs to turn his body around. "What was that?"

Rennick stood, no longer pale and weak like he was earlier. "This is how we make our exit." He smiled and bowed with a flourish.

Colton stared at him wide-eyed. Had he lost his mind? There had to be more to the plan than just explosives. Rennick's hands were still covered with blood. If all he did was plant explosives, it didn't explain the wind. Something cold dug into his waist and he looked down to see Mary had squeezed the barrel of a gun out between the ropes of chain that bound her.

"Think you can help me out here?" she asked.

"I would but—" He pulled at the chains that bound his hands together again.

"Might want to lean back a bit then."

Colton eyed the gun currently jammed in his waist and shifted his body to the side with his legs. Mary was able to push the rest of the gun out between the chains.

"There we go. Now, Colt," she whispered, "I'm about to cut us loose. Do you think you can keep us from hitting down too hard?"

He looked down into the black maw beneath their feet. "I can try."

She smiled then leaned forward and planted a kiss on his cheek. "You can do better than that, can't you?"

His eyes went wide and a flush moved up his cheeks, but before he could answer, a series of shots rang out. The two of them were flying through the air. They were falling. Colton realized the chain around his wrists was no longer tight. He didn't have time to question or hesitate. Pulling her into his arms, he turned them mid-air so he would hit first. All the same, they hit the ground hard.

The air slammed out of his lungs and the flesh ripped apart on his back as they skidded across the stone. Then his head struck something hard and the world spun.

For several moments, everything was blurred and distant. Mary got to her feet, still bound tight by the chains Kaga had used on her. She no longer had her pistol, though the hand that had held it was bloody and raw, likely from the impact. He couldn't hear anything, but he saw the pain in her face. She looked down at him; her lips were moving, but he didn't understand what she was saying. All he could hear was a high-pitched scream. It took a moment for him to realize the noise was coming from Kaga.

Mary must have shot through his chains, but Colton had no clue how she made that work. The momentum of the recoil had steered them clear of the pit, but it certainly hadn't saved them. It merely bought them time.

"Get up!" Mary cried. This time Colton could hear her clearly.

The back of his head felt wet from the impact and his back was raw, but he was able to breathe again, so he got to his feet. The ground felt like it was tilting sideways. He wasn't sure if his head injury was fully to blame because stalactites and debris were falling from above. The entire cavern was collapsing. Colton looked to Rennick in the distance, but he was a far more difficult prey for Kaga to catch than Colton and Mary.

Chains flew everywhere, whipping left and right, but Rennick was too quick. In the blink of an eye, he would move from one location to the next, and Kaga's chains were too slow to keep up. Then he noticed Kaga's body dragging in places. A few of his spidery legs dragged instead of holding his body up, and his head lolled to the side.

"It's too much for him," Colton said, his head still foggy and dimly aware of a warm wetness trickling down the back of his neck. "He's losing control of his body."

It required energy and concentration to control so much, and Rennick's speed was pushing the spirit to his limits. Kaga's grand performance at playing a demon was turning out to be his downfall. Colton spotted the entrance to the tunnel that lead to the surface; it was no longer blocked. Another tremor shook the cavern, and Mary nearly fell to the ground. She was having trouble keeping her balance with her arms pinned to her sides and leaned heavily against Colton.

He extended his black claws and cut carefully through the chains. The links didn't cut easily; Colton's claws were made for slicing through bone, not metal. Once Mary was free, he tore through the two chains still hanging from his own wrists and together they started for the tunnel.

A few steps into the entrance of the tunnel, he paused. "What's taking him?" he asked.

"I don't know," she muttered. "He just said to make it look good, and at the first chance, run for it. I have no idea what he's done."

Colton had never heard of any ritual that could bring forth an earthquake. A few simple symbols and a bit of blood shouldn't be able to bring forth that kind of power. He had caught Rennick's gaze a couple of times since he and Mary had reached the entrance of the tunnel, but his partner didn't look keen on catching up with them. Instead, he was keeping Kaga in the center of the chamber; but Colton could see him occasionally crouch down whenever he was at Kaga's back. He wasn't sure what Rennick was doing at first, then the first stick of dynamite exploded.

All around Kaga, dynamite went off like firecrackers. Each one blew off a chunk of his body and made a gaping hole in the rocky ground. Rennick leapt off the platform with a cry, "Judico!"

Out from each of the five symbols on the walls exploded yellow beams of light, surrounding Kaga in a brilliant sphere. A few of his spidery legs flew through the air as more explosions rocked the cavern. Soon, everything was obscured by clouds of dirt and smoke, then Rennick emerged from the haze.

"What did you do?" Colton asked.

"We destroyed him, of course!" Face covered in debris, Rennick smiled. He was panting, but he looked quite pleased. "I had to make sure he stayed on that platform, though, otherwise—"

"Look!" Mary cried.

The strange breeze cleared the smoke. A ball of light floated in the air. Kaga's body was a heaping mass of shredded flesh on the ground near the circle of bodies from earlier. Although his body was gone, his spiritual form, what must have been his true human form, hovered within the ball of light. He was a tall, gaunt man dressed all in black. At his throat were two rectangular pieces of white cloth that draped down to his chest. His eyes were dark. He grinned at the three of them.

Kaga was laughing. Not in their heads any longer, Colton could hear his deep voice reverberate against the stone walls.

"Very good!" he cried, "I'm most impressed! I didn't expect you to have any skill in the dark arts, but here you are."

Rennick was stunned. "I don't get it. That ritual is supposed to destroy him!"

"Perhaps it works on your lesser spirits, but not on me." When Kaga smiled, even though his face had a human appearance, the similarity to the gruesome smile of his grotesque form was uncanny. "I'll admit that you trapped me, but I'm in no rush. I will exist far longer than these stone walls will. All I must do is wait for them to crumble."

"But that's not possible," Rennick muttered, stepping forward. He turned to Colton and Mary with eyes wide. "That's simply not possible. It was supposed to bring judgment!"

Colton put a hand on his partner's shoulder, but he addressed Kaga. "That's fine, we'll just have to contact the Agency to take care of you, now that you're contained."

Kaga's smile faltered.

"If they can't destroy you, then I'm sure they can find something to do with you. Maybe lock you in a lamp, or trap you in a painting. Either way, you'll wish you could die by the end of it."

Mary stood on the other side of Rennick. "Come on," she whispered, "don't let him get to you."

Rennick looked crestfallen. He wouldn't budge when they wanted to head back up top. Colton was about to pick him up, regardless, when the ground shook beneath their feet. The back wall behind Kaga came tumbling down.

It was the opening Colton had stood in front of earlier when trying to spot Kaga, but once the whole wall fell, they could see how large the tunnel was. Farther into the tunnel, were the other bodies Rennick had mentioned. He was glad he hadn't entered it earlier. The entire chamber shuddered again. Colton expected it to be the start of many other collapses, but it wasn't. The strange breeze died down and a rhythmic sound like drums filled the air.

"What is this?" Kaga asked, his voice small and trembling.

A hissing noise came. At first, Colton thought it sounded like a steam leak. Something he might normally hear near the railroad. Then he realized it came in a breathing pattern, in and out. An enormous fist slammed down amid the rubble, right next to where Kaga was held. With wrinkled skin the color of grayish blue stone, it reminded Colton of elephant hide.

"Rennick?" he asked, but his partner looked just as dumbfounded.

Out of the opening came a creature larger than anything Colton had ever seen in his life. It walked out onto the center platform, knuckles dragging on the ground like a gorilla. It looked like a man, but so large it filled the tunnel opening. It had a long snout with eyes on either side of its head like a deer. Its eyes gleamed a dim yellow like the fires of lanterns. Giant antlers stuck out from the top of its head. Dirt fell from the ends.

"Colton, remember that cave we found the other night?" Rennick's voice was hoarse. "Remember how I thought I felt like an insect in front of it?"

A chill went down Colton's spine. He remembered the feeling of its gaze on his back as they fled across the desert. "Is this... an unexplainable?"

Rennick nodded in mute terror.

"I don't believe it," Mary whispered, stepping forward. "It's like the Jogahs, like the Gahongas, and Odhows. My mother used to tell me stories about them. My father used to say they were nature spirits. But they were so small in the stories, never like this."

The creature lifted its head and sniffed the air, and its massive antlers dragged against the cavern ceiling, tossing down more debris. Its large eyes searched the cavern, and that was when Colton noticed movement around the antlers. The hissing noise he had thought was its breathing was actually a swarm of tiny, buzzing, insect-like creatures flying around the spirit's horns like a swarm of bees. There must have been hundreds of them, and they gave off a dim light like blue-green fireflies.

"What are those?" he asked. Something about the little sprites was entrancing. Watching them fly through the air brought about a strange calm. He felt dazed as he watched them drift.

"They look like its minions." Mary's face was transfixed with wonder and she had tears in her eyes. "The Odhows,

Mother used to say, they prevent the spirits of the underworld from rising to our world. They're defenders, protectors of our world. Maybe that's kind of what this is."

The large creature shook its head, and more of the little minions emerged from the antlers. Like a swarm of butterflies they flew around the cavern, taking in everything, examining all parts of it. A few flew in circles around one of the hanging corpses. With streaks of blue-green light, the minions circled the symbols Rennick had marked into the walls, and then around the beams of yellow light holding Kaga in place.

"Stay back!" Kaga warned, flattening himself on the opposite side of his spherical prison. "Stay away from me!"

Slowly, the unexplainable took in the entirety of the room. Colton had the impression of a general surveying a battlefield. Every step it took shook the chamber. It stared down at the pile of bodies in the center of the cavern near Kaga's hovering form, and at the mound of flesh that remained of Kaga's body, its nostrils flaring.

The swarm of minions moved toward the corpses like a flock of birds. They covered the them like bees on a honeycomb. The giant creature turned its head toward Kaga and its eyes gleamed brighter. Abruptly, the flock moved towards Kaga.

"Stay back!" Kaga cried again when several minions flew easily into his cage. He flung an arm out at one, but even though it was flung away, the others flooded in. "Don't come any closer." He sobbed. The tiny minions began to cover him.

Colton's heart thundered in his chest. "What are they doing? I don't understand. Why is he frightened of them?"

Mary had a hand over her mouth. "They're herders of the dead. They prevent them from causing harm, and punish those that do."

"My God," Rennick whispered. "I didn't know..."

Suddenly, all the minions pulled away from Kaga. When they did, each pulled off a tendril of shadow; each tendril looked like black, wet taffy, and reminded Colton of the gunk that had filled Rennick when he had been possessed.

Kaga screamed.

The flying minions moved so quickly Colton couldn't keep track of them. They zoomed around Kaga and he looked like a giant blue-green bonfire of light. Kaga's cries shifted into shrieks of pain. Each time they flew by, the flying minions tore out another piece of him, pulling free another tendril of black ooze and dropping them like strands of hair to the ground. There must have been hundreds of them, and like a series of razor blades, the minions dismantled Kaga piece by piece, much like he must have done to his victims.

The little girl, the one Colton had tied up, was still in the corner and still struggling to get loose. He had completely forgotten about her and panic heated in his chest. Kaga's wails echoed to a higher pitch and the cavern floor was littered with strands of black tendrils. The creature turned its head toward the girl.

Colton's mouth went dry. He didn't want to see her taken apart like Kaga. It wasn't fair, she didn't have a choice in what she became. She was a victim pulled into Kaga's madness. He took a step forward, but Rennick's fingers dug into his shoulder.

"Don't," Rennick warned. "We have to let them decide. Besides, they could kill you in an—"

One of the minions moved so quickly Colton barely had time to register it. The girl's head toppled to the side and blood oozed from the stump of her neck. Mary gasped. A scream caught in the back of Colton's throat as the girl's head rolled across the ground.

Numbly, he said, "I don't understand. Why?"

"I don't know." Rennick's voice was hollow.

The minions were spreading out to the rest of the bodies. One of the werewolves that hadn't been killed with silver fell to black ash at a single touch.

"We need to get out of here," Mary whispered, her voice tight. "Now."

"Come on," Rennick urged, pulling at Colton's shoulder.

He turned, trying his best to ignore the horror that threatened to overwhelm him. He picked up Mary and ran up the tunnel as fast as he could. Rennick could have easily outpaced him, but instead stayed close.

He ought to be keeping his ears alert for any more surprises, but his mind, instead, replayed the image of that little girl's head falling off her shoulders. Kaga wouldn't harm anyone else again. That much made him pleased, but this was no victory. Anything that ended in such cruelty couldn't really be considered a success, could it?

CHAPTER 33

UP FOR AIR

THE BREEZE TOLD HIM THEY WERE NEAR THE surface. After being underground for so long, the air felt strange, but Colton was grateful to see the brilliant night sky above them. They stopped just outside the exit of the tunnel.

He put Mary down and leaned against the wall of the decrepit shanty. The wood was bent from exposure to the elements, and layers of it flaked off like a pastry. He opened his mouth to speak, but Mary held a finger to her lips. When she started toward her home, Colton took one last look down into the dark tunnel they left behind. There was no noise, not a single indication of the dangerous battle that had taken place underground. He pushed a hand through his hair and shook loose the dirt, frowning when he felt the blood on the back of his head. Deciding it was best not to bring it up yet, he joined Rennick in following Mary's lead.

They had taken one hell of a beating down there. The back of Colton's head throbbed and his neck felt wet and chilled from the air. His back was still raw from skidding across the stone. He would heal, but it would take time and food. Mary still cradled her bloodied hand against her chest, but she hadn't said a word about her injury.

Out of all of them, Rennick was the least injured. He had a gash along the side of his face that curved around up to his forehead, likely made by one of Kaga's chains. He looked paler, too, though that could be the moonlight playing tricks. He still had blood on his arms and hands, possibly from the ritual, and losing his three illusions had taken a toll on him.

The wind had gotten stronger as night descended upon Peridot and it cut through him. He took a deep breath and stared up, relieved to once again see the stars. The black sky was littered with them and the nearly full moon was enormous at its apex. It was beautiful. Between the shanties he could see the distant rocky crags on the horizon and the rolls of dunes that led up to them. He hadn't realized how much being underground had eaten away at him, how much it had worn away his spirit, and how claustrophobic he had felt especially when Kaga had closed them inside his chamber. The loose sand was sturdy beneath his feet compared to the uneven, treacherous platforms they dealt with below.

He thought of the many who had fallen under Kaga's control. He, Rennick, and Mary must have fought off dozens of his minions. Dozens of lives had been wasted. There was no telling how many more had been lost. Colton thought of the man in the tunnels, whose fingers had been worn to nubs; the enormous werewolf who had still maintained his fighting prowess even when under Kaga's control; and he thought of that little girl who had lost her mind.

They hadn't deserved such a cruel fate. They hadn't deserved to be slaughtered for some reckless spirit's sick entertainment. Regardless of what pack those werewolves were part of, they hadn't deserved that kind of treatment. He didn't have much love for the pack that had tried to kill him twice since he arrived at Peridot, but they were still his kin. Hadn't he come close to being drawn into Kaga's hold as well? In the end, they were lucky Kaga found them amusing enough to live.

He didn't want to rely on luck, but he couldn't argue how much of it they had on this mission. In his brief time in the Agency for the Betterment of Supernatural Creatures, though, he had found it necessary on more missions than he liked. He could train, prepare, and even make grand plans, but in the end the Agency often had only a vague idea what their agents were up against. He had to be smart, quick, and adaptable in order to survive the work. It was possible one of the victims down there had been a previous agent. Perhaps that was why the Agency sent a pair of agents this time around. It didn't matter if they were strangers to each other, the backup had been necessary. The Agency couldn't have sent in a whole team. Peridot was a fairly small town. Too many new arrivals would have raised suspicions. The whole point of the organization was to do the work without letting on to the people who lived alongside the supernatural world.

The Agency would want a report. They would want a clear explanation of the events and how Kaga was eliminated. They would send in others to do any necessary clean up, a detail Colton appreciated. He had no interest in going underground again, regardless of how much his superiors might press him.

It was early evening yet, when much of Peridot's night life got started. On a normal day, Rennick would probably be heading to the theater around this time and Mary would be preparing for some play. Colton noted Rennick had folded his bloody hands into his armpits as they got closer to civilization. It was silly, really. There was no way to hide the fact they had been in a bad scrap. The back of Colton's neck was sticky with blood and so were Mary's skirts. Though maybe they weren't such an unusual sight in a strange town like Peridot.

When they reached Mary's home, Rennick and Mary headed inside quickly to avoid any dubious looks from people they might know out on the street. But Colton had no such qualms. He stayed outside and walked over to visit Tahoe. She seemed happy to see him, and much calmer than she had been the day before. He wondered if she had encountered any of Kaga's puppets on her journey back to civilization. Her mane was full of debris from her time in the desert, and Colton felt neglectful leaving her out here by herself for most of the day. She probably felt as trapped as he had been underground.

Reaching around, he untied her harness. She didn't break away or even seem to care one way or the other, seeming perfectly content being tied to a fence post.

It bothered him. He wasn't sure why, but it grated on his nerves. She had been tied to the post here all day. Why didn't she appreciate freedom when she had it? Didn't she want to explore anything? Didn't she want to run?

"Go on then," he said and took a step back.

Her big brown eyes stared at him while her ears flicked back and forth. She was nervous. Maybe she heard the anger in his voice or smelled the blood on him and wasn't sure what it meant. Maybe she didn't trust him. Maybe she was mad at him, and this was how she got back at him.

"Do you want to get tied up again?" He held up the tack.

Tahoe just stared back at him, frozen, as though Colton was a wild animal. She was such a docile horse, such a tame thing compared to the flicking fire that always burned in his heart, wanting to run free.

Her calmness baffled and annoyed him. No animal should prefer a cage, regardless of how comfortable. He pointed toward the dirt road just opposite the fence. "Go on," he whispered, trying to keep his annoyance out of his voice. She gave a high-pitched, fearful whinny before trotting away down the street. After she went a few feet, her ears went back and she pawed at the dirt. Colton shook his head and tossed the tack to the ground.

"You're welcome," he whispered, though Tahoe didn't seem very appreciative.

His thoughts led to Kaga's puppets. What did it feel like to be stripped of freedom? Rennick said he couldn't even turn away when he didn't want to look at something. If Colton had been bound like those other werewolves, would he have been forced to obey Kaga's every word? Would he have blindly followed his every step like some false deity? He liked to think those puppets no longer had a mind, but Rennick's experience said otherwise. Colton wanted to believe they were beyond saving, but that didn't feel like the truth. He thought of those minions and how easily they had severed that child's head from her shoulders, how with merely a touch they turned the other werewolves into ash, and how Kaga screamed while they tore him apart.

Colton leaned heavily on the wooden fence beside him. The weathered cracks pinched his skin, but he welcomed the mild pain. He needed something steady, something to ground him, and the rickety fence looked more stable than he felt. The realization of all they had lost fell on his shoulders and its weight nearly toppled him. Colton had been doing this job for five years, but this was the first time he had ever questioned himself.

The front door of Mary's shack squealed open and closed, and he recognized Rennick's footsteps coming down the stairs.

"Are you alright? I thought you would want to clean up."

"Do you know why I joined the Agency? I did it to help people." Colton shook his head. "I hated what I had become, but at least, I thought I could help others. But after tonight..." He expected Rennick to interject, but instead he was silent. Colton hung his head and pursed his lips before asking the true question. "Did we save anyone tonight? I want to believe we did, but..."

Rennick sighed and leaned back against the fence and looked Colton in the eye. He had scrubbed the blood from his hands and washed much of it out of his hair as well. "If I said yes, you wouldn't believe me. You would think me callous, putting the lives of these people above the ones below." He gestured toward downtown Peridot before biting into an apple.

"No, I wouldn't."

Rennick smirked. "You wouldn't have to *say* it. I can read between the lines, you know. I'm actually pretty good at it, and there's a lot to read between yours." He looked down to work with the stem, twisting it between his fingers.

"I just... we must have killed close to twenty people. All of them were possessed, like you were. Couldn't we have convinced Kaga to release them? Would that have been so hard, instead of watching him get killed by those horrible insects?"

Rennick shook his head. "No, that's not fair. That was an unexplainable, probably a nature spirit and its minions, not horrible insects. They're not cruel, they're simply not invested in our interests."

Colton scoffed. "Don't give me that bureaucratic talk."

"Alright then, they only care about spirits who prey on the living. That's it. They don't care about what's fair, what's unfair, or what three measly folks like us want. All they do is hunt the world for spirits like Kaga who have grown far beyond their place."

"Their place? What was Kaga's place? To wander the world in limbo for eternity? To find some meaning in death that he could never see when he was alive? At the end of the day, Kaga was only human. Granted he was a terribly cruel, disturbed shadow of a man, but he started off no better than the rest of us."

"Most of us, you mean. I'm not fully human; I've never been fully human. And there are a bunch of agents like me."

Colton sighed. "You see my point."

Rennick's smile faltered. "If you're expecting me to have all the answers, you're sorely mistaken. If you want me to tell you that it really isn't that bad, and the world really is a place of good intentions, then I will. You know I'd be lying, though. The world is no more right or fair than the unexplainable back there. You've got bandits, sadists, victims, and the vast majority of the oblivious and apathetic. Somewhere in there, you have those of us who are doing the best we can with what little we have."

"If you're saying that the only purpose that little girl had was to be that foul bastard's victim, then I think you've got a simplistic view of things."

Rennick sighed. "Now you're being melodramatic."

"No, I'm being realistic. How are we any different from how Kaga used to be? We allowed creatures with unearthly powers to take out a man who was misled, cruel, and confused. He thought he was some fallen angel, when really he was just a power-hungry lost soul. How do we know someone won't sic something like that nature spirit on us one day? It's a blurry line between what we do and what he became."

"Like what? How many monsters are there in the world that would care to challenge us? That nature spirit only polices spirits. That's it. They're not horrible, like you want to make them out to be. As long as you don't go on a murderous rampage after you die, I think you'll stay clear of their path."

Colton pointed a finger in the direction they had come. "We saw them kill. Those werewolves weren't dead, and neither was that little girl. They could have been saved. In my book, that means they're just as dangerous as Kaga. More dangerous than us."

Rennick tossed his apple up and down, looking to be considering Colton's words.

"What if even that wild nature spirit couldn't stop him?" Colton asked. "What if he was too far gone even for them? It isn't that far of a stretch to see us in the same boat one day."

Rennick laughed. "You want to go down and ask them? I'd be fine with not seeing them again after tonight."

Colton sighed and flexed his hands. His palms were sore from clutching the splintered wood. He rubbed them together. "I'm sorry. These last few nights have been rough."

"I know. Trust me, I agree with you. I'll be happy when we can just send off our report and put our backs to this city."

"*Our* backs?" Colton grinned, "You mean you actually want to work with me again?"

"I'd say so." Rennick smiled. "You're rather terrible at acting, but you're a useful distraction. I think that was an excellent tactic. When in trouble, just toss in the werewolf."

"Distraction? I think I was—"

"Alright, alright. I'll admit that speech you gave was quite convincing. Not acting, really, but it got his attention. I don't know how reliable that is, though. I don't think you could have performed so well, if you hadn't realized Kaga was a human and not a demon."

"Keep your voices down." Mary hissed behind them. Colton turned to see her walking down the steps in a faded green dress. She had cleaned up and bandaged her hand. "You want the whole street to know what happened?

Talking about nature spirits and demons is going to cause some talk."

She pulled a shawl close around her shoulders. "So, how soon are we heading out of here? I don't have much to pack, but I will need one of Ren's horses. Unless we'll be traveling by train, that is."

Rennick sputtered. "Wait, what? You're not coming with us."

"And why not?" She eyed him.

"I mean, you're not a member of the Agency," Rennick said, "You can't just tag along like a little sister or something..."

She laughed. "Is that how you think of me? A *little sister*? That's certainly telling."

"What he means to say..." Colton cleared his throat. "Is that you'll have to have an escort. Single women shouldn't be traveling across the country on their own, after all. It's dangerous."

Mary smiled and cocked her head to the side. "Are you offering to be my chaperone, Mr. Fen?"

He shrugged. "Sure, you're definitely good at working with us. You certainly saved me back there. And you're a better shot than either one of us."

Rennick rolled his eyes and Mary grinned at him. "Thanks, Colt. I appreciate it." She glanced to Rennick. "That's perhaps the kindest thing a gentleman has ever said to me."

"Don't look at me." Rennick laughed. "He's the one who has to explain to the Agency why we'll need an extra ticket for our next assignment. I'll be curious to see how you get Mr. Tep to sign off on that."

"He won't need an extra ticket," Mary said with a mischievous glint in her eye. "I'm sure you would be kind enough to pay for it, wouldn't you, Ren?"

"What? I never said—"

"If you sell my house, I'm sure you can get a pretty penny off of that. This shack won't give me nearly as much, but if you add the theater on top of that, well..." She smiled. "I'm sure you get the idea."

"Wow." Rennick nodded and a slow smile spread across his lips. "I do have a soft spot for a lady who can wrangle me out of money." He narrowed his eyes. "Though, somehow, I don't think you really want me to sell your home. It was in your family for how many generations?"

"Five, on my father's side. My mother's tribe was on the east coast." Her smile faltered, "In all seriousness, we can find someone to keep it for us, can't we?"

"Of course, I can," Rennick smiled. "What about the theater, though? You wouldn't really sell it, would you?"

"No, not if you actually do buy my ticket to wherever you're going. I figure what the Agency doesn't know can't hurt it."

"You know that won't last forever," Colton muttered. "They'll find out that you're working with us at some point."

"And? What are they going to do? Fire you? Somehow, I don't think they find many folks willing to do this kind of work."

Colton exchanged a look with Rennick. Then Rennick shrugged and laughed.

"I mean, she's got a point. She would pretty much be volunteering to help the Agency out, which I can't see them getting too bent up about. It's only if she ever wanted to be compensated that it could be a problem."

"I'm not averse to getting cash under the table for my services, Ren."

Rennick tapped a finger on his apple. "You are a good shot."

Colton shook his head with a chuckle. While he had appreciated her help underground, he hadn't even considered what would happen once their assignment was completed. He couldn't deny being happy she would be joining them. His cheeks burned at the memory of the kiss she had planted when they were held precariously over that underground trench.

"Now, where is Tahoe hiding?" Mary asked. "I pulled out a whole basket of apples for her, and it looks like she's gone and run off on me."

Colton frowned. "She... I let her loose."

Mary turned to him with wide eyes.

"I thought she wanted to be free to run after being cooped up here for so long." He backed out of the yard, his face burning in embarrassment. "I'll—go get her. She couldn't have gone far."

COLTON JOGGED DOWN THE STREET, WHISTLING for Tahoe. Rennick shook his head and Mary chuckled after him.

"He's a funny man, isn't he?" Mary whispered.

"That does seem to be your type." Rennick pursed his lips.

She arched her eyebrows. "Oh, I see how it is."

Rennick sighed and pushed away from the fence. "It doesn't bother me if you want to date him. You've got the man wrapped around your finger, as you already know."

She stared off down the empty street. "I kissed him down there, Ren. I didn't mean to. It just sort of happened."

He smiled and gave a short nod. "So..."

"I don't know, Ren! He's a werewolf!"

"And I'm a half-vampire. That didn't stop your interest before." He gave her a wink; she huffed.

"You know what I mean. Like what happens on a full moon? How communicable is it? I think I need to learn a lot more about him before I even consider actually dating him." She glanced to him. "Then there's you."

"Then there's us," he corrected her. "I don't know where we stand anymore."

She gripped a fold of her dress and twisted it around her fingers. Far in the distance Colton tried to wrangle a still nervous Tahoe. His rope trick wasn't nearly as effective on an actual horse as it had been on the girl underground.

"I still love you, you know," she whispered.

"I know." Rennick sighed. "Let's not put a name on it though, okay?" He watched her for a moment before biting his lip. "We're still friends, aren't we, Mary? You're not still mad at me."

She shook her head. "I ought to be, but I don't blame you anymore. I guess it's hard to live like you two do. But I guess I'll get to see that firsthand, won't I?"

He put a hand on her shoulder and squeezed. "Are you sure you want to join us? It's dangerous, like you saw, and I can't promise your safety, ever. Even if Colton says he can always keep you safe, don't believe it. We never know what we'll be up against, or even if we'll survive from one assignment to the next."

"Honestly, Ren, that sounds exciting, and I've needed some real adventure in my life for too damn long. I'm tired of pretending to be a hero in a smelly theater. I want to try to be a real one."

In the distance, Colton finally calmed Tahoe. On the opposite side of the street, three drunks watched, giving him horrible advice. When the wind came right, it carried music from the Crimson Theater along with the foul scent of horse manure. Above them, the stars spread like a blanket across the endless night sky.

The series continues in the upcoming book:

The Woman Who Sang to Monsters

Acknowledgments

Of all the books I've written thus far, this one certainly had the longest journey. I wrote the first draft of this book in a single month back in 2012, writing with a fury I hadn't realized I possessed shortly after the publication of the novelette prequel, *Night Feeders*. I dove headfirst into the world and hoped that it would quickly get picked up for publication.

I found myself dealing with a publishing house that offered me a not-so-great contract. I had to get a lawyer to help me interpret it. A big thank you to the attorney T.K. Read for her help in navigating those treacherous waters.

A few years after that, I pulled out the manuscript and dusted it off to present to the incredible agent, Cherry Weiner. While I ultimately decided to self-publish this book, she gave me some wonderful insight and helped me believe in this novel.

Throughout the twelve years that I've gone back and forth with this novel, I've had several people give me help with it and motivate me to keep going. My sister, Kelley, encouraged me to revisit it even after I gave up on it again and again. She saw the potential with this book and this series. She wanted to see it succeed. I'm incredibly grateful to her.

Early in my writing career, I got the help from the writers at Scribophile where I learned some valuable lessons in building a world set in the Old West. They set me on the path of doing intense research, of verifying my facts, and on double checking my descriptions. I especially appreciated R.M. James who went on to become a dystopian author herself. It was basically a starting point for several of us as we figured out our first books, and I'm so incredibly grateful for the help and insight I found there. Thank you to my editor, Lara Zielinsky, who helped shape this book into its final form.

I must thank my parents, John and Connie, who are always incredibly supportive of whatever wild idea I write about next. My aunt Charmaine has always been one of my top supporters throughout my entire writing career and I'm so thankful to her. Finally, I have to thank one of my amazing Ko-Fi supporters, Donna.

Donna was one of the first reviewers of my novelette, *Night Feeders*, back when it came out in 2012. She loved it and gave me some incredible feedback. When I reached out to her years later about my Stolen series, thinking she wouldn't remember me at all, she remembered me and my work and was excited for what I had next. Ever since then, she has been a steadfast supporter, always there to cheer me on with my next book. I'm so very fortunate to have her support and her friendship.

Colton Fen's first novel took over a decade to see publication, but I sure hope the next book in this series doesn't take as long. I see this world as episodic like my favorite comic books when I was a teenager, full of fun, excitement, drama, romance, and a fair dose of danger. I always loved dropping back in for the next issue to see what wild adventure waited next, and I hope you do the same.

Thank you for joining me on this adventure. I hope you come back for the next. Colton's story is far from over.

Monstrous Creatures Series
> *Young adult, horror, sci-fi, dystopian*
> The Seeking

Ominous Hour Series
> *Horror, short stories, standalone*
> A Beautiful Specimen
> Undertow

Standalones
> *Short stories, horror, dark fantasy*
> The Impostor and Other Dark Tales

Mystery, film noir, humor, short story
> The Mysterious Disappearance of Charlene Kerringer

The Blade Filled with Stars

A kingdom is under siege from a familiar enemy. Families and friends are pitted against each other without reason. Slaughter is imminent while the winged Queen Khafil soars overhead. Desperate and terrified, Anna works with her sister, Lilah, to summon aid from their mother's ancient spell book.

Determined to save their people, the sisters

summon Death to help them, but Death is not easily swayed. Neither of the sisters are prepared for the consequences.

Want a peek behind the scenes?
Want to preview my books before they get released?

Get exclusive access to book goodies, giveaways, and cover reveals by joining my mailing list. Not only will you get notified of all my new releases, you'll get an exclusive copy of The Blade Filled with Stars.

Subscribe to the Mailing List at:
http://marlenafrank.com/mailinglist/

Support Me On Ko-fi

Follow me on Ko-Fi for regular updates on my writing progress.

Monthly subscribers get access to sneak peeks at stories way before anyone else. They also get access to cover reveals, monthly shout-outs on social media, and thanked by name in the acknowledgements in my books.

http://ko-fi.com/MarlenaFrank

About the Author

Marlena Frank is the author of young adult fantasy and horror novels, short stories, novellas, and book series. Many of her books have hit the bestseller charts, including her debut novel, Stolen. Readers' Favorite has praised several of her books with 5-star reviews. The Reader's House featured her work in March 2024, and De Mode of Literature Magazine in November 2021. Her stories have appeared in anthologies such as The Darkest Lullaby, Emporium of Superstition, Heroic Fantasy Quarterly, Georgia Gothic, and The Librarian Reshelved.

Although born in Tennessee, Marlena has spent most of her life in Georgia. She has various professional memberships, including the Atlanta chapter of the Horror Writers Association and the Science Fiction and Fantasy Writers Association. She enjoys cosplaying, gaming, and spoiling her adopted cats. Her drink of choice is a dairy-free chai latte. As a wildlife enthusiast, she can share a plethora of weird animal facts and talk about her favorite cryptids.

Follow her at: MarlenaFrank.com

www.ingramcontent.com/pod-product-compliance
Lightning Source LLC
Chambersburg PA
CBHW011125190726
48289CB00012B/2904